LIVE TO TELL

THE GOOD SISTER

"A chilling, captivating and all-too-timely
tale of suburban suspense, *The Good Sister* is
guaranteed to keep you up at night—and
keep a closer eye on your kids, too!
I couldn't put it down."
Alison Gaylin, *USA Today* bestselling author

"Taut, tense, and incredibly suspenseful. This
chillingly creepy psychological thriller is the
perfect page-turner. Staub's powerful and timely
story-telling is captivating!"
Hank Phillippi Ryan,
Agatha, Anthony and Macavity-winning author

"Intense! Wendy Corsi Staub once again
delivers a masterful psychological mystery that
is both chilling and thrilling. You will not be
able to put *The Good Sister* down until the very
last page."
Allison Brennan

"I haven't been this frightened for the citizens
of Buffalo, New York, since I was born there!
Wendy Corsi Staub weaves a tale of good sisters
and fallen angels as terrifyingly chilling as the
winter winds off Lake Erie!"
Chris Grabenstein, multiple award-winning
mystery author

BLUE
MOON

By Wendy Corsi Staub

Mundy's Landing Series

BLUE MOON
BLOOD RED

And

THE BLACK WIDOW
THE PERFECT STRANGER
THE GOOD SISTER
SHADOWKILLER
SLEEPWALKER
NIGHTWATCHER
HELL TO PAY
SCARED TO DEATH
LIVE TO TELL

WENDY CORSI STAUB

BLUE MOON

Mundy's Landing
Book Two

WILLIAM MORROW
An Imprint of HarperCollins*Publishers*

Map courtesy of Brody Staub.

Excerpt from *Bone White* copyright © 2017 by Wendy Corsi Staub.

BLUE MOON. Copyright © 2016 by Wendy Corsi Staub. All rights reserved. Printed in the United States of America. No part of this book may be used or reproduced in any manner whatsoever without written permission except in the case of brief quotations embodied in critical articles and reviews. For information, address HarperCollins Publishers, 195 Broadway, New York, NY 10007.

First William Morrow mass market printing: August 2016

ISBN 978-0-06234975-0

William Morrow® and HarperCollins® is a registered trademark of HarperCollins Publishers.

16 17 18 19 20 OPM 10 9 8 7 6 5 4 3 2 1

For my beautiful sister, Lisa Rae Corsi Koellner,
on her fiftieth birthday.
And my guys, Mark, Morgan, and Brody.

Acknowledgments

I'm thankful to my editor, Lucia Macro; her assistant, Nicole Fischer; publisher Liate Stehlik; and everyone at HarperCollins who played a role in bringing this book to print; to my literary agent, Laura Blake Peterson, her assistant, Marnie Zoldessy, and my film agent Holly Frederick at Curtis Brown, Limited; to Rick Gennett; to Betsy Glick of the F.B.I. Office of Public Affairs; to the special agents at the F.B.I. Headquarters in Manhattan; to Margery Flax and Mystery Writers of America; to International Thrillerwriters, Sisters in Crime, and Romance Writers of America; to Carol Fitzgerald and the gang at Bookreporter; to Cissy Hartley and the gang at Writerspace; to Peter Meluso; to my supportive fellow authors; to enthusiastic booksellers, librarians, and readers everywhere; to Mark Staub and Morgan Staub for the manuscript feedback and marketing support; and to my newly minted high school graduate, Brody Staub, for painstakingly mapping Mundy's Landing.

Peace on Earth

The Archer is wake!
The Swan is flying!
Gold against blue
An Arrow is lying.
There is hunting in heaven—
Sleep safe till tomorrow.

The Bears are abroad!
The Eagle is screaming!
Gold against blue
Their eyes are gleaming!
Sleep!
Sleep safe till tomorrow.

The Sisters lie
With their arms intertwining;
Gold against blue
Their hair is shining!
The Serpent writhes!
Orion is listening!
Gold against blue
His sword is glistening!
Sleep!
There is hunting in heaven—
Sleep safe till tomorrow.

—William Carlos Williams,
1913

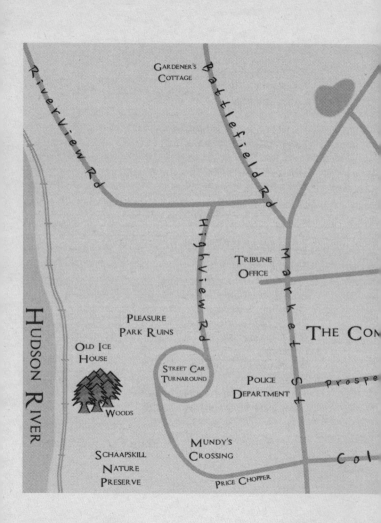

MUNDY'S LANDING

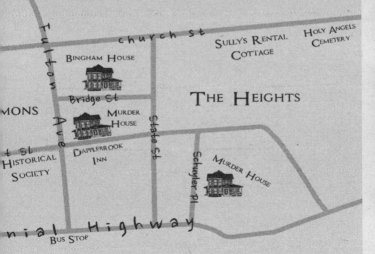

church st

Sully's Rental
Cottage

Holy Angels
Cemetery

Bingham House

THE HEIGHTS

Bridge St

Murder
House

Fulton Ave

State St

MONS

Murder House

Historical
Society

Dapplerook
Inn

Schuyler Pl

nial Highway

Bus Stop

From the Sleeping Beauty Killer's Diary
August 1, 1893

Perched, as I am in this moment, between childhood and adulthood, I have decided it might be wise to keep a journal over the course of my trip. One day, I will surely reflect upon this adventure with fond nostalgia. Perhaps, from that distant vantage, I shall even peer through the gray mists of age and time to view this very day as a pivotal crossroads in what I dearly hope will be a long and prosperous life.

I pen this entry from the famed Richelieu Hotel in Chicago, where I have taken up residence for the next two weeks. Too restless with excitement to adjourn to my room just yet, I sit in a conservatory that connects the front and rear wings of this massive building. Above my head is a skylight that allows me to see the waning moon above Michigan Avenue.

It has been a long day. I disembarked at Central Station just before dawn, thus concluding a liberating solo journey that began on my birthday last week, when Father transported me to the rail station in Hudson to board the New York Central.

He was reluctant to be left alone in the house so soon after the funeral, and I again encouraged him to accompany me as initially planned. He in turn begged me to reconsider. But despite the sad circumstances, I had no intention of forfeiting the opportunity to see the World's Fair. If truth be told, I welcomed the opportunity to escape the house—always oppressive but now unbearably so.

As we stood waiting upon the platform, I clutched my favorite book, Walt Whitman's Leaves of Grass, *in my left hand. Father pressed several bills into my right. It was indeed an unexpected gesture, what with our recent loss, and the country itself in the midst of the worst depression ever seen. He bade me to return home safely and on schedule to resume my studies in September. Of course I promised that I shall, and he was pleased, I know. Yet he remains critical and I, in turn, found myself more resentful with every mile that fell between us.*

The bitterness dissolved, however, when I received my first glimpse of the splendid midway, with the inventor George Ferris's enormous rotating wheel as its centerpiece. I contentedly roamed among strangers until darkness fell.

An audible gasp went up in the crowd as the landscape was illuminated in a brilliant and instantaneous flash. There were at least two hundred thousand electric bulbs, enough to outline every manmade structure in the vicinity. The resplendent moon and all the stars in the heavens could scarcely compete with the shimmering White City.

I returned to the hotel for a late dinner in the sumptuous café, settling into a leather-upholstered mahogany seat surrounded by fellow fairgoers. Many were alone, as am I. A curious camaraderie sprang amongst those of us who had traveled for days to witness this modern marvel. Lacking familiar companionship, the others shared with me their day's adventures, and some included tales of the lives they'd left behind. I refrained, unwilling to solicit sympathy, curiosity, or attention. It felt rather as if I were hiding in plain sight, a refreshing change from my stifling existence of late.

As I prepare to make my way up to bed, I shall close with a fitting quote from the great Whitman:

This is thy hour O Soul, thy free flight into the
      wordless,
Away from books, away from art, the day erased,

the lesson done,
Thee fully forth emerging, silent, gazing, pon-
dering the themes thou lovest best,
Night, sleep, death and the stars.

Prologue

Sunday, October 25, 2015
Mundy's Landing, New York

"**H**ere we are," the Realtor, Lynda Carlotta, announces as she slows the car in front of 46 Bridge Street. "It really is magnificent, isn't it?"

The Second Empire Victorian presides over neighboring stucco bungalows and pastel Queen Anne cottages with the aplomb of a grand dame crashing a coffee klatch. There's a full third story tucked behind the scalloped slate shingles, topped by a black iron grillwork crown. A square cupola rises to a lofty crest against the gloomy Sunday morning sky. Twin cornices perch atop its paired windows like the meticulously arched, perpetually raised eyebrows of a proper aristocratic lady.

Fittingly, the house—rather, the events that transpired within its plaster walls—raised many an eyebrow a hundred years ago.

Annabelle Bingham grew up right around the corner, but she stares from the leather passenger's seat as if seeing the house for the first time. She'd never imagined that she might actually live beneath that mansard roof, in the shadow of the century-old unsolved crimes that unfolded there.

For the past few days, she and her husband, Trib, have

taken turns talking each other into—and out of—coming to see this place. They're running out of options.

Real estate values have soared in this picturesque village, perched on the eastern bank of the Hudson River midway between New York City and Albany. The Binghams' income has done quite the opposite. The only homes in their price range are small, undesirable fixer-uppers off the highway. They visited seven such properties yesterday and another this morning, a forlorn little seventies ranch that smelled of must and mothballs. *Eau d'old man*, according to Trib.

"*Magnificent* isn't exactly the word that springs to mind when I look at this house," he tells Lynda from the backseat.

She smiles at him in the rearview mirror. "Well, I'm not the professional wordsmith you are. I'm sure you can come up with a more creative adjective."

Annabelle can. She's been trying to keep it out of her head, but everything—even the tolling steeple bells from nearby Holy Angels Church—is a grim reminder.

"Monolithic," pronounces the backseat wordsmith. "That's one way to describe it."

Murder House, Annabelle thinks. That's another.

"There's certainly plenty of room for a large family," Lynda points out cheerily.

Optimism might be her strong suit, but tact is not. Doesn't she realize there are plenty of families that don't care to grow larger? And there are many that, for one heartbreaking reason or another, couldn't expand even if they wanted to; and still others, like the Binghams, whose numbers are sadly dwindling.

Annabelle was an only child, as is their son, Oliver. Trib lost his older brother in a tragic accident when they were kids. Until a few months ago, Trib's father, the last of their four parents to pass away, had been a vital part of their lives. He'd left them the small inheritance they plan to use as a down payment on a home of their own—a bittersweet prospect for all of them.

"I just want Grandpa Charlie back," Oliver said tearfully last night. "I'd rather have him than a new house."

"We all would, sweetheart. But you know he can't come back, and wouldn't it be nice to have a nice big bedroom and live on a street with sidewalks and other kids?"

"No," Oliver said, predictably. "I like it here."

They're living in what had once been the gardener's cottage on a grand Hudson River estate out on Battlefield Road. The grounds are lovely but isolated, and they've long since outgrown the tiny rental space.

Still . . . are they really prepared to go from dollhouse to mansion?

"There are fourteen rooms," Lynda waxes on, "including the third-floor ballroom, observatory, and servants' quarters. Over thirty-five hundred square feet of living space—although I have to check the listing sheet, so don't quote me on it."

That, Annabelle has noticed, is one of her favorite catchphrases. *Don't quote me on it.*

"Is she saying it because you're a reporter?" she'd asked Trib after their first outing with Lynda. "Does she think you're working on an article that's going to blow the lid off . . . I don't know, sump pump function?"

He laughed. "That's headline fodder if I ever heard it."

Lynda starts to pull the Lexus into the rutted driveway. After a few bumps, she thinks better of it and backs out onto the street. "Let's start out front so that we can get the full curb appeal, shall we?"

They shall.

"Would you mind handing me that file folder on the

floor back there, Charles?" Lynda asks Trib, whose lanky form is folded into the seat behind her.

He'd been born Charles Bingham IV, but as one of several Charlies in kindergarten, was rechristened courtesy of his family's longtime ownership of the *Mundy's Landing Tribune*. The childhood nickname stuck with him and proved prophetic: he took over as editor and publisher after his dad retired a decade ago.

But Lynda wouldn't know that. She's relatively new in town, having arrived sometime in the last decade. Nor would she remember the era when the grand homes in The Heights had fallen into shabby disrepair and shuttered nineteenth-century storefronts lined the Common. She'd missed the dawning renaissance as they reopened, one by one, to form the bustling business district that exists today.

"Let's see . . . I was wrong," she says, consulting the file Trib passes to the front seat. "The house is only thirty-three hundred square feet."

Can we quote you on it? Annabelle wants to ask.

"I can't imagine what it cost to heat this place last winter," Trib comments, "with all those below-zero days we had."

"You'll see here that there's a fairly new furnace." Lynda hands them each a sheet of paper. "Much more energy efficient than you'll find in most old houses in the neighborhood."

Annabelle holds the paper at arm's length—courtesy of advancing farsightedness—and looks over the list of specs. The "new" furnace was installed about fifteen years ago, around the turn of this century. The wiring and plumbing most likely date to the turn of the last one.

"Oh, and did I mention that this is the only privately owned indoor pool in town."

She did, several times. Some potential buyers might

view that as a burden, but Lynda is well aware that it's a luxury for Annabelle, an avid swimmer.

Still, the house lacks plenty of key items on her wish list. There's a ramshackle detached garage instead of the two-car garage she and Trib covet. There is no master suite. The lot is undersized, like many in this historic neighborhood.

"You're never going to find exactly what you want," Lynda has been reminding her and Trib from day one. "You have to compromise."

They want a home that's not too big, not too small, not too old, not too new, not too expensive, not a rock-bottom fixer-upper . . .

Goldilocks syndrome—another of Lynda's catchphrases.

This house may be too old and too big, but it isn't too expensive despite being located in The Heights, a sloping tree-lined enclave adjacent to the Village Common.

Its owner, Augusta Purcell, died over a year ago, reportedly in the same room where she'd been born back in 1910. Her sole heir, her nephew Lester, could have sold it to the historical society for well above market value. But he refused to entertain a long-standing preemptive offer from the curator, Ora Abrams.

"I'm not going to cash in on a tragedy like everyone else around here," he grumbled, adamantly opposed to having his ancestral home exploited for its role in the notorious, unsolved Sleeping Beauty case.

From late June through mid July of 1916, a series of grisly crimes unfurled in the relentless glare of both a brutal heat wave and the Sestercentennial Celebration for the village, founded in 1666.

Forty-six Bridge Street was the second home to gain notoriety as a crime scene. The first was a gambrel-roofed fieldstone Dutch manor house just around the corner at 65 Prospect Street; the third, a granite Beaux Arts mansion at 19 Schuyler Place.

No actual homicide took place inside any of the three so-called Murder Houses. But what had happened was profoundly disturbing. Several days and several blocks apart, three local families awakened to find the corpse of a young female stranger tucked into a spare bed under their roof.

The bodies were all posed exactly the same way: lying on their backs beneath coverlets that were neatly folded beneath their arms. Their hands were peacefully clasped on top of the folded part of the covers. Their long hair—they all had long hair—was braided and arranged just so upon the pillows.

All the girls' throats had been neatly slit ear to ear. Beneath each pillow was a note penned on plain stationery in block lettering: *Sleep safe till tomorrow.* The line was taken from a William Carlos Williams poem published three years earlier.

The victims hadn't died where they lay, nor in the immediate vicinity. They'd been stealthily transported by someone who was never caught; someone who was never identified and whose motive remains utterly inexplicable to this day.

Ghastly death portraits were printed in newspapers across the country in the futile hope that someone might recognize a sister, a daughter, a niece. In the end, their unidentified remains were buried in the graveyard behind Holy Angels Church.

Is Annabelle really willing to move into a Murder House?

A year ago, she'd have said no way.

This morning, when she and Trib and Oliver were crashing into porcelain fixtures and one another in their tiny bathroom, she'd have said yes, absolutely.

Now, staring up at the lofty bracketed eaves, ornately carved balustrades, and curve-topped couplets of tall, narrow windows, all framed against a blood red foliage canopy of an oppressive sky . . .

I don't know. I just don't know.

"Since you both grew up here, I don't have to tell you about how wonderful this neighborhood is," Lynda says as the three of them step out of the car and approach the tall black iron fence that mirrors the mansard crest.

A brisk wind stirs overhead boughs. They creak and groan, as does the gate when Lynda pushes it open. The sound is straight out of a horror movie. A chill slips down Annabelle's spine, and she shoves her hands deep into the pockets of her corduroy barn coat.

The brick walkway between the gate and the house is strewn with damp fallen leaves. For all she knows, someone raked just yesterday. It's that time of year, and an overnight storm brought down a fresh barrage of past-peak foliage.

Yet the grounds exude the same forlorn, abandoned atmosphere as the house itself. It's the only one on the block that lacks pumpkins on the porch steps and political signs posted in the yard.

Election Day looms, with a heated mayoral race that reflects the pervasive insider versus outsider mentality. Most residents of The Heights back the incumbent, John Elsworth Ransom, whose roots extend to the first settlers of Mundy's Landing. Support for his opponent, a real estate developer named Dean Cochran, is stronger on the other side of town, particularly in Mundy Estates, the upscale townhouse complex he built and now calls home.

A Ransom for Mayor poster isn't all that's conspicuously missing from the leaf-blanketed yard. There's no For Sale sign, either.

Trib asks Lynda if she's sure it's on the market.

"Oh, it is. But Lester prefers to avoid actively soliciting

the 'ghouls'—not the Halloween kind, if you know what I mean."

They do. Plenty of locals use that word to describe the tourists who visit every summer in an effort to solve the cold case. The event—colloquially dubbed Mundypalooza— has taken place every year since 1991. That's when, in conjunction with the seventy-fifth anniversary of the cold case, the historical society first extended a public invitation: *Can You Solve the Sleeping Beauty Murders?*

So far, no one has—but every summer, more and more people descend to try their hand at it. The historical society sponsors daily speakers, panel discussions, and workshops. Even Trib conducts an annual seminar about the sensational press coverage the case received in 1916.

He turns to Annabelle. "That's something we'd have to deal with if we bought this place."

"You're right. We'd be inundated with curiosity seekers. I don't think I want to—"

"Just in the summer, though," Lynda cuts in quickly, "and even then, it's not a big deal."

"This house will be crawling with people and press," Annabelle points out.

A Murder House isn't just branded by century-old stigma; it bears the brunt of the yearly gawker invasion. No local resident escapes unscathed, but those who live at 46 Bridge Street, 65 Prospect Street, and 19 Schuyler Place are inundated.

"Let's just walk through before you rule it out," Lynda urges. "A comparable house at any other address in this neighborhood would sell for at least six figures more. I'd hate to have someone snatch this out from under you."

The odds of that happening are slim to none. Lester, who insists on pre-approving every showing, requests that prospective buyers already live locally. Not many people fit the bill, but Annabelle and Trib passed muster and they're here. They might as well look, even though Annabelle is sure she doesn't want to live here after all. She'd never get past what happened here during the summer of 1916, let alone what will happen every summer forever after, thanks to Mundypalooza.

They step through the massive double doors into the dim, chilly entrance hall. So far, so *not* good.

Before Annabelle can announce that she's changed her mind, Lynda presses an antique mother-of-pearl button on the wall. "There, that's better, isn't it?"

They find themselves bathed in the glow of an elegant fixture suspended from a plaster medallion high overhead. Surprisingly, it *is* better.

There's a massive mirror on the wall opposite the door. In it, Annabelle sees their reflection: Lynda, a full head shorter even in heels, bookended by herself and Trib, who could pass for siblings. They're similarly tall and lean, with almost the same shade of dark brown hair and light brown eyes—both attractive, if not in a head-turning way.

Their eyes meet in the mirror, and he gives her a slight nod, as if to say, *Yes, let's keep going.*

"Just *look* at that mosaic tile floor!" Lynda exclaims. "And the moldings on those archways! And the woodwork on the grand staircase! We haven't seen anything like this in any of the houses we've looked at, have we?"

They agree that they haven't, and of course wouldn't expect to in their price point.

Annabelle can picture twelve-year-old Oliver walking through those big doors after school, dropping his backpack on the built-in seat above the cast-iron radiator with a *Mom? I'm home.* As she runs her fingertips over the carved newel post, she envisions him sliding down the banister curving above.

The long-dormant old house stirs to life as they move through it. One by one, doors creak open. Spaces beyond brighten courtesy of wall switches that aren't dime-a-dozen rectangular plastic levers. These are period contraptions with buttons or brass toggles or pull-pendants dangling from thirteen-foot ceilings. Lynda presses, turns, pulls them all, chasing shadows from the rooms.

Annabelle's imagination strips away layers of faded velvet and brocade shrouding the tall windows. Her mind's eye replaces Augusta's dark, dusty furnishings with comfortable upholstery and modern electronics. Instead of mustiness and cat pee, she smells furniture polish, clean linens, savory supper on the stove. The ticking grandfather clock, dripping faucets, and Lynda's chirpy monologue and tapping footsteps are over-shadowed by the voices Annabelle loves best, echoing through the rooms in ordinary conversation: *Mom, I'm home! What's for dinner? I'm home! How was your day? I'm home . . .*

Yes, Annabelle realizes. This is it.

This, at last, is home.

PART I

And the moon like a twisted torch
  Burned over one lonesome larch;
  She passed with never a sound.

  Three times had the circle traced,
  Three times had bent
  To the grave that the myrtle graced;
  Three times, then softly faced
  Homeward, and slowly went.

—Madison Julius Cawein,
  "The Eve of All-Saints"

Holmes's Case Notes

It took less than an hour to drive to Albany from Mundy's Landing with no traffic. Just past midnight, I arrived in Albany and parked down the road from her house. I assumed she was long gone by then.

She always takes the bus home from Wal-Mart after she finishes her shift at seven o'clock on Friday nights. It stops right there on the corner, a nice little perk in a low-income neighborhood that's seen better days.

Sometimes, when I was watching her through the windows, memorizing her routine, I would see her make dinner for herself and eat it alone at the kitchen table. Her stepfather, Tony, is long home from his factory job and parked in front of the television by then. They don't talk much. I doubt he'll miss her.

Next, she always goes upstairs to try to make herself pretty. She isn't. Her hair is an unnatural shade of yellow with dark roots. Her eyebrows are too thin; her eyeliner too thick. She dresses all wrong: snug tops tucked into equally snug pants or skirts with a fat wedge of belly spilling over at the waist.

By nine o'clock, she leaves the house again. Snow, rain, it doesn't matter: she goes on foot. She turned seventeen back on March 31, but I don't believe she has a driver's license. Or maybe her stepfather won't allow her to drive his car. She can't afford to buy one—a high school dropout working as a cashier.

In the beginning, last summer and into the fall, I used to follow her to see where she went every night. It was never to a restaurant, a movie, or concert. None of that for her. She just visits friends in the neighborhood. She stays until two or three in the morning, and then walks home alone. Sometimes, I can tell that she's overindulged in liquor and drugs by the way she weaves and sways back up the block in the dark.

On any of those nights, it would have been easy, so very easy, to make my move. But it wasn't time yet.

I had to wait until today, May 21, when the moon was full. Full, and blue.

Not true blue, of course. Certainly not blue in color. And not blue by modern astronomical calculations, which define a blue moon as a second full moon occurring within a single calendar month. By that definition, the blue moon that occurred last July was the first in three years, and there won't be another of those until January 2018. But a hundred years ago, a blue moon was defined as the fourth full moon within a single season, as it is now.

It was a marvelous sight in those hours before dawn, perched high above that dismal neighborhood. I was anxious to see her bathed in its light as she walked home. I waited for her as long as I could, until the moon faded into morning. But she never came. I had to drive back without her.

I'll return tonight.

What if she doesn't come? What will I do? Everything—everything I've worked for—depends on this girl. On this date. On this blue moon.

Chapter 1

Saturday, May 21, 2016
Mundy's Landing

The moon hangs low in the blue-black night sky. Lying on her back on the hard ground, staring up at it, Indi realizes that it's blue.

She may have been flunking earth science—flunking everything, really—when she dropped out of high school. But this, she knows.

There's only one blue moon in all of 2016, and it's tonight.

"Blue moon . . . you saw me standing alone . . ." Her mother, Karen, used to sing to her when she was a little girl.

She'd been named for the one beneath which she'd been born on March 31, 1999.

Indigo Selena Edmonds.

Indigo means blue.

Selena means moon goddess.

Edmonds is Tony's last name.

He's not her father. He never even adopted her after he married her mother. He makes sure he reminds her of that every chance he gets. But they're stuck together under the same roof, living separate lives that seemed miserable until tonight, when she was abducted by a stranger.

I shouldn't have gone out. I didn't even go to work. Why did I go out?

She's been sick in bed for the last few days. Strep throat, probably. It's going around. Several of her coworkers at Wal-Mart have had it lately, but she couldn't afford to go to the doctor for antibiotics. Nor could she afford to miss her shift two days in a row. But by the time her friends texted tonight, she felt a little better. She got out of bed, fixed herself up, and headed out the door.

She hadn't even reached the corner when the dark SUV pulled up alongside her. The driver rolled down the window to ask for directions in a pleasant voice she hasn't heard since.

The next thing Indi knew, she was waking up in a puddle on the floor of a musty-smelling rowboat, her hands tightly bound behind her. The boat was bobbing, and she could hear the oars thumping and splashing in the water. She was so terrified it was going to capsize— she can't swim—that she couldn't even wonder how she'd gotten there.

Now she's back on dry land, flat on her back, panic threatening to overtake her.

You can't let that happen. You have to stay calm, she tells herself as she stares at the sky. *Think about the moon.*

It can't be a coincidence that it's blue tonight, just as it was the night she was born. That's a sign that she's going to survive this . . . this . . . whatever is going on, here.

The moon. Think about the moon.

Its creamy, mottled surface reminds her of baby deer.

They're small. Sweet. So vulnerable.

Helpless, really.

They have big, soft, Disney eyes, and ears that stick out sideways, and . . .

What else? What else?

Their mothers protect them. Yes, when you come across a fawn, you can be sure a doe is nearby, even when you don't see her. She hovers close to her baby, making sure nothing hap—

"Get up!" The gruff command shatters Indi's attempt to comfort herself.

"Please. I'm so tired. I just—"

The night sky sways away as rough hands grip her shoulders. She's back on her feet, pushed from behind, again stumbling over rutted ground on a path through the dark woods.

An owl hoots from an overhead bough, joined by the distinct yowl of a feline in heat. Indi thinks of other creatures that lurk in the forest, and dread slithers in, binding her in its clammy embrace.

No. Think about the gentle deer, the fawns. What else about them?

Think. Think.

She's never seen one before in real life. There are no deer, old or young, roaming the streets of Albany. Other creatures do, though. Dangerous predators, and Indi is the fawn: small, sweet, helpless.

I want my mommy.

The thought leaps through her brain and lingers, nosing at the periphery.

Two years have passed since she lost her mother. But the woman who gave birth to her at sixteen was never *Mommy*. She insisted that Indi call her by her first name, Karen, so that she could pass her off as a little sister back when she was dating, before she met Tony.

Forget Karen, forget Mommy, any mommy. Indi would give anything, *anything*, if Tony were here with her now.

She'd never had much use for her lug of a stepfather, but she'd always assumed that since her late mother had loved him, he must have some redeeming characteristic.

She'd never have guessed that the one thing she hates most about him—that he takes "no crap from nobody," including his stepdaughter—would become the one thing she'd desperately need.

Tony would get me out of here so fast that this . . . this . . . creature's head would be spinning.

"Come on, move it! Move!"

"I'm . . . I'm trying."

The rocky terrain is tangled with vines that twine around Indi's legs, bared to her thighs in a short skirt. Thick with the foreboding organic perfume of old leaves and mud, the very air she sucks into her lungs is a stark reminder that things die, that dead things are buried, dead people are buried . . .

Am I going to die?

A leafy rope snares one of her stiletto heels like a trap, turning her ankle sharply. She stumbles, falls forward.

If only she could land in her sickbed and wake to find that this was all just a terrible nightmare, courtesy of feverish delirium.

If only the earth would open and swallow her whole.

It doesn't. She hits the ground hard, her face slamming into an unforgiving layer of damp leaves, sticks, rocks. Something deep in her ankle pops with a residual explosion of nausea.

"Get up!" the voice growls.

She finds her own, small and tinny. "Please . . ."

The plaintive appeal is greeted with laughter, cruel and guttural, and a sharp tug on her long hair. She's yanked into the air like a limp, battered plaything dangling from a feral cat's paw. Her feet fumble, stumble, find the ground at last.

"Walk!"

Her own slight weight on her ankle is too excruciating to bear. She's down again, this time flat on her back.

The full moon shines through branches that stretch

above her like gnarled fingers. She wonders if it will be the last thing she ever sees.

It isn't.

She'll only wish it had been.

Thursday, June 23

Annabelle flips the turn signal and brakes for the stop sign at the brick-paved intersection of Fulton Avenue and Bridge Street, hoping the ice cream didn't melt in the trunk. It's been there much longer than she intended.

Mundypalooza doesn't even begin until next week, but traffic was already much heavier than usual as she ran her morning errands.

This year marks the twenty-fifth annual historical society convention and the hundredth anniversary of the murders, along with the 1666 Founder's Day gala officially dubbed ML350. Buzz has been building for months. Judging by the abundance of far-flung license plates in the crowded Price Chopper parking lot, people are willing to travel for days for a shot at cracking the case that has eluded professionals and amateurs for almost a century. The historical society even offers a significant reward—intended, of course, not to capture a dangerous criminal, but as an expensive publicity stunt. The dollar amount has substantially increased with every passing year, along with the size of the crowd and media attention.

After buying groceries, Annabelle had to drive around the block several times looking for a parking spot near the dry cleaner's, and again at the pharmacy. Then there was a fender bender at the busy corner of Prospect and Fulton, adding insult to injury with a lengthy detour around the perimeter of The Heights.

But at last she's home, and home is looking particularly lovely on this sunny, breezy morning. In the fluid, dappled shade of swaying maple boughs, with its clapboards and trim painted in muted sepia shades, the house looks like a vintage daguerreotype come to life.

Little has changed since it was built in 1870. She knows, because there *is* a vintage daguerreotype of the house, framed and prominently hanging in the Mundy's Landing Historical Society.

She pulls into the driveway, efficiently avoiding the deepest ruts. Someday, they'll repave it.

Home ownership, she and Trib have discovered, is accompanied by plenty of *somedays*.

She parks around back beside the old carriage house that was listed as a detached garage—laughable, as a gaping root cellar is visible beneath the few rotting floorboards that are still in place. They wouldn't dare walk in there, much less drive a car inside, even if it weren't crammed with old books and magazines Lester was supposed to have removed before the closing.

They opted not to press the point, as the process had already dragged on. They'd made their initial offer in early November, but Lester had already left for the Sarasota condo where he spends the winters. In no hurry to close, he was presumably holding out for more lucrative offers that never came, all the while refusing to entertain any from Ora Abrams over at the historical society.

When he did at last accept the Binghams' offer, he insisted on adding a restrictive covenant to the sales contract stating that they would use the house solely as their private residence. Their lawyer, Ralph Duvane, wasn't thrilled, but at that point, they all just wanted the sale to go through.

They finally closed on the property over a month ago. "The most expensive Mother's Day gift you're ever going to get," Trib teased Annabelle as they signed the papers.

"Darn. I had my heart set on a Tuscan villa for next year," she quipped, and Ralph Duvane laughed along with Trib. Even the seller's no-nonsense attorney cracked a brief smile, though the seller himself remained stoic.

"Maybe Lester's just grieving the loss of his aunt, or the house his ancestors built," Annabelle told Trib later, when they were discussing how the man's dour demeanor had cast a pall over the proceeding. "After all, it's the end of an era for that family."

"Oh, come on. He's been waiting for Augusta to die, and I bet she knew it. I don't think they'd even spoken in years. I'm surprised she didn't just leave everything to her cats."

Augusta was the quintessential small-town spinster whose many feline companions outranked and outlived her human loved ones, Lester aside—if he, as the least lovable guy in town, could even be included in that category.

Annabelle opens the car trunk and runs a hand through her short dark hair, feeling sweat begin to trickle at her forehead. This is typical June weather in the Hudson Valley, warm and sunny with a slight breeze whispering through abundant foliage of ancient trees.

Checking her watch as she reaches for the groceries, she notes that Oliver will be home from school soon. He's had half days all week, and tomorrow he'll just go in for an hour to get his report card.

She hurriedly carries several grocery bags to the house, juggling them to unlock the door. The large, narrow, and old-fashioned key is conspicuously different from the others on her key ring. Lester claimed this is the only key his aunt had to this door, so Trib can't even get in when it's locked. They tried to have it duplicated, but it's obsolete, according to the locksmith they consulted.

"I can't duplicate it. You're going to have to replace the whole lock. But you really need to rekey all the other exterior locks, too, for security."

Annabelle and Trib looked at each other. "How much will that be?" she asked, already anticipating the answer.

Too much.

That locksmith, too, was relegated to the *someday* list—way down at the bottom. Despite its brushes with violence, Mundy's Landing prides itself on being the kind of small town where no one ever locks their doors.

Except most of the time, we do.

She steps into an enclosed service porch, where there are two additional doors. One leads to the kitchen, the other to the indoor pool—both of which entail far more *somedays* than they can possibly accomplish in this lifetime on their budget and do-it-yourself schedule.

"Do you think it's too much house?" they'd asked each other when they first considered making an offer, and again, repeatedly, when they were preparing to move in.

The answer was always clear—of course it's too much house for three people. But their perspective varied depending on the day and the amount of time they'd spent rolling fresh paint across acres of walls and ceilings. In some moments, they were certain they were making a huge mistake; in others, they were convinced that too much house is preferable to too little house.

Still, sometimes—like right now—I don't know how I feel about it.

She steps into the kitchen and, as always, catches a faint whiff of cat. Even now, strays show up on the steps expecting to be fed. Both Annabelle and Trib grew up with pets and wouldn't mind adopting one, but Oliver is skittish around even the friendliest furry creatures.

Stepping around stacks of moving boxes that have yet to be unpacked nearly a month after the move, she wedges the bags into a skimpy patch of counter space. Then she walks through the hushed rooms to open the front door for Oliver.

Most of the time, the place feels cozy and homey despite its vast size. But once in a while—like right now—she has a vaguely uneasy feeling about living here.

After the closing, Trib brought home yellowed editions of 1916 papers from the *Tribune* archives. She pored over articles pertaining to what happened under this roof.

It was a warm July morning—a few days after the Fourth—when Florence Purcell discovered the dead girl eerily tucked into a vacant bed upstairs. That was the second of the three corpses that turned up in Mundy's Landing during that frightening time.

As Annabelle reaches out to give the old-fashioned lock a clockwise turn, she imagines the many hands that have touched it. Primarily Augusta's over the past couple of decades, to be sure. But on a summer night a century ago, Augusta's mother turned this brass lever counter-clockwise and assumed that her children would thus be safe within these walls.

And they *were* safe, Annabelle reminds herself. It isn't as though someone broke in during the night and slaughtered them all in their beds. The Purcell family wasn't physically harmed. But surely they suffered the psychological consequences for a long time afterward. Probably for the rest of their lives.

A large studio portrait of the family hangs in the historical society. Annabelle walked past it countless times without paying much attention, but after moving into the house, she revisited the image online, wanting to familiarize herself with the people who once lived here.

Taken in 1915 against a staged foliage backdrop, it depicts a classic pose of the era. Augusta stands between her seated parents, and her baby brother, Frederick, is cradled on her mother's lap. All of them, even the baby, focus solemnly on the camera.

Five-year-old Augusta is a pretty child, with corkscrew

curls topped by a big, loopy hair bow. She wears a sailor middy, white tights, and shiny black shoes. Her hand rests on her father's shoulder.

George is handsome and dignified in a shirt and tie, his suit coat neatly buttoned over a waistcoat. His dark hair is parted in the middle and combed back, and his eyes stare from behind small, wire-rimmed glasses.

Florence is impressively dressed. Her long skirt matches a smart tailored jacket cinched with a belt at the waist. A white lace blouse frames her attractive face, and her pale hair is upswept beneath an elaborate hat, its brim decorated in flowers and ribbon. Her right hand clutches the white-gowned baby. Her left is pressed to her heart, alongside a delicate scallop-edged locket on a long chain.

Annabelle thinks of them, of their lives here, as she touches the carved mahogany newel post at the foot of the stairs. Soon after moving in, she'd noticed that the knob's fluid scrolls and looping ribbons are interrupted by a deep, linear score about two inches long. She runs her fingertips along the scarred wood, gazing up at the shadowy second-floor hallway.

Did he wait, on that fateful night, for the family to retire before slipping up the stairs? Who was he, the deranged intruder who violated this house with his presence, with his gruesome cargo? Who was *she,* the young girl whose throat had been neatly slit from ear to ear? Why had she been killed? *Where* had she been killed? Why had she been left *here*, posed in such a macabre way? Why had this house, this family been chosen?

According to the *Tribune*, those were the questions bandied over porch railings and backyard fences like tennis balls on the courts at the newly built Valley Cove Electric Pleasure Park off Colonial Highway. Surely those same questions roamed Florence Purcell's mind as she lay awake in a dark, neighboring bedroom on nights that followed the incident. Surely she, like everyone else in Mundy's Landing, wondered what if . . . ?

What if he comes back?

He did, once. To 19 Schuyler Place; not here.

And then . . .

Never again.

He simply disappeared, along with the oppressive heat that had suffocated the village for weeks. A fresh season blew in from the west. Lush greenery changed fleetingly to golden red and orange before succumbing to a dry, dead brown, scattered on bracing river gusts. The old year turned; the new brought harsh winter snows and violent spring storms until summer loomed once more, and villagers reconnected over fences and porch railings.

By then, the country had been dragged into the raging global conflict and the new Selective Service Act required all men between the ages of twenty-one and thirty-one to register for the draft. Concern over the eerie events of last summer gave way to more pressing threats. Yet still the unsettling memory remained, as indelibly etched on the communal consciousness as the jagged scratch on the newel post.

A sudden clicking sound reverberates just a few feet from Annabelle's ear, startling her. She gasps and whirls around, expecting to see . . .

Someone.

But it's just the grandfather clock, preparing to play the Westminster Quarters.

With a black walnut longcase, mercury pendulum, and hand-painted roman numerals on an ivory face, the clock rises against the stair wall where it's stood since the house was built. Lester Purcell offered it to Annabelle and Trib, along with a monstrous vintage telescope and the player piano in the front parlor, as if he were bestowing a tremendous favor. Clearly, though, he had no use for the antique monstrosities in his Florida condo.

"Do you know what it would cost him to have these things shipped a thousand miles?" Trib grumbled. "We should just say no."

But Annabelle was nostalgic. Her childhood home, like many in The Heights, had housed an upright piano, and she'd taken lessons as a girl. She decided she might like to play again, or teach Oliver.

The telescope, perched in the cupola on top of the house, still works, and the grandfather clock suits this house better than their own furniture. Most of it is plenty timeworn, but not retro-cool or antique. Just old.

So they kept the telescope. They kept the piano, with its crumbling paper rolls stashed in the bench and keys badly in need of tuning. They kept the clock, its chimes now tolling a reminder that Oliver will be here any second, and the melting ice cream needs to be resuscitated.

She stashes it in the ice-crusted freezer. Then she heads into the storm porch and stops short.

The back door is slightly ajar.

Did she leave it that way?

She must have. Right?

Right.

She opens it, closes it firmly, and goes down the steps through sun-speckled shade toward the open trunk of the car. She can hear the clock's final chime through the open window screens. Songbirds trill high overhead. A lawn-mower hums on a distant block.

Somewhere nearby, a twig snaps.

About to reach for the last couple of grocery bags in the trunk, Annabelle pauses. She looks past the pair of cheap aluminum lawn chairs perched on the cracked concrete apron beside the carriage house—a makeshift patio, she and Trib joked when they sat there the other night for as long as Oliver—and the mosquitoes—would let them.

The sound came from the rear thicket of overgrown shrubs and trees. Probably another stray cat, she thinks. They keep coming around, looking for Augusta and a kibble handout.

But as she looks at the foliage, she realizes it isn't a cat at all.

A human silhouette is distinctly visible among the trees.

She blinks, but it's still there.

What do I do?

"Mom? I'm home! Mom?"

Oliver. He's calling to her from inside the house.

She grabs the bags, slams the trunk, and hurries toward the back door, shooting an uneasy glance over her shoulder when she reaches it.

The shadow is gone.

Inside the house, she locks the back door, drops the groceries on the counter, and finds Oliver in the front hall. He's putting his backpack and a brimming tote bag on the built-in bench, right where she'd imagined him doing just that the day they'd looked at the house . . .

Back when it was still Murder House, and not home.

"We cleaned out our lockers. Look at all this stuff I found!"

She smiles and ruffles his hair. "Terrific. Why don't you take it into the kitchen and go through it while I put away the groceries and make lunch?"

Agreeable, he heads toward the back of the house. She starts after him and then hesitates, thinking of the shadow that had come and gone in the yard.

Whoever was lurking there might have realized he'd been spotted, or slipped away at the sound of her son's voice, or . . .

Or she imagined it in the first place.

Or perhaps it was a ghost.

"Do you think the place is haunted?" Trib asked her just the other night, when she tried to describe the uneasiness she sometimes experiences when she's alone here during the day. "I read about a resident ghost in one of the old newspaper accounts of the murders."

"You know I don't believe in that stuff."

No, and he doesn't, either. They're both much too pragmatic for that.

"I thought you might have changed your mind."

She hasn't. But sometimes—like right now—a restless spirit is the lesser of the evils that might lurk under this roof. Standing utterly still, she pictures an imaginary prowler warily doing the same, hovering in one of the shadowy rooms branching off from the hall.

For a century, the weird facts surrounding the Sleeping Beauty murders have been ingrained in the lore of this town, kept alive in the memories of earlier generations and by the historical society. Maybe ghosts don't inhabit the house, but it's certainly haunted by a collective awareness that lingers among the living heirs to the strange and sorrowful legend.

Yes, and maybe Annabelle was wrong to think that a Murder House can ever truly become a home.

Either way . . . we're stuck with it.

In this town where no one ever locks their doors, she gives the antique knob a firm counterclockwise turn.

From the Sleeping Beauty Killer's Diary
August 2, 1893

Father has always told me, in a rather accusatory fashion, that I was born during a total eclipse of the sun. Given the dramatic circumstances of my birth, I have always supposed he might have imagined, or at the very least exaggerated, that fact.

Whilst roaming the fairground today, I discovered that he did not. Among the educational displays, I came upon astonishing photographic evidence depicting the sun on the date—perhaps at the very moment—of my birth, having been virtually obliterated by the moon. That in turn led me to seek astronomical exhibits, scattered as they are throughout the great expanse of the fair. I concluded my visit in the North Gallery of the Manufacturers Building, where I encountered various telescopic instruments.

As I watched a splendid full moon rising through a magnified lens, I found myself questioning the future Father has prescribed for me. Now that I have grasped the world that lies beyond my little village, wouldn't it be grand to explore the rest of the universe?

I have, like the tormented man in W. B. Yeats's poem, dreamed of Faeryland, and I have found it here, in the White City—

Where people love beside star-laden seas;
  How Time may never mar their faery vows
  Under the woven roofs of quicken boughs:
The singing shook him out of his new ease.

And thus, I fear my wistfulness is slowly transforming into fury at the thought of dutifully returning home to Father and Mundy's Landing.

Chapter 2

Friday, June 24

Early morning mist hugs the sleeping village as Holmes drives through the quiet streets and out onto Colonial Highway toward the river. He parks, as always, in the Price Chopper lot at the Mundy's Crossing Shopping Plaza. The store is open twenty-four hours, so even pre-dawn, his SUV won't arouse suspicion.

Nor will he, dressed for an early hike, wearing cargo pants and carrying a backpack. If, however, anyone glimpsed the items he's stashed inside the pack and his pockets—well, then they'd certainly be curious, if not downright suspicious.

But he encounters no one as he treks the mile along the highway to his destination. It would be simpler and faster to have parked down by the water and gone over via the kayak he keeps stashed in the back of his SUV. But at this hour, there are too many fishermen out on the river. They all know each other, and some might know Holmes, too. They'll realize he doesn't belong there with them, and they'll wonder why he'd want to visit this godforsaken patch of land.

Years ago, a traveling carnival set up here for a few days every summer. Local families descended to ride the rides, play games of chance, and eat grease-slicked, sugar-sticky fair food. But those days are long gone. The spot is now visited only by woodland creatures and by Holmes.

That isn't his real name, but it's the one the world will know when this is over. For now, he keeps his secret identity carefully masked as he goes about his daily business, just as his historic counterpart did.

As a late nineteenth- and early twentieth-century true crime aficionado, Holmes has long been captivated by S.B.K., as he refers to the Sleeping Beauty Killer in his notes. For himself, he chose a pseudonym that honors a trio of famous Holmeses who lived during that era.

The first, Cornelius Holmes, was the mayor of Mundy's Landing during S.B.K.'s reign of terror.

Both other Holmeses were mythical.

One is Sherlock Holmes, the fictional literary hero created by Sir Arthur Conan Doyle, arguably the world's most famous detective.

The other is H.H. Holmes, America's first documented serial killer, the lethal alter ego of an inconspicuous man named Herman Mudgett.

Perhaps S.B.K. crossed paths with H.H., who hunted his victims amid the Chicago World's Fair of 1893. S.B.K. was there in August of that year, according to a notice printed in the *Mundy's Landing Tribune* noting "the intrepid traveler's safe return to our warm fold, ruddy from the prairie sun and bearing adventurous tales."

Imagine—just imagine!—if Sherlock and H.H. had matched wits to solve the S.B.K. case in some alternate universe where fact meets fiction.

Ah, well, in *this* universe, past meets present. Detective meets predator. The legendary Sherlock and the murderous H.H. have melded into one cunning creature. Mundy's Landing's arrogant new mayor Cochran will soon find himself in his predecessor Mayor Holmes's shoes, as an eerily familiar crime spree unfolds in The Heights . . .

Thanks to me. I'll be the most famous Holmes of all.

As he scuffles over familiar ground with his flashlight, he hears the faint, mournful toll of a foghorn somewhere downriver. The first songbird's trill joins the steady hum of insects lurking in tall grasses. Glancing over his shoulder, he notes faint shreds of pink tainting the blue-black eastern sky.

Just few days past the solstice, dawn comes early, at 5:21 a.m.

On June 30, the sun will rise at 5:24 a.m.

On July 8, at 5:28 a.m.

July 14, at 5:33 a.m.

For Holmes, as for S.B.K., time is as crucial as place.

Before the summer of 1916, this pastoral swath of riverfront land was nearly as overlooked as it is now. Located at the end of the streetcar line, its small picnic grove was obscure to all but a smattering of locals.

Wealthy New Yorkers summered in the area, but rarely ventured from their grand Gilded Age estates. Urbanites who boarded trains seeking respite from their sweltering city apartments bypassed Mundy's Landing, which lacked a depot.

Then came June 1916. Valley Cove Electric Pleasure Park opened in the height of the golden amusement park era and drew people from miles around.

If only I'd been alive to see it in all its splendor, Holmes thinks wistfully, imagining this spot teeming with men in straw boaters, women in shirtwaists, children everywhere, boys in knickers, and young girls in middies with hair ribbons.

Was he really there?

To some, the notion might seem like sheer lunacy. Yet the past—specifically 1916—lives so vividly in Holmes's mind that the line between imagination and memory often blurs. When it does, Holmes perceives that reincarnation and time travel, every history buff's fondest fantasies, are not only possible, but probable.

He's been visiting the abandoned Pleasure Park for well over a year now, and so far, he's had it all to himself. Given its prime location near Colonial Highway's growing commercial sprawl, it's only a matter of time, he supposes, before the wildflowers and woodlands are paved over.

But that won't happen overnight. His secret is safe for now. The spot remains overlooked by developers, tourists, and history buffs. Even vintage amusement park enthusiasts focus on other regional historic parks, like Coney Island and Rye Playland, that are still open for business. Those who prefer exploring defunct sites can visit bigger, better ruins.

You would think this location might attract the Mundypalooza crowd, many of whom consider themselves crime aficionados. Yet in their efforts to solve the case, they focus solely on the historical society and Murder Houses in The Heights. How can they be so oblivious, quite literally clueless, to this hallowed ground and its pivotal role in the "frightfulness"?

Frightfulness—that's how Holmes refers to it in his case notes. The vintage word would be unfamiliar to anyone lacking the highly evolved vocabulary in which he takes great pride. Translated from the German *Schrecklichkeit*, it was originally used during the Great War to reference the army's terrorizing tactics toward civilians.

How appropriately it describes the havoc S.B.K. wreaked upon Mundy's Landing a century ago.

Unbeknownst to the rest of the world, it all began in this spot.

And so it shall begin again, Holmes thinks smugly, right here under their noses.

Right here . . . with me.

Annabelle awakens to a man-scream—the most blood-curdling kind, preternaturally high-pitched and hoarse.

Trib.

Trib is screaming.

Her heart slams into her ribs.

Why is Trib screaming?

Something horrible must have happened to Oliver in the night. Dear God. Dear God.

She bolts from the bed and rushes into the hall, bracing for the worst.

But—there's Oliver, safe, framed in the doorway of his bedroom, looking terrified. "What's going on? Where's Daddy?"

"I'm not sure." She rests a calming hand on his pajama-clad shoulder, seized by a new dread: that her husband stumbled across a dead schoolgirl tucked into bed in one of the spare bedrooms.

"Trib?" She struggles to keep her voice steady. "Trib, where are you?"

"In here," he calls from behind the bathroom door.

There is no bed in the bathroom; therefore, there can be no dead girl.

And this is 2016, not 1916, and of course there is no dead girl—what the hell was she even thinking?

"Trib? What's going on in there?"

"Nothing."

Hearing an audible curse and a muffled thump, she raps cautiously on the bathroom door, conscious of Oliver's gaze. Without his glasses, he looks young and vulnerable.

Even *with* his glasses, he looks young and vulnerable.

Because he is.

Diagnosed several years ago with generalized anxiety disorder, Oliver is plagued by irrational worries. Mundane activities others take in stride are monumental tasks for him, and ordinary days? Forget it.

She can no longer remember, much less hope for, days free of sheer panic over activities other kids take in stride or even enjoy. She often feels as though she's strolling through the park one moment and on a harrowing detour through a minefield the next, her child clinging to her for dear life.

"Trib?" she asks, hearing another thump behind the bathroom door.

"Everything's okay," he calls, not convincingly. "Go back to sleep."

"But what are you doing?"

He jerks open the door. Like Oliver, he's not wearing his glasses—he's wearing nothing, in fact, but boxer shorts. He doesn't look young or vulnerable; merely exasperated, waving a rolled-up magazine.

"I was trying to kill a mouse."

"A *mouse*? That's why you screamed?" Ordinarily, rodents make her shudder, but not today. Not when she was thinking of schoolgirl corpses.

"*You* try not to scream with something furry crawling over your bare toes while you're brushing your teeth."

"It crawled on your *toes*?" Oliver asks in dismay.

"It did."

"But then you killed it, right?" Annabelle shoots Trib a pointed look—his cue to say yes, regardless of the truth.

"Nope. I missed."

Missed his cue, missed the mouse. Terrific.

"I'm afraid," their son announces in a small voice.

Annabelle steeples her hands and presses her fingertips into her forehead. It's too early for this, and *this*—whatever this is . . . it's just too much for a kid like Oliver.

For his mom, too.

"Dad, where did the mouse go?"

"I don't—" Trib breaks off, seeing the look on Annabelle's face. He'd obviously intended to complete his sentence with *know*, but instead, he pats Oliver on the shoulder and continues smoothly, "—want you to worry about this."

I don't want you to worry about this? Yeah, right, Annabelle thinks grimly. They never want him to worry about anything, do they? Yet Trib knows as well as she does that curtailing an anxiety attack once it's begun is like attempting to intercept a torpedo with a butterfly net.

"Oliver, the mouse is long gone. Right, Trib?"

"Right. I scared the heck out of him with this." He waves his weapon: a copy of *Family Handyman*. He'd subscribed when they bought the house, in full-on manly and capable mode—though he now appears to be feeling anything but.

"You didn't kill it?"

"We don't need to kill it. It ran away. It's outside now. That's—"

"It's going to come back!"

At the telltale escalation in Oliver's pitch, Annabelle and Trib exchange a glance; his apologetic, hers resigned. They've done this a thousand times before, and unless something changes drastically, they'll do it a thousand times more. Occasionally, Trib defuses the panic attack; more often, she does. It all depends on which of them has more strength, time, and patience—not that those things are guaranteed tactics to see Oliver through a crisis.

"I've got to get into the shower." Trib shoots Annabelle the guilt-laced farewell glance of a soldier spared deployment while his buddy boards the copter to the battlefront, then quickly closes the door.

She puts both hands on Oliver's bony shoulders and turns

him away from the bathroom. "Come on. The alarm won't go off for another half hour, and I know you were up late last night watching the end of the Yankee game with Dad."

At eleven, she left the two of them eating ice cream and went up to bed. Now, she regrets not dragging Oliver along with her, regardless of the game in extra innings. Overtiredness always heightens his anxieties.

Behind the bathroom door, the pipes groan. She tries not to resent Trib, stepping into a steamy shower, as Oliver clutches her arm. "I don't want to go back to bed."

"It's still early, and you need more sleep."

"I don't."

"Well, *I* do," she says reasonably, steering him down the hall to his room, "so how about if you just hang out in your bed until the alarm goes off?"

"No, I don't like it there."

"You don't like your bed? But you picked it out. You said it was the greatest bed ever," she reminds him, silently adding, *and it had better be, since it cost us more than a mortgage payment.*

He'd long been asking them for a captain's bed like his best friend Connor's, built atop a wooden platform with storage underneath. Instead of just drawers, Oliver's bed also has a deep cupboard.

"This would've been good if I still played hide-and-seek!" he said.

"You still can," she reminded him.

"Nah." He never plays anything other than video games. Long gone are the days of hide-and-seek and board games.

He and Trib once had a month-long Battleship tournament that ended abruptly when Oliver learned about the *Lusitania* in social studies.

"I don't like it," he said, "because it makes me think of torpedoes and shipwrecks and that scares me."

"But you're not going to sea," Trib pointed out. "You're playing a game. You've never even been on a boat."

There is no reasoning with Oliver's anxiety. Battleship was history.

Now, he tells Annabelle, "I like the bed. I just hate the room."

He'd chosen it as well, with far less enthusiasm. He'd waffled between a large room down the hall with a fireplace and window seat, and this much smaller one at the top of the stairs, across from their own.

Trailing him between the two, roller and paint cans at the ready, Trib had tried to maintain a jovial attitude in an attempt to head off their son's anxiety. But it grew more strained by the minute, and he finally forced a decision.

"Come on, kiddo, enough is enough. We're moving in tomorrow. You can always change to a different room if you don't like it. There are plenty to choose from."

Oliver glumly decided upon the room next to theirs, as Annabelle had anticipated he would.

"It's more like home," he said—meaning the rented cottage they'd left behind. "You'll be able to hear me if I need you in the middle of the night."

"I'd hear you even if you were down the hall, sweetie," she reminded him, though she could see that he was methodically counting the steps from his doorway to theirs. "And this is home now."

"It doesn't feel like it." Behind his glasses, his wide brown eyes—so like her own, and Trib's—darted nervous glances around the hallway. He took it all in: burnished wallpaper, towering ceilings and amber light spilling from ornate sconces. "It feels like the library."

"You *like* the library."

"I don't want to *live* there."

Fair enough. It's a lovely old building, yet as a child, Annabelle always felt a little uneasy being there. Back then, the historical society was located in the basement. She'd visited its exhibit devoted to the Sleeping Beauty murders and she knew—all the kids in town knew—that the collection also included certain artifacts that weren't on display. Gruesome items related to the crimes that occurred a century ago . . .

In our own home.

But we'll eventually settle in and get past it, she assures herself as she escorts Oliver into his room, now painted a buttery shade of yellow with fresh white trim that matches his new bed.

Before moving in on Memorial Day, they'd stripped the house of its smelly, claw-tattered draperies before realizing that the windows are much too tall for standard shades or curtains. Expensive custom treatments are just one more item on the massive to-do list. The windows remain bare in all but the bedrooms, where Trib installed temporary cheap vinyl shades that leave a wide gap above the sill.

Beyond the wedge of exposed glass, Annabelle sees that it's still dark outside. She fiddles with the toggle light switch on the wall, not yet accustomed to the old-fashioned fixtures.

"There we go," she says cheerily as the room brightens. "See? Look how cozy it is, Oliver."

His television, with the prized Xbox console, is on the dresser along with his video games and favorite books. All were neatly stacked when they moved in. Now the games are tossed haphazardly, the books untouched. There are plenty more stacked in the cupboard beneath the bed, along with outgrown toys he didn't want to part with, and boxes filled with baseball cards. His wooden baseball bat is propped in the corner just inside the door, with his glove draped over the top. It's been a while since he's touched either.

On the bed, the navy and turquoise patchwork quilt is entangled with the sheets. A pillow lies on the floor beside it, evidence of his hasty departure at Trib's scream.

Stupid mouse, she thinks, in lieu of *stupid Trib*.

Sometimes it's hard not to blame each other when their son's anxiety disorder rears its ugly head to strain their otherwise solid marriage. They rarely argue about anything other than how to handle Oliver's episodes amid their own frayed nerves. Those incidences have become more frequent since the move.

Oliver doesn't do well with change, to put it mildly. Or loss.

Naturally, they'd consulted his longtime child psychiatrist, Dr. Seton, before the move. He reminded them that they wouldn't be doing Oliver any favors by removing challenges from his life.

"Even if you managed to accomplish that, the rest of the world won't cooperate. He needs to learn to cope with adversity."

Once they'd made the decision to move, they did think twice about even looking at 46 Bridge Street. Remarkably, however, Oliver seems unbothered by its distant past. His fears tend to be quirkily specific, tied to the here and now. Plus, Connor Winston lives right down the street. That sealed the deal.

"Connor thinks it's cool that I'm going to be living in a Murder House," he reported proudly. "He thinks I'm really brave. Don't tell him I'm not," he added, tugging Annabelle's heart.

He hides his condition from even his closest friends. How many birthday parties has he missed because his crippling fear of the dark means can't see a movie or play laser tag? How many field trips has Annabelle chaperoned because he can't venture beyond his comfort zone without her? How many times has the school nurse sent him home

with a stomachache that fortuitously struck right before a
school assembly or classroom presentation?

But living in a Murder House? Ironically, he's been
okay with that. He did ask several questions about the
historic crimes, seeking reassurance that the Sleeping
Beauty Killer is no longer a threat.

"Absolutely not," Annabelle told him. "He's probably
been dead for at least fifty or sixty years now."

"But nobody even knows who he was, so how do you—"

"It doesn't matter *who* he was. It happened a hundred
years ago. Whoever did it can't possibly still be alive. You
know that, right?"

"Because he would have been old, like Grandpa Charlie?"

"Much older. Grandpa wasn't even born when it happened."

"And dead people can't come back."

No, they can't—something Annabelle would have
done well to remember herself a few skittish minutes ago.

She attempts to coax her son back into bed, but he
grabs her arm like a toddler. Acute separation anxiety
is part of his diagnosis. They've come a long way since
he used to wrap himself around her, screeching, at the
kindergarten bus stop . . . but not nearly far enough.

"Do you want me to stay here with you for a few
minutes?"

"No, please, Mom . . . I don't want to stay here."

"All right. You can get up. It's fine."

"No, not that . . . I want to go home."

"You *are* home, Oli—"

"No!" Tears fill his eyes. "I want our old house!"

"I know you miss it, sweetheart, but—"

"I can't stay here with mice!"

"There were mice in the cottage, too."

"No, there weren't."

Yes there were, but she and Trib made sure he never

knew. They were experts at navigating around potential
triggers in their old home.

Life in the new one is fraught with uncertainty. Here,
there are mice, stray cats, unfamiliar sounds, workmen,
and deliverymen . . .

Yes, and a shadowy visitor lurking in the backyard
yesterday, she remembers uneasily. Her eyes may not be
what they were, thanks to middle age, but she's positive
they weren't playing tricks on her.

If Oliver hadn't been there, she'd have gone back outside to investigate. Instead, she busied herself putting
away groceries, making lunch, sorting through a year's
worth of locker clutter, unpacking more boxes, returning
phone calls. There were a million things to do, as always.

Yet she couldn't quite forget that someone had been
boldly spying through the trees. She meant to tell Trib,
but fell asleep before he came to bed—and woke up to
his scream.

I'll mention it to him today, she decides.

Right now, she has to ease Oliver's mouse concerns.

At least it wasn't a prowler, she thinks wearily.

Or a dead schoolgirl.

In the predawn murkiness, Holmes's flashlight beam
picks up traces of the old trolley turnaround among the
pervasive sumac plants. As always, he wonders what
treasures—potential clues—might still lie scattered
along the arc of rusted rail.

Searching the area in broad daylight, he's already unearthed a handful of antique buttons and coins, including
his cherished 1916 buffalo nickel.

It's just an ordinary coin, as opposed to a rare double
die 1916 version worth tens of thousands of dollars to
collectors.

To him, however, this one is priceless—well worth the

rash he developed from brushing against the poisonous weeds.

Buffalo nickels were date stamped in a vulnerable raised spot that tended to wear off very quickly once in circulation. Any coin with clearly legible numbers, like the one he found, couldn't have been passed from hand to hand over a span of years, or even months.

Clear as day, he can see that nickel tumbling, shiny and brand-new, from pocket or purse as someone stepped off the streetcar here that summer, the summer everything changed.

Someone—perhaps a Sleeping Beauty herself?

Five cents was considerable currency at that time, half the daily admission price or round-trip trolley fare. Losing that much money could very well have left a young woman stranded and vulnerable. Vulnerability could have led to an ill-fated connection with a killer.

His superior logical analysis skills have thus led him to believe that this very nickel, his nickel, might have been the catalyst that led at least one victim to her doom.

He was meant to find it.

Or maybe he found it because he already knew where it was. Maybe he, in another lifetime, actually visited the Pleasure Park. Maybe he encountered S.B.K. Maybe he *was* S.B.K.

Preposterous?

No more preposterous than the great General George S. Patton's belief that he'd gone to battle with Napoleon in a past life.

Maybe that's how Holmes arrived at the truth behind the unsolved murders—not just by carefully weighing all the facts and then piecing them together in a way that makes perfect sense, but courtesy of insider knowledge floating in his brain. Maybe he didn't just solve the perfect crime—he committed it.

He carries the nickel wherever he goes, to remind him of that possibility. Tucked into his pocket, it's wrapped in a fitting shroud: a small piece of white muslin torn from one of the victims' nightgowns.

Alas, the fabric scrap isn't bloodstained. It *is*, however, authentic, stolen from a police evidence file on the case. Plenty of people around here would love to get their hands on it.

Ignorant, all of them. They never bothered to dig beyond the surface of the case, as Holmes did. They never even considered the details. The people. The *timing*.

Deep in the woods above the river, he makes his way to a small graffiti-covered stone building adjacent to the crumbling foundation of the old dance hall.

Having made it his business to learn every possible detail about Valley Cove Electric Pleasure Park, he knows that it was last used for storage, undoubtedly filled with chairs and music stands before the dance hall burned down back in the 1920s.

By then, the Great Depression was looming and the park was past its heyday. It remained closed the summer following the stock market crash—and forever after.

Like the adjacent field, the woods are dotted with its remains.

Some are transient. When the waterline is low, you can see the tops of pilings that once propped the large amusement pier beneath the bluff. In winter, when the ground is bare, the old picnic pavilion's slate slab emerges from the carpet of living foliage and dead leaves.

Other relics are visible year-round: a wrought-iron stairway that leads nowhere, a rusted, twisted metal heap that was once a Ferris wheel, and this sturdy stone structure nestled in the trees on a bluff above the river.

Back when Holmes first came upon it, the door stood ajar as if to beckon anyone who happened along. Inside the windowless room, he encountered countless spiders, rodent droppings, and rampant evidence of teenage decadence: spray-painted graffiti, broken beer bottles, cigarette wrappers and butts, used condoms.

He replaced the exterior door with a steel-enforced look-alike and padlocked it. For a long time, he wondered whether someone would come along and remove it, but no one ever did. The partying kids moved on to more accessible haunts.

Removing the key from his pocket, Holmes swiftly unlocks the door and slips inside. His flashlight beam falls on a trapdoor in the wide-planked floor. There used to be a large iron pull ring in the middle, but he removed it, in case a random person should come across the building and manage to break in—although why would anyone bother? Still, if it happens, the trapdoor will no longer be easy to spot at a glance.

Originally built as an icehouse, a deep cellar lies beneath the floor. Frozen blocks were cut from the river and stored, layered in straw, until they were needed in the summer months. Intended to provide added insulation in warm weather, the building's thick walls, floors, and roof have rendered it virtually soundproof.

For over a year after Holmes first secured it, the building sat undisturbed, waiting . . .

Ready.

No longer empty, the makeshift dungeon has served its purpose for over a month now.

It won't be long until the next part of the plan is underway—although every second must seem like an eternity to the trio of Beauties hidden beneath the trapdoor.

Holmes's Case Notes

I had a close call at 46 Bridge Street yesterday morning. I was in the upstairs bedroom—that bedroom—when I heard a car pull into the driveway. I rushed to the window and spotted Annabelle Bingham getting out of the driver's seat.

I heard her enter the house just as I reached the first floor. I intended to dart out the front door. But through the glass, I saw a neighbor at the curb with a leashed dog.

Trapped, I crept instead toward the back of the house, unaware that Annabelle was making her way to the front. Our paths crossed in the front parlor. Had she glanced in my direction, she'd have seen a pair of human legs between the wooden piano legs. Luckily for me—and indeed, for her—she did not.

She disappeared into the foyer, and I scurried for the back door. I was hiding in the trees, still trying to catch my breath, when she emerged from the house again.

She did glance my way for a long, heart-stopping moment. Had she called out or approached, I'd have treated her to a hastily concocted cover story.

If she hadn't bought it . . .

Yes, then she would have been an obstacle, and I'd have been forced to deal with her accordingly.

But she simply stared before reaching for the rest of the groceries. If she'd spotted me, she wasn't going to let on.

That intrigues me. I'd dismissed her as a stay-at-home mom no different from the others who populate this town—useless creatures who cry for help at the slightest incident and show little interest in anything that doesn't revolve around themselves or their precious offspring.

Does it matter that Annabelle appears to be different?

Not in the long run.

Hence, I note my resolve here, lest I find myself tempted to check in on her again in the days ahead. Now is hardly the time to take chances.

Chapter 3

The morning that began so precariously before daybreak has yet to right itself.

Annabelle finally managed to calm Oliver and wrestle him off to school, but the struggle left her in a volatile mood. Trib, too, was cranky before he departed for work. Even the weather is unstable—hot and humid, with sun and black clouds alternately staking a claim in the sky.

Fittingly, the computer desk in the front parlor wobbles slightly as she sits. This is one of the few recent furniture purchases they've made: a faux wood piece Trib bought on clearance at Home Depot. It came in a cardboard box and he assembled it hurriedly with a screwdriver, a few too many curse words, and a few too few plastic connector pieces. They were missing when he bought it.

"What do you expect for thirty-nine ninety-nine? It might collapse any second," he warned Annabelle when he placed it in the front parlor, in the piano's shadow.

The tumbler of ice water in her hand, slick with beaded moisture, nearly slips from her grasp as she plunks it down without a coaster. She still hasn't gotten around to unpacking them, and who cares if the glass leaves a ring on a desk that might collapse any second?

I feel the same way.

Wilted in the muggy weather and awakened far too early, she's also deprived of her morning caffeine. She'd been too caught up in Oliver's drama to brew her usual pot, and by the time he was gone, it was too hot to drink coffee. Without it, she doesn't have the energy to go swim her laps at the gym as she'd planned to do as soon as Oliver was off to school.

Reaching for the computer mouse, she thinks again of the real one Trib encountered in the bathroom.

That thought leads her directly back to the dead schoolgirls.

How, she wonders, did the Purcell family manage to go on after their horrific experience? How did Florence tuck her children into their beds every night after someone had crept into the house while they were sleeping? How did any of them ever sleep soundly again?

If something like that had happened now, here, with Oliver . . .

Of course it won't.

History can't repeat itself. The Sleeping Beauty Killer isn't lurking, waiting to strike again.

Dead people can't come back.

No, but if Oliver starts noticing strangers prowling in the yard, he might change his mind about that. It's going to be a long summer for both of them unless she finds a pleasant diversion to get him out of the house.

He's too old for the town day camp he's attended since kindergarten, and most of his friends are going to sleepaway camp instead. Back in February, when their friends were glibly filling out registrations and sending in deposits for their sons, Trib thought they should do the same for Oliver.

Annabelle was incredulous. "You're kidding, right?"

"It would be good for him. Every kid there is going

to be homesick, and then they'll get past it. That's what happens at camp."

"It isn't just homesickness. He's not like every kid," she pointed out for the millionth time. "We've finally got him used to the middle school, and we're going to be moving by summer. That's a lot for him to handle."

And for Annabelle herself. It isn't easy to raise a child who can be calm one moment and frantic the next; a child who harbors fears so irrational it might be laughable if it weren't so tragic; a child who can cling to you in terror at an age when his friends are not only long past such behavior but are prone to ridiculing anyone who betrays infantile conduct or weakness of any kind.

"You can't protect him forever, Annabelle," Trib said. "He's not a helpless kitten being attacked by a bear. He's a kid who's got to grow up and leave us someday whether we—whether *he*—likes it or not."

He doesn't like it. But separation anxiety is a medical diagnosis, and Dr. Seton agrees with Annabelle that it isn't a good idea to add more upheaval right now.

In the end, Trib was fine with that decision. "It's not like I'm hell-bent on sending him away. I just don't want him to miss out. I loved camp."

Annabelle suppressed the urge to remind him, yet again, that Oliver is different—different from Trib, different from the other kids they know. Same old conversation, and it would have become the same old argument had they let it progress. They've had a lot of practice avoiding it, pushing silently past the small hurdles and moving on, saving their energy—and their voices—for the huge ones.

Years ago, as a competitive swimmer, Annabelle learned to choose and set goals, then focus on doing whatever it takes to reach them. But you can't control and excel at every aspect of training, let alone a meet. That will only dilute the overall effort.

"It's better to zero in on a couple of areas and work on them until you're exceptional than to be mediocre at everything," she told her students back when she was working as a swim coach at Hadley College

She's tried to use the same principle in parenting Oliver. He's never going to be entirely fearless, but he can focus on mastering a few things that scare him: the school bus, gym class, even a sleepover at a friend's house, which he has yet to attempt.

Most days, she wishes she were as competent a mother as she was a swimmer and coach. Unfortunately—and ironically—she had to give up her job because Oliver suffered when she was on the road with the team. She's been rearranging her daily life to accommodate his needs ever since. She has to be there for him when he needs her.

Which, lately, feels like all the time.

He would be perfectly content to stay here with her all day every day, but Dr. Seton didn't think that was a good idea, either. He cautioned her about allowing Oliver too much screen time.

She and Trib do limit his electronic privileges. They've relaxed the rules since the move, though, because they're busy, and because—healthy or not—Oliver's anxieties ebb when he loses himself in a game or television program.

She told Dr. Seton that there will soon be a functioning swimming pool in the new house to help keep Oliver occupied. Water is one of the rare things some kids fear that he does not. Shipwrecks, yes. Swimming, no. He's always relished that bit of bravado, much as he has the peer respect that comes with moving into a Murder House.

Then again after this morning, thanks to the mouse, he's no longer interested in living here at all.

Wondering where she'll find the strength to resume the inevitable *I want to go home/You* are *home* conversation later, Annabelle turns her attention back to the matter at hand. Dr. Seton advised her that it's not a good idea for Oliver to spend months of uninterrupted time with her at home, pool or not, and he's right.

But she dropped the ball on this, too busy with the impending move to make arrangements when she should have. Now, with summer vacation officially beginning in—she checks her watch—fifteen minutes, she's desperate. Desperate, yet distracted.

She inhales deeply as she opens a search window on the computer. The antique woodwork is particularly aromatic in the muggy heat, infused with the sweet old-fashioned perfume of mock orange, honeysuckle, and peonies blooming beyond the screens.

Is this the same scent Florence Purcell breathed on that awful morning a century ago?

Fingers poised on the keyboard, she fights off morbid curiosity. Additional information about the Sleeping Beauty murders is the last thing she needs right now. Instead, she types *Mundy's Landing summer programs for 12-year-olds* and hits Enter, then scans the results.

Mundy's Landing has overshadowed her other search terms, and is, predictably, synonymous with Mundy-palooza. Every hit revolves around the upcoming extravaganza, with its well-publicized daily schedule of events, everything from a "Forensics Expert Q&A" to a "Whodunnit Roundtable"—whatever that is.

She deletes *Mundy's Landing* and presses Enter again. This time, she gets a number of promising summer programs for kids—but none located in this geographical region. A third search yields several local options Oliver might enjoy, but all are past the enrollment deadline, filled to capacity, or too expensive.

Frustrated, she leans back in her chair and sips her ice water.

What am I going to do with him?

The rubbery-gravelly sound of a car floats through the screened windows behind her. Rather than driving on past, it slows in front of the house. Turning, she spots an unfamiliar black SUV lingering in the middle of the street. She can't see the driver, but she can feel him watching her.

No wonder Augusta Purcell cloaked the windows in layers of heavy fabric.

I'll ask Trib to install those vinyl shades down here, too, she decides. *I don't even care what it looks like. I don't want to be a sitting duck for snoops all summer.*

At last, the shadowy driver moves on down the street.

But I'm sure he'll be back, she thinks as she resumes her dogged online search.

This is what it must feel like to be high on drugs, Holmes decides, as he turns the corner from Bridge onto State Street.

Unlike his idol Sherlock, who dabbled in cocaine and morphine, he doesn't use illegal substances. He prefers to derive pleasure from being squarely rooted in every moment. Surely no chemical-induced sensation could rival his exhilaration when he saw Annabelle Bingham sitting in her parlor. It was all he could do to move his foot from the brake to the gas pedal and drive on past 46 Bridge.

To think he almost hadn't allowed himself to detour through The Heights this morning. He'd promised himself he'd stay away, but the house pulled him like a magnet, as always.

There she was, plainly visible through the front parlor window.

Once again, he could have sworn she'd seen him.

Once again, she didn't let on. She didn't jump to her feet and rush to the window, or disappear from view.

Until now, he hasn't wasted much time wondering what makes Annabelle Bingham tick. There are too many others to worry about.

The Beauties are becoming a problem.

"Shut up!" he hollered this morning, amid their incessant wailing. "I can't hear myself think!"

A pity, because frankly, one of Holmes's most pleasurable pastimes is hearing himself think. And speak.

"I love the way your mind works," he says aloud, a perfect imitation of his mother's admiring tone. She often said those very words to him. Now that she's gone, Holmes carries on the tradition.

"There's nothing wrong with talking to yourself," he adds, driving on down State Street. "How else can you be assured of an intelligent speaker and attentive audience?"

Of course, if you are alone, some errant eavesdropper might misinterpret one-sided conversation for loneliness, or even mental illness. Holmes suffers from neither affliction, though when he was in London a few years back, he was memorably accused of the latter. He quite sanely and methodically set matters straight, though his efforts went unappreciated by the accuser, lying as she was in a puddle of her own blood.

No raging madman, Holmes.

He goes sensibly yet stealthily about his business just as his predecessor did a century ago. How else can one expect to hide in plain sight?

With a satisfied smile, he drives on through The Heights. The infamous dates—three of them, spaced about a week apart—loom as tantalizingly close as the trio of Murder Houses themselves.

June 30: 65 Prospect Street.

July 8: 46 Bridge Street.

July 14: 19 Schuyler Place.

The agenda is set for S.B.K.'s return visit to Mundy's Landing, and the clock is ticking.

Whenever it gets to be too much—the gnawing hunger in her belly, the terror growing like mold in the darkest corner of her soul—Indi makes up stories. She lets her imagination fly her away to a world where she's a princess, or a rock star, or just back home in Albany, New York.

Home . . .

She squeezes her eyes closed, not that it matters in the pitch black, and pretends that she's lying in her own bed. She tries to ignore the dank chill in the air and the fiery ache in her twisted, shackled arms. In her fantasy, she's just awakened on a warm summer morning, the kind of morning where your hair sticks to your forehead and neck, and your pajamas are damp, and you slept with the covers thrown back.

Indi shivers, longing for warmth, longing for home . . .

No, you are home. You are.

Yes, she's back in the duplex apartment she shares with her stepfather, Tony. She can hear him snoring through two closed doors and see the plastic glow-in-the-dark stars and moon—a full moon, sloppily painted in blue Day-Glo—stuck on the ceiling above her bed. She can hear the old box fan cranking away in the window. Its dusty plastic blades stir sticky air laced with hot asphalt from the highway below her bedroom window.

They're always paving at this time of year. Heavy machinery incessantly makes that *beep . . . beep . . . beep*ing backing-up sound. It grates on her nerves, but not today. Today, it would be music to her ears.

"Blue moon . . . you saw me standing alone . . ."

Karen is singing to her.

If only it were real.

Please let it be real. Please, please . . .

She opens her eyes to blackness.

This is real: being imprisoned in some kind of underground bunker deep in the woods.

For a long time, she was alone here. Then Juanita came, followed by Kathryn. Both had also been abducted by the man in the black SUV.

When they showed up, one right after the other, Indi figured it, too, was a fantasy. Maybe all that time alone in the dark had taken its toll and she'd lost her mind.

But she hadn't. Not yet, anyway.

"I want to go home, goddammit," she whispers into the darkness.

"I wish you wouldn't do that." A devout Christian, Juanita protests whenever Indi takes the name of the Lord in vain.

Sometimes Indi apologizes. Today, she's feeling prickly. "Yeah, well, I wish a lot of things."

Juanita says nothing to that.

Kathryn, too, is silent. She's probably out cold again.

Younger, smaller, and frailer than Indi and Juanita, she's fading fast. Whenever she loses consciousness, Indi worries that she might not wake up.

"I hope I don't. At least it's a way out of this hellhole," Kathryn told her a few hours—or was it a few days?—ago. It's all just a blur of hunger and exhaustion, the dark and the cold. They aren't wearing watches, and he took their phones away. He took everything except the clothes on their backs.

If only Indi had been wearing a fleece jacket and jeans that night. What she wouldn't give for a layer of protection against the clammy gloom and the creepy-crawly bugs and the metal restraints that gouge her wrists and ankles.

Yet she told Kathryn, "Come on, you can't give up. The police have to be looking for you, for all of us."

"They're never going to find us here."

"She's right," Juanita said. "We're buried alive."

"*Alive*, though," Indi reminded them. "As long as we're alive . . ."

"We might as well be dead."

"How can you think that, Juanita?"

"How can you not? Ask me to choose between heaven and hell . . . I'll take heaven."

Maybe Indi would feel the same way if she were as devoutly Christian as Juanita. But she's not even certain there's an afterlife. And if there is . . .

She's not sure where she's headed. Lately, she's done some stuff that won't guarantee her a fast pass through the Pearly Gates. She's rung up beer for underage friends at the store, and she's drunk too much of it later. She's smoked cigarettes and worse.

But one sin weighs far more heavily on her now: last year, she terminated an unwanted pregnancy because she didn't want to end up like her mother. If Karen had done that, Indi wouldn't be alive.

Maybe she isn't supposed to be. Maybe this is her punishment.

She closes her eyes, not wanting to believe that. It wouldn't be fair. She's not a bad person. She was just stupid, and afraid.

Juanita is sobbing loudly. She does that a lot, wailing to herself in Spanish.

Indi doesn't understand most of what she's saying, but some of it sounds like prayer. She may have failed Spanish—not to mention moral goodness—but even she knows what *Dios* means.

Dios doesn't seem to be paying attention. They can pray all they want; they can screech and beg until they're hoarse, and no one listens.

"I can't hear myself think!" their captor bellowed the last time he visited—maybe yesterday, maybe a week ago.

Whenever they hear footsteps overhead, they start screaming, in case it's a rescuer. It never is. The trapdoor opens, and it's he. They can't see him, but he can see them. He shines a blinding light into the hole. They can hear him muttering to himself as he tosses down food and water. Sometimes it rolls just beyond their reach, no matter how hard they strain. When that happens, they go without. He doesn't care. He just closes the door and disappears again.

Since Indi has been here, he's lowered a ladder to climb down into the hole twice: once to deliver Juanita; again to deliver Kathryn.

For a long time, she thought others might join them. Or that he was going to descend and do terrible things to them. You hear about depraved perverts who keep young girls imprisoned or sell them as sex slaves.

But this isn't like that.

What is it?

That's the thing. It doesn't make sense. He hasn't raped them. And he can't possibly be holding them for ransom, because the other girls' families are even more impoverished than Tony is.

He wants something else.

Something, she fears, more ominous than anything she'll allow her mind to conjure.

She closes her eyes.

I'm home . . . I'm home . . .

Please, please let me go home . . .

From the Sleeping Beauty Killer's Diary
August 14, 1893

I have spent the vast majority of my time at the Exposition immersed in astronomical delights. Each time I visit the grounds, there is something new to discover, much like the universe beyond our earthly boundaries.

As time grows short, I have made an effort to experience the fair's most notable attractions, lest Father accuse me, upon my return, of having avoided the educational experience I'd promised to seek here.

Father and the great Jules Verne would be glad to know that yesterday I visited, in quick succession, pavilions unique to each of forty-three states and territories and nearly two dozen countries. Hence, like a modern-day, breakneck Phileas Fogg, I traveled around the world in not eighty days but just one.

This morning, wilting beneath the incessant Midwestern heat, I found refreshing respite in the waters of the natatorium.

Later, within the brightly lit Electricity Building, I witnessed remarkable demonstrations of every appliance imaginable, projected to change the way we shall live our daily domestic lives in the distant future.

Finally, as the blazing prairie sun set over the midway on this final night, I purchased a ticket to ride Mr. Ferris's Great Wheel. I know what Father would say about my splurging fifty cents on such folly when the banks are failing and the nation's economy is a shambles. But I had coins at the ready and I seized the opportunity that will become, as I see it, my last untethered moment for the foreseeable future.

Having gaped at the engineering marvel with my feet firmly rooted on the dusty ground for days on end, I waited rather impatiently for my turn to soar. By the time I boarded a car, the sunset had given way to a delicate sliver of golden moon suspended in a dusky indigo sky.

As the wheel carried me up, up, up into the heavens, my fellow passengers exclaimed over the view below. I must agree that the array of sparkling yellow lights against deep blue shadows of land and lake was indeed breathtaking. Yet as we arced over the top of the wheel, I was dumbfounded by what lay above and beyond.

Arms outstretched, awash in the strange sensation that I would catapult into that twilight sky, I strained to pluck the moon for my pocket, a most fitting souvenir.

Alas, too soon, I was whisked back down to earth, that golden crescent well beyond my grasp once more.

Twilight sinks down from above us,
Swiftly all the near is far:
But first shining high above us
Radiant is the evening star!
Everything is drifting vaguely,
Mist steals upwards to the height:
And the still lake mirrors darkly
Black abysses of the night.

—Johann Wolfgang von Goethe

Chapter 4

Stepping out onto the front porch, Annabelle nearly changes her mind about going to meet Oliver at the bus stop. The house may not be air-conditioned, and it seemed stuffy while she was trapped inside, but at least it's shaded by trees and sturdily built enough to ward off the blazing midday heat. The world beyond is hot, bright, and preternaturally still. She wades down the steps through soupy air sonorous with cicadas and window air conditioners.

She spent the morning poring over old news accounts of the historic crimes and keeping an eye out for Peeping Toms when she should have been doing other things. Laundry, cleaning, unpacking, searching for the elusive window fans . . .

All that can wait. Right now, she needs to get out of the house; needs a distraction from her growing obsession with Florence Purcell, trespassers, and murdered schoolgirls.

Glad she remembered to grab her sunglasses, she puts them on and feels them instantly slip lower on the sweat-slicked slope of her nose.

Mundypalooza might be looming, but Bridge Street is deserted. Her flip-flops make a slapping sound against the concrete as she walks toward the corner. There's not a car or pedestrian in sight, no joggers, dog walkers, or stroller-pushing moms. Even the elderly porch sitters have been driven indoors by uncomfortable weather.

The bus stop is two blocks away, at the intersection of Fulton Avenue and Colonial Highway. She walks down every morning with Oliver, who balks at leaving the house alone. The only way to get him out the door is to go with him.

Before the move, she always met him after school as well, since he was the only kid getting off at the old bus stop. But here in The Heights, he disembarks with a gaggle of neighborhood kids. By that time of day, in the swing of being away from home and Annabelle, he contentedly makes his way back to Bridge Street with his best friend, Connor Winston.

Annabelle never worries. It's broad daylight, the boys don't have to cross the highway, and the neighborhood is as safe as it was when she was growing up here, with plenty of familiar faces out and about. Today, though, she feels uneasy at the thought of her child wandering the streets of Mundy's Landing unsupervised, unprotected. As much as she tells herself she's out here for her own sake—a change of scenery, a diversion, a breath of not-so-fresh air—she really just needs to shepherd her son safely home along streets once prowled by a predator.

Somehow, it doesn't matter that the murders took place a century ago, or that the victims were all female, and not even local residents. Today, it's hitting too close to home.

She rounds the corner.

Perched on the Village Common and lined with storefronts, Fulton Avenue marks the border between The Heights and the business district. The *Mundy's Landing Tribune* building is across the leafy green, tucked on a side lane off Market Street, so close to home that Trib could easily walk to and from the office. He never does, needing a car on hand so that he can dash to breaking news scenes.

The subject of today's front-page story, however, is literally a stone's throw away: it's about the intersection of Fulton Avenue and Prospect Street, which Annabelle is about to cross.

Throughout her childhood, the crossing had just a two-way stop sign. That became a four-way stop with a crosswalk as a result of the increasing traffic brought on by Mundypalooza. Now there's a traffic signal that flashes yellow most of the year and red during the hectic summer season.

Nonetheless, people—almost exclusively out-of-towners—tend to either speed through the intersection or get distracted gaping at the historical society on the corner. The flashing red light is ignored or overlooked, resulting in an increasing number of near-pedestrian misses and fender benders at the spot, with the latest accident yesterday morning resulting in minor injuries.

Prominent orange traffic cones and a cop have since been posted there for the duration of the visitor onslaught.

Annabelle recognizes the young uniformed officer stationed on the opposite corner today. Ryan Greenlea is a local boy.

Man, she corrects herself, taking in the badge, broad shoulders, blue visor, and aviator sunglasses. Just yesterday, he was a scrawny kid in a Cub Scout cap and thick wire-rimmed glasses. Little boys grow up quickly. But will Oliver? It's hard to imagine him manly and capable.

Officer Greenlea beckons her to cross the street.

"I'm on my way to the bus stop," she tells him, after they agree that it's a hot one today. "It wasn't so long ago that you were on the school bus yourself, was it?"

His mouth quirks into a smile and he shrugs. "It seems like a lifetime ago to me."

"I bet it doesn't to your mom," she says, and makes a note to tell Trib that it's happened: she's officially become one of the old-timers who goes around town telling young people how quickly they've grown up and how time flies.

She and Officer Greenlea tell each other to have a good day, and she starts to walk on, then turns back, remembering.

"I just want to mention something."

But does she really?

Too late to back off now. He's waiting expectantly.

"My husband and I bought the house at 46 Bridge."

He nods. He's local. She doesn't need to explain that it's a Murder House. He gets it.

"Yesterday afternoon, I found someone on the property."

"In the house?"

"No. God, no." She shudders at the thought. "I just glimpsed him in the trees behind the house. And this morning, a car stopped in front of the house and someone else was kind of . . ."

"Spying?" he guesses when she trails off, and she nods.

"I just thought I should mention it, because it's that time of year, and I have a little boy, and it makes me nervous to have strangers hanging around watching the house. I mean, I get why they do it, but . . ." Hearing the rumble of large tires and a whoosh of brakes, she looks over her shoulder and spots the school bus.

"Do you want to file a report?"

"No, nothing happened. I just thought I should mention it. I'm sure it's par for the course, living in one of . . . the houses." She can't bring herself to say the word *murder*.

She glances again toward the bus, seeing the flashing lights go from yellow to red. Kids are bounding off. She doesn't want Oliver to come walking up in the midst of this conversation.

"I'll mention it at the station. We're stepping up patrol in The Heights anyway over the next few weeks, but if you see anything else suspicious or feel as though you might be in danger, don't hesitate to call. We can have someone there in a matter of minutes. Sometimes even seconds," he adds, and his mouth smiles, as does hers.

But her eyes, masked behind the sunglasses, are wide. *Danger?*

Does Officer Greenlea think there's danger?

Of course not, she assures herself. The danger came and went a hundred years ago. This is nothing more than a nuisance. She probably shouldn't have mentioned it at all.

As always, the precinct bustles with activity this afternoon. But the NYPD Missing Persons Squad is going to have to get along without Detective Sullivan Leary for the next two weeks. Only one short stack of case paperwork stands between her and her summer vacation.

As she reaches for the document, her cell phone rings for the fourth time in the past half hour.

She groans. "Now what?"

The first time it was her landlord; the second, her building's maintenance supervisor; the third, the electrician who will be doing some long overdue work on her apartment while she's away. Each call brought fresh aggravation.

"Maybe it's FDNY calling to say your place is on fire," her partner, Detective Stockton Barnes, comments without looking up from his own paperwork.

"You say that like it would be a bad thing."

"Yeah, what do you care? You've got someplace else to stay for the next few weeks." He scribbles his signature on a report as she pulls her cell phone out of her pocket. "And if that doesn't work out, what do I care? In about two minutes, I won't be around to listen to you complain."

Barnes, too, is anxious to call it a day, though his upcoming vacation is as drastically different from hers as—well, everything else about the two of them.

Sully is a petite, fair-skinned redhead with a quick

temper and an affinity for the simple things in life: baseball, television, burgers, and beer. She likes to stay close to home. World traveler Stockton is a strapping, movie-star handsome African-American man with gregarious charm and a fairly extravagant lifestyle despite a cop's salary.

"Trust me, you wouldn't hear me complaining if my place burned down," Sully informs him, glancing down at her phone to see who's calling. "Everything I care about is loaded into the trunk of my rental car, and—oh good."

"It's not about the apartment?"

"Nope. It's Nick."

"The Knicks?"

"You know who I mean."

"Saint Nick? Nick Nolte? Nick—"

"Hi, Lieutenant Colonomos," she says into her phone.

"Please, call me Nick," he reminds her, and she wastes a smug smile on the back of Barnes's head.

"Sorry, I keep forgetting. And please call me Sully."

When they first met back in December, she was following a case that led up to Mundy's Landing in the Hudson Valley. After the arrest, she was so enamored of the village that she looked forward to return visits to wrap up the case. Barnes, however, complained every time they made the hundred-mile drive from midtown, and can't understand why she wants to spend her long-awaited vacation there.

"Are you on your way?" Nick asks Sully.

"Not yet. I got a little bogged down in paperwork. You know how that goes."

Barnes looks up with a snort and rolls his eyes at Sully, who ignores him. Her partner has little respect for their Mundy's Landing law enforcement counterparts, based on their cushy headquarters on the village square and a crime blotter that typically features trespassers and pooper-scooper violations.

"John Patterson just stopped in to say he's headed out of town," Nick tells her, "but the cottage is all set for you. He left the keys under the front doormat."

John owns the place she's renting for the next two weeks in Mundy's Landing. Like many locals, he flees town when the summer crowds descend, funding his vacation—and then some—by renting out his home in The Heights.

Just before Christmas, she'd casually mentioned to Nick that she'd love to visit the village again in nicer weather. He said that Ron Calhoun, the police chief, lives across the street from a place that had just become available again for the last week in June and first week in July. Nick showed Sully a couple of photos of the gingerbread cottage, painted lavender and gray, with window boxes and an ivy-covered chimney.

"You probably don't want to waste much time making up your mind," Nick advised. "Whoever was supposed to rent it just backed out last night, and John's about to list it again. It'll get snapped up right away. So if you don't have other vacation plans . . ."

"She does," Barnes spoke up. "She always spends those weeks down the Jersey Shore."

He was right about that. Sully used to go with her husband when she was still married, and kept up the tradition with her single friends after the divorce. Last summer, she wound up going by herself, which was . . . fine. Relaxing. Just not exactly fun.

After some debate, she told Colonomos, "Maybe it's time for a change of scenery. I guess I'll take it."

If you were to listen to Barnes—and Sully really does try not to listen to Barnes—you'd get an entirely different account of that conversation.

According to him, Sully was so eager to rent the place that she whipped out her checkbook on the spot, gushing to the dashing cop about how she couldn't wait to see him again.

"I said the *town*. Not him. And I never carry my checkbook around. And gushing? I was *not* gushing."

"You were gushing harder than ye olde fountain in ye olde town square, Gingersnap."

"The fountain wasn't gushing. Everything was frozen solid. It was ten degrees."

"Well, it'll be gushing in summer, and so will you if you go back there and hang around with Dudley Do-Right."

Barnes was wrong. Not about the fountain, with its patinaed copper sculpture of Horace J. Mundy. It's probably gushing away by now. But she isn't in the mood. Her landlord told her this morning that he's raising her rent again on September first. She's paying a fortune to live in a concrete box that's not much bigger than the holding cell at Central Booking.

For now, though, she only wants to think about vacation.

"It's probably not a good idea for John to leave the keys under the mat," she tells Nick. "Maybe there's a neighbor who could hang on to them for me? Or maybe . . ."

She trails off, hoping he'll volunteer to meet her at the house himself.

He says only, "Don't worry. People do that all the time here. It's safe. Not like the city. You'll see."

Right. Trespassers and pooper-scooper scofflaws. She doesn't remind him that they met in the first place because she was there investigating a grisly homicide. Last winter's serial killer was an anomaly. So was the one who struck the village exactly a hundred years ago next week.

Who knows? Maybe Sully will be the one to solve the Sleeping Beauty case and claim the reward. An extra fifty grand would allow her to tell the landlord to go to hell and . . .

And rent a slightly larger concrete shoebox in the sky. Swell.

"Good luck getting settled," Nick tells her. "Holler if you need anything. I'd offer to show you around when you get here, but I've got my hands full with the commotion around here. We're all working overtime, and then some. Safe travels."

Overtime, and then some?

She thanks him, wondering if she's just been given the brush-off.

It isn't that she was expecting him to wine and dine her. Especially on her first night in Mundy's Landing. Because of course she's not going up there solely to see him. Or to see him at all.

It just would have been nice if he'd been a little more accessible, as a fellow cop. And, okay, as a *man*. An available man. She knows he's single, and he doesn't seem to have a girlfriend.

Hanging up, she sees Barnes watching her.

"What?"

"Just wondering what Tall, Dark, and Handsome had to say? Or not say?" he adds, obviously having read her mind, as usual.

"I thought *you* were Tall, Dark, and Handsome, Barnes."

"I may be taller and a helluva lot darker, but pretty boy's got me beat on the handsome."

"You don't honestly think that."

"No, but you do."

"Don't put words into my mouth, Barnes." She pockets her phone, pushes back her chair, and picks up the paperwork. "Come on. It's time to get out of here. You want to walk me to my rental car?"

"You want to give me a ride to JFK?"

"On a Friday in the summer? Are you out of your mind?" She shakes her head. "I'd help you flag a cab, but we both know you'll never find one at this time of day in this heat. Hope you brought something to read on the airport bus. I hear *War and Peace* is a real page-turner."

"I was just kidding about the ride." He picks up his own paperwork and reaches for the handle of a rolling bag parked beside his desk. "I've got a limo taking me to the airport this trip. Kicking things off in style, baby."

"Same here. I went with the compact-class rental car instead of economy."

"Good choice, considering you *are* compact."

"And class. Don't forget it. I'm all class."

"You're *in* a class all your own, Gingersnap."

"Ditto, Barnes. Who's footing the bill for the limo?"

"Remember that sweet little old lady I met on Sutton Place a few weeks ago? The one who was struggling with the purse snatcher?"

"The sweet little old lady whose mother was a Vanderbilt and whose purse cost more than I make in a year?"

"That's the one. She took me to lunch last week to thank me, and when she heard I was going on vacation, she insisted on sending her driver to take me to the airport."

Sully rolls her eyes and shakes her head.

"What?" Barnes is all innocence. "That's not violating any rule about accepting gifts on the job. I wasn't on duty. I was just being a Good Samaritan who happened to come along while she was being mugged."

"And you were on Sutton Place because . . ."

"Because that's where Jessica lives."

"I thought you broke up Memorial Day weekend."

"We did. I was picking up all my stuff."

"And then you conveniently dropped it off at Mrs. Vanderbilt's? Is she your girlfriend now?"

"Hilarious." He shakes his head. "And she isn't Mrs. Vanderbilt. Her mother was a Vanderbilt. Her name is—"

"What I want to know is how you managed to dump Jessica and yet somehow still get to take this fabulous vacation to . . . where are you going again?"

"A tiny island in the South Pacific. Jessica's not going with me."

"No, but you were supposed to, and she paid for the plane ticket and you're staying at her timeshare."

"I told you, we ended things amicably, and she insisted I go."

Of course she did. In Barnes's charmed life, someone—usually a female someone—always seems to be jetting him to a resort or carting him around by chauffeur. Or at the very least, sending him pricey bourbon from a nearby barstool. In Sully's not-so-charmed life, the drunk on the next barstool always seems to be puking on her shoe. Though that hasn't happened in at least a few months. Maybe her luck is changing.

Five minutes later, stepping out into glaring sun, she and Barnes find Seventh Avenue transformed into a sauna writhing with too many bodies.

"Good Lord." Squinting, Sully feels around in her pockets for her sunglasses as Barnes lowers his over his eyes. "It's hotter than Hades out here."

He holds out his hand, palm up. "Ten bucks."

"What?"

"You swore you'd never complain again about being too hot. I bet you would. We shook on it. You owe me ten bucks."

"When was that?"

"January. Remember?"

"Hell, no. My brain was numb from New Year's until Easter."

Winter had record lows, and spring came late. When

it did arrive, it lasted maybe a day before blasting ahead into full-blown summer.

The city in summer, the city anytime, has never really bothered Sully before. She's a native New Yorker, born to the breed: her father was NYPD, and so were his brothers, his father and grandfather. Same on her mother's side.

This is the only home she's ever known. But she doesn't find it very appealing under the rippling sheen of sun and heat. The heavy air is ripe with sweat, tar, and garbage. Sirens wail incessantly. Crime goes up with the temperature. The streets are clogged with honking traffic, the sidewalks with cantankerous humanity. Everyone but the tourists would rather be someplace else.

Luckily, she's about to be.

She pulls a crumpled ten from her wallet and hands it to Barnes. "Here you go."

"Nah, it's okay. Keep it."

"No, give it to that resort masseur you keep talking about, and tell him to give you a couple of extra-hard slaps from me."

"You mean *her*."

"What makes you so sure it'll be a woman?"

"I saw the Web site photos. She's an exotic babe in a coconut shell top."

"Pffft. That's the Web site."

"Jealous, Gingersnap?"

"Jealous? Me?"

Okay, so maybe she secretly hopes the masseuse turns out to be a masseur. Or at least a jolly, roly-poly old woman instead of an exotic babe—only for his own good, of course.

Like her, Barnes swore off serious relationships after his divorce. But he likes to flirt, and women enjoy flirting back, including those who think they can lure him for the long term.

Luckily for Sully—and perhaps for Barnes—she isn't one of them. As far as she's concerned, partners should never become romantically involved. She and Barnes learned the hard way that fellow cops often make lousy spouses. Reality isn't changed by the fact that they get along far better with each other than they ever did with their respective exes.

"There's my car." He points to a black sedan waiting on the curb across the street.

"Wow, aren't you fancy, Mr. . . . Baines."

"What?"

She points to the white sign in the car's window.

"*Baines*," he reads aloud. "Yeah, I'll be Mr. Baines. Hell, I'll be *Mrs*. Baines as long as that car has A.C. Where's your rental, Sully?"

"Twelve blocks up and around the corner on Eighth. Ready for a fast getaway, facing uptown."

"Want a ride?"

"Nah, your car is headed in the opposite direction. Listen, you be careful, Mrs. Baines."

"Of what?"

"The last thing you need is to fall in love with some hula chick masseuse who lives across the globe."

"Right now, a hula chick masseuse is *exactly* what I need. How about you?"

"I don't give massages. And I don't hula."

He laughs. Too hard. "I gotta admit, the thought of you jerking around in a grass skirt is . . . interesting."

"*Jerking? Interesting?* Hey, I *could* do a mean hula if I wanted to."

"A mean hula? Want to demonstrate?"

She gives him the finger.

"Yeah, that *is* mean. Anyway, what I meant is, what did the doctor order for *your* vacation? Maybe a strapping stable boy?"

"Stable boy? What am I, a cradle robber?"

"A strapping mature farmhand, then."

"Where do you think I'm going, Barnes? Iowa?"

"I *know* where you're going, Sully. Just remember what I said."

"Yeah, yeah . . . nice place to visit, but you wouldn't want to live there."

"Not even a nice place to visit. And *you* wouldn't want to live there." He points squarely at her. "Trust me. You might think you would, but you wouldn't. Just take care of yourself and put everything behind you." He wraps her in a quick bear hug. "I want you back, okay?"

Touched by the unexpected flash of sincerity, she stands watching him jaywalk across the avenue to his waiting car.

She turns abruptly and starts shouldering her way around the sightseers who insist upon walking four or five abreast. Holding hands. Jerks.

I want you back, okay?

When they first visited Mundy's Landing in December, she was just busting Barnes's chops when she said she was so fed up with city life that she'd consider moving there.

But now, six months later, after everything that's happened, the *everything* Barnes wants her to put behind her . . .

You never know.

"Move, lady!" a guy bellows in her ear, jostling her from behind. The Don't Walk sign has changed to Walk. Sully walks, headed north.

Holmes's Case Notes

To most people, the three Murder Houses are a matched set, having played equal, chronological roles in the historic crimes.

But those people don't know what I know.

One crucial detail makes 46 Bridge Street unique. Because of it, I find it difficult to stay away even now that the Binghams have moved in.

Augusta was still alive back when I began investigating the Sleeping Beauty murders in earnest, but she would never have invited me past the threshold.

She lived alone even at her advanced age, but caregivers came and went on a regular schedule that was ridiculously easy to discern.

One night, certain Augusta was the only one in the house, I crawled through a broken basement window and stealthily made my way to her bedroom.

For a long time, I stood over her and watched her chest rise and fall, swept by a reverence akin to what I experience whenever I gaze at the historical society's special exhibit.

To think that the ancient crone, with her wispy white hair and translucent tissue-paper skin, had once been a round-cheeked, brunette six-year-old! I longed to awaken her just so that I could stare into those eyes—or better yet, see what she had seen. As the last surviving witness, she was a living artifact.

She passed away not long after my first stealthy nocturnal visit. By then, I'd found a spare set of keys in a desk drawer and used them to familiarize myself with the floor plan, laying the groundwork for things to come.

It isn't the same with the other two Murder Houses, for the aforementioned reason and many additional ones. They're both equipped with alarm systems that will alert police headquarters, conveniently located a block away. Plus, the Yamazaki family, who live at 65 Prospect Street, has a large dog.

Forty-six Bridge Street is readily accessible and has conveniently stood empty for months while it was on the market. During that time, I often spent the night in the small room that opened off the master bedroom. It was there, in the dark, that my plan took shape.

Chapter 5

"**T**onight?"

"Tonight," Annabelle confirms as she hurries past Trib, dragging a chair around the obstacle course on the floor.

"What time are they coming?"

"Six-thirty." She tiptoes on the chair to fetch the olive oil and vinegar. She can't reach most of the shelves in the dark wood cabinets even though she's an agile five-seven.

"It's six-forty."

She glances at the stove clock as she climbs down. He's right. Damn. The Winstons will be here any minute.

Trib shakes his head, still rooted a few feet inside the door he'd walked through less than a minute ago, wearing khakis and a blue chambray button-down, loosened at the collar and sleeves rolled up. He's always exhausted on Fridays and was probably looking forward to a low-key evening in front of a televised Yankees game.

"So you're cooking dinner for them?"

"Me? No. What gave you that idea?" Sarcasm isn't usually Annabelle's style, but it's hot as hell and she's irritable.

Like the rest of the house, the kitchen is still cluttered with boxes that have yet to be unpacked. Somewhere among them are several window fans. Today would have been a great day to come across them.

"Easy there, Cruella," Trib says mildly. "What are you making?"

"Couscous-stuffed chicken breasts." Well, she'll be making them as soon as the homemade angel food cake, to be served for dessert with strawberries and ice cream, comes out of the oven.

"On a ninety-degree day? What were you thinking?"

"I was *thinking* that school is out and we should celebrate with Oliver, and Connor is leaving for camp tomorrow morning so they won't see each other until August."

She doesn't add that it will take their son's mind off the mouse—which he hasn't forgotten. Or that it might be his last bit of fun for the next two months, since she failed to find a summer program for him.

"You don't have to make yourself crazy. We could have just gone out for pizza."

"I'm not making myself crazy"—*lie*—"and there's no way we'll get into any pizza place tonight. The village is jammed with people."

Truth.

"Anyway," she goes on, tiptoed on the chair, rummaging through the contents of the shelf, "they want to see the house."

Also truth. Kim Winston has been texting all week. She was out on the porch steps waiting for Connor when Annabelle trailed the boys home from the bus stop, and she all but invited herself over tonight with her husband and their kids.

It seemed like a good idea at the time. Now . . . not so much.

Annabelle plucks the oil and vinegar from the shelf, climbs down, and looks around for a place to put them. There isn't one. Removing a stack of unopened mail from the counter, she sets the bottles in the cleared space and thrusts the heap of bills and catalogs into Trib's hands. "Can you please stick this someplace?"

"Where? Or will I be sorry I asked?" He flashes the wry grin she fell in love with almost thirty years ago.

She returns it, albeit fleetingly. "There's just too much clutter on the counters, and I'm in way over my head with this dinner."

"No way, really?"

He steps over to the dryer—the laundry facilities are in a kitchen nook—opens the door, and puts the mail inside on top of the load of dry towels she hasn't had time to fold.

As she rushes past him again, dragging the chair back to where it belongs, she decides that one of the best things about Trib—and there are *many* best things about Trib—is that he's unflappable. She appreciates that, being largely unflappable herself, though not tonight.

"Trib," she says now, "yesterday when I—"

The stove timer goes off a split second before the doorbell rings, and the moment is lost.

leaving the city on a Friday afternoon in the summer, Sully expected to hit some traffic. But she could have walked faster than this. Stuck on the Taconic in stop-and-go, she's had plenty of time to think.

Which, lately, is the last thing she wants to do.

Working Missing Persons and the occasional homicide, she's witnessed her share of tragedy over the years. But what happened a few weeks ago rocked her to the core.

She and Barnes were in a rough neighborhood, interviewing the family of Roland Mitchell, a teenage kid who hadn't been seen in a few days. As it turns out, he was a runaway. He turned up last week, safe and sound, in Newark. Roland's story—unlike Manik Bhandari's—ended happily.

A couple of wasted-out-of-their-minds punks were joyriding down the boulevard, saw Sully and Stockton on the sidewalk talking to the locals, and opened fire for kicks. Sully has a scar on her temple where a bullet nicked her before hitting the kid sitting on the stoop behind her.

Manik Bhandari was a seventeen-year-old honor student, about to graduate high school and become the first in his family to go to college. He died at her feet in a pool of his own blood, tinged with hers, and his tears, and her own. He died crying for his father. Sully, who never cries if she can help it . . .

Sully cried. She's still crying.

Whenever she climbs into bed at night and closes her eyes, she can see his: teary, terrified, pleading . . . and then fixed on the gray summer sky. The memory keeps her up at night, haunting her in a way few others have.

She stops at a crosswalk, watching the traffic fly by.

Does it help that both punks were swiftly apprehended and will likely be behind bars for the rest of her lifetime, if not their own?

No. Not really. Not this time.

Nothing helps.

They say sooner or later it happens to every cop, every fireman, every first responder: the one tragedy that hits you hard. The one that's just too much to bear. The one that makes you wonder whether—

The car behind her blasts its horn, and she sees that the one ahead of her is moving. She takes her foot off the brake, only to jam it down again as the traffic halts.

At least they're not going backward. Sometimes that's how she feels back home, dealing with the challenges of city life and this job she's always had, the only job she's ever known or wanted, the job she was born to do. And every day, every night, she thinks of Manik, and her head throbs with a terrible ache that no amount of Advil can ease.

The surface wound is almost healed. Her doctor ruled out a concussion. He thinks the headaches are from stress.

"Go on vacation and forget about what happened," he advised her at her checkup a few days ago. "You'll be good as new after a week or two of rest and relaxation. If you're not, you'll need to see someone."

Someone. A shrink.

Sully has already seen one. Protocol. Yeah, that didn't help, either.

Right now, her only option is vacation. And if that doesn't work . . .

No, it'll work. Because what is the option? Giving up?

Sully will never give up.

She'll just get away: from the daily chaos and violence, from being on high alert 24/7 because danger can strike at any moment.

At last, the car ahead of her moves forward.

Mundy's Landing, here I come, she thinks, only to hit the brakes again and sigh, shaking her head. *Eventually.*

The Village Common, a leafy park with fountains, statues, and meandering brick pathways, is sandwiched between Church and Prospect Streets to the north and south, Market Street and Fulton Avenue to the east and west. As this first busy summer weekend gets under way, every diagonal parking spot on the Common's perimeter is filled, as are most spots in nearby municipal lots.

Glad to be a pedestrian, Holmes strolls the brick sidewalks taking it all in, grateful for the late day sun that makes sunglasses an unobtrusive and essential accessory. Not technically a disguise, but they preclude eye contact with passersby or diners at sidewalk cafés.

As he crosses the street, he gives a casual wave at the

uniformed police officer directing traffic at the corner of Prospect and Fulton. The busy intersection lies in the long shadow of the Mundy's Landing Historical Society at 25 Fulton Avenue and is, like many things here or in any small town, the subject of controversy. According to today's *Mundy's Landing Tribune*, a local citizens' brigade is campaigning for *immediate*—which is laughable—installation of a regular traffic light and speed bumps.

Charles Bingham wrote an accompanying editorial implying that traffic woes are the most urgent problem facing the village. Ironic, because Holmes was prowling through Bingham's house right around the time the latest fender bender occurred at Prospect and Fulton.

"Excuse me, mister, would you like to buy a candy bar for the Sunrise Project?"

Turning, Holmes sees a kid seated at a card table in front of Vernon's Apothecary.

"It's a good cause," she goes on, "and they're only five dollars."

Only five dollars? Well, *that's* rich.

And I'm not, Holmes thinks, yet he stops walking and pastes on a pleasant smile. "What's the Sunrise Project?"

"It's our troop's community service project."

She's wearing a Girl Scout uniform and accompanied by another uniformed kid who's pressing buttons on a sleek cell phone.

Two vaguely familiar women hover nearby—the kind of women whose good looks are strictly courtesy of cosmetics, grooming, fashion, and the gym. Oblivious to kids and candy bars, they're spending this ostensible mother-daughter bonding time in deep discussion with each other. From the sounds of it, they're shredding a fellow mom whose parenting skills aren't up to their lofty standards, as she's allowed her daughter to wear "inappropriate" clothing. Whatever *that* means.

Holmes thinks of Indi, so scantily clad on that May evening when he lured her into the SUV. She's had plenty of time in the weeks since to reconsider every move she made on that fateful night. Chances are, she blames her plight on what she chose to wear—or rather, not to wear.

Maybe I'll let her go on thinking that. Or maybe I'll tell her the real reason I wanted her and only her.

There are plenty of provocatively dressed young women out and about on any warm spring night. But that night was special—and so is Indi.

"What kind of community service project?" Holmes asks the young girl holding the candy bar. Not because he cares about her cause, but because he's fascinated by the mother's utter lack of interest in her daughter's interaction with him.

Evidently, they feel safe despite Mundy's Landing's deplorable track record when it comes to young girls. These two women are all about appearances, and Holmes doesn't merit an admiring or even a critical glance.

I don't seem like a threat, and so they don't consider that there might be more than meets the eye. Idiots.

Holmes focuses on the Girl Scout. She takes a deep breath and begins speaking as if she's reciting from a PowerPoint presentation: "The troop project is to plant flowers and paint the benches around the stone monument at the Settlers' Landing Overlook on the bike path at the—" She breaks off to ask, "What's it called, Lauren?"

Her fellow Girl Scout doesn't look up from her phone. "What's what called?"

"The place."

"What place?"

"You know . . . the flower-planting place?"

"The bike path?"

"No, what's the park called? Where the settlers landed?"

Lauren shrugs to indicate that she either doesn't know

or doesn't care. The Girl Scout turns to the chattering women. "Mom?"

"Please do not interrupt, Amanda."

"But I have a customer who wants to know about the project. What's the park called?"

Amanda's mother flicks a gaze at Holmes. Her expression conveys that she is above all this—whatever *this* is. Her attitude is so abhorrent that Holmes wishes she were chained to the cellar wall alongside Indi and the others right now. Not because she fits into the plan, but because he would enjoy making her suffer.

"It's the Schaapskill Nature Preserve," she tells Amanda, then turns back to her friend.

Ah, the nature preserve. It's adjacent to the site of Valley Cove Electric Pleasure Park.

"That's where we're going to plant flowers next Thursday morning at sunrise," Amanda tells Holmes.

"Hence, the Sunrise Project." He nods, thinking that next Thursday happens to be June 30—the date the first body will be discovered.

"Hence?"

Modern kids, and their limited vocabularies, he thinks, rolling his eyes behind his sunglasses. "That's a beautiful place and a great cause. I'm happy to contribute. I'll take three candy bars. You can keep the change."

"Thank you." She carefully puts the twenty-dollar bill into the metal cashbox and reaches for the chocolate. "Are you going to eat these all by yourself?"

"No, they're for my girls."

"You have three girls?"

"I do." His mouth curves into a smile. "And they're always happy when I bring them a treat."

"Well, candy bars aren't healthy and you should only have a little taste. That's what my mom says."

I'll bet, Holmes thinks. The woman, whose skeletal

frame is on full display in a sleeveless dress, looks like she's never dared touch a candy bar in her life. She could stand to eat one. Or three.

Immersed in her gossipy conversation again, Amanda's mother—whose name, Holmes has discerned, is Bari—doesn't give him another glance.

Hmm.

Maybe I'll make her regret that later, just for fun.

"Yes, practice does make perfect."

"What?"

Seeing Amanda's inquisitive expression, he realizes he spoke aloud. He thinks back, trying to remember what they were even talking about. Ah, yes.

He improvises, "I *said*, it's important to practice good healthy eating habits."

"I think I was the one who said that." Amanda hands him the candy bars. "But thank you for your contribution anyway."

"Thank *you* for the chocolate anyway."

"Remember not to give them to your girls unless they eat a good dinner," she calls as Holmes heads off down the sidewalk, "and then they should only have a little taste."

Aren't we the bossy little twit.

The apple doesn't fall far from the tree.

Holmes pockets the candy with a smile. When was the last time his three Beauties tasted anything sweet and delicious?

But they don't deserve a treat. This morning, they were a little too restless for his taste. He'd expected them to resign themselves to their fates by now. They might, if he were to tell them what lies in store. Perhaps they'd be comforted knowing they won't be forgotten when this is over. Would they be struggling to escape if they knew they were about to take featured roles in the greatest crime of the twenty-first century?

Possibly. But even if they mustered the herculean

strength to break free of their steel shackles, they'd still be imprisoned. The windowless stone building is padlocked from the outside. It's so remote that no one would ever hear their cries for help even if they hadn't already screamed themselves hoarse.

No need to check in on them again tonight, Holmes decides, as a mosquito buzzes around his damp forehead. The woods will be buggy in this heat.

Instead, he'll detour past the historical society, maybe even pop inside to pay a little after-hours visit. Dear sweet Ora Abrams never knows he's there.

It was Ora who first issued the challenge that consumed Holmes for the better part of a lifetime.

Can You Solve the Sleeping Beauty Murders?

The answer—Holmes's ultimate answer, anyway: *Yes, I can . . .*

And I have.

Like the Binghams, Kim and Ross Winston were born and raised in Mundy's Landing. Ross likes to tease Annabelle that she used to babysit for him, which is true. She was thirteen at the time, and he was a toddler.

Now he's a middle-aged man, still handsome, but with a slight paunch that strains the horizontal stripes of his polo shirt. Kim, a petite, fine-featured blonde, dresses and often sounds younger than she is. She delights in comparisons to her look-alike daughter, Catherine, who just finished eighth grade.

Judging by the look on the girl's face as she steps over the threshold, she's none too thrilled about being here on this first official Friday night of summer.

"Do you want to go upstairs with the boys?" Annabelle asks her, as Oliver and Connor make a beeline for the game console in Oliver's room.

"No way."

"You mean 'No, thanks,'" Kim admonishes her, handing Annabelle a bottle of chilled sauvignon.

"No, thanks."

Noting that Trib and Ross are already caught up in some manly conversation about woodwork or wiring, Annabelle invites Catherine to come to the kitchen.

"No, thanks," she says again.

"Catherine!"

"What? I said, 'No, thanks,' Mom!"

"But if Mrs. Bingham needs help in the kitchen, you'll come help."

"Oh, it's okay. I have it all under control." Not exactly the case, but Annabelle isn't eager to turn the dueling mother-daughter duo into sous chefs.

She settles Catherine in the back parlor and turns on the television, but the girl seems much more interested in texting on her phone.

"Wow, what a great space!" Kim looks around the kitchen. "Just imagine what you can do in here. It could be amazing."

Annabelle and Trib had thought the same thing the first time they saw the expansive room. But a renovation isn't in their budget, and Annabelle has come to realize that even the small galley kitchen in their rental cottage was more efficient than this one.

Though the room is large, its design is sorely outdated. The cabinets are ancient—but, like the Binghams' furniture, not in a retro-cool, kitschy way. Just in a flimsy, ugly way. They have to go. So do the green laminate countertops and scarred appliances, especially the refrigerator that smells of spoiled food no matter how many times she scrubs the shelves and bins and replaces the box of baking soda.

"I really hope you're not starved," Annabelle tells

Kim, sliding a tray of chicken into the oven and setting the timer for forty-five minutes.

"I'm not, but I could use a drink after the day I've had."

"I'll open the wine. I know there's a corkscrew around here someplace." She hunts through drawers until she finds an old butterfly one imprinted Mundy's Landing Wine & Liquor. The store is still open on Market Street, but a few years ago, new owners changed the name to Mundy's Landing Fine Wine & Spirits.

Seeing the corkscrew, Kim laughs. "My mother the packrat has one of those. My dad teases her that she should donate it to Ora Abrams for the museum, which Mom says she'll do that over her dead body."

Annabelle nods, knowing Kim's parents—and Kim herself—are among the longtime locals who'd prefer that the historical society focus attention on the village's illustrious past, rather than its tarnished one.

But Annabelle has a soft spot for Ora, a close friend of her late mother's. In fact, she's been expecting her to show up any day now wanting a tour of the house. Maybe she's just been too busy planning Mundypalooza.

Annabelle opens the sauvignon and pours two glasses, handing one to Kim. "Do you think Catherine would like something cold to drink?"

"As much as I'd like to improve her mood, I don't think getting her drunk is a good idea."

Annabelle laughs. "I was thinking of iced tea or lemonade."

"No, just let her be. We need a break from each other."

"So she's the reason you've had a bad day?"

"Is there any other reason lately?"

Between sips of wine, Kim tells her that Catherine had been invited to a pool party over in Mundy Estates, a luxury townhome development off Battlefield Road by the high school. But when Kim called to confirm the details with the mother of the teenage hostess, she discovered that boys would be there, and the parents wouldn't be home.

"You know how that goes," she tells Annabelle. "Things can happen."

She does, indeed, know how that goes. She may have been a straight-A athlete in high school, but as she tells Kim now, she went to her share of unsupervised parties.

"We all did," Kim agrees, watching Annabelle take produce from the fridge and line it up beside the salad bowl on the counter. "But things are different now. There was no way I was going to let her go."

"I get that. But you don't have to make her stay here. I can send food home with her if she wants to—"

"No, we had a big fight about that right before we got here. I don't want her there alone."

"Oh, Kim, I don't want her to feel trapped here. She'll hate me."

"Don't think that she doesn't."

"What?"

"It's nothing personal. She hates everyone." Kim picks up a paring knife and a tomato. "Especially me."

"*Hate* is a strong word. I don't think she *hates* you."

"That's what she said. *I hate you.*" Kim pokes the knife tip around the tomato stem. "It killed me. Has Oliver ever said that to you?"

"No."

"Connor hasn't, either."

"I'm relieved Connor doesn't hate me," Annabelle says wryly, and Kim laughs.

"Just be glad you don't have a thirteen-year-old daughter. They're impossible."

So are twelve-year-old boys with anxiety issues. But Kim wouldn't grasp the extent of what Annabelle goes through with Oliver. Unaware that he's been medicated for a few years and under a child psychiatrist's care, she only knows he sometimes worries excessively.

Annabelle isn't willing to entrust the truth even to her closest friends, who wanted to know why Oliver isn't going away to camp.

She blamed the fact that he's staying home this summer to the chaos of the move and their limited finances. Not because she doesn't trust the moms to protect Oliver's secret, but because she doesn't trust their children, should the secret go farther than she intended.

It isn't that the other boys are mean-spirited. But kids are kids. If they ever knew that Oliver spends so much of his time sobbing and cowering in sheer terror . . .

But they won't know. Nobody can know. The Binghams stoically shoulder their burden in isolation.

"So that's why you made Catherine come over here?" she asks Kim. "Because you were afraid she'd sneak out to the party after you left?"

"No, she knows better than to try something like that. We'd ground her until college."

"Then why didn't you want her home alone?" Annabelle pours some olive oil into a jar for the dressing. "I thought she's been babysitting for Connor for a few years now."

"Yes, but . . . you know. *Brianna Armbruster.*"

Kim is referring to the pretty redheaded teenager who disappeared from a neighboring block in December. Her remains have yet to be found, but bloodstains matching her DNA were found in the serial killer's van.

A chill seems to permeate the steamy kitchen as Annabelle thinks again of yesterday's backyard interloper. She'd assumed that incident was connected to the Mundypalooza gawkers, but what if . . .

No, that's ridiculous.

"There's no psycho lunatic on the loose in Mundy's

Landing," she says firmly, as much for Kim's benefit as for her own.

"There was one six months ago—"

"Who is no longer a threat."

"—and there was one a hundred years ago, too."

"Right. But not now." Her hand trembles a little as she adds some balsamic vinegar to the jar.

"No, now there are just hordes of sketchy strangers hanging around, and more on the way. Hundreds more. Maybe thousands—that's what I heard the other day." She rolls her eyes. "Ora Abrams must be thrilled."

"Well, it *is* a fund-raiser. The more people who show up, the more money the historical society gets. Anyway," she says, changing the subject, "you and Ross are still going to the gala with us next Thursday night, right?"

"I've been looking forward to it for months. I bought my gown in February. What are you wearing?"

"A dress, I guess. I didn't even wear a gown at my wedding."

"What did you wear?"

"You know—a dress."

"Like—a cocktail dress?"

"No, it was long, but . . . I wouldn't call it a gown. It was simple. What?" she asks, seeing the look on Kim's face. "I *like* simple."

"But this is a black tie affair at Hudson Chase, Annabelle," she points out, referring to the country club out on Battlefield Road. "Trib is wearing a tux, right?"

"Yes. He rented one. Too bad I didn't tell him to rent me a gown while he was at it."

"Catherine and I can go shopping with you. It would be fun."

Annabelle, who's never been much of a shopper, just shakes her head. "Don't worry. I'll figure it out."

She has nothing against the gala, which kicks off the

ML350 celebration, marking three hundred and fifty years since the village was officially settled—*officially* being the operative word, according to a recent newspaper interview with Ora Abrams.

On Thursday night, Miss Abrams will present the mayor with a time capsule sealed and buried in a vault beneath the village common during the celebration in July 1916. For years, there was a stone marker on the spot.

1916—2016
Mundy's Landing Sestercentennial Vault
To Be Opened 2016

Fifteen or maybe twenty years ago, a group of Hadley College students tried to steal the time capsule. The police caught the drunken vandals before they got very far in their dig. The old chest, still sealed, was unearthed the next day and carted off to the police station for safekeeping. There it remained until just a few weeks ago, when it was placed on display in the historical society.

Many people in town believe that it should be opened in mid-July, exactly a hundred years to the date after it was sealed. But Ora convinced the new mayor that it would be much nicer to open it during the June 30 gala.

Trib is one of the featured presenters that evening. Annabelle has no choice but to attend with him. That would be fine with her if it didn't mean leaving Oliver home with a sitter.

That's something they rarely do—and haven't done at all since Katie Mundy, their babysitter, graduated high school and left for college last August. Luckily, she's home for the summer and Annabelle reserved her for next Thursday night.

"Anyway," Kim says, "Getting back to Mundy-palooza . . ."

"Must we?"

"I think it's time to move on."

"Then why are we still talking about it?"

"No, I mean enough is enough. The historical society needs to stop creating such pandemonium every summer." Kim gestures dramatically with the paring knife in her hand, and Annabelle can't help but think of the poor lost girls whose throats were slit.

As Kim goes back to cutting the tomato, she asks, "Does it make you nervous, living here?"

"You mean because of all the people driving by looking at the house?"

"I mean because of what happened upstairs."

Annabelle hesitates only briefly before saying, "Not really."

"You're a lot braver than I am."

"It happened a hundred years ago. I don't believe in ghosts, and it's not like we're in danger."

"No, I know, but I mean, it's a Murder House. I just . . . can't . . . even."

She sounds like Catherine, who punctuates many a sentence with "I can't even."

"She can't even . . . what?" Annabelle once quietly asked Kim, who shrugged and explained simply, "They all say it. It's a *thing*."

Annabelle adds salt and pepper to the jar, screws on the top, shakes it vigorously, and sets it aside. Done. For now.

"Come on," she says. "I'll show you around my Murder House."

From the Sleeping Beauty Killer's Diary
August 16, 1893

When I heard the learn'd astronomer,
When the proofs, the figures, were ranged in
    columns before me,
When I was shown the charts and diagrams, to
    add, divide, and measure them,
When I sitting heard the astronomer where he
    lectured with much applause in the lecture-
    room,
How soon unaccountable I became tired and
    sick,
Till rising and gliding out I wander'd off by
    myself,
In the mystical moist night-air, and from time to
    time,
Look'd up in perfect silence at the stars.

It was with a discerning eye this morning that I found myself rereading these lines from Whitman's Leaves of Grass, *as the locomotive hurtled me into the glaring sunrise above an eastern mountain range. Can this be the same volume that so captivated me as the train steamed west into the prairie sunset? Intellect assures me that it is indeed the same book, yet in the course of one remarkable fortnight, my perspective of this passage has transformed just as drastically as my direction.*

Can one not possess the soul of a poet and the brain of a scientist? Are not the two disciplines opposite sides of the same coin, born of the intrinsic yearning for unrestricted exploration beyond the confines of our realm?

Indeed, Mr. Ferris's Great Wheel embodies both

artistic masterpiece and scientific genius. This very train does the same, both in its form and in my perception of that form. Just two weeks ago, I fixated upon its gleaming modern design, its power and speed. I find it less impressive in retrospect, as I was able to ride the far more innovative elevated electric rail at the fair.

On this return trip, I focus not on the scientific prowess of this locomotive. Rather, I see it as a black dragon puffing smoke through its snout as it carries me—unwilling prey snatched from a happy land— back to the dreaded abyss.

And so I shall, for now, set aside Leaves of Grass. *Before I left the hotel, an erudite gentleman from Massachusetts—with whom I had shared many a silent evening in the hotel's reading room—brilliantly suggested that we exchange books we'd finished reading. Though I kept* Leaves of Grass, *I willingly parted with two other volumes, and came away with a pair. One is Sir Arthur Conan Doyle's* The Adventures of Sherlock Holmes, *which I have been longing to read ever since it was published last year.*

I've never heard of the other book, entitled The Fall River Tragedy, *though I have read in the papers about the unsolved double axe murders that took place a year ago this month. Miss Lizzie Borden was acquitted in December, but there are some who believe she committed the most heinous crime imaginable: the cold-blooded murder of her own flesh and blood.*

Chapter 6

As the daughter of the venerated Hadley College history professor Dr. Theodore Abrams and the grandniece of the Mundy's Landing Historical Society's previous longtime curator, Miss Etta Abrams, Ora Abrams has a favorite catchphrase: "History is the family business."

Not just history. Local history.

Her given name is Aurora, after the princess in Charles Perrault's original Sleeping Beauty fairy tale. It was a not-so-subtle nod to the crimes that captivated her father, his aunt, and fellow hometown historians. Her mother—not quite as captivated, but overruled by her strong-willed husband—insisted upon shortening it to Ora.

Great-Aunt Etta helped Papa care for Ora after Mama died. In her mid-thirties when the crimes were committed, Etta shared her perspective, her theories—and her private stash of mementos. She lived into the 1950s, at which point Ora inherited that secret trove along with curatorship of the official public collection. At that time, the museum consisted of dusty relics unceremoniously crammed into the basement of the Elsworth Ransom Library, suitably named after a nineteenth-century descendant of Priscilla Mundy Ransom, one of the village's original settlers.

If Great-Aunt Etta had been passionate about the cause,

then Ora was obsessive. Under her stewardship, the non-profit has gained world renown, sealed Mundy's Landing's place on the map, and moved into the elegant Conroy-Fitch mansion, a space befitting its extensive collection.

Winded from the long day's final climb up the grand stairway, Ora sinks onto a maroon velvet-upholstered bench in the second-floor hallway. There's another flight to go before she reaches her private quarters, but she's too worn out to continue just yet.

"I'm getting old, Rosie," she tells the cat who trailed her up the stairs and now sits perched at her feet.

The cat's full name is Briar Rose. Waiting patiently to continue the journey, she offers a slow blink of under-standing. Ora reaches down to pat her furry head and is rewarded with loud purring.

Among the historical society's best-kept secrets, Briar Rose has lived here in the mansion for the past few years. Ora keeps her tucked away in a storage room during museum hours, with plenty of food and water, toys, and a cozy bed.

If word were to get out that she's here, plenty of people would instantly know where she came from. Female orange tabbies are relatively rare, but Augusta Purcell's collection of wandering cats has included gingery gals for many generations.

Ora is nearly certain that Briar Rose is directly descended from Marmalade, Augusta's childhood pet. The two felines have strikingly similar markings. Marmalade was pictured in one of the numerous newspaper articles about the Sleeping Beauty murders. Her presence in the house at 46 Bridge Street on the night of July 7, 1916, is noted in court documents.

For that reason, Ora simply had to have her. The ancestral connection makes Briar Rose a treasured addition to Ora's private collection.

It wasn't very difficult to obtain her. Augusta's cats roamed The Heights long before her death, and Ora often left food for them on the doorstep of the annex behind the mansion. When she heard Augusta had passed away, she simply brought this sweet orange girl inside for the night, and has kept her here ever since.

Some might consider that a kitty-napping. As far as Ora is concerned, it's both a humane act and a community service. Neighbors complained about Augusta's wandering felines. They raided garbage cans, howled mating cries into the night, and delivered litters under porches. After his aunt died, Lester Purcell reportedly rounded up as many of her pets as he could and delivered them to the pound.

"But not you, Rosie," Ora says, petting her soft coat. "You're a V.I.C."—Very Important Cat—"and you belong here with me. I'm just sorry you were cooped up so long tonight."

Ordinarily, she locks the massive front door promptly at five o'clock. But today's visitors included latecomers who'd traveled a great distance to settle in before the festivities officially get under way next week.

Ora's personal policy, established back when she was sprightly enough to sustain a longer day without missing a beat, is to allow guests to browse to their hearts' content once they're here.

But oh my. If she's this exhausted now, whatever will she do next week, during the convention?

Late day sun still shines brightly through the window on the stairway landing. Yet all she wants is the strength to complete the journey and climb into bed.

How the mighty have fallen.

She'd been younger by a good sixteen years when she'd decided to locate her office and private quarters in the expansive attic. She darted up and down two flights of steps day in and out, often lugging boxes, without a second thought.

Now that she's well into her eighties, she leans heavily on her favorite walking stick, a bone-handled rosewood piece she'd confiscated from the museum collection. Whenever she experiences the slightest touch of guilt for that indiscretion, she reminds herself—as with the kitty-napping—that the deed was justified.

It isn't as though she's made off with a priceless antique. The cane isn't going anywhere and neither is Ora, unless it's the great beyond—in which case, all her worldly goods will be left to the historical society anyway.

As for the society itself, who knows what will become of it after she passes away? She doesn't like to think about that.

She considers of herself as keeper of the flame—and yes, keeper of the many secrets that cloak her hometown's history. She always thought she'd carry them to her grave, but now that her grave isn't as distant a destination as she'd like, well . . .

"I'll decide," she informs the empty second-floor corridor. "I'll decide whether to tell."

Unless, of course, someone finally rises to the challenge she issued twenty-five years ago.

Can You Solve the Sleeping Beauty Murders?

The visitors who descend every summer assume that the key must lie somewhere in the extensive exhibit devoted to the crimes. Behind the wall against which Ora now leans her aching spine, mounted yellowed newspapers and police reports are displayed. They include hundreds of original photographs of the crime scenes, the investigation process, the people involved at all stages.

The large adjoining room holds glass cases containing other crime-related artifacts: household items from the three homes where the bodies were found, bits of evidence collected by the detectives, notes purportedly written by the killer, and an antique barber's blade similar to the suspected murder weapon, which was never found.

Farther down this side of the hall lies a bedroom graced with an almost identical layout to the guest quarters at 19 Schuyler Place where the third dead girl appeared. Ora recreated that room in this one, using authentic furnishings donated by a grandson of Julius and Lydia Palmer, who lived in the house at the time.

The final room in the Sleeping Beauty exhibit is located at the far end of the hall. She opens it only during Mundypalooza. Within are photographs and other items Ora long ago deemed too grisly for a family museum; too fragile and sacred for a permanent exhibit. That's where guests linger longest, transfixed by a blood-tainted nightgown and hair ribbons found on the Sleeping Beauties' corpses. Those items, along with a yellowed note found beneath the pillow of one of the victims, have long been on loan from the local police department.

The visitors who closely study every item are looking for clues. They're thinking they might unmask the long-dead murderer by picking up on the one detail everyone else has missed. Craving notoriety, superiority, and cold hard cash, they pepper Ora with questions they assume she hasn't been asked thousands of times before.

She patiently answers every single one.

Some more truthfully than others.

She's so confident that the case will go unsolved that she offered an exceptionally large reward this year to anyone who can unmask the killer. In the unlikely event that some genius pieces things together, Ora will have one less secret to decide whether she should keep or share.

With a sigh, she steadies her cane and hoists herself to her feet. Slowly, with the orange tabby trailing a step behind, she makes her way up the steps to her quarters.

This flight is steeper than the first and much narrower, dimly lit and enclosed by walls rather than carved rails.

Clutching the simple banister with one hand and her cane with the other, she's nearly reached the top when she hears a creaking sound far below.

There are many things about Ora's old body that are failing: her legs, her dexterity, her eyesight. But her hearing is still sharp. So is her mind.

Ora stands poised, frowning. The cat, too, has turned back, her ears back and twitching.

After a few moments, Ora hears the creaking again. It's faint, but she didn't imagine it.

Someone is downstairs.

Like the rest of the house at 46 Bridge Street, the natatorium was built on a grand scale. It wasn't added until the 1950s, when Augusta Purcell's doctor prescribed swimming as physical therapy for her arthritis, but the design reflects the home's Victorian architecture.

Three walls consist of beveled casement windows above built-in wrought-iron benches. The canopy of branches casts eerily fluid shadows through the glass. They move like phantoms across the mosaic tile floor, swallowed by the yawning rectangle in the middle.

The fourth wall, which runs along the back of the house, is plaster, painted in a mural. It's cracked and faded, but you can still make out a World War I–era scene at an outdoor pool surrounded by arched brick columns and foliage. The women wear striped bathing dresses and bloomers, the men one-piece tanks.

"This is the coolest thing ever," Kim tells Annabelle, looking around.

"Right now, it feels like the hottest thing ever."

Broken portions of the gabled leaded glass ceiling are

covered in plywood, but late day sun falls through the rest, creating an uncomfortable greenhouse effect.

"When's the first pool party?"

"Probably not this weekend." Annabelle's tone is as dry as the pool, which hasn't been used in at least fifty years. The tile border is motley and missing so many pieces that it's impossible to distinguish a pattern, let alone discern the colors. A network of fissures covers the plaster walls, and the sloping bottom is strewn with rubble.

"You hired someone to fix it, though, right?"

"I wasn't going to. But Trib and I ran into Steve Reed at the hardware store the other day and he offered to come over and take a look."

Kim raises an eyebrow. "Did Trib tell him to get lost?"

"He probably would have, and not because I used to date Steve. He's more worried about our household budget than some old boyfriend almost thirty years later. But I told Steve to come on over, and he did. He said a job had just been postponed and he can't start the next one for a few weeks, so he can squeeze us in."

"What did Trib say to that?"

"He wasn't here. When I told him, he said there's no way we're spending money on a pool. But Steve is giving us a rock-bottom deal as long as he can do it right away, and if we don't jump on it, we'll never be able to afford to do it."

"Was Trib okay with that?"

"Not really. He still thinks the pool should be at the tail end of the to-do list. But he gave in." Only after several arguments she'd rather not remember, or discuss.

"Just remind him of all the money you'll save when you drop the gym membership so that you can swim laps at home," Kim tells her.

"I did. And he reminded me of all the money we'll

spend on repairs and maintenance. Anyway, Steve starts tomorrow. But you might not want to mention that in front of Trib."

"I'm glad I'm not the only one with marital discord."

"We don't have marital discord—and neither do you!"

"Don't be so sure." Kim sips from the wineglass she topped off before the tour. "All we ever do lately is argue about the kids. Well, mostly one kid. You can't imagine the stress it's causing between me and Ross."

Annabelle says nothing to that, watching Kim tap across the floor in her heeled sandals, stepping around a box of tile samples. Her shoulders and long legs, bare in a short sundress, are already tanned, and her toenails are painted a bright coral shade to match her dress.

Wearing as little as possible due to the heat—a tank top, shorts, and flip-flops—Annabelle is underdressed alongside her friend. She spends her days quite comfortably in swimsuits and athletic wear, but there's something about Kim that always makes her feel vaguely inadequate.

Suddenly, she feels utterly exhausted by the sheer . . . imperfection of it all. Her marriage, her house, her finances, her child's health . . .

Nothing is perfect, she reminds herself. *Nobody's life is perfect.*

Kim is struggling, too. She just manages to look good doing it.

Annabelle watches her pause to inspect a pair of enormous stone planters containing brittle stalks that were once the trunks of lush palm trees. "You should fill these with flowers, Annabelle. And—ooh, what's that?" She points to the carved white angel on a small stone platform just above the illegible depth marker on the deep end.

"Lynda Carlotta thinks the pedestal was originally meant to hold a diving board. But Augusta must have put the statue there instead."

"Not to be morbid, but it looks like a tombstone sitting in front of an open grave. Is it supposed to be some kind of memorial to the Sleeping Beauties?"

"I doubt it."

"I bet it is."

Annabelle shrugs. She hadn't given it much thought, nor even considered that possibility, until this moment. But it's in the back of her mind as she goes on talking about the expensive filtration system Steve is giving them at cost.

"Too bad you can't take what you would have spent on it and install central air-conditioning." Kim wipes sweat from beneath her blond bangs as she peers into the shadowy chasm at the deep end.

"We wouldn't have spent anything at all on it—not for years," Annabelle reminds her. "Anyway, I'd rather have the pool. We'll get more use out of it, since I can swim three hundred and sixty-five days a year, and it's hardly ever this hot around here."

"No, but when it is, you die." Kim fans herself with a hand, and Annabelle takes the hint to move on with her tour, the word *die* echoing darkly in her head.

"Who's there?" Ora calls from the top of the third-floor stairway.

No reply.

Not surprising. If someone is downstairs, then he broke in. And if he broke in, he's hardly going to announce himself.

Still, she calls a little louder, "Hello?"

Again, she seems to hear a faint creaking sound far below. The cat must have heard it, too, because she dives past Ora with a nervous meow-growl and disappears into the third-floor shadows.

Hmm. Should she call the police?

No. Goodness knows they already have their hands full with the crowds in town tonight. Besides, if they arrive before she works her way down all those stairs, they might break down a lovely original oak door or, God forbid, shatter a stained glass window. Better to investigate on her own first.

Armed with her walking stick, Ora painstakingly creeps back down to the first floor, pausing every couple of steps to listen for creaking or footsteps. She hears not a sound.

But someone is here. She can feel him.

The thought makes her uneasy, but not afraid.

She's quite accustomed to visitors who come snooping around after hours at this time of year, although they typically don't find their way inside. She's also had a few stray visitors who'd become so absorbed in an exhibit that they failed to exit when the others did, before Ora locked the doors.

She's usually careful to make sure that everyone who comes in goes out. But she could have overlooked someone tonight. Her mind isn't what it used to be. Maybe she should start counting heads as people enter and then again as they exit . . .

Oh, nonsense, she tells herself even as that thought enters her head. *You're much too busy to stand around counting all day long.*

She should probably install an alarm system. She's been meaning to do it, but it never seemed necessary until now.

She eyes the wooden chest prominently on exhibit in the front parlor. The Mundy's Landing Sestercentennial Time Capsule, scheduled to be opened at the gala next Thursday night, is temporarily on exhibit here. Years ago, vandals tried to steal it from its burial place in the Common. What if someone is after it now?

Concerned, she makes her way from room to room, peering beneath tables until she grows tired of stooping, and poking behind draperies for as long as her old bones can stand it.

Finally, she decides to curtail the inspection, certain that she and Rosie are quite alone in the mansion.

And if by chance they're not . . .

She'll just have to hope the intruder is more interested in browsing the collection than stealing it. There might be valuable antiques on the first floor and sealed in the wooden chest, but the most priceless relics are as securely tucked away as Ora's secrets.

Holmes's Case Notes

Poring over historic photos, I am struck by the physical differences between Annabelle Bingham, with her willowy frame and dark, boyishly cut hair, and her 1916 counterpart.

Florence Purcell was fair-skinned, buxom even for her time, and wore her pale hair elaborately twisted upon her head. Perhaps to compensate for life's limitations, she was impeccably groomed and had the finest clothing her husband's handsome salary could buy. Photos taken during the investigation that summer show her wearing the latest styles: belted waists, tiered skirts fashionably cut above her ankles, hats trimmed with ribbon and ostrich plumes.

All dressed up, as they say, with nowhere to go. That was Florence. For the twelve years that spanned 1904–16, she was locked away in the house with her children and her secrets, like a beautiful butterfly still ensnared by its cocoon.

Only after the frightfulness did she emerge to spread her wings. She was no stranger to speakeasies and became a vocal proponent for women's rights, which is how she met the famed feminist journalist Ruth Hale, an Algonquin Round Table regular. It is said that she introduced Florence to artists and writers including the great Dorothy Parker.

For all her socializing and gallivanting, Florence never spoke of the past. Who could blame her, when the slightest misstep might incriminate her?

Chapter 7

As she leads Kim through the first-floor rooms, Annabelle can't stop thinking about the stone angel.

In any other house, the piece might feel quirky, perhaps ostentatious. In a Murder House . . .

It *does* look like a tombstone that would suit any of the three dead girls buried in Holy Angels Cemetery. Annabelle has seen their graves, unceremoniously marked by slabs etched with the year 1916.

Was Augusta Purcell thinking of them—at least, of the one found in this house—when she had the stone angel placed on the diving pedestal?

According to the local grapevine, Lester is sticking around for the summer. If she runs into him, she can ask him about it. Or maybe there's some information in the historical society archives—though if she mentions the statue to Ora Abrams, Ora will probably want to add it to her collection.

She and Kim find Catherine still sprawled on the couch in the back parlor, texting her friends.

"Can I get you some cold lemonade or something?" Annabelle offers.

"No, thank you."

"Look up from your phone when someone is speaking to you, please, Catherine."

She looks up, but only to glower at her mother.

"If you change your mind, help yourself from the fridge," Annabelle tells her, and they move on.

Beyond the open screens, the evening air is hushed, still thick with heat. The sounds that reach Annabelle's ears are likely the same ones Florence Purcell heard on that fateful night: the hum of katydids, a dog barking, and children playing in a neighboring yard. There are no traffic noises, no lawnmowers; nothing to jar her from past to present.

As Kim pauses at the foot of the stairs to check out the grandfather clock, Annabelle rests a hand on the scarred newel post, thinking of Florence Purcell and July 7, 1916.

According to the *Tribune*, the family's kitten, Marmalade, had gotten out of the house earlier that day and poor little Augusta was beside herself. Marmalade's mother had recently escaped and been mauled, perhaps by a coyote. Just before bed, Florence had found the kitten and brought her back inside. She'd locked the door, extinguished the gas lamps, tucked in her children, and climbed into bed with a book.

Annabelle can imagine an intruder creeping into the house just as the clock struck midnight and—

"Annabelle?" Kim's voice breaks into her thoughts.

"Hmm?"

"I said, if you ever need money, I'll bet you can get a fortune for this clock."

"We don't want to sell it." She's already as attached to it as if it were her own family heirloom. "It belongs in the house. Come on, let's go upstairs."

As they ascend, the silence behind Oliver's closed bedroom door is punctuated by electronic sound effects and staccato outcries—the boys are still playing a video game. *Ah, welcome back to the twenty-first century.*

Overhead, heavy footsteps thud across the third floor. Trib must be showing Ross the old ballroom.

It's warm downstairs and hot up here, but it must be downright sweltering above. Annabelle went up this afternoon to open the windows and air out the space, but found that they were painted shut there as well as in the cupola above. Since central air-conditioning is out of the question and even window A.C. units would be a fire hazard without hiring an electrician to rewire the outlets, the third floor is out of commission for the time being.

There was a terrible heat wave a hundred years ago, too, when the crimes unfolded. The house would have felt just like this: hot and close and still, its occupants wrapped in a suffocating wet blanket.

Kim admires the antique floral wallpaper and sconces, then asks, "So which room was it?"

"We're not sure," Annabelle lies.

"Haven't you ever seen the pictures at the historical society?"

She grimaces. "Who hasn't?"

There are photographs of the corpses in the bedrooms of all the Murder Houses, but Annabelle never studied them closely until she moved into one. She was, like everyone else, far more captivated by the dead schoolgirls than by their surroundings.

The backdrops had been similar enough that none would stand out in the mind's eye of a casual observer. All three photos showed vintage wallpaper, perhaps a bureau or bedside table. In one or two or maybe all of the images, there are hints of a fireplace or a tall fabric-festooned window. Those identifying characteristics made it easier for Annabelle and Trib to not only pick out which of the three rooms belongs to their house, but also which room was the scene of the crime.

"We should go down there tomorrow and look at the pictures again."

Ignoring Kim's suggestion, Annabelle opens the door at the top of the stairs. "This is the master bedroom."

"Wow. It's a great size for an old house—it's a lot bigger than ours." Kim and Ross did extensive renovations on their charming Queen Anne Victorian down the block, transforming six small second-floor bedrooms into three that are larger, but hardly spacious.

"We knocked out a wall. There was an adjoining room right there." She points to the rectangular alcove that holds an armoire and dresser. "It's the only major work we did before we moved in. If we hadn't done it, pretty much the only thing that have would fit in this room is our bed."

Kim pokes around the alcove. "Do you think this was the guest room back then?"

Annabelle hesitates, but decides against letting her believe that. "No, it didn't even have a window. It was probably used as a nursery. Lester's father, Frederick, was just over a year old in 1916 and he was the last baby born in this house, so he was probably still sleeping there when it happened."

"*If* it was a nursery."

"Right. Either way, that room only opened into the master bedroom, not the hall, so whoever left the body probably wasn't going to lug it past the Purcells in the middle of the night."

"I can't *even*." Kim shudders. "You sound like a detective. Maybe you'll solve the crime and win the reward. I bet fifty grand would come in handy, right?"

"Definitely."

"So there were just the two kids in the house then? The baby and old lady Purcell? How old was she when it happened?"

Old lady Purcell. Annabelle winces. She, too, used to call her that. But ever since she moved into this house, it rankles. Now when she thinks of Augusta Purcell, she imagines her as the cherub-cheeked child in the 1915 family portrait.

"Augusta was six. Her bedroom was down at the other end of the hall."

"How do you know?"

"Because when we looked at the house last fall, that was the only room that had been lived in for years. She had a part-time caregiver once she could no longer get up and down the stairs, because she didn't want to move her bedroom to the first floor, let alone leave the house. Lester's lawyer told Ralph Duvane that his aunt spent every night of her entire life in the same room."

"Can I see it?"

Annabelle leads the way down the hall and shows Kim the large, pleasant space with the window seat and fireplace. It's empty now, other than a few sealed moving boxes and stacks of old newspapers in one corner. But when Augusta Purcell lived here, it was filled with mahogany bedroom furniture and framed family photos.

"So it wasn't this room," Kim says, "and it wasn't the nursery and it wasn't the master bedroom. That leaves two other possibilities on the second floor for the guest room, right?"

Annabelle nods.

"And one is Oliver's room?"

Again, she nods.

"Does he know that there's a fifty-fifty chance there was a dead body there a hundred years ago?"

"We don't really talk about that."

"Connor said Oliver knows what happened here," she confides in a hushed tone, as if it might be news to Annabelle, "and that it doesn't even bother him."

"No, but—" She breaks off, hearing footsteps descending the stairs from above. A moment later, Trib emerges from a door midway down the hall, followed by Ross.

Spotting Annabelle, he gives her a thumbs-up. "Hey. Nice observatory and ballroom."

"Observatory? Ballroom?" Kim echoes. "Seriously?"

"Servants' quarters, too," Ross tells her.

"Okay, first of all, it's not really an observatory," Annabelle points out. "It's just a cupola with an old telescope in it. And it's not like we're hosting balls in the ballroom. Or like we have servants."

From Trib: "Unless you count me."

"Come on, Annabelle, show me your ballroom so I can start planning Catherine's sweet sixteen party. Maybe by then she'll be speaking to me again."

"Trib can take you back up, since he's the servant and all," Annabelle tells her. "I have to go check on the chicken."

"It's about four hundred degrees up there," Trib says. "If it's not ready yet, you should stick it upstairs for a few minutes."

Excusing herself, Annabelle heads back down the hall.

Kim is one of her dearest friends. She doesn't blame her for being curious, asking questions. Still, she can't help but feel protective of the old house. It's an architectural masterpiece, a warm and sturdy haven for the families who lived beneath its turreted, iron-crowned roof. Yet despite what might otherwise be an illustrious hundred-and-fifty-year history, most people are interested only in its role as a backdrop to one dark, horrific night.

All but caressing the silky banister as she starts down the stairs, she can just imagine the resentment aging Augusta Purcell must have felt over the widespread curiosity in her ancestral home. She can even summon sympathy for curmudgeonly Lester, who probably—

Hearing movement at the foot of the stairs, she's startled to see Catherine there. She's holding her phone like a camera, aimed up the stairway.

Seeing Annabelle, she guiltily lowers the phone. "Sorry, I just . . . I was texting my friends that I'm in a Murder House and they wanted to see a picture, so . . ."

"Oh." Annabelle's hand leaves the banister to rake through her short, dark, sweat-dampened hair.

Catherine grins. "Don't worry. You're not in it."

Gratified that she's not scowling for a change, Annabelle decides to go with Catherine's presumption that her gesture was vanity, rather than frustration. "Good. I was afraid you'd post it somewhere."

"You mean on social media? I don't do that."

"I thought everyone does."

Catherine shrugs. "Well, I don't do it that often."

Yeah. Sure.

"It's just, we're new to living in . . ." *Say it. You might as well. It wouldn't be the first time.* ". . . a Murder House. We're still trying to settle in and get used to it. It's not easy with the Mundypalooza invasion, so . . . you know. I'm just trying to maintain a little privacy wherever I can."

"I totally get that. I'm so sorry. My friends just wanted to know what it's like inside."

Annabelle fights the urge to tell her that it's okay, and add that she won't tell Kim, but . . .

Tell her what?

That her daughter was taking a picture of your house? Big deal. Or that you just had a conversational exchange with the sullen, silent teen? That she doesn't seem to hate you after all?

Anyway, it isn't okay. She feels as violated as she did this morning, when she found that her Web surfing had been transformed into a spectator sport.

"Can you do me a favor?" she asks Catherine.

The girl doesn't immediately agree, but the remnants n are still on her face, albeit joined by a wary n in her blue eyes. "What is it?"

"I just need help with the strawberries for dessert. I forgot to cut them up. Do you mind?"

"Oh . . . not at all."

"Great. Come on." Annabelle escorts the girl to the kitchen, thus ensuring that there will be no "Inside the Murder House" photos floating around in cyberspace for the time being.

When Ora returns to her third-floor apartment, she finds her feline companion blissfully snoozing at the foot of the bed. So much for relying on the animal's instinct to tell her whether something is amiss in the house. Rosie doesn't even stir when Ora nudges her feet beneath the warm, furry weight on the coverlet.

Maybe nothing *is* amiss.

Having lived in old houses all her life, Ora knows that their joints creak and groan as much as her own do these days. Pipes rumble and clang, foundations shift, eaves shake . . .

So why was she so quick to conclude that there was a prowler tonight? Because the cat was spooked and ran?

I'm probably the one who scared her when I called out.

Ora sighs and turns over, wondering if perhaps she's finally gone senile. Papa did when he wasn't nearly as old as she is now. Illness claimed Mama long before dementia could have. Great-Aunt Etta prided herself on having all her marbles "and then some," as she liked to put it, until the day she died.

But Papa—her distinguished, dignified, brilliant, and scholarly papa—was reduced to childlike confusion in his final years on this earth.

If I were senile, Ora reminds herself, *I wouldn't know it.*

Her father never did. Ora humored his delusions, even when he insisted on talking to people who either weren't alive anymore or had never been alive at all. His imaginary friends included Rip Van Winkle, whom he frequently insisted was playing ninepins in the living room, making quite a racket.

"Do you hear it?" Papa would demand, clasping his gnarled hands over his ears. "Tell him to quiet down in there!"

Ora would tell him that she did hear it, and duly swallow back her sorrow to scold the imaginary visitor.

Is it possible that she's now entertaining imaginary visitors of her own?

The idea seems preposterous. But Papa would probably have said the same thing, had she tried to convince him that Rip Van Winkle and the others weren't really there.

Earlier, as she went through the mansion opening closets and peering into corners, she honestly hoped she was going to come across someone lurking. Unpleasant as it might have been to confront an intruder, at least she'd have known that she can still count on her senses, her brain, her instincts.

Now . . .

I can't count on anything at all.

Ora rolls onto her back and stares at the shadows playing across the ceiling. Glumly, she wonders what will become of her if she truly is beginning to fade away.

Holmes hadn't lingered long in the mansion after Ora plodded back upstairs. Once the potential thrill of discovery had dissipated, his visit was as entertaining as hanging around a concert after the headliners have played their final encore.

Hands in his pockets, he whistles softly to himself as he walks up the steep slope of Prospect Street, away from the historical society.

He doesn't slow his pace as he passes the old stone house across the street, at number 65.

Back in detective mode, expertly gathering information with a mere sidewise glance, he notes that the lights are on and the Yamazaki family is home. All three of their vehicles are parked in the driveway: a pair of SUVs and a sedan with physician's plates that read Vani-T. *Vanity*, Holmes discerned long ago. The car belongs to Dr. Yamazaki, a plastic surgeon.

The house has central air-conditioning, but despite the closed windows, he can hear the family's dog barking from somewhere within. It's an Akita, which is not a breed known for being yappy. Perhaps it senses change. They often do. With luck, the dog will soon become accustomed to increasing activity level surrounding the house.

What fun it was to stay one step ahead of Ora Abrams as she made her way around the house like a geriatric superhero. He was tempted to really spook her—maybe knock over something in her path, or whisper from the shadows. But he refrained. Now is the time to tread carefully.

Really, his hat is off to the old gal. Unfortunately, it's merely a baseball cap, as opposed to the houndstooth deerstalker Sherlock would have doffed. He couldn't resist buying one when he visited London, but he doesn't dare wear it out in public.

Ora didn't seem particularly fearful. Perturbed, maybe. Inquisitive, yes. But afraid? No.

Holmes wonders what it would take to really scare Ora Abrams.

Outside the Dapplebrook Inn, a pair of women stand chatting with the female driver of a car parked at the curb with the engine running. They all glance in his direction and wave. He waves back, not slowing his pace.

"Good to see you," one of the women calls. "How have you been?"

"Very well, thank you." He's learned not to return the question unless you really want to know the answer. Holmes never does.

He walks on, reaching the intersection of Prospect and State. His SUV is parked straight ahead, way out beyond The Heights, near the elementary school.

Meanwhile, off to the left . . .

No. It's a bad idea. Visiting the historical society tonight had been foolhardy. He's lucky he made it out of there, just as he was lucky yesterday in the Bingham house.

Still . . .

He wouldn't actually go inside this time. He'd just stroll by. Just to see. Just to . . . anticipate. No harm in that, is there?

If someone were to notice him strolling through The Heights now, they might remember and become suspicious later, when the frightfulness begins anew.

Plenty of people are wandering through The Heights this weekend.

But look at S.B.K., who had boldly existed amid the flurry without ever arousing suspicion. What fun it must have been to look befuddled investigators in the eye while wearing a mask of innocence and respectability! How glorious to answer their questions one moment and make them dance like marionettes the next, amid the chaotic fear that accompanied the discovery of each new corpse.

Soon, Holmes will know exactly what that feels like.

For now, all he can do is savor the anticipation.

Go ahead. You're entitled. You've worked so hard.

He makes a left, heading up State Street toward Bridge.

Ah, yes, it was the right decision. The neighborhood is alive on this warm night. Extra cars are parked in driveways and bumper to bumper along the curbs. The old houses are brightly lit inside and out. Conversation spills out to the sidewalk from some porches, where candles flicker and gliders creak. Kids are still playing in their yards, gleefully celebrating summer vacation.

Holmes passes a dog walker, a teenage couple, a jogger. All nod pleasantly, caught up in their own little worlds, as is he. No one gives him a second glance.

He's just like S.B.K.

No.

He *is* S.B.K.

Locking the front door after the departing Winston family, Annabelle turns to Oliver. "Up you go. Brush your teeth and get your pajamas on."

"But it's not a school night."

"I know, but you were up way too late last night and way too early this morning."

His protest is swallowed by an enormous yawn.

Trib grins and pats him on the head. "Get moving."

Oliver dutifully heads up the stairs, and Annabelle and Trib return to the kitchen. Looking at the pans in the sink and the dishes and leftovers crammed into patches of counter, she groans.

Trib starts to speak, but she cuts him off.

"Don't say I told you so. Please?"

"I was just going to say go to bed. I'll clean up."

"Really?"

He nods, giving her a squeeze. "You made a great dinner, and you were right. It was nice to have people here. It's starting to feel more like home."

"It is, isn't it?" She lingers to discuss the evening— fun, they agree, despite the disorganization, the heat, and Catherine's mood. The girl had been cheerful and even chatty while helping Annabelle prepare the strawberries in the kitchen. But as soon as her mother reappeared, she was back to ornery and combative. Stressed, Kim polished off the wine she'd brought and part of another bottle before the evening was over.

"I can't really blame her," Trib says, rinsing plates as Annabelle hunts through the cabinet beneath the sink for Brillo. "She could have said, 'It's warm out tonight' or 'It's Friday' and Catherine would have jumped to contradict her."

"I know. Earlier, when she said Catherine hates her, I thought she was exaggerating. Now I'm not so sure. Do you think Oliver's going to put us through that?"

"Not you. Me. At that age, boys resent their dads, and girls resent their moms."

"According to Kim, girls resent everyone."

"Did you?"

"My father died when I was twelve. I wouldn't have had the heart to hate my mother after what we'd been through. It was me and her against the world."

"You were always a sweetheart, though."

"You don't know that."

He grins. "Sure I do. Everyone always thought that, including me."

He's a year older, but their circles of friends overlapped. In high school, he had a steady girlfriend who graduated with him but was on the swim team with Annabelle. She, in turn, was dating Steve Reed, who was Trib's age and wrote the sports column for the school newspaper—badly.

By contrast, Trib's articles were always thorough, well-researched and flawlessly written. His byline was on the front page beginning freshman year, he was news editor junior year, and named editor-in-chief as a senior. Steve resented that, complaining that Trib was appointed because his family owned the *Tribune*.

Even back then, long before Annabelle ever imagined he could possibly be her future husband, she championed him: "I think he deserves it. He's a good writer and he wants to become a reporter."

Steve, who wanted to become a professional athlete and fancied himself a talented writer as well, lasted one semester at Cortland State before flunking out.

Of course, as a swimming pool contractor, he's far wealthier than she and Trib will ever be.

Annabelle finds the Brillo, and Trib takes it out of her hands. "Go upstairs. You're tired."

"So are you."

He shrugs. "I'll sleep in tomorrow. You won't."

He's right about that. Her inner alarm clock always goes off at the same time. Hopefully tomorrow morning, she'll be able to head to the gym to swim her laps. She'd missed this morning's swim thanks to the mouse.

Remembering, she almost asks Trib what he thinks about hiring an exterminator. But she decides against it. She's too tired to talk about the never-ending to-do list right now. Anyway, Oliver was so caught up in the excitement of having a friend over that his rodent fears have evaporated for the time being.

She kisses him on the cheek and starts out of the kitchen. Then, remembering something else, she turns back.

"Go to bed, Annabelle. I've got this."

"No, it's . . . I forgot to tell you something. Yesterday morning, I saw someone in the yard."

"What do you mean?"

Quickly, she explains as Trib scrubs the chicken pan without missing a beat.

He doesn't say *So?* but he might as well.

"It's going to happen," he tells her with a shrug. "The gawkers are back in town. It's nothing new. We knew what we were getting into when we bought this place."

"No, I know."

She's never been thrilled by the traffic congestion and overall lack of parking spots, restaurant seats and common courtesy. But it's much worse when your home is the target of their fascination. Especially when you can't even draw curtains to shield yourself from the prying eyes of amateur detectives, crime buffs, curiosity seekers, press, and plain old nutcases who descend like droves of stinkbugs every summer.

"Maybe we should talk to the Yamazakis or Mr. Hardy," Trib suggests, vigorously scrubbing a stubborn spot in a pan.

The Yamazaki family lives at 65 Prospect Street; Bill Hardy at 19 Schuyler Place.

"What would we say to them?"

"We'd ask them for some helpful hints for surviving Mundypalooza when you live in a Murder House, I guess."

Annabelle shrugs. "That's not exactly what I had in mind."

"What did you have in mind? Do you want to call the cops?"

"I already told them."

Trib stops scrubbing. "You called the cops and didn't tell me?"

"No, I ran into them—well, one. Ryan Greenlea was directing traffic near the bus stop and I mentioned it to him."

"What did he say?"

"He asked if I wanted to file a report."

"And you said no?"

"Right. But it bothered me to see someone standing there staring at the house, especially with Oliver around. If it happens again, I'm calling the cops."

"For a trespasser?"

"I'm sure people have been calling them at the drop of a hat ever since the Armbruster thing."

"Is that why you're so rattled by this?"

"No. I don't know. Maybe." She shoves her fingertips through her sweat-dampened hair, pushing it off her forehead. "I'm so tired I can't remember why I was so rattled. But I thought I should mention it."

"You didn't tell Oliver, did you?"

"Are you *crazy*?"

"Just making sure. Good night, sweetie."

"Good night." She gives a little wave and heads upstairs, yawning.

For a long time, Holmes was stationed in a clump of bushes beneath the brightly lit dining room windows at 46 Bridge Street.

Like many of their neighbors, the Binghams had company tonight. The windows were open, and he clearly heard every word spoken at the table.

The conversation rotated around agonizingly dull subjects: food, sports, and television shows, for the most part. He expected talk to turn to the hot topic in town, Mundypalooza, but that was too much to hope for.

One interesting detail did emerge as he listened to the voices mingling amid clinking silverware and china: the visitors have a teenage daughter whose name is Catherine.

Just like his young friend hidden beneath the floor in the icehouse.

Coincidences, Holmes has learned, are never really coincidences. But most people aren't smart enough to realize that. Most people accept circumstances for what they are, never bothering to dig beyond the surface for true meaning.

Holmes is different. Smarter.

He watches the girl leave with her family. Now that he sees the parents more clearly under the street lamps' glare, he vaguely recognizes them. He doesn't know

their names, just that they're locals, and they live in
The Heights. But he isn't interested in them, nor in
their son.

Like his Kathryn, this one is tiny and fair. But she's
healthier, prettier, with pert features, perfect white teeth,
and a long-waisted, slender build. As she trails her parents
and brother, she's focused on the illuminated screen of
the cell phone in her hand.

Holmes slips over to the shrub border along the front
of the property and leans over the black iron fence. The
mother, Kim, is swaying a little, hanging on to the father's
sleeve. The boy has picked up a stick and is swatting it
along fence posts that border the sidewalk. His sister
scolds him. His parents ignore him. The woman's giggle
reaches Holmes's ears. She wobbles and nearly falls off
her high-heeled sandals.

The girl says something to her. Holmes can't hear
the words, but he appreciates the sharpness in her tone.
Clearly, she agrees with him: her mother is ridiculous.

Halfway down the block, they turn to head into a small
Queen Ann Victorian.

Catherine is the last one to disappear into the house.
Standing in the glow of the porch light, she turns back to
look out into the night. Holmes knows she can't see him
here, but he pretends that she can. For a long, delicious
moment, he imagines that she's looking into his eyes, and
that she *knows*.

Then the door closes between them, and he's left alone
in the dark to ponder this new development.

Catherine.

Sullivan Leary has never sat on a porch swing in her life.

But she's quickly gotten the hang of this one, bracing
her bare feet on the painted floorboards to gently push it
back and forth. It makes a pleasant rhythmic squeaking,

like something you'd find in a movie set in the perfect small town.

Back in December, when she first saw Mundy's Landing curtained by fluffy snowflakes, she decided it could stand in for Frank Capra's Bedford Falls. As she and Barnes trailed their serial killer to a bloody last stand, the scene grew decidedly Hitchcockian. But now it's reverted back to Bedford Falls, minus the snow—and minus the snide remarks from Barnes.

At the moment, he's boarding the first leg of a seventeen-hour flight to an island resort in the South Pacific. In its own way, her little refuge is as remote as Barnes's island getaway. More so, considering that unlike his beach hut, this place lacks wi-fi, daily maid service, and a resident masseuse.

But she wouldn't trade an ocean view for gliding on this quiet porch and watching fireflies dart above the disproportionately broad front lawn of this tiny house.

Perched on the Church Street rise in the historic Heights neighborhood, it was built in the late 1800s behind a mansion that burned down years ago and was never rebuilt. The cottage remains, set quite a distance back from the street, dwarfed between a turreted stone mansion and the steeple of Holy Angels Church. Its abbreviated second floor is tucked beneath a low gabled roof with dormers and an ivy-covered chimney. The clapboards and trim are painted in shades of lavender, cream, and gray, with magenta pansies trailing from scalloped window boxes.

Ordinarily, Sully isn't a frou-frou kind of gal, but in this case, the frills are nicely balanced by the no-frills. A laminated handwritten sign in the kitchen warns against running the microwave and vacuum cleaner simultaneously. The porch is missing a few spindles, one of which is being used to prop open a window. And that particular window has a cracked pane.

None of that matters.

Having swapped a shoebox for a storybook cottage, neon for a porch light, and wailing chaos for crickets, Sully isn't exactly homesick. Her head is feeling better already despite minimal rest and relaxation.

What should have been a two-hour drive up from the city turned into nearly five in Friday night traffic. She spent another hour jostling a cart through the crowds in Price Chopper, stocking up on groceries and several summer thrillers from the mass-market rack near the magazines. Famished and too exhausted to cook, she bought dinner from a fast-food drive-through on Colonial Highway and gobbled it on the five-minute drive over here.

It was the best cheeseburger she's tasted in a long time. And the cold Bud in her hand is going down more smoothly than the finest whiskey, quenching her thirst and easing the kinks out of her muscles. She'll probably sleep better tonight in the queen bed tucked beneath the gabled roof upstairs than she has in her own bed lately.

This isn't home. But it could be, if it were for sale.

Which it isn't.

And you're not considering leaving New York, she reminds herself. *Barnes needs you back, remember?*

She drains the last of her beer, sets the empty bottle on the floor, and leans her head back against the cushions, trying to muster the energy to retire for the night. Compared to Manhattan, this is a ghost town, but the streets of The Heights aren't quite deserted. From her front porch perch, she's watched people stroll by: retirees, young families, even a teenage couple furtively sneaking off into the shadowy graveyard behind the church.

"Okay," Sully can hear the girl saying, "but only ten minutes, or my mother will kill me."

The boy's voice is a low rumble, met with a giggle. "You're right. But I'm kind of freaked out. Everyone says it's haunted, and I mean, it's not like it's romantic with all those dead bodies hanging around . . ."

Sully rolls her eyes. Kids.

Those two don't know how lucky they are, living around here, where there's no risk of being gunned down in a random shooting . . .

Talk about haunted. There it is again, the awful memory, slipping into her thoughts just when her headache was starting to ease up.

Manik Bhandari . . .

Brianna Armbruster, too.

Bad things can happen anywhere, Sully reminds herself.

Standing and stretching, she decides to call it a night. Maybe she'll actually get some sleep for a change.

As she walks toward the door, she hears footsteps behind her on the concrete and hears a voice.

Turning, she sees a solitary figure walking by. From this distance, he's little more than a shadow. He's alone, head bent, baseball cap pulled low, and hands shoved in his pockets. She could have sworn she heard him say something. Poised in the doorway as he passes, she hears it again—a male voice, muttering.

So he *did* say something. Maybe he's on the phone, talking into an earpiece. Probably. Because this is Mundy's Landing, not the city.

Back home, she often comes across wandering vagrants who talk to themselves. Most of them are harmless, though once in a while . . .

But bad things can happen anywhere, Sully thinks as she steps inside and bolts the door. Even here.

PART II

Into this wild Abyss the wary Fiend
Stood on the brink of Hell and looked a while
    Pondering his voyage; for no narrow frith
He had to cross.

—John Milton,
Paradise Lost

From the Sleeping Beauty Killer's Diary
March 31, 1904

At precisely 7:43 this morning, the moon entered its full phase for the second time within the calendar month.

This astronomical phenomenon is certainly nowhere near as rare as Halley's comet, yet it is one that has not been witnessed on earth in nearly three years.

At that moment, I heard tortured screams escape the windowless room. They filled the house, despite obstetrical efforts to ease the violent labor.

At 8:30, scarcely an hour after the lunar phase commenced, the child was born.

The exquisite timing was hardly a coincidence, yet I must marvel at its near-precision. Certainly, I was aware that the herbal remedy she'd unwittingly swallowed would certainly induce uterine contractions, but how soon? My research was inconclusive. Thus I feared the child would make its appearance before it was time.

Good fortune smiled upon us.

She was caught off guard by her labor pains when they struck just a few hours after she'd sipped her evening tea.

I smiled when I overheard her conversation last night with the maid. "It tastes peculiar," she said. "Did you do something differently?"

"No, ma'am," Mary said in that insufferable brogue of hers, and blamed the strange flavor on the mistress's delicate condition. " 'Twas the same brew as always."

Ah, but it was not. Unbeknownst to either woman, I had replaced it with dried blue and black cohosh. The plants grow wild in the picnic grove beside the trolley turnaround west of town, and were used centuries ago by Native Americans to induce labor.

I'd gathered the leaves in the autumn wood, swallowing the bittersweet memory of the unexpected seduction on a night when a harvest moon shone through the pane. Soon after that night—much too soon, of course—she said that she was expecting a child. In June, she claimed, not meeting my eye, though the evidence was already visible beneath her dress. I suspected that the child would be born in April, or perhaps early May.

That was not all I suspected.

Yet verbal accusations are unnecessary. This morning, I scribbled a few lines from George Meredith's sonnet, "Modern Love." At precisely 7:43 a.m., I slipped in to tuck the page beneath her pillow as she filled the suffocating little room with anguished shrieks.

Her eyes were guilty gates, that let him in
By shutting all too zealous for their sin:
Each sucked a secret, and each wore a mask.
But, oh, the bitter taste her beauty had!

I do not know whether she has read those words yet, but she will, soon enough.

Meanwhile, I cannot fathom how I shall go on now that the child is here.

I must do something.

I must.

Chapter 8

Kneeling on the kitchen floor in front of yet another large cardboard box, Annabelle reaches for her utility knife. She's been carrying it around in her back pocket for the past few days. It's come in handy in all sorts of situations: opening endless moving cartons, prying jutting nail heads from the parlor walls before preparing to paint, and even slicing around the sash of a painted-closed window in the half bath.

"You're a regular little handyman," Trib said approvingly when she waylaid him on his way out the door this morning to show him that the window now slides easily up and down in its frame. "Maybe you can do the same thing up on the third floor. It's still an oven up there."

She promised she would, but so far, she hasn't had a chance. She's been busy unpacking, finding forgotten belongings she can't imagine ever needing again, like complicated kitchen gadgets, baby clothes, and craft supplies. There are way too many books: stacks of novels that weren't even compelling the first time around, plus cookbooks, atlases, and outdated almanacs rendered obsolete thanks to the Internet.

But here, finally, is something she can actually use.

No, not a gown suitable for tomorrow night's gala—though that would have been nice. Not the still-missing window fans, either.

According to Trib's Sharpie-scrawled label on the top of the box, it contains swim gear. She has her own goggles, swimsuit, and cap, but hasn't been able to find Oliver's and Trib's, or the pool towels and beach bag.

She flips open the blade, slices the taped flaps, and opens them to find . . .

Huh? Winter boots, umbrellas, flashlights, gloves . . .

Storm gear, she realizes. Trib has lousy handwriting.

She sits back on her heels, frustrated. So where is the swim gear? And where the heck is she going to store all this storm gear?

"Mom? I'm bored."

Oliver is standing in the doorway. Again.

And this is only day five of his summer vacation.

At least Trib was home for the first two. He did his best to engage Oliver in father-son household chores, but they all seemed to trigger anxiety.

Oliver didn't want to go outdoors to hose off the walkways or water the grass because there were bees. Afraid of spiders and mice, he wasn't interested in anything that had to do with the basement, crawlspaces, or rooms beyond their immediate living area. He couldn't hand Trib tools while Trib fixed things because he didn't like the sound of hammering. And he was reluctant to be alone in any room, including his own, because Steve Reed was there working on the pool. Strangers make Oliver nervous.

In the end, Annabelle and Trib tag-teamed hanging out with Oliver on Saturday and Sunday. On Monday, Trib went back to work, and their son has been all hers ever since.

"Did you sort your T-shirts?" she asks. "Figure out which ones you don't want to keep?"

He nods and hands her one shirt.

"That's it?"

"We already went through my clothes before the move," he says with a shrug.

He's right. The chore was pure busywork. Anything to keep him out from under, and away from video games and television. She allowed him to indulge in extra screen time on Monday and Tuesday while she was trying to catch up around the house. Last night, she promised Trib—and herself—that she won't rely on electronics to entertain Oliver all summer, but it won't be easy.

"If I get home at a decent hour, maybe I can take him to the park to practice hitting and catching. We haven't done that in a while."

No, they haven't. Oliver loved playing baseball before he got too old for Little League, and he was surprisingly decent at it. But he was too afraid to try out for the travel league with his friends because it would mean overnight trips. So he gave it up.

"Why don't you want this?" she asks, unfolding the shirt and seeing that it's a new one she bought him at Kohl's in May. The tags are still on it.

"It looks like it's for a little kid."

"You said you liked it when I asked you."

"I didn't want to make you feel bad."

"I don't," she assures him, and it's mostly not true. She tosses the shirt onto the table with the rest of the castoffs.

"What are we going to do now, Mom?"

"We're going to pack all that stuff into bags to donate to charity. And then we're going look for the box that has all the swim stuff. If we find it, we can head over to the pool this afternoon and go swimming."

"Which pool?"

There are two: the indoor one at the private gym where she swims year-round, and the outdoor public pool over near Schaapskill Nature Preserve, which belongs to the town. One is strictly for laps, the other for sunning, splashing, and socializing.

"The town pool."

His face brightens. "Do you think anyone will be there?"

"We'll be there."

Not what he meant. But of course every kid his age is either away at camp or enrolled in a fabulous summer program. Oliver is stuck with a mom who couldn't get her act together.

"It's just going to be a bunch of moms and little kids. I'd rather go swimming in our own pool."

"So would I, but it's not going to be finished for a few more weeks."

"Why is that guy taking so long?"

"You mean Mr. Reed? Because there's a lot of work to be done." Steve has been here working since before six this morning, but he should be wrapping it up soon. He has to leave early today, he said, on personal business. She wonders if he's already left.

"Come on, let's go look at the pool," she tells Oliver.

"I don't want to—"

"No, come on, you have to see." She puts a hand on his shoulder and leads the way before he changes his mind. The natatorium, like the other unfinished rooms in the house, gives him the creeps.

At the doorway, he shrinks back. "It's dark."

"Not that dark. It's just the tarp. Look up. See?"

She points to the glass roof. Steve covered most of it with a large blue tarp so that he can work on replacing the broken panes. What little gray light there is falls through the ceiling to illuminate the large, empty pool in the middle.

"What's that?"

"What's what?"

"That music."

"Oh—Steve hooks up his iPod to speakers when he's working."

She recognizes the song—old Bon Jovi, a throwback to their high school years. Either some things never change, or he's feeling nostalgic.

"Steve?" she calls. "Steve?"

She spots him through the window. He's out in the side yard, hosing off some equipment in the grass. His shirt is off, hanging on a nearby rhododendron bough.

That's because he didn't want to get it wet, and not, she reminds herself, because he stripped down for her benefit. She's married, he's married.

He's tanned and muscular, with tattoos. His jeans have holes in the knees. His hair is wavy and shaggy—not long, but collar-length. If he were wearing a collar.

He's nothing like Trib, not her type at all. She finds it hard to believe that he ever was. But back in high school, everyone thought he was cute—*including you*, Annabelle reminds herself. It's not as if she was immune to his charms. Steve was fun-loving and easygoing, the life of the party embodied in loud music, fake ID, a souped-up car . . . she was flattered that he paid attention to a straight arrow like her.

She watches him pause to drink from the hose. She doesn't realize that Oliver, too, is watching until he says, "I don't like him."

"That's not a nice thing to say."

Oliver shrugs. "He's not a nice guy."

"Why would you say that?"

"Because he drank from the hose."

"So?"

"So you're not supposed to do that."

"No, *you're* not supposed to do that."

"But he can?"

"Grown-ups have different rules."

He considers that. "What happens to people who drink from the hose?"

"You know what? I don't know. It's just one of those things my mom wouldn't let me do when I was a little girl, so I passed the rule along to you. But I guess you can drink from the hose if you want to."

"I don't want to," Oliver says with a scowl, "and I don't like him."

Hmm. Maybe he somehow found out that she and Steve used to date. Did Trib mention it to him? Or did Oliver hear her and Trib talking about him this morning?

Well, not about Steve, exactly. But about the tiles.

Rather than replace the missing squares in an effort to replicate the original pattern, as they'd discussed, Steve had removed them all on the first day.

"I was never good at puzzles," he told Annabelle, when he showed her, "and it would be too hard to match the exact shade. I'll replace the whole border with new tiles, and I'll give you a deal on the materials. Sound good?"

"Sure," she said, because what was she supposed to say?

"That feels like a bait and switch," Trib said that night when they surveyed the progress after he left.

"It isn't."

"How do you know?"

"Because it would have cost us more to pay him for the legwork and the time it would have taken to piece together the old pattern."

"Did he tell you that?"

"No, it's common sense. He's not trying to take advantage of us, Trib."

"Why didn't he at least dump the old tiles, then?" Trib asked, pointing at the ceramic squares that hadn't cracked or crumbled, now heaped atop a drop cloth in the far corner of the room. "What are we supposed to do with all that?"

"Maybe we can use them somewhere else in the house."

"Where?" He was grouchy.

So was she. "I don't know. Maybe I'll piece together a beautiful mosaic backsplash for the kitchen."

"Are you crazy?"

"I was being sarcastic, Trib."

He managed a smile. "Sorry. I just feel like this house is whipping our butts."

"It'll be worth it when it's done."

"Keep reminding me of that," he said, and they trudged wearily up to bed, arm in arm.

She's barely seen him since. With Mundypalooza officially kicking off tomorrow, he's been working late, putting together a special retrospective issue of the *Tribune*.

Late last night, trying to stay awake until he came home, she'd puttered from room to room finding storage for their meager belongings. Their rented cottage might have been small, but its built-in storage made up for the Binghams' lack of furniture. Unlike this massive house, it had had a linen closet, bedroom bookshelves and corner curios, closet cubbies, a medicine cabinet, and plenty of kitchen drawers. Here, the floors in otherwise empty rooms are littered with stuff.

There are heaps of dirty laundry and clean, folded clothing and linens that won't fit into meager drawer and shelf space. There are bundled old newspapers waiting to be recycled and much, much older newspapers destined to return to the *Tribune* office archives. There are moving boxes she wishes she hadn't opened and boxes she doesn't dare open because it will only mean finding a place to put everything.

As she attempted to tackle it, Annabelle imagined that every little noise and flitting shadow signified someone lurking in the house. It was always only the wind, a passing car, a squirrel in the downspout . . .

Still, strangers have been driving and walking by the house for days, blatantly stopping to stare. It's unnerving.

Now, she keeps an eye on the yard through the windows as she and Oliver look around the natatorium. Steve is alone out there. If he weren't around, would she see someone watching the house from back there in the trees?

Steve's presence might unnerve Oliver, but Annabelle decides it might not be a bad thing to have a man hanging around the house during the day.

"When will there be water in the pool again, Mom?"

"Hmm?" She turns to see that he's turned his attention to the pool itself. "I hope soon."

"How soon?"

"Before the summer is over, for sure." She describes what it will look like when it's finished, but it's hard even for her to imagine.

Like the rest of the house, the natatorium is in disarray. Steve's tools and supplies are everywhere. Two-by-fours are stacked on the floor, and large sheets of plywood lean against the wall, covering the mural.

In addition to restoring the pool and the surrounding area, he offered to frame in a small shower stall and changing room in the far corner. The plumbing is already in place, and he assured her that it won't be very complicated or expensive.

"Famous last words," said Trib, who threw up his hands in resignation when he heard about that last-minute addition.

"What are these for, Mom?" Oliver crouches beside the pile of discarded tiles.

"They used to be part of the border on the side of the pool, but we can't use them there anymore."

"Can I have them?"

"I guess so, sure. What do you want to do with them?"

"I don't know. They're kind of cool."

"They are, aren't they?"

"They would make a good floor. Can I take them up to my room?"

"Sure," she says, picking up an empty cardboard box— no shortage of those around—and hands it to him. "You can put them in here."

She stands watching him contentedly picking through the tiles. Funny how you never know what's going to strike a child's fancy.

The door opens, and Steve walks in. She's glad to see that his shirt is back on. "Hey, Annabelle. And is this your son?"

"This is Oliver. Oliver, this is Mr. Reed."

"You can call me Steve."

"Oliver, stand up and use your manners." Terrific, she sounds just like Kim talking to Catherine.

"Nah, it's okay," Steve says quickly. "I guarantee you don't want to shake my hand right now, buddy. I'm pretty grubby. Looks like you're having fun with those tiles, though, right?"

Oliver says nothing.

"Mr. Reed is talking to you, Oliver."

He looks up. "What?"

"No big deal. Listen, Annie, I've got to get out of here. The wife is waiting for me, and it ain't pretty when I'm late."

Annabelle has never met the woman he married, nor does she remember her name. He only refers to her as "the wife." She remembers that she isn't from here, and they don't live here now—they're across the river near Kingston.

"Thanks for everything," she says. "I'll see you tomorrow?"

"Bright and early. Have a great night."

He leaves with a wave, and a moment later, she hears him pulling out of the driveway.

"Why does he call you Annie?" Oliver asks, without looking up from the tiles.

"You know . . . for short. Like sometimes I call you Ollie."

"Not anymore. When I was little."

"Right. And a lot of people called me Annie, back when I was a kid. I knew him then, so . . . that's what he calls me."

"You knew Dad, too. He doesn't call you that."

"No. He's not big on nicknames. For other people, anyway," she adds. "Probably because he was stuck with one himself."

"I like Trib. I don't like Annie," Oliver decides.

Right. He doesn't like it, and he doesn't like Steve. Point taken.

Oliver goes back to sorting tiles, and Annabelle wanders across the room, stepping around a ladder and a bag of cement.

She's gravitating toward the stone angel, she realizes. She'd all but forgotten it, but now she finds herself curious all over again.

Up close, she can see the meticulously sculpted details. The angel has long corkscrew curls, high cheekbones, arched brows, and an exceptionally full lower lip. This must be a replica of some famous statue, because its features look vaguely familiar to Annabelle.

She runs her hand along the base, admiring the realistic curve of the bare foot and wondering, again, how it came to be here. It's an odd thing to find in a room like this, much more suited to a garden. Or, yes, a graveyard.

As Annabelle starts to turn away, she notices that something is etched at the base of the statue. She leans in for a closer look, but it's hard to make out without her reading glasses.

"Mom!" Oliver's voice interrupts as she squints at the series of letters and numbers. "It's too heavy!"

Turning, she sees that he's struggling to lift the box filled with tiles.

"I'll help you," she says. "Just a second."

"What are you looking at?"

"I'm trying to see what this says, but the print is too small."

"I think you need glasses."

She does. Her aging eyes are getting worse by the day, but optometrists aren't covered by Trib's meager health insurance policy. Nor are psychiatrists. Oliver's Dr. Seton costs them three hundred dollars an hour out of pocket. Her deteriorating eyesight is the least of their medical worries.

"Can you help me, Oliver?"

He dutifully comes over, giving a wide berth to the empty pool. Bending over the base of the statue, he reads, "Z . . . D . . . P . . . 3 . . . 31 . . . 04 . . . 7 . . . 7 . . . 16. What does that mean?"

"Good question. Is that all it says?"

"Uh huh. But there are dots after the letters and slashes between the numbers, like initials and dates."

"Can you read the numbers again with the slashes?"

He does, informing her that there's also a hyphen between the two sets of numbers, "Just like on Grandpa Charlie's grave."

Then . . . are they birth and death dates?

If so, whose?

And where—

"Is it a gravestone?" Oliver asks worriedly, taking a step back.

"No, of course not."

"But it has dates. If it's not a gravestone, then what is it?"

Good question.

"It's just a memorial marker. You know, like the one down by the water where the first settlers landed."

"Oh." Oliver looks at it again. "So it must be for something that happened from March 31, 2004, to July 7, 2016, and—hey, wait a minute. The . . . what do you call the statue carver guy?"

"The sculptor?"

"Yeah, the sculptor must have made a mistake, because this is only June."

He's right. And then it hits her: July 7, 2016, may not have happened yet, but July 7, 1916, has. That was the eve of July 8, 1916—the date the second Sleeping Beauty corpse turned up, right in this very house.

Holmes's Case Notes

It has long been public knowledge that the line written on the notes S.B.K. left beneath the Sleeping Beauties' pillows came from a William Carlos Williams poem.

I don't believe that anyone investigating the case in 1916—or in years since—ever grasped just how significant a puzzle piece it was. But any detective worth his salt will examine every aspect of the case, and that is precisely what I did. The poem—rather, poetry—became a key factor that allowed me to confirm S.B.K.'s identity, though I had long had my suspicions.

The Williams poem was entitled "Peace on Earth," published in his collection called *The Tempers* in the fall of 1913. A century later, I found the book still sitting on a shelf, overlooked and perhaps untouched by anyone but S.B.K. throughout the interim. I imagined that it had been handed to me from behind the veil.

I analyzed the poem stanza by stanza, then line by line, then word for word. I came to realize that in a twist on the title, "Peace on Earth" is not a joyful or gentle missive about gossamer angels trumpeting goodwill toward men. Rather, it's about a great unrest teeming in the heavens. It's about Orion, the hunter, and the three sister stars at his belt. It's an astronomical diatribe.

On another shelf sat Alice Meynell's *Poems of the War*. Beneath that, a row of carefully preserved and yet well-thumbed issues of *Poetry Magazine*, dating back to its inaugural issue in 1912. The collection ended abruptly with the volume published the precise month of S.B.K.'s death—among its poets, a young man named Ernest M. Hemingway, too green to have been listed on the cover.

I painstakingly searched them all, and found that by far the most dog-eared issue was, quite tellingly, published in June 1916. One page was folded over to a poem entitled "The Dead Child" by Madison Cawein. The following four lines had been lightly underlined in pencil:

The sunlight went. And then they fell asleep,
And lay beneath one covering white and deep.
Now all at once the garden wakes to light.
And still the child sleeps on clasped close in the
    night.

Chapter 9

Sipping the day's third cup of tea as she strolls along sun-splashed Market Street, Sully doubts that the weather can possibly be this lovely back home in the city. She's been completely unplugged here—hasn't even bothered to charge her cell phone—so she doesn't know about the forecast or anything else that's going on back home. But one thing is certain: a sunny, breezy, eighty-degree morning feels different in a bucolic village than it does in midtown Manhattan.

She feels different here, having spent the past couple of days trying to forget that she even has another life. A life that's perpetually in jeopardy, when you really think about it.

So don't. Just be in the moment. Isn't that the whole point of this vacation?

Ah, yes. And the moment is picture perfect.

The heat and humidity that gripped Mundy's Landing over the weekend are long gone. Last night, the temperature dipped down below sixty. Sully kept the windows open, just as she has every night here. She still isn't sleeping soundly through the night, but at least she hasn't had nightmares about Manik Bhandari, and she hasn't woken up with a headache.

Life—this life—is good.

Even the tea is good: whole leaf jasmine, brewed at the Gingersnap Sweet Shop around the corner. She also bought a dozen chocolate chip and peanut butter cookies displayed on trays in the glass case. The girl behind the counter put a couple of extras into the box.

"We always throw in a gingersnap or two," she said with a smile.

Gingersnap—that made Sully think of Barnes.

She wonders how he's making out at his island resort. He probably *is* making out, with his coconut bra hula babe or some vacationing billionairess. He'll want to tell her all about it when they get back. He'll want to hear all about her trip, too—mostly so that he can tell her all the reasons he doesn't like small towns, and she shouldn't, either.

Yet she can't help but miss the man. That's what happens when you spend nearly all your waking hours with someone. It isn't healthy. Nothing about her daily existence back home is healthy.

If I lived here, things would be different, she thinks as she arrives at the brick opera house facing the Common. Transformed into an art house movie theater, it's showing a film that opened a couple of months ago in the city, but still.

See, Barnes? There's culture here.

The Mundy's Landing Police Department is located in the theater's basement, which isn't underground. Rather, it sits a few steps below the sidewalk, with full-sized windows, just like the first-floor apartments in the brownstones back home.

Sully looked at one of those the last time her landlord raised her rent. It was a surprisingly affordable studio with high ceilings, parquet floors, and a fireplace. But there were bars on the windows, and she felt as though she was in jail even before Barnes vetoed the place. Naturally, he'd come with her to see it, and naturally, he informed her that it wasn't safe, bars or no bars.

"You can't live on the ground floor in this neighborhood."

"This neighborhood is up and coming."

"When it's up-and-come, we'll talk. Until then, it's down-and-out—and out of the question."

He was right, and Sully remains stuck with her sky-high—in every way—concrete cell.

If she moved up here, she could sleep in a gingerbread cottage every night, with screens instead of bars on the windows. And she could work in this spacious, light-filled police station with hardwood floors and the kind of wooden furniture that you polish, as opposed to the kind that you try to keep from wobbling by sticking folded gum wrappers and bottle caps under the shortest leg.

She'd also be able to see Lieutenant Nick Colonomos every day.

He stopped by on Sunday afternoon to bring her a bottle of wine and say a quick hello. On Monday, she visited him here—another quick hello, as he was busy. Yesterday, she didn't get to see him at all. She stopped by—twice—but he wasn't here. She only came because he'd told her on Monday not to be a stranger.

"I know you're busy this week, though."

"It'll slow down eventually."

By then, she'll be long gone. So here she is, wearing mascara on vacation, along with her nicest, slightly clingy T-shirt—not being a stranger.

Wilbur Morton, the recently hired new desk sergeant, who looks like someone's jolly uncle, greets her with a warm smile and calls her by name. Not Sully, and not Gingersnap, of course, but Detective Leary. Wishing she still had official business here as she did back in December, she reluctantly tells him that she's just stopping in to see Lieutenant Colonomos. Again.

"I think you're in luck this time. He's in." Sergeant Morton picks up the phone. "Hey, Nick? Detective Leary from the NYPD is back . . . yeah . . . yeah, okay. I'll tell her." He hangs up. "If you want to wait a few minutes, he's finishing something."

"Sure."

She sits on a comfortable chair sipping her tea and making small talk with Wilbur until at last Nick appears. He's accompanied by a familiar-looking uniformed cop.

"Detective Leary, it's good to see you. Do you remember Sergeant Ryan Greenlea?"

She does, of course. Back in December, Barnes had dubbed the rookie cop Babyface—privately, of course.

He *is* young, with a ruddy complexion that still shows remnants of acne. Tufts of sandy hair and large ears stick out from under his cap. She finds herself thinking that Barnes was right when he said New York would eat this kid alive. But when he strides over to greet her, his handshake and tone are authoritative. "It's good to see you again, Detective Leary."

"You too. Oh, and I brought these cookies—they're for all of you, so help yourselves," she adds, tossing her empty cup into the garbage and holding out the white bakery box, tied with red string.

"I'll take a couple," Greenlea says appreciatively. "I'm on the tail end of a double shift and that's just what I need to keep me going."

He opens the box, helps himself to a couple of cookies, and passes it to Nick, who shakes his head.

"No, thanks. Leave them on Wilbur's desk where people can help themselves. And listen, Ryan, if they give you any problem, tell them I sent you. Good luck."

Sergeant Greenlea thanks him and leaves, and Nick escorts Sully down the hall to his office.

"I only have a few minutes," he says, sitting and gesturing for her to take the chair across from his desk.

"I'm guessing Greenlea will call me in back to say they're giving him a problem."

"Who's 'they'?"

"The Marranas. They own the Trattoria down the block."

Sully knows the place. She's been trying to eat there since she arrived, but like every other restaurant in town, the wait for a table is always too long.

"They have a sidewalk café license," Nick goes on, "but someone just called to say they set up too many tables out there today, and one of the petunia planters is too close to the door of the building next door again. This is the third time we've had to send someone over there this week."

"Is he going to make an arrest?" Her question is tongue-in-cheek, but the irony seems to escape him.

"An arrest? No, but we have to fine them this time." He shakes his head. "I've known Mrs. Marrana all my life, and she's respectful, but she likes to do things her way. Yesterday, she sent us a tray of meatball subs and a note saying she was sorry and it wouldn't happen again, but now . . . here we are. I think I'm going to have to handle it myself. It's turning into a real problem."

Sully can just imagine what Barnes would have to say about a "real problem" that consists of a box of wayward petunias and bribery with meatball sandwiches. Back home, it's dodging bullets.

Or not managing to dodge them at all.

"I know it must seem small-time for you, coming from the city," he says as if he's read her mind. "But with all these people flooding into town, we have to stay on top of everything. And believe me, an event like this draws a lot of nutcases."

"I'm sure it does. I think I've seen a few of them."

"I'm sure you have, staying in The Heights. That's why a lot of people who live there get out of Dodge whenever Mundypalooza rolls around, and this year is worse than ever. Especially for the poor folks who live in the three houses where the crimes took place."

"Do they leave town, too?"

He hesitates. "It varies. They worry about break-ins—with good reason, since burglar alarms at two of the houses have gone off every night this week."

"So there were break-ins?"

"Attempted. It might have been just kids—you never know. But it makes people nervous."

"I'm sure it does."

"Don't *you* worry, though."

"Me?"

"Staying where you are, alone at night. You really are safe there. People are only interested in—"

Nick's phone rings before she can assure him that she's not afraid, and is perfectly capable of defending herself against the mischievous kids of Mundy's Landing, if it came down to that. She gets the feeling that if he hadn't been interrupted, he'd have called her "little lady," or something along those lines.

As he reaches for the phone, she says, "I'd better let you get back to work."

He doesn't protest. Nor does he tell her not to be a stranger. He just answers the call and gives her a distracted wave as he tells whoever's on the phone that he'll be there in about ten minutes.

She makes her way back to Wilbur's desk, where he brushes crumbs from his jowly face. "Make sure you come back and see us again, Detective."

"Oh, you just like me for my cookies," she teases.

He grins. "I do have a weakness for sweets—but for sweethearts, too."

"Funny—not many people call me that back home."

"I find that hard to believe."

"Yeah, well, you haven't met my partner, Sergeant

Barnes. He calls me a lot of things, and 'sweetheart' isn't one of them."

Nor, thank goodness, is "little lady."

As she heads for the door, she promises Wilbur she'll come by again, but she isn't so sure.

After all, she isn't in Mundy's Landing to spend time with Nick Colonomos. She's here to relax and heal her wounds and enjoy the bucolic village and the beautiful weath—

Oh.

She stops short in the vestibule, seeing that the sunshine has given way to a drenching downpour. Caught without an umbrella, she wonders how long it's going to last. Not that she's in a hurry to get anywhere. She lingers, watching people and cars splash through the rain.

If she had her cell phone with her, she'd be checking the forecast online. She does that a lot in New York. You can find out how long rain is going to last right down to the minute.

Here, who cares?

Let it rain. If she feels like it, she can kick off her sneakers and splash barefoot all the way back to The Heights.

Yeah, she doesn't feel like it, though.

She turns away from the glass door, and her gaze falls on the bulletin board. It's covered with notices: a memo about parking restrictions for the next couple of weeks, a schedule of events for ML350, a wanted flier, and a couple of missing persons fliers.

They of course remind Sully of the job, but she finds herself leaning in to read them anyway.

Both are females, both from the Hudson Valley.

Juanita Contreras, an eighteen-year-old who worked at a mall in White Plains, hasn't been seen in over two weeks.

Indigo Selena Edmonds—whose nickname is Indi—disappeared in Albany over a month ago. She's a minor,

Sully calculates—born January 31, 1999, which makes her seventeen.

She shakes her head. It never ends, and you can't escape it. Not even here.

For some reason, Holmes can't stop thinking about the girl he saw leaving the Bingham house on Friday night. She was young, barely a teenager, he's guessing, and just the same size and coloring as his Kathryn.

Yet unlike his Kathryn, whom no one seems to have reported missing even now, this girl would trigger an immediate Amber Alert. Especially after what happened to Brianna Armbruster,

He's been hoping to catch a glimpse of the other Catherine ever since, but he hasn't. Today, he crept through the yard of her house to look for her, but she wasn't around.

"Such a disappointment," he says aloud, to himself, thrumming his fingertips on the steering wheel. He would never have gotten away with abducting her, but it's fun to pretend otherwise.

Stuck in traffic on the way to Home Depot on Colonial Highway, he's counting on the store to be just busy enough to guarantee that he—and his last-minute purchases— won't stand out like a sore thumb.

Yes, he's been prepared for months. He thought he had everything he'll need for tonight.

But he forgot one thing.

"Come on, come *on*," he mutters at the brake lights stretching ahead through the rain-spattered windshield. "I don't have all day."

No, he has other things he's supposed to be doing; other places he needs to be.

But once an idea pops up in Holmes's head, it's as entrenched as the poison sumac taproots that choke the old trolley turnaround.

And that's typically a good thing, he reminds himself. Call it what you may—perseverance, or obsession—it's what enabled him to unlock the key to the greatest un-solved crime in the history of the world. He'd simply made up his mind that he was going to do it, and he did.

At first, he was motivated by the challenge, and the reward money, and the respect that would come with solving the case. But as time went on, he realized that there was far more to it.

It was all so real to him. The past. The more convinced he was that he'd actually been there, the more he grasped his true mission.

And now, at last . . .

Tonight's the night. And this last small detail will make it go off without a hitch.

If I ever get to buy it.

Finally making it into the parking lot, drives up and down the rows in search of a space. The store is busy, all right. Why are all these people at Home Depot in the middle of a weekday morning?

Because it's raining, and they can't find anything better to do?

Losers, all of them.

Holmes strides into the store and snatches a cart from the few that are left in the vestibule, avoiding eye contact with everyone he passes. Most appear to be out-of-towners, and those who are not wouldn't be suspicious, seeing him here. But he's all business, rolling up and down the aisles, maneuvering around meandering customers who appear to be browsing as if they're in a fancy dress shop.

He grabs a couple of random items—flashlight batteries, lightbulbs, some nails—to camouflage the one he really needs. Reaching for a box of garbage bags—not the target purchase but always handy—he bumps arms with a fellow shopper.

"Sorry," they say simultaneously.

"Oh—how are you?" she asks, as if she knows him.

He reluctantly allows himself to look at her. She's vaguely familiar, probably a local. But he can't place her, which means she's insignificant.

"I'm fine," he says briskly, tossing the garbage bags into his cart. "How about you?"

"I can't complain."

Sensing she's about to, he says, "That's good. Have a great day!" and rolls on to the next aisle.

A few minutes later, he joins the shortest checkout line. Ahead of him are a couple who are, in his opinion, far too pasty and flaccid to be buying a tent and other outdoor gear.

When it's their turn, the cashier, a friendly older woman with a broad face and kinky yellow hair, asks if they're going camping.

"Unfortunately, yes," the woman says. "We just drove all the way up here from Tennessee for Mundypalooza. We figured if we got here a day early we'd find a place to stay, but everything is sold out."

Holmes is quietly appalled. Did they honestly think they could just show up in town for Mundypalooza at the last minute and get a hotel room?

Even the cashier finds it inexcusable. "You'd have to get here a *year* early, guys. That's how long ago everything was booked."

"We didn't know."

Seriously? Ever hear of the Internet?

Barely able to mask his disdain, Holmes shifts his weight and studies a counter display of pocket knives.

Rhythmically running their items over the scanner, the cashier asks, "So you're going to camp?"

"We don't really have a choice," the man drawls. "But after we buy all this stuff, we're going to be broke. Any idea where we can find a cheap campsite?"

"Those are all full, too. Even up where I live, in Hudson. But I'll let you in on a little secret." The cashier stops ringing and leans toward them. "About a mile down the highway on the right, there's a big field and some woods behind it. There are no facilities, but you can pitch your tent for free if you do it way back in the trees above the river."

The woman raises her overly plucked brows. "Isn't that trespassing?"

"Trust me, no one ever goes back there. I mean, maybe the cops check it out the rest of the year, but right now, they're busy with crowd control right in town. But you didn't hear about this from me, okay?"

Naturally, they agree and thank her.

Still staring at the knives, Holmes shoves his clenched fists into his pockets.

Don't panic. All you have to do is keep the Beauties tucked away a little longer.

The situation is certain to become less complicated in the weeks ahead. After tonight, there will be only two captives in the makeshift dungeon; after July 8, only one; and by July 14 . . .

None at all.

"If we get that reward money, we'll stop by and take you out to lunch," the man promises the cashier.

Fat chance of that, with a pair of idiots who know so little about Mundypalooza that they didn't even bother to find lodging before driving a thousand miles.

Holmes closes his pocketed fist around his lucky buffalo nickel, wrapped in aged muslin.

Good thing he happened to be in the right place at the right time to overhear this exchange. Otherwise, those two dimwits might have found themselves in the wrong place at the wrong time tonight. As pleasurable as it would be to get rid of them, he doesn't need the distraction tonight, of all nights.

When they move on, the cashier greets Holmes pleasantly as he places his items on the conveyer.

"Haven't seen you here in a while. Guess work is keeping you busy these days?"

"Sure is," he returns cordially, resisting the urge to crush the package of lightbulbs he's holding.

Why did she have to talk to him as if she knows him?

And why the hell did she have to tell those outsiders about his special place?

Purchases paid for, he grabs the bags and pushes the cart toward the door.

"Excuse me, are you done with that?" asks a harried-looking woman. "There aren't any left."

"All yours." He gives the cart a shove. It careens toward her.

"Geez," she says, jumping out of the way, and then, belatedly, "Thanks. I guess."

Ignoring her, he steps out into the parking lot. The rain is coming down much harder now.

Good.

Even the annoying cashier wouldn't question why someone might need a large plastic tarp on a day like this.

The rain started coming down just as Annabelle and Oliver were about to head to the pool for a swim. She promised him that they'd go as soon as it lets up, and he returned to his room and the box of leftover pool tiles. She has no idea what he's doing with them, but at least he's been busy while she unpacked another couple of boxes and thought about the stone angel.

Now, she sits down at the computer in the parlor and opens a search window. The logical thing to do is type in the letters and numbers exactly as they appear at the base of the statue.

Z.D.P. 3/31/04—7/7/16

She isn't surprised when that search yields nothing of relevance.

Z.D.P.

If those are initials, then it stands to reason that the P stands for Purcell. She'll start there, ignoring the dates for now.

She logs into the Ancestry.com Web site, where she has an account. Last year, Oliver's social studies teacher gave an assignment in which students were supposed to trace their family back at least three generations.

She helped Oliver comb the Web site's databases for birth and death records, immigration manifests, and censuses taken by the federal government every decade and by New York State in 1905 and 1915. It was fairly challenging to uncover Annabelle's lineage. Her ancestors had emigrated from Europe through Ellis Island in the early 1900s and worked in New York City as household servants or laborers. Her parents moved to Mundy's Landing before she was born, having discovered the area when visiting her grandmother, hospitalized for years in a nearby tuberculosis sanitarium.

By contrast, Trib's family has been here for generations, and is well-documented back to the first Charles Bingham in the 1800s, and well beyond. The same is probably true of the Purcells.

Listening to the pleasant sound of the rain pattering on the roof and into the foliage beyond the screened windows, she begins the search with Augusta.

There are, she discovers, several Augusta Purcells in the ancestry database. Honoring previous generations with namesakes appears to be a tradition in their family just as it is in many others. She herself was named after her father's grandmother, and her mother's family tree is as laden with Marys as the Purcell family tree is with Augustas.

Annabelle's Augusta—Augusta Amalthea Purcell—
was born on January 18, 1910. The federal census
shows only three people living at 46 Bridge Street that
year: George H. and Florence Purcell and their infant
daughter.

Another Augusta, George's sister, Augusta Pauline, had
been born in July 1875. She appears on the 1890 census,
living in this house with her brother; her father, Floyd;
and a number of servants. The 1900 census shows George
and Floyd and an even larger collection of servants, two
of whom were named Mary. There was no Augusta Pauline at that point, but Florence had joined the household,
married to George before Christmas in 1899.

Annabelle double-checks for servants listed on the
1905 and 1910 censuses. There are none. What happened
to the household staff over that decade?

She'd been under the impression that the Purcell
family had always been well-to-do. Maybe they fell upon
hard times. Or did George Purcell release the servants
after he married so that the new mistress of the house
could handle all the chores?

"That must be it. Poor Florence," Annabelle murmurs,
shaking her head.

She moves on, looking for more information on the
other women in the family. Finding a death certificate
for George's mother dated July 29, 1878, the day he was
born, she realizes that childbirth must have killed her.
A death certificate for his older sister, Augusta Pauline,
reveals that she died just shy of her eighteenth birthday
in 1893.

So many tragedies back then. How did anyone bear it?

Annabelle turns her attention to the next Augusta on
the list. Born to a different branch of the family in 1852,
Augusta Elizabeth Purcell married a man named Isaiah
Nelson and died in New York City on Christmas Day

in 1909. Perhaps Augusta Amalthea Purcell, born just a month later, was named for her.

All right.

Now that that's settled, who the heck was Z.D.P.?

Annabelle opens another search and uses the first and middle initials Z and D along with the last name Purcell. Too broad. The site recommends adding another factor, such as a known relative or a location. She types in Mundy's Landing.

At a glance, she doesn't see anything that fits. Then something catches her eye: a link to a *Tribune* obituary from February 1904 for a woman named Griselda Jane Purcell—"affectionately known as Zelda."

Hmm. What if another Purcell baby was born on March 31 and named after the one who had just passed away?

She enters the name Griselda Purcell along with the birthdate 3/31/04 and Mundy's Landing.

Nothing.

She removes Mundy's Landing.

Still nothing.

When she takes away the date as well, she finds plenty of hits for Griselda "Zelda" Purcell, along with another Griselda who had lived earlier in the nineteenth century.

Definitely a family name.

She leans back in her chair, mulling it over as a rumble of thunder accentuates the steady rain.

If the dates on the stone angel are indeed initials, birth and death dates, then Z.D.P. was born in March 1904 and died twelve years later—Oliver's age—on the very date a Sleeping Beauty turned up in this house.

That can't be a coincidence, Annabelle thinks, her heart racing as she takes her cell phone from her pocket to call Trib.

His phone rings right into voice mail. She decides not to leave a message. He's busy.

She texts instead: *How's your day going?*

She doesn't expect an immediate reply, and she doesn't get one.

That's okay.

She opens her e-mail account and looks for Lester Purcell's address in the file of documents related to the closing. Hopefully she didn't delete it.

No, there it is.

She starts typing.

Hi, Lester . . .

No. Too informal. He's old, and pompous. She probably shouldn't be reaching out to him at all, but she can't help herself. She wants to know.

Dear Mr. Purcell,

I'm wondering if you have any information about the stone angel statue located beside the swimming pool in your aunt's house. I noticed something interesting carved on it, and I thought it might have something to do with . . .

No. Thinking better of it, she deletes that last sentence. Better to see whether he responds first, and wait until then to reveal what she found.

Instead, she writes:

I have a feeling it might have an interesting history and I wondered about its origin.

Sincerely,
Annabelle Bingham

She scans it, and hits Send before she can change her mind. Good.

There is one other person who will be interested to know that she might be on her way to unlocking the Sleeping Beauty case.

She logs off the computer, pushes back her chair, and goes in search of the umbrella she'd unearthed in the box of storm gear. It's going to come in handy after all.

"Can you do it?" Indi asks Kathryn, and holds her breath for the answer.

There is none, but in the dark, she can hear Kathryn trying. Her breath comes quickly, punctuated by grunts and Juanita's whispered prayers.

Indi, too, is praying, in her own way: *PleaseGodplease, pleasepleasepleaseGodplease . . .*

"I can't," Kathryn wails at last. "I'm sorry! It hurts."

Juanita lets out a sob of despair; Indi a frustrated curse.

"Are you sure?" she asks. "It'll only hurt for a few seconds. It's the only way . . ."

"I can't! Stop making me try."

Indi bites her tongue to keep from lashing out in anger. Kathryn starts to weep, softly, and Juanita goes back to praying in Spanish.

Kathryn is their only hope. She was thin to begin with. Now her tiny frame is skeletal, hands and wrists almost withered enough to slip through the shackles. *Almost.*

Every time she gives up, Indi allows her to rest before coaxing her to try again. She knows it isn't pleasant; knows Kathryn's skin is rubbed raw from her attempts.

But if she can just free herself, she might be able to escape this dungeon and go for help, before—

Overhead, she hears a distant thumping noise.

Her breath catches in her throat.

The others fall silent; they heard it, too.

Sure enough, footsteps creak overhead.

He's back.

From the Sleeping Beauty Killer's Diary
June 15, 1916

Each day inflicts fresh trauma. I can no longer bear the sight of her. The situation has grown intolerable. Even the cat desperately tries to flee every time someone opens a door, spurred by the tension sizzling in the air like one of the newfangled electric pendant lights gone awry.

Seeking reprieve, I visit the newly opened Electric Pleasure Park west of town.

The sight of its midway, complete with a towering Ferris wheel, brings to mind my journey to the World's Fair in Chicago. Who would imagine that less than a quarter century later, such an extravaganza of modern attractions would exist so close to home? Already, the park draws crowds from throughout the Hudson Valley and well beyond.

Many arrive by horse-drawn carriage or bicycle and a few via motorcar. Most, however, come via steamboat or train. They disembark the New York Central Railroad in Hudson to the north or Rhinecliff to the south, where they're met by a free shuttle service sponsored by enterprising local business owners. Crowds are dispatched on the Village Common in the hope that they'll shop and spend before boarding the streetcar for the short ride out to the park.

There, they stroll the boardwalk, sun themselves along the riverbanks, and cool off in the water. They indulge in root beer and ice cream on the concession pier, ride the carousel and Ferris wheel, and try their luck at arcade games. In the gloaming, they take in vaudeville acts or visit the dance hall, where the new foxtrot is all the rage. A pianist plays jaunty ragtime or an orchestra serenades with Tin Pan Alley favorites.

Tonight, strains of "By the Light of the Silvery Moon" float on the river breeze as the kaleidoscopic midway is illuminated by nearly three hundred thousand electric bulbs. The glare obliterates not just the moon but the thousands of stars and planets visible with the naked eye, yet no one seems to mind or note the irony.

Blind fools.

It is late. I've grown as weary of this day as I am of my predicament.

I must do something.

I must.

Soon. Not now.

My search for bedtime reading to pry my mind from my troubles yields these lines from last June's issue of Poetry Magazine—*a piece called "The Love Song of J. Alfred Prufrock," written by an immensely talented newcomer named T. S. Eliot:*

> Do I dare
> Disturb the universe?
> In a minute there is time
> For decisions and revisions which a minute will
>   reverse.
> For I have known them all already, known them
>   all:
> Have known the evenings, mornings, after-
>   noons,
> I have measured out my life with coffee spoons;
> I know the voices dying with a dying fall
> Beneath the music from a farther room.
> So how should I presume?

Chapter 10

"**B**ut I thought we were going to go swimming," Oliver grumbles as Annabelle, holding an umbrella high over their heads, takes him by the hand to lead him across Fulton Avenue.

Yes, he's twelve years old, and yes, there's a four-way stop sign, but some of these tourists drive like maniacs. As they were preparing to leave the house, she heard sirens, an unnervingly commonplace sound in The Heights this week.

When they got outside, they saw that a police officer had pulled over a car with out-of-state plates. Maybe it had blown the stop sign; maybe it was speeding. One thing is sure: the Mundy's Landing Police are on high alert right now.

"We can't go swimming in the rain," she tells Oliver. "If it stops, we'll go to the pool. Right now, we're going to the historical society."

"But why?"

"I told you—I have to ask Ms. Abrams about something. It won't take long. Afterward, we can go get lunch."

"Where?"

She hesitates. Their choices are limited to the town proper, since they're on foot. She's barely ventured away from the house these past couple of days, but Trib told her that the town is so overrun that it's impossible to even buy a sandwich at the deli.

"We'll get pizza," she says, hoping the lunch crowd will have dispersed at Marrana's Trattoria by the time they get there.

Even in the rain, there are plenty of people out on the streets of The Heights, some wearing raincoats or carrying umbrellas, others heedless of the downpour. Many are carrying what appear to be folded yellow fliers, cross-referencing them against street signs and house numbers.

"What are those papers they have, Mom?"

"I'm not sure I even want to know," she says, shaking her head.

A teenage boy in an orange rain slicker is directing cars trying to maneuver the small parking lot alongside the stately Dapplebrook Inn. Lunch is being served in the dining room at this hour, and the wide veranda is crowded with patrons dining al fresco or waiting for tables.

A few doors down, a small crowd has also gathered on the sidewalk along the low stone wall in front of 65 Prospect Street. The Yamazakis, a married couple, share the home with their college-aged kids. Beyond the tall wrought-iron gate, there's a Cadillac and an SUV parked in the driveway. The house, like most in the historic neighborhood, lacks a garage.

She wonders how the family feels about this lineup of strangers staring at their home like zoo spectators at the polar bear cage.

Noting that they all have matching stickers on their jackets, Annabelle realizes it's an organized tour group led by an older man, whom she doesn't recognize. As he talks about the house, voice raised over the sound of a dog barking inside, people snap cell phone photos. Several are selfies: broad grins with the Murder House in the background. One man has a camera set up on a tripod and is training an enormous telephoto lens on the house.

"Look!" someone is saying. "I think I just saw a curtain move up there!"

"Where?"

"Which window?"

"I think someone just looked out! Do you think that's the room?"

An untended child reaches through the bars of the driveway gate to pluck a blooming peony from the Yamazakis' carefully tended flowerbed.

There's a similar clump on the Binghams' property. Leaving home, Annabelle paused to admire the flowers, telling Oliver they're like "pretty maids all in a row."

Now she watches as the wayward kid tosses aside the delicate bloom and promptly picks another, and then another, apparently intent on deadheading them all. She wants to reprimand him, but the conflict would upset Oliver.

Knowing it's only a matter of time before the group finds its way to 46 Bridge Street, she clenches her jaw and propels her son on toward the historical society, looming at the corner of Prospect and Fulton.

When she was a little girl, she always thought the Conroy-Fitch mansion was a castle. It doesn't have a drawbridge and a moat, but it does have turrets and is made of stone.

Back then, Rudolph Conroy, a concert pianist, lived there. On still summer nights, lilting music spilled from the open windows. Annabelle could hear it from her bedroom windows, mingling with her parents' voices as they sat companionably on the porch.

After Dad died, her mother never sat out there anymore. If the sound of Mr. Conroy's piano seeped in through the screens, she shut the windows. Music reminded her of Dad. Everything reminded her of Dad.

The historical society grounds are, not surprisingly, teeming with strangers. An easel placard lists the day's workshops and discussions, all of which are taking place in the annex building behind the museum and required preregistration. Attendees are requested to pick up their wristbands each morning and wear them when they return within the designated time slot.

The line that runs from the front door to the sidewalk, protected from the rain by a striped awning, awaits general admission to the museum exhibits.

As Annabelle and Oliver shoulder their way past, someone calls, "Hey, lady, the tour line starts back there."

She bristles. "I'm not here for a tour."

"Yeah, right," he mutters.

"Don't worry," someone else says, "they'll set her straight inside and she'll be back out here in the rain with the rest of us."

To Annabelle's relief—and delight—she finds a familiar face manning the door.

Rowan Mundy, a childhood friend, gives her a big hug, and then hugs Oliver. She was his fourth-grade teacher a few years ago and is well aware of his anxiety issues, as is her daughter, Katie, which is why Annabelle has always trusted her to babysit.

"What are you doing here?" Annabelle asks, after complimenting Rowan on her hair, back to her natural red after she went blond for a while. Now she looks much more like her old self—a relief, considering the ordeal she and her family endured back in December. Annabelle thinks of asking her how everyone is faring, but doesn't want to bring it up in front of Oliver, much less the eavesdropping strangers.

"Ora talked me into volunteering," Rowan tells her. "I thought I'd be dusting display cases or something, but basically, I'm a bouncer."

"What's a bouncer, Mrs. Mundy?" Oliver asks.

"Oh, you know . . . a bouncy person," she says with a grin. "Actually, I'm giving a workshop tomorrow about daily life in pre–World War I Mundy's Landing. But Ora had a visit from the police first thing this morning when they saw how many people were out there waiting to get in. She asked if I'd come over to count heads so we don't violate the fire laws."

"Fire?" Oliver asks and darts a nervous look at the house, and then at the crowd snaking behind them. "Is there—"

"No, no, kiddo," Rowan cuts in, resting a hand on his shoulder. "No fire. That's why I'm here. I make them all listen to me and follow the rules. I'm really good at that, right, Oliver?"

He cracks a smile. "Right."

"Katie's really excited about babysitting for you tomorrow night, Oliver."

Like a light on a dimmer, the smile fades. "That's tomorrow night?"

"I told you, remember?" Annabelle initially brought it up over the weekend, and has been reminding him ever since of all the fun he and Katie will have.

Oliver's brows furrow above the rim of his glasses.

"Katie can't wait to see you again," Rowan tells him. "She missed you while she was away at Cornell."

Yeah, Annabelle thinks wryly, sure she did. College kids always pine away for anxiety-ridden neighborhood kids they leave behind.

"Maybe if Katie's around later, she'd like to stop by to say hello," she suggests to Rowan. "It's been so long since we've seen her."

"I'm sure she'd love to if she's up for it. She's been a little under the weather the last couple of days. She was still in bed when I called home just now. But I'm sure she'll be much better by tomorrow," she adds, seeing the expression on Annabelle's face.

"What if she's not? Then you can't go, right, Mom?" Oliver asks.

"She'll definitely be better," Rowan assures Annabelle. "You know kids that age. They're up all night, and they want to sleep all day. So what brings you out in this deluge? Are you here for the exhibit? Or did you want to catch a glimpse of the famous time capsule before it's opened tomorrow night? It's on display in the front parlor."

"I just wanted to talk to Ora for a minute, but I'm guessing she's busy."

"No, you caught her at a good time. She was exhausted, so I made her sit down with a cup of tea, and my son Mick is on his way here with some minestrone soup from Marrana's."

"Is he still working there?"

"He is, but his shift doesn't start until four."

"We're going there for pizza after this," Oliver tells her.

"Hmm. Mick says it's crazy there," Rowan tells Annabelle. "It'll take you forever to get a table. I'll text him to pick up some pizza for you while he's getting the soup."

"You don't have to do that."

"Don't be silly." Rowan pulls her cell phone from her pocket. "What do you want on it?"

"I'll take a couple of slices with pepperoni," the big-mouthed guy in the tour line calls.

"He called my mom 'lady,'" Oliver tells Rowan in a low voice. "I don't like him."

"I heard him," Rowan replies, ignoring the man and texting their pizza preference to her son. Then she stands back and holds the door open. "You can go on in."

"Is Ora up in her office?"

"No, she wasn't up for climbing all those steps. She's in the kitchen. You know the way."

"Thanks, Rowan." Annabelle can't help but feel smug as she and Oliver step over the threshold, leaving the crowd of strangers outside in the rain.

Blinking into the harsh glare of light that spills from above, Indi wishes the others would shut up. But they both started screaming when the trapdoor opened, ignoring their captor's guttural commands for silence.

Above the screams and his voice, she hears a telltale scraping sound overhead. The ladder.

He's bringing another girl to join them, she realizes, opening her eyes.

The light is indirect now; not nearly as harsh. It still makes her eyes ache, but she forces them to stay open, watching as he lowers the ladder into the cell.

But he doesn't descend grunting and lugging a limp female figure.

He comes alone, leaving the flashlight propped overhead so that the cell is illuminated.

His face is twisted into a hideous scowl.

He reaches into the bag he's carrying and tosses several objects at Indi's feet. A bottle of water and some bread. He drops the same beside Kathryn, cowering and wailing on the ground.

He fixes his gaze on Juanita, kneeling between them, screaming in Spanish for God to save her.

Indi watches as their captor removes a key ring from his pocket and strides over to her.

"Shut your mouth, Juanita, and open your eyes. *Now.*"

Those words, laced with a lethal calm, reach her. She falls silent and still.

Indi sees the object in his hand before Juanita does. Blinking away the unrelenting darkness, she gazes up at him, but she can't possibly see the pistol pointed squarely at her head.

"You're going to do exactly what I tell you to do. All of you. If you don't . . ." The sound of a weapon cocking is unmistakable.

Juanita gasps. Kathryn shrieks. Indi swallows a lump of bile, trying to think logically.

He has the keys.

Is he going to let them go?

No—he let them see his face. They're never getting out of here alive. Either he's going to shoot them all right where they are, and unlock their shackles so that he can dispose of them . . .

Or he's going to unlock us first, and take us someplace else to kill us.

If that happens, then the first two who are freed can try to overpower him while he's unlocking the third. It might work if he saves tiny Kathryn for last. If not . . .

It's still worth a try, unless . . .

Indi looks at the ladder. If he were to unlock her first, would she be able to climb it before he could shoot her?

That's unlikely.

It's even more unlikely that if she did manage to make it to the top, there's a wide open door to freedom. Trapped up there, she'd be a sitting duck for him and his gun.

Much better for two of them to jump him. Maybe they can wrestle the gun away, or grab the ladder and hit him with it.

She tries to catch Juanita's eye to convey the plan, but her head is bowed, and he's holding the gun pressed to her temple with one hand while he fumbles the keys with the other. She's trembling violently, hyperventilating, and Kathryn continues crying hysterically.

"Don't move, do you hear me?" he tells Juanita, as the keys clank against her shackles. "Don't you dare move. Stay still."

He manages to unlock first one arm and then the other. She stays utterly still, crumpled on the floor.

Indi holds her breath. *Please let me be next. Please-pleaseplease . . .*

Kathryn is still shrieking. He gives her a hard kick. "Shut up! Shut up!"

Her cries abruptly give way to a yelp of pain, and then a forlorn whimper.

He turns away, satisfied.

I'm next, Indi thinks as he looks toward her. Thank goodness.

Even if Juanita doesn't rise to the occasion, she'll try to take him herself. Adrenaline rushes through her veins. She's good and ready, bracing herself. When he puts the gun against her forehead, she can't lose focus. She has to stay calm, ready to attack.

"Let's go," he says, prodding the gun into Juanita's neck. "Get up. Now."

Wait—what is he doing?

"No," Juanita sobs, staggering to her feet. "No, please . . ."

"Start climbing. Climb!"

He's taking her, Indi realizes. *He's taking her, and he's leaving us. But why?*

It takes Juanita several tries to make it up even a few rungs. Every time she falls, he kicks her hard and forces her up again. He jabs her with the gun, right behind her.

Finally, she makes it to the top. He gives her a hard shove, pushing her up and over the edge. Then he scrambles after her. The trapdoor slams with a thud, and the light is gone.

For a long moment, left behind, Indi is bitterly disappointed.

Then relief trickles in, along with the certainty that she'll never see Juanita again.

Clasping a mug of chamomile tea on the antique kitchen table, Ora wishes she'd brewed a cup of strong Earl Grey instead. A few months ago, when she was having heart palpitations, her doctor warned her to stay away from caffeine, and she's heeded that advice ever since. But today, she could use a little something to pep herself up.

She was awake late last night putting the finishing touches on her special handout: "A Walking Tour of The Heights." She proofed it several times, making sure she hadn't left out any sites relevant to the 1916 crimes.

No, they were all there: the three Murder Houses along with countless local landmarks that had played a role, from the site of the old police station, now a private home, to the cemetery behind Holy Angels Church where the three victims are buried. She added a time line and graphic imagery that included several artifacts that are part of the exhibit. After printing several hundred copies of the guide on yellow paper and folding them pamphlet style, she finally collapsed into bed.

She'd deliberately waited until the last minute to create the maps, knowing that the locals won't be pleased. She hadn't even mentioned the project to her committee members or volunteers, knowing she'll hear nothing but complaints once the community gets wind of it.

So far, that hasn't happened. She's spent the morning chatting with the visitors who have filled the place and assuring every police officer and fireman who's stopped by that she's strictly adhering to the occupancy laws. People aren't thrilled about being kept outside in the rain, but they're resilient enough to wait. And so far, no one has complained about the map—probably because none of the visitors live around here. Today, the locals wouldn't be caught dead in—

"Ora?"

She looks up.

Well, speak of the devil, she thinks, seeing a familiar face peeking into the kitchen. She knows the woman—

yes, of course she does—but it takes a moment to place her. That's because she's cut her hair very short, Ora realizes, and she's coloring it brunette again after having gone gray. The chic, sporty style looks wonderful on her, taking years off her pretty face.

"Mary! It's wonderful to see you!"

The woman's smile fades. "It's me, Annabelle. Mary was my mom."

"Annabelle! Of course. I'm sorry, dear. That's what I meant."

It is *what I meant*, Ora assures herself.

Of course she knew it wasn't her dear friend Mary, who passed away years ago. This is Mary's lovely daughter, who recently bought the Purcell house after that old sourpuss Lester refused to sell it to Ora.

"Come in. Is this your son?"

"Yes, this is Oliver."

"You're growing up, young man. How old are you now? Eight? Nine?"

Dismayed, he says, "I'm twelve."

"Ah, of course, you're twelve." Lest they conclude that she's senile, she explains that because she never had children of her own, she sometimes finds it impossible to guess their ages.

Annabelle seems to buy that explanation, though the boy still seems offended.

"I know you're busy, Ora. I'm sorry to just show up in the middle of all this."

"At least you've announced yourself. That isn't always the case."

"What do you mean?"

"I've had a few late night visitors this week. It's that time of year, isn't it?"

Annabelle looks down at her son. "Oliver, did we tell Mrs. Mundy we wanted pepperoni on the pizza?"

"We said plain."

"Would you run and tell her we'd like pepperoni, please?"

"I don't like pepperoni."

"But I do. Tell her we'll just have it on half."

He hesitates, eyes wide behind his glasses, looking over his shoulder at the expanse of rooms that lie between here and the door.

"Come on, Oliver. I'll walk you back to Mrs. Mundy. Then you can hang around with her and help her count people while I talk to Ms. Abrams."

"I don't think she needs help counting. She's a great counter."

"Well, so are you. Let's go," his mother says firmly.

Good for her. She seemed to be coddling the boy for a moment there, not doing either of them any favors. But now she seems to have remembered who's in charge.

Mother and son disappear for a few moments, and Annabelle returns alone. Whatever she wants to discuss is obviously unsuitable for a child's ears. Ora's interest is piqued.

"Sorry, Ora. He gets spooked easily."

"Yes, well, who doesn't?" she asks with a smile, though the truth is, *she* doesn't.

Two nights ago, she again heard noises on the first floor after she'd gone up to bed. That time, they were distinct footfalls. But she was too darned tired to go down to investigate.

Or maybe she was afraid she wouldn't find anything if she did.

An intruder, she could handle. But no one at all—or worse yet, Rip Van Winkle. Or Papa . . .

Hearing things, seeing things: that's the beginning of the end.

If it's going to happen, just let me get through this last convention.

But maybe it isn't going to happen. Maybe there really was someone there. That's why she mentioned it to Annabelle, hoping she'd agree and maybe even mention that she, too, has experienced prowlers this week.

"I know this is the worst possible time to barge in on you, Ora, but believe it or not, this might have something to do with . . . well, the case."

"What is it, dear?"

"You know Trib and I moved into the Purcell house, right?"

"I do. In fact, I've been meaning to bring you a little housewarming gift, but I haven't had a chance."

"Have you ever been inside the house?"

Ora shakes her head firmly. "Never. Augusta and Lester made sure of it. And their parents, before them, kept Aunt Etta away as well."

Annabelle seems to believe her, because she says, "I don't think it was just you and your aunt. I think they probably just guarded their privacy after what had happened. Especially Florence, raising young children. That reminds me—did you know that according to the 1900 census, the Purcell household had six live-in servants before she married into the family? And no servants at all in 1905 and 1910?"

Ora did know. And of course, it makes perfect sense. But not for the reason Annabelle is thinking, nor the one Ora provides for her.

"Domestic life changed drastically after the European immigration wave slowed down. Factories popped up and hired men and women who would have otherwise been working as household help. Then the war came. By then, the servant class dwindled all over America, Annabelle, to half of what it had been."

"But I'm not saying the Purcells went from a full staff to fifty percent. I'm saying they had *none*."

"And you know this . . . ?"

"Because of the census."

"Perhaps the census taker didn't bother to count the servants."

"He was supposed to count every person in the household, and he did in every other house on the block. I checked."

"The Purcells' staff may have lived out."

"Maybe, but they lived there in 1900. There's a huge servants' wing upstairs. I think that after poor Florence came along, her husband and his father decided she should do all the work."

She goes on about poor, put-upon Florence Purcell, until Ora can't help but tell her that by the summer of 1917, the woman was marching up Market Street behind Carrie Chapman Catt.

"Who was she?"

"The president of the National American Women's Suffrage Association." Ora doesn't add that the historical society's photo archives clearly show that a Votes for Women banner isn't all that was visible against Florence's starched white shirtwaist that summer.

"She became a suffragette? Good for her." Annabelle gives an approving nod.

"Yes, she was the same age as my aunt Etta, and they shared interest in feminist literature." She doesn't mention that a few weeks before the murders, Florence had borrowed Aunt Etta's copy of a recently published book called *Poems of the War*, by the noted British poet and essayist Alice Meynell, an early supporter of women's rights. Ora later perused its musty pages for passages that provoked Florence's later metamorphosis and tragic final days.

"I couldn't find much information about the rest of her life," Annabelle is saying, "other than a death certificate for the late 1930s. She died fairly young."

Ora shrugs. "People didn't tend to live into old age

back then. My aunt Etta knew Florence. She was ill for many years, and she was widowed back in the early 1920s. Now, why were you asking about whether I've visited the house, dear?"

"Because I found something . . . interesting."

"Oh?"

"Do you know anything about a stone angel statue?"

"A stone . . . angel? No."

She listens intently as Annabelle tells her about the one that sits beside Augusta Purcell's indoor swimming pool, looking for all the world like a gravestone.

"Is that what you think it is?" Ora asks, careful to keep her voice level. "Do you think someone is buried beneath the pool?"

"It did cross my mind," Annabelle admits. "I even thought it might have been one of the Sleeping Beauties, but I know they were laid to rest at Holy Angels. I mean, that's well-documented, isn't it? There's no chance one of the bodies wasn't actually buried there?"

"No, Aunt Etta was at the service when they were buried. They're all there, in the cemetery. Why would you think it might be one of them?" Ora asks, her pulse racing to keep up with the possibilities darting through her head.

"Because of the birth and death dates on the statue. I mean, I'm assuming that's what they are. For someone who died at only twelve years old."

Ora's breath catches in her throat.

"The death date is July 7, 1916," Annabelle goes on, "which is the day the dead girl was found in the Purcell home. She was described as a young teenager. I know she was never identified, but there are letters on the statue, too, and I thought maybe they were initials. Maybe Lester knows something about it. I was hoping he would—"

"What are they?" Ora cuts in. "The initials? And the birthdate? What is that?"

"Z.D.P. The date is March 31, 1904. I'm probably reading too much into this, and maybe they're not initials at all, but if they are, then I'm guessing the P stands for Purcell, and the Z—well, there were two Zeldas in earlier generations of the Purcell family."

"Yes, there were," Ora murmurs.

"What do you think?" Annabelle is asking. "Am I way off base with all this?"

Ora lifts her mug, feigning casual indifference, but feeling as though she's just run a marathon. Her hands are trembling so badly that she quickly sets down the tea before it sloshes over the rim.

"I have no idea what it might mean," she tells Annabelle. "But if I were you, I wouldn't mention anything to Lester. Or anyone else, for that matter. Not with so many curiosity seekers around town right now. You don't want someone to decide the angel would be a nice Murder House souvenir and make off with it. And you don't want Lester to decide it has sentimental value and take it back, do you?"

"I doubt that will happen. He left behind every clunky thing he didn't want to bother moving—the clock, the piano, and that ginormous telescope in the cupola."

"A telescope?" Again, Ora plays it cool. "Really? Is it in working order?"

"Yes. If you want it for the museum, I'd be happy to donate it."

"That would be nice, dear. We'll talk about it after all this hullaballoo dies down."

I'll offer her a nice sum to take that old statue off her hands, too, Ora decides. *That will be the crowning glory of my personal collection.*

Holmes was planning to wait until after dark to move the first Beauty from the icehouse. But after overhearing the Home Depot cashier recommending his sanctuary as a free campground, he realized he'll have to do it in broad daylight. Hopefully, it won't take long.

He's well prepared. He keeps a rowboat stashed in the tall reeds along the riverbank, near a dirt parking lot used by the predawn fishermen. They're long gone by now.

"Why did you unlock me?" the girl asks him in accented English, still lying on the floor beside the trapdoor.

He ignores the question, busy answering a text on his phone. He shouldn't be here. He should be—

"What are you going to do to me?"

"Shut up!" he says, sending the text with a *whoosh* and shoving the phone back into his pocket.

"Please . . . Please don't—"

He shuts her up with a good hard kick, and she cries for her mother.

"I want my mommy," he mimics, shaking his head in disgust.

Her name, he knows, is Juanita Contreras. He'd chosen her because she was an easy target: walking alone through the nearly deserted parking garage of a White Plains mall. If it hadn't been her, he'd have found someone else who fit the bill physically. They only have to be small enough for him to carry, and pretty, with long hair.

Oh, and they can't be from affluent families. People who have money can hire private detectives if the police don't give high priority to a missing persons case. Then again, they invariably do just that when an upper-middle-class female goes missing.

Yet not for young women like Juanita Contreras and Kathryn Donaldson and Indigo Edmonds. They're a dime a dozen as far as Holmes is concerned, and the authorities feel the same way. They come from impoverished or broken homes. They hang around with the wrong people.

As a result, sometimes they run away; sometimes they walk away. It makes little difference in the end, right?

Of course Holmes has seen the missing persons posters for Juanita and Indigo, but most people won't even look twice.

And Kathryn—has anyone even noticed she's missing?

A fragile wisp of a girl, she's the true throwaway case. Born to a prostitute junkie who's been in jail for years, she's bounced around the foster system from Albany to Buffalo and back again. Her frame is scrawny, her skin is sallow, and her teeth are bad—crooked, one broken, another missing. Almost fifteen, she looks a few years younger. All she does is cry, cry, cry.

For Holmes's purposes, she and Juanita are interchangeable. When he descended into the vile-smelling pit with a flashlight and pistol to fetch the first of the three Beauties, he wasn't even sure which of them he was going to choose.

But then he thought of Catherine, the girl he'd seen the other night on Bridge Street, and he decided to let the other Kathryn live a while longer. Just because . . .

"Because I can," he says aloud with a shrug.

Juanita is filthy, with matted hair, wearing rags. It's going to take considerable cleaning to make her presentable for tonight.

I don't have time for this now. Dammit.

"Get up!"

She whimpers.

"Or don't," he says with a shrug. "It's fine if you don't want to get up. You can be on your hands and knees if it's easier. Go ahead."

He prods her with his black dress shoe, pushing her in the right direction. She scuttles away from him like a frightened kitten darting for a safe corner. "That's right. Over there. A little more."

The blue tarp makes a crinkling sound as she crawls onto it. Hearing it, she goes still.

"It's all right," he tells her. "I put that down so that we don't make a mess of the place, and I'll be able to wrap you up and take you right down to the boat. No fuss, no muss."

"No! Please, no . . ."

"Be quiet," he snaps, and just like that, she is.

He reaches into his pocket for the antique razor blade.

The weapon is as synonymous with Mundy's Landing as Lizzie Borden's axe is with Fall River. A hundred years ago, S.B.K. used one. Six months ago, in a delicious turn of events, so did another vengeful killer who visited Mundy's Landing—like an opening act, Holmes thought at the time.

Now, at last, it's his turn to take the stage.

He leans over the cowering, violently trembling girl. She's in a fetal position now, her arms, their wrists rubbed red and raw from the shackles, clutched against her forehead.

He wonders, belatedly, whether S.B.K. shared any profound words before dispatching the three victims. Interesting. What should one say at a time like this?

An apology might be fitting, but for Holmes, it wouldn't be sincere.

He isn't sorry at all. Nor does he have any misgivings.

He felt very much the same the last time he found himself in this situation—only then, it was a spontaneous act.

It happened not long after Mother died. Needing a change of scenery, he'd taken a long-awaited trip to London. Sherlock Holmes might have been a fictional character, but Baker Street, where he'd lived, is a real place. So are plenty of other settings Sir Arthur Conan Doyle used in the mysteries.

When Holmes set out to see them all, he was armed

only with a map. But he soon picked up a couple of souvenirs the detective would have carried, according to the author: a pipe, a walking stick, a riding crop.

Somewhere along the way, on a murky, midnight street, he crossed paths with an ugly whore who first propositioned him, then accused him of being crazy when he turned her down. There may have been more to the conversation, but that's what Holmes remembers.

Get away from me, you crazy son of a bitch!

That, and the rain.

And calmly beating her to death with the riding crop.

How satisfying to leave her on the cobblestone pavement in a puddle of rain and blood. The block, little more than an alleyway, was deserted. He strolled back to the hotel, cleaned up, and caught his scheduled flight home a few hours later.

His only regret was having to part with the riding crop, tossed into a Dumpster behind a nearby pub. By the time anyone found it, Holmes would be an ocean away.

Even his detective hero could never have traced that crime to him.

As for this one . . .

Grinning down at Juanita Contreras, Holmes lifts the blade.

Holmes's Case Notes

Going about my business today, I crossed paths with Mrs. Rowan Mundy. I immediately recognized her due to her role in last December's incident, when a notorious criminal mastermind intended to make her his next victim.

It was Mrs. Mundy who once suggested that I be tested for—among other things—a cognitive condition called prosopagnosia, also known as face blindness. To Mother's credit, she told Mrs. Mundy to mind her own business. Mother assured me that I simply don't bother to pay attention to most people because they are insignificant. She said that I have no reason to note, much less find reason to memorize, the facial features of those who will never matter.

This may or may not be the case. I'll confess that I have since done some research into prosopagnosia and wondered whether Rowan Mundy did indeed have a point.

There are many people whom I fail to recognize on sight no matter how many times I've met them. When they seem to know me, I pretend to know them.

In any case, despite this potentially crippling disability, I've proven myself to be a superior detective. I excel at scrutinizing people who matter.

Annabelle Bingham does, now that she and her husband are living at 46 Bridge Street. Like a handful of other steadfast locals, she's lived in Mundy's Landing all her life and probably intends to die here, too. That may happen much sooner than she imagines.

It's not part of the plan. S.B.K. didn't harm the residents of the homes he visited. But if an unforeseen obstacle pops up, I'll have no problem adjusting accordingly.

Chapter 11

Annabelle's cell phone rings as she and Oliver walk up the puddle-pocked driveway with their cardboard pizza box, under the disconcerting scrutiny of strangers congregated out on the sidewalk.

Here, at least, the flowerbeds lie well within the property, beyond reach of any hands that might grasp through the bars of the tall black fence. But the peonies that had been lush and lovely when they left the house have since been bent by pelting rain—pretty maids keeled over all in a row, delicate pink heads lying in the mud.

Annabelle takes the phone from her pocket, hoping it's not Kim, who's been texting her for the past two hours.

It isn't.

"Good, it's Dad," she tells Oliver. As they were walking, she'd made the mistake of wondering why he hadn't responded earlier. Naturally, Oliver had immediately assumed something awful must have happened to him. That's how his mind works: zero to sixty. She's been trying to reassure him ever since.

"Hey," Trib says, "Sorry I didn't get in touch earlier, but I've been holed up trying to finish an op-ed. What's going on? Did you get a chance to fix those third-floor windows?"

"Not yet. Oliver and I went for a walk and stopped at the historical society."

"Today? Really? Why?"

"Rowan was working and I wanted to say hi," she improvises, not wanting to bring up the stone angel in front of Oliver.

"Did you see the time capsule?"

"We did." They'd snuck a quick peek at the large, prominently displayed wooden chest, before they left. "Did you finish writing your speech about it?"

"Not yet."

"When are you going to do it? The gala's tomorrow night."

"I know when it is, Annabelle," he snaps.

Trib is scheduled to address the crowd during the evening's featured event. He'll recap the *Tribune*'s historic coverage of the time capsule's creation and burial ceremony in 1916, all front-page news written by his great grandfather, the first Charles Bingham. Then, as the capsule is opened, Trib will read from the itemized catalog of its contents.

It's an honor, but hardly a welcome one. Never comfortable in the spotlight, he's been concerned about the pivotal role ever since Ora Abrams invited him.

Changing the subject, Annabelle says, "Listen, you'll never believe what Ora Abrams did."

"What did Ora Abrams do?"

"She made a map of The Heights to hand out to people. Our house is prominently featured."

"I'm not surprised," he says mildly. "It's not as if people can't find us anyway, right? We expected the gawkers."

"Yes, but this is . . . I mean, she might as well load them into buses and drive them past giving a bullhorn tour."

"I thought you liked Ora."

"I love Ora," she assures him, glad she found out about the map long after she'd left her old friend in the kitchen.

When she collected Oliver at the door on her way out, a nice man at the head of the line was teaching him how to fold a paper airplane under Rowan's watchful eye. They were using a yellow sheet of paper that Oliver carried along with him. When he sailed it into a puddle—splat—Annabelle fished it out for him, and was dismayed to see what it was.

Still talking to Trib, she herds Oliver into the house, locking the door behind them.

"Leave your shoes right here on the mat," she tells him, and he obediently steps out of them as she explains to Trib, "The driveway is a mess, and we're covered in mud. Good thing we're in for the rest of the day."

"The rain is letting up," he comments, crunching something in her ear. "Maybe you can still go to the pool."

"I don't think so. We're basically trapped in our own house."

Oliver looks up at her, alarmed.

"I don't mean *trapped*."

Yes, she does.

"Oliver, go upstairs and find some dry clothes, okay? You're soaked. No video games, though. Come right back down. I'll heat up the pizza."

"Pizza? How'd you get pizza?" Trib asks, as Oliver heads for the stairs and she carries the box to the kitchen. "I can't get near any restaurant in town. My lunch is a stale granola bar I just found in my drawer."

She explains about Rowan Mundy's son, Mick, which reminds her—"I just want to give you a heads-up that Katie hasn't been feeling well. In case she bails on us tomorrow night."

"Why do you sound like you *want* her to bail on us?"

"Of course I don't. But you know Oliver. He's already a little freaked out about our going out for the night."

"He'll be fine. He's twelve."

"He's Oliver." She puts a couple of pieces of pizza on a

plate and sticks it into the microwave, then makes her way to the front parlor. "And you're not here, Trib. You can't see what's going on, thanks to this map. There are hordes of people out there looking at us."

"Hordes?"

"Okay, not hordes. There were hordes in front of the Yamazaki house, though."

"I heard they left town."

"Really? Where'd you hear that?"

"One of the neighbors saw them packing their car last night. Mr. Yamazaki said they were fed up, but they don't want anyone to know they're going away because the house will be empty."

"So the neighbor told the local reporter?" she asks as she leans over the computer, clicking the mouse to wake the screen.

"He mentioned it because we live in one of the Murder Houses. I promised I wouldn't tell anyone about the Yamazakis. Make sure you don't, either, okay?"

"Who would I tell? Oliver?" She sighs, waiting for her e-mail to load. "Maybe we should go, too."

"Where?"

"I don't know . . . a hotel?"

"There isn't one, unless we drive for miles. And I have to work. You and Oliver can go. Although we can't afford it."

"Forget it. It's just that I feel like people can see us through the windows."

"We'll cover them with sheets or something tonight. Why don't you get out of there for now?"

"And go where?"

"What's Kim doing?"

"She keeps texting me, wanting to know if I want to go to the mall with her and Catherine." And Annabelle's been ignoring the texts, hoping she'll get the message.

"You should go."

"What about Oliver?"

"What about him? Last I heard, he hadn't been banned from the mall."

"Very funny. He'll be bored."

"At least he won't be scared."

True. The mall is one place he never minds going. That's because there's a video game store, and a place where you can buy pretzel nuggets to dip into warm icing.

"Kim will want me to try on dresses for the gala."

"You *need* a dress for the gala."

"I *have* dresses. I spent the whole morning looking through boxes of clothes."

"And did you find a dress?"

"No," she admits. "But what about dinner? It's getting late, and—"

"And I won't be home for dinner. Go shopping, Annabelle. Buy something for tomorrow."

"With what money?"

"You always have Macy's coupons, and you can put it on the store charge. That's not maxed out, is it?"

"Nope. Only the Home Depot one."

"Awesome," he says flatly. "Listen, I have to run. I'll see you . . . late."

Not later. *Late.*

"I miss you," she says, and expects him to say something like *You just saw me.*

But he doesn't.

He says, sounding just as wistful, "I miss you, too."

They hang up, and Annabelle checks her e-mail, still standing beside the computer. No response from Lester. That's okay. She's no longer in the mood to solve mysteries.

Back in the kitchen, she stands in front of the microwave, watching the pizza spinning around through the glass window and thinking about Trib.

It isn't just that he's working late again tonight.

It isn't even that she misses him, exactly.

No, I miss us. *The way we used to be.*

Perfectly in sync. Perfect for each other. There was a time when they *had* time.

"We've got nothing but time," they'd say. That, and each other. What more did they need?

Back then, not much.

These days, Trib's working so hard to keep them afloat financially, and to keep a locally owned newspaper thriving now that most people get their news—even local news—online.

He'd dreamed of a big career, graduating with honors from one of the top journalism colleges in the country, Newhouse in Syracuse. After working abroad for a year as a foreign correspondent, he came back to Mundy's Landing when his mother became terminally ill. It was supposed to be temporary.

His return coincided with Annabelle's graduation from Iona College. She'd been recruited as a Division I swimmer and received a full scholarship—good thing, because her mother couldn't have paid tuition. She'd majored in business and been accepted for grad school at Columbia, but had to defer a year in order to afford it. Only when she was home again did she realize that as much as she'd enjoyed the past four years, she'd had enough. Enough academia—for a while, anyway—and enough time spent in the New York City area. She wanted to settle in her hometown, get married, and raise a family.

The marriage part came naturally. She and Trib ran into each other almost immediately after their mutual return, easily and swiftly finding their way into each other's arms. The family, though, was hard-won. When, after a few years of marriage, they decided it was time for her to get pregnant, they were still young. They tried casually at first. Then earnestly. Then desperately.

It was no longer true that they had nothing but time. Time was running out.

They tried to convince themselves that if it was just the two of them forever, they'd be okay. Still together. Still a family.

The doctors claimed there was no good reason they shouldn't be able to conceive. It was "just one of those things."

They'd given up hope and were trying to figure out whether they could afford either infertility treatments or foreign adoption—coin toss—when she got pregnant just after her thirty-fifth birthday.

Now they're living happily ever after in this big old house with a child they love as dearly as they love each other.

Everything is good. Everything is *great*.

They have everything.

Everything that matters.

And yet . . .

Sometimes *everything* is just too much. Oliver's illness, the constant worry over their son's constant worry, the house, the overwhelming bills that go with all that.

They both had the potential to make far more money than they do—especially Annabelle, considering that her current income is zero. But having lost three of their four parents well before they married, along with Trib's older brother, who had tragically died in childhood, they learned early on the far greater value found in things money can't buy.

Now those things, too, seem to have fallen by the wayside, and their lack of money keeps cropping up to threaten their solid marriage and the perfect life they were supposed to be living.

The microwave dings and the pizza stops spinning.

Tomorrow night, out with her husband, wearing a new

dress . . . it's suddenly sounding pretty good. It will be so nice to escape real life for a while and connect with Trib again. So nice to talk about something other than the shared burdens that encompass every conversation.

She makes room for the pizza on the table, still heaped with unpacked items—nary a fancy dress among them—and reaches for her phone.

"Oliver!" she calls, opening Kim's last text message. "The pizza's ready! Hurry up and eat it, because we're going to the mall!

It will be a shame if there's no sunset tonight in Mundy's Landing, Holmes thinks, listening to the rain drip on the roof. It doesn't look as though the gray gloom is going to lift any time soon, though the forecast calls for clearing. He's been checking it constantly the last couple of days, hoping that the weather tonight will mimic the weather exactly a century ago: cool and clear.

Contentment settles over him as he works, unwrapping the tarp as the bathtub fills with steaming water.

He'd originally been planning to transport Juanita Contreras from the icehouse to the boat in one of those oversized contractor garbage bags. But the tarp was pure genius. It allowed him to wrap her body like a neat little package right where she lay after the kill, thus removing the bloody mess from the icehouse. Now there will be no DNA-rich stains on the wooden floor. Now forest animals won't smell fresh blood wafting in the air and start sniffing around, which in turn might draw curious humans.

He didn't encounter anyone along the journey from the icehouse to the boat. If he had, though, he'd been prepared to offer a cover story. And if they didn't buy it, well . . .

He still had the razor blade in his pocket.

Not anymore, though. It's clean and stashed away until he needs it again on July 7.

"Now it's your turn to be cleaned and stashed away," he tells Juanita, lifting her from the tarp and carrying her to the tub.

He bathes her carefully, washing the blood from her corpse until the deep slashes in her neck are all that mar her appearance. Well, those, and her gaping eyes that watch him in mute horror. But he isn't ready to close them just yet. Not until she's dressed and ready to be tucked into bed, a Sleeping Beauty at last.

He dries her gently with a towel and dresses her in a simple cotton nightgown similar to the ones S.B.K.'s victims had worn.

The nightgown's high ruffled collar nicely hides the gashes in Juanita's neck.

Now it's time to braid her long dark hair. He practiced with three lengths of rope until he'd mastered it, but when the moment finally arrived, he couldn't get it just right. It's different when you're wrestling with a thick mass of individual strands, damp and tangled and attached to someone's head.

He looks at his fifth or sixth lopsided attempt, and then at his watch. He can't stay here indefinitely. This will have to do.

He hurriedly washes the tarp, and places her on it once again. Reaching down to close her eyes for the last time, he finds that he's made a terrible mistake. They're fixed in their wide-open position. Rigor mortis is setting in. He attempts to push the lids down, but can't do so without disfiguring her face.

Luckily, her arms are still pliable. He's able to fold them, hands clasped over her bosom.

There. She's ready.

As he starts to fold the tarp around her again, his phone rings. He checks his watch, and then the caller ID, and knows he'd better answer it.

He does, with his name, same as always—his real name, of course.

"Where are you?"

Keeping his voice calm and casual, he says, "Stuck in traffic. This town is crazy. I can't get anywhere." He gives the tarp another tug. It makes a telltale crinkly sound and he freezes.

But the caller doesn't seem to have heard, updating him on a few routine matters and then saying, "All right, well, I guess I'll see you soon."

"I hope so. I'm getting really fed up with all this traffic and commotion."

"Yeah? You're not the only one. You know the Yamazaki family?"

Holmes's breath catches in his throat. "Yeah?"

"They packed up and left town this afternoon. They've had it."

After attempting to wait out the rain in the police station vestibule this afternoon, Sully had decided it wasn't a good idea. When Nick Colonomos ventured out of his office on the way to go wherever he'd told the person on the phone he was going, she wouldn't want him to think she was . . .

Well, she's hardly stalking him, so of course he wouldn't think *that*. It's not even within the realm of possibility. Nor is she pursuing him, exactly.

Yes, he's handsome. And no, she wouldn't mind getting to know him better—say, over dinner one night. But mostly, she stopped in to see him because he's one of the few people she knows in Mundy's Landing. He doesn't seem to mind. He just hasn't taken the initiative to show additional interest in her. Romantic interest.

Probably because he's not interested. So why are you? And didn't you swear off cops after you divorced one?

But who else is she going to meet? In the city, the dating pool for women her age is notoriously limited. In her experience, single men in their forties or fifties are either unattached for a very good reason, or newly single and interested in dating women who don't need bifocals, hair dye, shape-wear, beauty sleep—or have the emotional baggage strewn in the wake of any failed marriage. Not to mention a bullet scar and the nightmares to go with it.

On the job, she meets cops, cops, and more cops. Oh yes, and perps. Plenty of eligible bachelors in *that* pool.

Here in Mundy's Landing, she hasn't met anyone at all.

A solo vacation might be just what the doctor ordered, but she has to admit, if only to herself, that it is a little lonely. A person can only read so many novels—she's finished three thrillers since Saturday—before she starts to crave human companionship.

Yesterday, she stopped by to see Rowan Mundy, a local woman and the December serial killer's intended victim. Rowan invited Sully to join her and her husband tomorrow night at the local gala.

"It's the least I can do for you while you're here, considering you saved my life," she said and—laughably—told Sully to feel free to invite a date, as well. "We have two extra tickets. My daughter and her boyfriend were supposed to join us, but they broke up and she doesn't have a date, so she's babysitting. You know how it goes when you're that age."

Or when you're me, Sully thought, and thanked Rowan for the invitation, but said she doesn't have anything formal to wear, much less a date.

"You don't need a date, and you and I are about the same size. You can borrow something from me. Please think about it."

Sully promised that she would.

She also promised she'd try to visit the historical society while she's here. Rowan is volunteering there.

"I'll be around all day tomorrow. You should stop by and tour the special exhibit."

After leaving police headquarters in the rain, Sully decided to do just that. She almost changed her mind when she rounded the corner onto Prospect Street and spotted the line waiting to get in. But they were under an awning, and what else did she have to do?

Rowan was glad to see her, and she spent the last couple of hours immersed in local lore more riveting than the page turners on her nightstand. It turned out to be the perfect diversion for a stormy summer afternoon.

Now, as she steps back outside, a fine drizzle still falls from a sky that's gone from charcoal to chalky gray. It feels good, though, after the stuffy museum crowded with too many people—though technically not, according to the elderly curator. Sully overheard her assuring a local police officer—not Nick, nor Sergeant Greenlea—that she was keeping a careful count of visitors.

On the way in, Sully had helped herself to various handouts, including a walking tour of The Heights. Now she consults the map and then looks at the row of large homes across the street. She can't read the house numbers from here, but it's easy to tell where the first dead girl turned up exactly a hundred years ago tomorrow morning.

Sixty-five Prospect Street is the house where the crowd is gathered along the curb. It's been there for days, but growing steadily. At this point, she wouldn't be surprised if some opportunist started hawking hotdogs and souvenirs to go with the map.

The Mundy's Landing Historical Society has it down to a science: "it" being what amounts to the commercialization of murder.

Yes, it all happened a hundred years ago. It's not as if

the victims' families are forced to be privy to the exploitation. Even then, the victims' families were spared that ordeal, since all three of the Sleeping Beauties were Jane Does.

Certainly that factor contributes to the crimes' mystique. Dead bodies—even grotesquely posed bodies of unidentified young women—aren't exactly unheard of in Sully's line of work. Maybe it doesn't happen all the time, but it happens frequently enough that she's encountered two—no, three—this month alone.

Missing persons investigations have come a long way since 1916, thanks to forensics, media, and Internet databases. If the Sleeping Beauty case were to unfold today, every one of those victims would have been ID'd sooner or later.

Mulling the possibilities, Sully steps over a gutter river to cross the street and eyes the mansion where the first body was found. In 1916, Dr. Silas Browne and his wife, Viola, lived there along with their teenage sons, Benjamin and Lewis. Their daughter, Maude, was summering abroad, and the corpse was found tucked into her vacant bed.

Sleep safe till tomorrow, read the note left under the pillow in that house and in the other two.

How, Sully wonders, did any of those families ever truly sleep soundly in their own beds after the trauma had passed? Were they, like Sully herself, plagued by insomnia and nightmares?

"The gate is opening!" someone shouts, as if announcing that a herd of elephants is making its way down Prospect Street. The crowd stirs with anticipation as, sure enough, the electronic iron gate across the driveway begins to move.

A moment later, a small Honda pulls into the driveway and parks behind the SUV and a sedan whose New York State vanity plate reads Vani-T in an apparent nod to vanity plates themselves. They seem to be more popular up here than in the city, as are bumper stickers. Sully notes that there are two on the Honda: a paw print and one that reads Dog Lover on Board.

The crowd is stirring with excitement over the new arrival.

"Who is it?"

"Hey, lady, do you live there?"

"Can we come inside with you?"

Ignoring the strangers staring at her from beneath dripping umbrellas, a young blonde wearing pink scrubs gets out of the car. She pops open the trunk, takes out a large sack, and carries it toward the house.

"What is that?"

"It looks like Puppy Chow."

"Is that the daughter?"

"Come on, does she *look* like her name is Evelyn Yamazaki?"

Sully rolls her eyes and walks on. She does turn back, just once, in time to see the young woman press the electronic keypad beside the front door, carefully positioning herself to block the spectators' view of her fingers on the numbers.

You don't have to be a detective to figure out that she's there to feed the family pet. Sully wonders where the Yamazakis are. There are two cars in the driveway, but there was another SUV, too, the first couple of days she was here. The oversized gas guzzlers are also much more prevalent here than back home in the city. Probably because people travel farther on a daily basis, and winters can be treacherous on rural roads.

Apparently, the Yamazaki family has left town like John, who owns her cottage, and every other Heights resident unwilling to deal with this circus.

Ron Calhoun, the local police chief, is an exception. Sully hasn't seen him since December, but Monday night she spotted him dragging a garbage can out to the curb at the house across the street. She went out to say hello.

Ron is about fifty, with more hair in his bushy gray mustache than there is on his head. "Well if it isn't Detective Sullivan Leary. I heard you were my new neighbor. How do you like the 'hood?"

"I wouldn't exactly call it the 'hood."

"The Heights, the 'hood . . ." He shrugged. "Same difference."

"I like it here," she told him.

"Even right now, with the invasion of crazies?"

"I live in the city, sir. This is nothing."

"Call me Ron. And you'd better be careful, Detective."

"Call me Sully. And why should I be careful?"

"Because this place grows on you. Ask your friend Colonomos. He came to visit from Boston and never left."

"Unfortunately," Sully told him, "I have to leave."

Calhoun just smiled, and told her to holler if she needs anything. She hasn't seen him since. He must be working overtime, like every other law enforcement officer in town.

As she steps off the curb to cross onto the next block, a car barrels around the corner. She jumps back to keep from being hit, landing squarely in a puddle. Terrific.

"Slow down!" she shouts after the car, wishing her *friend* Colonomos would materialize with sirens wailing.

Her sneakers make a squishing sound as she walks on up the hill toward Church Street. Her hair is plastered to her forehead, starting to drip into her eyes. Forgetting she's wearing mascara, she wipes them, and her hand comes away with black smudges.

Okay, she definitely does not want Nick to materialize after all.

She turns onto Church, covering the last steep block to the cottage. There are cars parked along the curb the entire way, and people are walking in the rain. More tourists. Holy Angels Church, right next door, is also on the map. The three so-called schoolgirls are buried in the graveyard behind it.

I'll have to go take a look when the sun comes out again, Sully decides.

Right now, she just wants to climb into a bubble bath with a book and a glass of the wine Nick brought her. She's given up the idea of sharing it with him.

As she cuts across the long stretch of grass toward the cottage, fishing her keys from her pocket, Sully suddenly feels as though she's being watched. Turning, she almost expects to see a crowd like the one at 65 Prospect Street. No, the sidewalk in front of the house is empty, and there's no one following her.

With the well-honed instincts of a longtime detective, she scans the street and the windows and porches of neighboring houses. There are people around, but no one is paying any attention to her.

She frowns, turning back toward the house. So much for well-honed instincts. A few days away from the job, and she's all out of whack.

But as she moves closer to the house, she sees someone sitting on the swing, watching her.

"It's about time you got back, Gingersnap," a familiar voice says.

At last the final visitors have departed the historical society, trailed by Rowan Mundy, who'd all but kicked them out, bless her heart.

"It's past closing," she told them, shooing them to the door an hour past closing, "and Ms. Abrams needs to rest up for tomorrow."

Ah, tomorrow. Tomorrow, the museum is open until eight o'clock, when the gala begins. As the unofficial hostess, Ora will have to stay until it ends at midnight, of course.

After locking the door, she lets Briar Rose out of the storage room. The cat rubs against her legs, purring loudly.

"I know, Rosie. It's been a long day for both of us. But it isn't over yet. Let's go upstairs. I have to show you something."

Up they go, one painstaking step at a time. Rosie used to bound up the stairs after a long day of being cooped up in the closet. Ora wonders whether she's taking her time out of loyalty, or if she, too, is getting too old to bound.

When they finally reach the third floor, Ora locks the door to her quarters. Some nights, she doesn't bother to do that, but tonight . . .

"This is exciting, Rosie," she tells the cat, who perches on the bed watching as Ora walks over to the built-in bookshelves that fill a gabled nook. Beneath them, a strip of baseboard molding that matches the rest of the room is actually the facing of a concealed drawer. You have to move a book on the bottom shelf to release the catch so that the drawer will spring open.

The title, of course, is *Sleeping Beauty*. It isn't the leather-bound first edition Ora bought years ago from an antiquarian book dealer. She keeps that copy locked in a case down in the parlor, where any thief who might recognize its value can break the glass and help himself without stumbling across something far more valuable.

This volume of *Sleeping Beauty* is a discarded 1980s-era children's library book she bought for a dime. There's nothing remarkable about it, other than the fact that its spine is sufficiently thick.

Ora plucks it from the shelf and presses the concealed mechanism, and a wide, fairly shallow drawer pops open. It's filled with archival boxes of all shapes and sizes, each carefully labeled. Some are much older than the others, with yellowed labels that bear Great-Aunt Etta's spidery handwriting.

What a shame that the treasures won't be passed to another generation who might cherish it as Ora and her family have. An only child, she'd never married, never had children of her own. She hasn't lacked for companionship—not with her work and the networking that goes along with it. But it's a shame that she doesn't have even a niece or nephew to take over where she leaves off.

For a long time, she hoped that someone might come along to fill that role as a surrogate—perhaps a local child, or one of the students at nearby Hadley College conducting research at the museum. Someone who would share her reverence for this place.

There was one promising prospect, years ago. But he had an air of superiority that rubbed her the wrong way.

Now, she fears it might be too late to find a young protégé.

After all these years Ora knows the contents of each box, but it still takes her a bit of searching to find the one she needs. It's on the small side, and labeled Jewelry.

She removes the contents, each a small packet wrapped in acid-free tissue. Carefully, she unfolds each one, searching.

Her parents' wedding bands are nestled together in the first.

Aunt Etta's ivory brooch, left to Ora in her will along with the vast majority of her worldly goods, is in the next.

There's Papa's gold pocket watch, followed by a jeweled hair comb that had belonged to his mother, whom Ora never met.

The oldest and thus most valuable artifact is a gimmal ring dating back to Elizabethan England. It's also known as a joint ring because it was made in interlocking pieces that could be worn separately by betrothed lovers, later joined on the bride's finger.

This one had belonged to James and Elizabeth Mundy.

They were among the small group of men, women, and children who sailed across the ocean from England in the spring of 1665. After reaching the New York harbor, they continued on up the Hudson River, landing at a spot now encompassed by Schaapskill Nature Preserve.

Over the summer, the colonists built a cluster of sturdy homes. The subsequent winter came early and the river froze over, stranding their desperately awaited supply ship until the spring thaw. When at last the reinforcements arrived, all but five of the settlers had died of starvation.

Only James and Elizabeth Mundy and their three children had survived—by feeding on the corpses of their dead neighbors.

Justice was carried out swiftly when their cannibalism was discovered by the newcomers. Accused of murder, the couple maintained that they had eaten only those who had already died. They said the ground was too hard to bury the corpses and eventually, desperate to save their children, they resorted to carving frozen flesh from human bones.

James and Elizabeth were nonetheless convicted of murder and sentenced to death by hanging in front of the entire colony, including their horrified children.

Traumatized, stranded in a foreign land populated by vengeful strangers and surrounded by dense wilderness, the Mundy orphans proved remarkably resilient. They overcame the stigma of their parents' supposed crimes and went on to become productive citizens who were ultimately embraced by the community. Two of the siblings, Jeremiah Mundy and Priscilla Mundy Ransom, lived to marry and have children of their own. Charity, the frail middle child, died not long after her parents.

Ora has always relished the fact that the village was named in honor of James and Elizabeth Mundy's great-great grandson Enoch Mundy, a Revolutionary War hero. It was, as she likes to tell museum guests, "the ultimate way to clear the family name and ensure that it would never be forgotten."

The cast-iron pot the doomed couple had supposedly used to make a human stew is on permanent display amid the museum's seventeenth-century artifacts. So are the handwritten parchment records from the trial and execution.

Ora's private collection contains more provocative relics related to the cannibalism incident, along with this gimmal ring. It had been taken from Elizabeth's finger after she was hanged, though it isn't clear who took it, or how it made its way back to the Mundy family.

Nor is it clear how Great-Aunt Etta happened to possess it when she died. Ora found it among her late aunt's belongings, its illustrious past carefully documented.

Aunt Etta was, like Ora herself, so passionate about preserving the past that she may have helped herself to an artifact here and there—not for personal gain, but to ensure that history wouldn't be forgotten, or recklessly tossed aside: the proverbial priceless treasure on a dollar table at a tag sale.

But Ora isn't looking for the gimmal ring today.

The object she seeks is, naturally, the very last one she opens, because that's how it always seems to go when one is impatient to locate something.

The gold locket is distinctly shaped: more or less an oval, but with scalloped corners. The metal is burnished. The back is scratched with wear; the front, etched with vines and roses and decorated with seed pearls. It's on a long chain, as was customary around the turn of the century, so that women could double or triple it to achieve a convenient or fashionable length.

Florence Purcell wore this very locket in every photograph Ora has seen of her after 1916.

Before 1916, she wore it only occasionally—most notably, Ora has always thought, in a 1915 family portrait after her youngest child was born.

In addition to that photo, prominently featured in the museum, the official collection contains prints of several Purcell family photographs. There's a sepia-toned wedding portrait of Florence and George, one of her with little Augusta, and several of the children, individually or together.

Ora's personal collection contains many pictures that were taken by Florence herself. Aunt Etta said she'd become an amateur photographer after her husband presented her with a Brownie box camera as a wedding gift. Some of her shots captured innocuous household moments rendered fascinating in retrospect: a table set for a festive meal, a decorated Christmas tree with gifts beneath, a nursery that appeared to have been lovingly prepared for a future occupant. Others revealed Mundy's Landing in all its early twentieth-century splendor: street scenes, store interiors, a schoolhouse, churches, homes, piers, and docks.

Many of her earlier photos included people—her husband, her father-in-law, even the servants Annabelle had mentioned this afternoon. A few showed Florence herself, self-portraits in a full-length mirror.

After a couple of years—by 1904, to be precise—the people faded away. She still took photographs, though.

Inside the locket, trimmed to fit perfectly beneath the rim, is a photo of a young girl in a sailor blouse. She has a round face and long hair worn in braids. Her eyes are gaping, but not in astonishment. They're just utterly vacant.

If anyone other than Ora—and before her, Aunt Etta—

had ever seen the photo, or even the girl herself, she probably wouldn't have been recognized. Not at a glance.

No, because when you look at her face, it's impossible to see past those empty eyes. The rest of it, even the braids—those telltale braids—becomes all but invisible.

But in the other photo—the famous photo, the one exhibited down on the second floor, the one that was printed in newspapers far and wide—her eyes are closed in death.

She lies in an unmarked grave behind Holy Angels Church, the second of the Sleeping Beauties to be found in Mundy's Landing in 1916.

Her name was Zelda.

Zelda D. Purcell.

From the Sleeping Beauty Killer's Diary
June 16, 1916

I must do something.

I must.

Soon.

I have been thinking of Miss Lizzie Borden. When I read The Fall River Tragedy *many years ago on the train home from Chicago, I was convinced of her innocence, finding it unimaginable that a fine, upstanding citizen might murder her own flesh and blood. Now, despite her acquittal, I am convinced of her guilt.*

Had she not acted in a rage, she might never have been accused and charged. I resolve not to make the same mistake, and shall ensure that suspicion will never be cast upon me. But how?

The answer came upon me this evening as I wandered the Pleasure Park, remembering my splendid interlude at the World's Fair nearly a quarter of a century ago. A lifetime ago. And yet I suddenly remember like it was yesterday the heady sensation of controlling of my destiny for the first time and perhaps for the last. Why, though, must it be that way?

There on the midway tonight, I couldn't help but remember a wonderful poem called "Chicago," published by a talent named Carl Sandburg a year or two ago in Poetry Magazine. *Here I share a bit:*

City of the Big Shoulders:
They tell me you are wicked and I believe them,
    for I have seen your painted women under
    the gas lamps luring the farm boys.

Fittingly, those very lines were running through my head when I spotted her in the crowd that encircled the Ferris wheel. Nearly everyone was watching the riders whirl into the air aboard a midway mainstay that had been a newfangled contraption in my youth. The young woman, however, was watching me.

Her dubious morality would have become evident in the course of our mercifully short conversation even if she had not been wearing rouge, with her skirt hemmed far higher on her calves than is the new fashion.

She mentioned that she'd taken the steamboat up from New York City. She introduced herself as Calliope, with music of the same tinkling in the background.

"Surely," I said, "that cannot be your real name."

"Of course not. I have done my best to forget that over the years. And you are . . . ?"

I glanced around for inspiration, and found it right there on the midway. "Ferris."

She threw her head back and laughed. "I hope to see you again, Ferris. I'll be here every evening."

When I questioned that, reminding her that train fare alone is fifty cents and admission a dime, she informed me that she could earn that in no time. "Or," she added with a wink, "I can take all the time you need."

I will confess that I hastened to escape her shockingly inappropriate advances. But I haven't forgotten her.

In parting, she said gaily, "Perhaps I'll see you again."

"I doubt that," I replied rather stiffly. "I am a respectable citizen."

" 'Tis what they all say," she told me, amused.

I shall return to look for her again, very soon. Or for someone quite like her.

I must do something.

I must.

Chapter 12

"**Y**ou have to admit, that was fun."

Seated in the passenger seat of Kim's SUV as they head east over the bridge across the Hudson, Annabelle smiles wearily. "That *was* fun."

For the first hour, anyway.

Never a fan of trying on clothes just for kicks, she'd quickly had her fill of the Macy's dressing room. In fact, she'd have bought the simple sleeveless black chiffon cocktail dress right off the rack if Kim hadn't insisted that she go put it on, along with an armload of others. Then she insisted that Annabelle step out and show her each one, as Oliver and Catherine sat in a pair of chairs—he playing a video game, she texting her friends.

She wound up buying the black dress, and Kim bought it in bright pink, promising she wouldn't wear it whenever Annabelle wore hers.

"As long as you don't wear it tomorrow night, you're safe," Annabelle said dryly.

At which point Kim tactfully tried to talk her into dressing up more often, and Catherine said, "Maybe you should try to dress *down* more often, Mom."

After that, they headed for the food court and video game store, with Catherine and Kim bickering incessantly, yet visiting every dressing room along the way and back again.

Now, at last, they're on their way back to Mundy's Landing. The pavement is still shiny, but the rain has stopped.

Annabelle's lone shopping bag is in the back of the SUV, accompanied by Kim's, and several that belong to Catherine. Oliver is dozing in the backseat, and Catherine is texting, texting, texting her friends. Annabelle wonders what they possibly have to say to each other.

She pulls her own phone out of her pocket to see whether she might have missed a text from Trib. No.

"Is he home yet?" Kim asks, glancing over.

"Nope. He said late, and I know he means *late*."

"Ross is working late, too. Which is nothing new."

"You must get sick of that," Annabelle says, putting her phone away. Ross works at a law firm an hour away, in Albany.

"No big deal. You can get used to anything. Listen, why don't you come over and have a glass of wine?"

"Wine sounds great. But you come to my house. I promised Oliver he can play his new video game when we get home."

"He can use Connor's Xbox."

"No, come to my house."

Annabelle doesn't elaborate. She's learned that once you start offering excuses, people respond with alternatives you don't want to consider.

Oliver would be uneasy about being in Connor's room without him. Period.

"Okay," Kim says with a shrug, "but Catherine will have to come, too."

"What will I have to do?" Suddenly, her daughter is all ears in the backseat.

"We're going over to Annabelle's house for a little while. You can play Xbox with Oliver."

"*What?*"

Ignoring her, Kim tells Annabelle, "It'll be nice for her to spend time with Oliver since Connor's gone."

"It's not like I even miss him! I'm psyched that he's gone, and—"

"This is the least you can do," Kim cuts her off, "after I bought you all that stuff."

"You never said I had to sell you my soul in exchange for it."

"Catherine! I just can't even—"

"Well, I just can't even, either."

"Hanging around playing a game with a sweet kid for an hour isn't selling your soul."

"You know what? Forget the wine. I'm tired," Annabelle says, hoping Oliver is still asleep, "and it's been a long day, and—"

"You just said you want a glass of wine. So we're having one," Kim tells her.

"Why can't I just go home?" Catherine asks.

"You know why."

"No, Mom, I really don't. This is ridiculous. You're treating me like I'm a little kid."

"I'm not going to spell it out for you again."

"If it's because of what happened to—"

It's Annabelle's turn to interrupt, not wanting Catherine to bring up the Brianna Armbruster tragedy.

"It's all right, Catherine. You don't have to—"

"Yes, she does," Kim says firmly.

"I *have* to babysit Oliver? Because a few days ago when I asked you if I could babysit for the Millers, you said no."

"Because they were going away overnight, Catherine, and you're thirteen. That's out of the question."

Her daughter talks over her as if she hadn't spoken. "And you're making me stay over at Jessica's tomorrow night while you and Dad go out, which is—"

"Catherine, stop right now. Just stop."

"If Dad's home can I go home?"

"He's not home. I'm going to the Binghams', and you're coming with me. End of story."

Catherine mutters something.

"I heard that," Kim says.

Annabelle, who did not, marvels at her friend's bionic hearing, and at the way mother and daughter have gone from inseparable to arch enemies. Oliver's illness is no picnic, but maybe it is better than blatant animosity.

"You heard what?" Catherine shoots back at Kim. "I didn't even say anything."

"Yes, you did. Don't you dare threaten me."

"I didn't threaten you. I knew you didn't hear anything."

"Yes, you did. You threatened that you're going to run away. And you'd better not try it, because believe me, you won't get far, and you'll be grounded for the rest of the summer. For the rest of the year. For the rest of your life. Got it?"

Catherine says nothing to that. Annabelle can feel her glowering back there.

"Catherine, listen," she says after a few minutes of silence, hoping to defuse the situation, "I'm going to pay you for hanging out with Oliver, okay?"

"You don't have to do that."

"No, she doesn't, and she won't," Kim says firmly.

"It wasn't my idea, Mom. She offered."

"I did offer, and I insist."

"That's not necessary, Annabelle. I don't want to hear another word about it."

Fine. Weary of conflict, and grateful for the reprieve

from full-time duty on the Oliver Entertainment Committee, Annabelle decides she'll just slip Catherine some cash later, before she heads home.

Beyond the steeples, treetops, and rooftops, the sky has gone from stormy gray to piercing blue to twilight navy. The birds, silenced by the day's storms, are singing themselves to sleep.

Walking briskly down Prospect Street, Holmes dwells on the Yamazaki family. How could they? How could they just leave town?

Upon hearing the news earlier, he'd clutched the phone hard against his ear, thoughts racing. "Where did they go?"

"Just down to New York City. They have family there."

"When are they coming back?"

"Who knows? Probably when this is all over."

Mid-July?

This means their house will be empty tomorrow morning.

There will be no screams from the upstairs bedroom, no frantic phone call to the police, no tsunami of terror sweeping the quiet streets of The Heights. The village won't hold its collective breath over the next eight days, wondering if . . .

No, *certain* that another Sleeping Beauty is going to turn up. And then another.

He's gone to all this trouble for nothing.

"No, that's not true," he mutters to himself. "It's just going to take some time, that's all."

And there is an upside, to be sure. Now Holmes won't risk a wee-hour run-in with the family when he's placing the body.

Ah, but wasn't the challenge a critical element in the plan? Perhaps as important as the dread the discovery of that first corpse would instill. Now it's just . . .

"Anticlimactic. That's what it is."

A woman walking her terrier along the curb turns to look at him. She's older, with thin, saggy legs and arms revealed by a T-shirt tucked into baggy shorts with a cinched waist. Realizing he must have spoken aloud again, he smiles pleasantly, as if he knows her. Perhaps he does.

"So glad the weather cleared up, aren't you?" he asks, like they were in the midst of a conversation already.

She smiles back, a bit warily, and nods. Her little dog barks at him as he passes.

Up ahead, he sees a couple of people on the sidewalk in front of the Yamazaki house. The group is considerably smaller than it was earlier.

There's a candle flickering on the sidewalk. As he walks closer, he sees that it's some kind of makeshift memorial.

A group of young women are gathered around it, arm in arm, staring morosely at the flame. They're earnest-looking, wearing Birkenstocks and no makeup. College students, he's guessing. And hardly Beauties.

Several cellophane-wrapped bouquets of supermarket flowers are heaped beside the lit votive, along with a sign that reads SB1—RIP—6/30/16.

The message is printed in black marker on a white rectangle of dry cleaner's cardboard, Holmes notices with disdain. If you're going to go to the trouble of creating this ridiculous tribute, why not do it right?

Because ordinary people don't bother with details. They don't have the patience or the intelligence.

As he approaches them, the girls glance in his direction.

"What's going on here?" he asks authoritatively.

"We're just paying our respects," one of them says. She's stockily built, with wire-rimmed glasses and short, frizzy hair.

"To whom?"

"You know . . . to the first Sleeping Beauty victim."
She indicates the sign.

"Was she a friend of yours?"

She raises an eyebrow and looks at the other girls.

"She, like, died a hundred years ago," a skinny brunette informs him. Her hair, he notices, hangs in a single braid down her bony back.

He thinks of Juanita.

"It was *exactly* a hundred years ago tonight," someone else puts in. "That's what this whole thing is a—"

"I know, ladies. I get it. I was kidding around."

"Oh. Right." The first girl spouts a nervous little laugh.

He tries to force a smile onto his face, but it feels like a silent snarl.

They turn back to their candlelight vigil.

"Ladies? I hate to rain on your little parade here, but you can't have an open flame out here on the street."

"It's just a candle."

"I told you, Lindy," one of the girls says. "It's a fire hazard."

"Okay, okay, I'll blow it out." The girl with the frizzy hair leans over the candle with puffed cheeks. It takes her a few tries to extinguish it.

He nods as if he's satisfied and walks on. But his hands are clenched again.

The Common is crowded with people. Most are gathered by the white-painted bandstand, where musicians are tuning up amid deafening feedback from the amplifier. The chamber of commerce sponsors a concert here every Wednesday night in July and August. They always feature some local ensemble—a polka band, a jazz trio, a couple of high school kids with guitars. Most are attended only by the musicians' families and friends and a smattering of senior citizens who walk to the park carrying lawn chairs.

Tonight's band, the Jitterbugs, are a quartet of older men wearing white T-shirts and leather jackets, with what's left of their hair greased back fifties style. You'd think they were the second coming of Elvis, judging by the throngs jostling for a good spot in front of the stage.

Yes, tonight is special. After the concert, there will be a trivia contest with prizes, and free coffee provided by the Valley Roasters Café on the square. But Holmes sees that there's a line out the café door right now, with plenty of people willing to pay for their coffee rather than wait for the freebies. Down the block at the Commons Creamery, the line for ice cream is even longer, disappearing around the corner.

Everyone is looking for something to do now that the museum is closed and they've had their fill of staring at the Murder Houses for the day.

Stuck in slow-moving mass of people clogging the sidewalk, he listens to snatches of conversation unfolding around him.

". . . and then afterward if it's not too late we can get a drink. I heard the Windmill is a good place to . . ."

". . . told him to meet us here, but he's not answering his cell and . . ."

". . . no, Amanda, I told you before, it's tacky and you can't wear it unless you want to look like a little tramp . . ."

Amanda. The name, the voice, the preachy tone—all familiar. It's the Girl Scout, he remembers. The one who was selling chocolate. And her annoying mother. Holmes turns his head slightly, scanning the faces behind him, not sure he'll recognize them if he sees them.

But he does.

They're wearing matching pouts, with identical red leather handbags slung diagonally across their shoulders to their hips. They have similar small, pinched features, and similar sleeveless blouses and walking shorts.

"And pull your shoulders back," the woman is saying. "Don't walk all hunched over. It doesn't look good."

"I'm not hunched over."

"You are. Straighten up."

The girl does. Seeing her long hair flip over her shoulders, Holmes imagines braiding it.

Then the crowd swallows them, and he walks on. Amanda has her Sunrise Project tomorrow morning, and Holmes has his Sunset Project tonight.

Beyond the nineteenth-century storefronts of Market Street, the orange rim slides toward the river like a curtain descending after the promising first act of an uplifting drama.

It will rise again on a horror show, he promises himself. The people of Mundy's Landing won't realize that right away, but when they do, it will be worth the wait.

"**W**here have you been?" Sully asks Barnes as he steps back into the cottage.

"Getting my luggage out of the car." He deposits it on the floor, where the rugged canvas bag looks as out of place between a doily-topped table and a Victorian-style sofa as a giant in a dollhouse. Which is what he told her he felt like before he stepped out the door.

"You were gone an awfully long time."

"Ten minutes."

"Were you smoking?"

"I quit smoking two years ago."

"That was a yes-no question, Barnes."

"I don't believe in those."

She sniffs the air for traces of tobacco, shakes her head and looks at his duffel. "Do you by any chance have a tuxedo in there?"

"Don't tell me—surprise wedding? Am I getting married? They say the groom is always the last to know."

"No, you're going to a gala tomorrow night, and it's black tie."

He raises an eyebrow. "Are *you* going to this gala, too?"

"No, you're going alone." She shakes her head, laughing. "Of course I'm going."

"So I'll be your date."

"In a manner of speaking, yes. But don't go getting any ideas, there, Barnes. I know I'm looking ravishing and all."

"You took the words right out of my mouth, Gingersnap."

Still sporting the hastily-towel-dried, drowned-rat look courtesy of having been caught in the downpour hours ago, she hands him a cold beer and clinks it with her own bottle. "Cheers."

"What are we drinking to?"

"To the typhoon. Although I'm guessing we're the only ones."

"*You're* the only one. I was looking forward to that vacation."

"You should have checked the forecast, Barnes."

He eyes her hair. "Look who's talking."

"Yeah, well, I was walking into town, not flying across the globe. And I have no connectivity here. No wi-fi, no computer, no cable."

"That's not a good excuse."

"It's not an excuse. I'm getting away from it all, remember?"

"Yeah, well, you can't get away from me."

"Looks that way."

In truth, she's grateful to the typhoon that had struck the South Seas island where Barnes was headed, grounding him on the mainland for two days. Otherwise, she'd be alone tonight. And going to the gala alone tomorrow night.

Well, alone with Rowan and her husband, Jake; a third wheel.

Instead, Barnes turned up in Mundy's Landing to salvage what's left of his vacation, thinking she'd be expecting him. Over the course of his long, segmented journey back, he'd reportedly left her a voice mail, texted, and e-mailed to say he was on his way.

"Did it not occur to you, when I didn't respond, that I might not have gotten the messages?" she'd asked this afternoon, ushering him into the cottage.

"I guess it might have if I hadn't been deliriously tired. Do you know how exhausting it is to travel around the world and back again in four days?"

"What do *you* think?"

"I think that between the Jersey Shore and this place . . . wouldn't it be nice to broaden your horizons and see how the other half lives?"

"If you don't like this place, then why are you even—"

"Sorry, I'm just tired and grumpy, Gingersnap. Give me a break, will you?"

She gave him a break.

That was a few hours ago—before he used up all the hot water taking an endless shower in the tiny bathroom where she'd planned to soak in a sudsy bath with a book and wine. Before he went out to get takeout for their dinner and came back an hour later, empty-handed, reporting that every place in town was mobbed. Before he fell asleep with his head down on the table while she was stretching her meager ingredients into a semi-palatable dinner for two.

He insisted on doing the dishes, for which she was grateful. But then he eyed the couch where he'll be sleeping tonight and commented that it was much too short to accommodate his long legs.

"You're out of your mind if you think I'm going to—"

"Relax, I'm not trying to jump into your bed with you."

"I was going to say if you think *I'm* going to sleep on

the couch," she informed him, feeling her face grow hot. That was when she offered him the beer, thinking she could use one—or two—herself.

Now, she invites him to come sit on the porch with her.

"Why?"

"Because it's what I do at night."

He peers through the screen. "It looks buggy out there."

"Those are fireflies."

"Fireflies aren't bugs?"

"Get your butt onto my porch swing, Barnes. If you're going to crash my vacation, we'll do things my way."

"Whatever you say, Gingersnap," he says amiably, and trails her outside.

"Why *are* you crashing my vacation, anyway?" she asks, settling on the swing, stretching her legs, and resting her bare feet on the railing. "Why didn't you fly to some fabulous vacation?"

"I tried. But the airline would only fly me back to New York, and it wasn't exactly direct. After forty-eight hours cramped into coach seats, I didn't feel like getting back on a plane."

"You mean Jessica didn't fly you first-class?"

"On the way out, yes. But it turned out she'd used points to buy my ticket, and—long story. Anyway, I figured I'd take a road trip."

"Yes, but . . . why here?"

"Because I had to choose whether to go north, south, east, or west, and this made the most sense. The Hamptons are booked, no one wants to go south in the summer heat, Jersey traffic is a nightmare, so . . ."

"So that leaves north."

"Right. I figure after a day or two here, we can head up to the Adirondacks. There's a nice resort in—"

"Oh, c'mon, Barnes. Don't you want to see how the other half lives?"

As she speaks, she hears police car wailing up a nearby street.

"Uh-oh," Barnes says. "Guess the meatball bribe didn't work."

She wishes she hadn't mentioned that over dinner, because she'll never hear the end of it. "Good to know that's probably all it is, don't you think?"

He's silent for a minute. When he speaks, the teasing tone is gone. "I think those sound like famous last words."

"What do you mean?"

"I mean, you seem to think this town is some kind of safe haven, but there's no such thing."

She has nothing to say to that.

The words linger in the air, mingling with the squeaking of the porch swing and the sound of sirens in the night.

Stepping into the backyard with two glasses of pinot grigio, Annabelle sees that Kim is no longer sitting in one of the cheap aluminum lawn chairs over by the carriage house.

"Kim? Where'd you go?"

"Over here," her friend calls back from around the side yard, over keening sirens.

Heading in that direction, Annabelle hopes that Oliver won't hear them and start worrying about Trib, who's still at work. He's up in his room with Catherine, and with any luck, they're wearing headsets to play the video game.

Walking around the corner of the house, she sees Kim on the driveway, talking to a uniformed police officer. Her heart beats faster as she hurries toward them.

What if something really did happen to Trib?

As she gets closer, she recognizes Nick Colonomos.

Around her age, he moved to Mundy's Landing right around the time she started dating Trib. He was from someplace in New England, and wore a Boston Red Sox

hat in the beginning, until some of the locals gave him a
hard time. She remembers being out at the Windmill—a
local bar that has long since dropped the word *Tavern*
from its name and traded cheap drafts and a pool table
for craft brews, exposed brick, and flickering white
votives.

She thought Nick was incredibly handsome, with
dark, close-cropped hair, a strong jaw, and long-lashed
dark eyes. Everyone thought he was handsome; he still *is*
handsome. He's a nice enough guy, but there's something
slightly standoffish about him.

"You just think that because your friends want to date
him, and he isn't interested," Trib said at the time.

That was partly true.

The other part might be that Nick possesses a strong
streak of Yankee reserve. One of her college swim team-
mates had grown up in New Hampshire, and as she put
it, "Where I come from, we believe in minding our own
business."

There's nothing wrong with that.

Why is he here, at her house?

Maybe he was driving by and spotted Kim, with her
blond hair flowing, wearing a snug tank top and frayed
denim shorts, a hemp bracelet tied around one ankle.

*Spotted her . . . and what? Stopped to see if she needed
directions to the nearest California beach?*

"What's going on?" she asks Nick, scurrying so
quickly that the wine sloshes over the rims of the glasses
in her hands. "Is everything okay?"

Of course everything isn't okay, she scolds herself. You
don't find a cop in your driveway if everything is okay.

"That's what I'm trying to find out, Mrs. Bingham," he
tells her. "You haven't had any trouble here, have you?"

"What kind of trouble?"

Even as she speaks, her gaze goes to the sidewalk in

front of the house. People were milling around beyond the iron fence when Kim picked up her and Oliver to go to the mall. They were still there upon their return, though fewer in number. Funny, though, how you can become accustomed to the intrusion. For a little while there, they'd become part of the landscape. An annoying part, like a neighbor's yappy dog or incessant weed whacking. But not exactly . . . *trouble.*

"I just came from 65 Prospect Street," Lieutenant Colonomos says.

"The Murder House," Kim adds helpfully—for his benefit? For Annabelle's? It's not as though anyone doesn't know the address.

"Why were you over there?" Annabelle asks. "Did something happen?"

"Just a bunch of nosy nellies hanging around, same as here. But the alarm just went off again, so I'm guessing someone went past the fence and the gate and got too close to a door or window. *Again.*"

"You mean someone tried to get into the house?"

"Probably just kids fooling around on the property. But I figured I'd better check in here and with Bill Hardy. He lives at 19 Schuyler," he adds, since apparently it's his turn to share information everyone in town knows.

That's the thing about Mundy's Landing: everyone seems to ·know everything about—well, everything. Especially when it comes to the Murder Houses.

A widower whose children have all moved away, Bill Hardy was a history teacher at Mundy's Landing High back when Annabelle was there. She never had him as a teacher, but Trib did.

"He seemed old back then," he said recently, when Annabelle suggested they go talk to him about moving into a Murder House.

"He was probably younger then than we are now."

"I know, but we don't *seem* old. Do we?" he asked, and she assured him that they don't.

But Mr. Hardy . . . he must be in his eighties by now, living all by himself in a big old house.

"I hope he's okay," she tells Nick Colonomos.

"He is, although he's not thrilled by all these false alarms."

"You mean his alarm is going off, too?"

"Yes. He told me he's sick of going up and down the stairs every time it rings, though, and he's going to just turn it off."

"Do you think that's a good idea?"

Nick shrugs. "Probably just kids, like I said. Or maybe the press snooping around. About fifteen, maybe twenty years ago, old lady Purcell opened a window and tossed a bucket of water on a camera crew."

"They were actually on the property?" Kim asks, and Nick nods.

"I heard that story," Annabelle says, "but I wasn't sure I believed it, since she had to be pushing ninety at the time."

"Believe it," Nick tells her. "I was on duty that night."

"She called the police?"

"No. She never trusted anyone, including us. One of the neighbors heard the commotion and called. The water ruined some of the camera crew's equipment."

"Good!"

"Um, Annabelle—you're married to a reporter," Kim points out.

"Yes, but Trib doesn't go around trespassing on private property. I did see someone in the backyard a few days ago, but whoever it was didn't get close to the house. I guess he might have tried if I hadn't been around. And I'd have been happy to toss a bucket of water on him if he was under my window," she adds, thinking of Oliver and how anxious he'd be if he spotted a trespasser by the house—or, for that matter, a camera crew.

But of course, the media isn't nearly as interested in the Bingham family as they'd been in Augusta Purcell, the only known survivor who had been in any of the three Murder Houses when the crimes occurred. Trib himself approached her for an interview many times, but she always turned him down, though more politely than she handled "outsider" reporters when they came calling.

"When did you see this person?" Nick Colonomos asks her.

"Last week. Wednesday, maybe? Or Thursday? It was broad daylight. I mentioned it to one of your officers."

"You called us?"

"No! Nothing really happened. When I ran into Officer Greenlea the other day I told him about it, but it really didn't seem like a big deal by then."

"Did you get a good look at whoever it was?"

"No. I . . ." She almost tells him that she isn't even entirely sure anyone was there. But she doesn't want him to think she's imagining things . . .

Just in case she isn't.

He asks whether it was a male or female, adult or child.

"I didn't get a good look at all," she tells him, shaking her head. "My eyesight isn't exactly twenty-twenty these days."

"Well, if it happens again, or if you see anything unusual, call us. We're right around the corner."

Wondering how he defines unusual, she eyes the people out on the sidewalk. Some are kids. Some aren't. They all appear harmless as Disney World tourists.

She sees the lieutenant following her gaze. "It's a public sidewalk," he says, almost apologetically. "Unless they're trespassing . . ."

"I know. It's just hard. They're not doing anything, but they're staring."

"I've lived on this street for years," Kim says, "and it was never this bad before. It's because of that huge reward. I wish someone would solve this damned crime already and we could stop dealing with this every summer. How about it, Lieutenant?"

"How about what?"

"How about solving the Sleeping Beauty murders? I'm sure you could use fifty grand."

His smile is perfunctory. "I'm sure everyone could use fifty grand."

"Annabelle and I are going to work on it. Right, Annabelle?"

"We are?"

Kim nods. "Maybe there's a clue in the house. We should look."

She'd forgotten about the stone angel. She could mention it to Kim—and to Lieutenant Colonomos. But something makes her want to keep it to herself for now. Even Trib doesn't know.

If he ever gets home, and we can have a real conversation, I could tell him.

Mundypalooza is disrupting every part of her life, and that includes her marriage. Thank goodness tomorrow night is date night, none too soon.

Holmes's Case Notes

In June 1916, the house at 65 Prospect Street was occupied by the esteemed obstetrician Dr. Silas Browne; his wife, Viola; their teenage sons, Benjamin and Lewis; and several servants.

The Brownes' vivacious and beautiful twenty-year-old daughter, Maude, was not in residence. She had gone abroad in the spring of 1915, to visit her mother's family in England. It was not uncommon in that era for wealthy families to send their privileged daughters off to Europe. But as war escalated overseas, passenger crossings became fraught with danger, and many anxious parents deferred lavish travel for their precious offspring.

The Brownes, however, had good reason to send Maude away. She sailed from New York a few days before the *Lusitania*'s fateful departure. Its sinking was disastrous for many in the Hudson Valley, but not for the Browne family. No one in Mundy's Landing questioned why she would remain in London rather than risk a return voyage in wartime. Presumably, no one ever knew of the illegitimate son she bore that autumn.

They had no access to the online records so easily available to me when I began my investigation.

Maude Browne never did return to her tainted bedroom. Both her brothers enlisted and served overseas. Lewis was killed in the German trenches. Silas and Viola, shaken by their ordeals—both public and private—went abroad after the war to visit his grave, and then to see their daughter and young grandson in England. Benjamin joined them, and there the family spent the rest of their lives, an ocean away from Mundy's Landing.

The house stood unused and vacant until the

early 1920s, when at last a willing buyer came along. Attracted to Dr. Browne's bargain price and proximity to the railroad and river, bootlegger K. J. Jones didn't care about the Murder House stigma.

The place changed hands again just after the Depression, and stayed in that family for generations until Dr. Yamazaki and his wife bought it in the early 1990s. He is a plastic surgeon, not an obstetrician, but still, he is a physician just as Dr. Browne was. He has one son, not two, but his daughter is almost exactly the age Maude Brown was in 1916, and she, too, is away, leaving a vacant bedroom in her parents' house.

I felt as though fate had explicitly engineered the situation to suit my purposes.

I was mistaken. Unlike the Browne family, the Yamazakis won't wake up on June 30 to find the body of a strange young girl tucked into their daughter's vacant bed.

Therein lies the problem.

Had I anticipated that they might leave, I'd have easily created some kind of deterrent. I truly believed I'd thought of everything. I am bitterly disappointed and disconcerted to find that certain circumstances are beyond my control.

However, I shall move forward as planned.

Chapter 13

Thursday, June 30

Eyes closed, Indi tries—she tries, really hard, desperately hard—to transport herself back home.

Yes, she knows she can't really will herself there.

But she's been able to get there in her head, and even if she knows it's not real, it helps make this hellhole bearable for another minute, or two . . .

An hour, or two . . .

A day, or two . . .

"How long has it been?" she asks in the dark, but Kathryn doesn't answer. She passed out again sometime while Juanita was being brutally slaughtered directly above their heads.

Indi heard everything, though.

She's been trying to transport herself home ever since. But this time she can't conjure her room. She can't see the glow-in-the-dark plastic constellations stuck to the ceiling over her bed and she can't smell the hot tar wafting through the window and she can't hear Tony snoring.

Dammit, dammit, she can only hear Juanita sobbing, Juanita begging for her life, Juanita dying.

Now she knows why they're here.

It's not about rape, or ransom. It's about—

Catapulted by an explosion of sheer terror in her gut, a sob bursts from her throat.

No, stop it. Crying won't get you out of here.

She swallows another sob, regaining her composure. She can cry later, when it's all behind her and she's safe—or when she's not. When he comes for her.

"Kathryn," she says sharply, her voice echoing in the damp cell. "Kathryn, wake up."

"Annabelle?"

She cries out, startled by a voice and a hand on her bare shoulder. Opening her eyes, she sees Trib standing over her.

"Hi," he says.

"You're home."

"You didn't have to wait up."

"I guess I didn't," she says, stretching and sitting up on the couch. She'd started out upright, watching TV here in the back parlor. That was after Kim and Catherine left, and she'd tucked Oliver into bed, after nine o'clock.

"What time is it?"

"Around midnight. How was your night?"

"I watched some reality dating show Kim told me I'd love. I didn't. And you would have hated it. How was your day? And your night?"

"Long. And longer." He sits beside her, leaning his head back and closing his eyes.

"Did you eat?"

"No. Is there leftover pizza?"

"No," she admits. "I only got a medium, and Oliver polished off the rest before bed."

She's been meaning to go to Price Chopper and stock up on groceries, but that's yet another chore left untended while she obsesses about the Purcell family's past.

"I can make you an omelet," she offers.

Trib makes a face. He's not a fan of eggs for breakfast, let alone a midnight supper.

"Canned soup? Macaroni and cheese?"

He shakes his head. "It's too late to cook. Is there bread and peanut butter?"

"Yes. And maybe jelly. Although . . . maybe not."

He nods, not moving, eyes still closed. "Good. I'll go make a sandwich in a second."

She could go make it for him. He'd do it for her, if the tables were turned.

But I'm exhausted, too, she thinks as a yawn overtakes her right on cue.

"You should have gone up to bed, Annabelle."

"I just wanted to make sure you got home okay."

"My office is a few blocks away."

"No, I know, but . . . it's been a weird night."

He lifts her head to look at her, concerned. "Weird, how?"

She tells him about the burglar alarms going off at the other two Murder Houses. But of course, he already knows that. It's news, and he does work at the newspaper.

"It's just kids fooling around."

"That's exactly what Nick Colonomos said. I hope he's right. He said he'll make sure officers patrol our house over the next week or two, just to keep an eye on things."

"That's good. And there's no crowd out in front right now. The whole neighborhood is quiet."

"Really? Where did everyone go?"

"Probably to the concert at the bandstand in the Common. Now they're all at the Windmill."

She yawns again. "That's good. But they'll be back. Promise me you'll help me cover the windows tomorrow morning, okay?"

He sighs. "Yeah. I promise."

"And Trib?"

"Mmm hmm?"

She was going to tell him about the stone angel, but his head is back again, eyes closed.

It can wait until tomorrow. Maybe by then, she'll have heard back from Lester. When she checked her e-mail before turning on the television, he still hadn't replied. That's probably for the best. She's no longer sure how much she's willing to share with him now that Ora advised her not to mention it.

She reaches out and rubs Trib's shoulder, feeling the knots. "You're so stressed. Why don't you come up to bed with me? I can give you a massage."

"You need a massage yourself. I saw all those empty boxes out back by the garbage. You did a lot of unpacking. It's really starting to feel like home, isn't it?"

She considers the question. She doesn't want to admit that after Nick Colonomos left, she'd felt overwhelmed by the house and all its baggage. They already had enough of their own. Her first glass of wine went down too quickly and led to a second, which led to her telling Kim they'd made a huge mistake, buying this place.

Kim, who works part-time as a medical office biller, assumed she meant a financial mistake and promptly said, "I can talk to my boss. He's looking for temporary help to cover the phones when people are on vacation this summer."

"I can't do that—I have Oliver home."

"It's part-time. He's old enough to stay by himself for a few hours."

"You won't even let Catherine stay alone and she's thirteen," Annabelle pointed out.

"But that's different. She's a girl."

"Girls are more mature."

"They're also more vulnerable," Kim said with a shrug. "In Mundy's Landing, anyway. But listen, if you wanted to start working part-time, I could let Catherine come over here and watch Oliver. It would keep them both out of trouble."

"How is it okay for her to babysit another child but not stay home alone?"

"Safety in numbers, right? Brianna was alone when she was abducted."

"You've got to stop dwelling on that, Kim. It's over. The killer's not going to harm anyone else."

"That doesn't mean there aren't others out there. Other girls have gone missing in the Hudson Valley recently. I saw a couple of fliers in town. I can't help it, Annabelle. I'm just worried about my child."

Aren't we all, she thought grimly.

Déjà vu seeps in as Holmes creeps through the night toward 65 Prospect Street. He listens to the crickets, breathes the earthy scent of wet grass and night crawlers, sees that distinct gambrel roof looming in the trees, and it's all so familiar.

He isn't merely imagining the wee hours of a Friday morning in 1916; he's remembering. Because he really was here.

It was much darker then; the moon was new. Tonight, it's a waning crescent set in a night sky that reminds him of sequin-studded blue-black satin.

"See? Already it wasn't going to be exactly the same," he mutters to himself. "You can't have everything."

He could have chosen to wait for the new moon, but then the dates would not have matched.

He moves forward step by step, struggling with the foibles inherent in this plan as much as with the burden of the bulky blue tarp in his arms.

For months, he's been lifting weights in preparation to carry his Beauties on their final journey. He's in peak physical condition. But she's heavier than he expected, and the distance is farther than it seemed on his empty-handed trial runs.

Maybe it's a sign. Maybe he should just—

No. You won't get this chance again. Not for another hundred years.

And everything else, every painstaking detail, is in place.

He'd parked around the corner in the large driveway behind a mansion that was converted to several apartments. He's been doing that for a while now, some-times leaving it there overnight, so that the people who live there will get accustomed to seeing it and assume it belongs to one of the other residents or to a regular visitor. Residents of The Heights—even the renters—tend to get touchy about parking once Mundypalooza rolls around. If someone were to spot an unfamiliar vehicle on private property tonight, they might call the police.

The deep lot behind the apartment house backs up to the Yamazakis' property, the rear of which is bordered by a wooden stockade fence. With a low grunt, he reaches up and heaves the tarp over the top. He hears it thud to the ground on the other side, quite literally a dead weight.

He easily lifts himself up and over the tall fence—not bad for someone who was once ridiculed for being incapable of doing a single pull-up in gym class. Holmes has often wondered what ever became of the phys ed teacher who was little more than an overgrown bully. Until now, he's been too busy to hunt him down. But maybe when this is over, and he'll find him and pay a visit.

He picks up the bundle again, pushing his way through the wooded part of the property. Now he has to cross a stretch of open lawn.

Three sets of French doors open onto the wide stone patio that runs across the back of the house. The carefully landscaped yard is dotted with spotlights that illuminate garden beds and specimen plantings. But leafy limbs shroud the view from neighboring windows, and there are no motion sensors or cameras in the yard.

The home security system is relatively outdated, limited to the doors and windows. When the alarm is tripped, an alert is sent to the monitoring company, who then alert the local police, who have, by now, had their fill with answering false alarms at 65 Prospect and 19 Schuyler.

Thanks to me.

This is it.

The time has come.

Holmes musters his strength and dashes across the yard.

He drops his burden beside the French doors that lie closest to the back stairway off the kitchen. It opens just across the hall from the room where S.B.K. left the first Sleeping Beauty one hundred years ago. Holmes is certain of that, having studied crime scene photos and police records.

Today, the bedroom is occupied by Evelyn Yamazaki, who attends Stanford University and stayed in California for the summer, leaving the room vacant, just as Maude Browne had done a century ago.

Inside the house, the Akita is barking. Holmes anticipated that, and he's prepared. In his pocket is a weapon chosen specifically for the occasion.

It isn't the razor, or his pistol. It's a large raw steak.

Unlike H. H. Holmes, who tortured animals, he would never choose to harm a pup. Sherlock, who'd had a childhood hound named Redbeard, was quite fond of them. In the mystery tale "Silver Blaze," the detective used his knowledge of canine behavior to deduce that the killer couldn't have been a stranger, because the dog hadn't barked.

Holmes never had a pet himself, but he familiarized himself with characteristics of the Akita breed during the research phase of this plan. They're not vicious guard dogs. Unlike other large breeds that will attack a stranger on sight, Akitas tolerate unfamiliar humans as long as they pose no threat.

They're also known to be receptive to bribes. Holmes will attain this dog's silent cooperation by offering the choice hunk of meat. If that doesn't work . . .

Well, there's always the razor. Or the pistol. But he hopes it doesn't come to that; really, he does. It would be such a pity if Holmes were forced to harm an innocent creature.

"Oliver . . ." Annabelle calls, finding his bed empty in the night. "Where are you?"

Seized by panic, she looks around the room. No sign of him.

She lifts the plaid comforter, certain he must be hiding underneath it, but he isn't. Looking around, she sees that the windows are bare. Beyond the glass, she can see a big full moon and stars . . . so many stars, shooting stars trailing effervescence across the sky.

It's a beautiful summer night.

But where is Oliver?

Oh! They must have been playing hide-and-seek.

"Olly olly oxen free!" she calls, the way she did when he was little and she'd pretend she couldn't see his little Velcro sneakers poking out beneath the curtains. He hid in the same spot every single time. "Time to come out, Ollie Ollie Oliver!"

Even the familiar childhood nickname doesn't lure him out.

She runs down the hall, opening doors, looking for him.

"Oliver . . . where are you?" She rushes up the stairs to another hallway lined with closed doors and opens one after another, calling for her son, calling, calling . . .

Up another flight of stairs. More doors. More stairs, and . . .

I don't remember the house being this big, she thinks, exhausted, confused as she climbs a steep flight that twists and turns. She can see a light glowing above, and she realizes that it's the cupola. He must be up there. Yes, she can hear the electronic sizzles and explosions of his new video game.

"Oliver? Oliver!"

But it isn't a light at all. And she isn't hearing high-tech sound effects.

The cupola is filled with shooting stars. Surrounded by their dazzling light reflected in all four windows, Annabelle is blinded.

"Mommy! Help me, I'm afraid!"

Relieved to hear his voice, and yes, even those familiar words, she feels her way to his bed. Why is it up here? she wonders. It's so strange, because it was just downstairs.

There's a large, human-shaped bump in the middle of the navy and turquoise patchwork quilt. She reaches out, laughing, to pull back the covers. "Gotcha!"

But it isn't Oliver at all. It's . . .

Annabelle awakens with a start. Her heart is racing as if she's just run miles, or . . .

Or climbed stairs.

Okay. It's okay. It was just a dream.

She finds herself looking at the bedside clock. It's well past four in the morning.

Trying to shake the nightmare, she rolls over to her husband's side of the bed. She won't wake him; she'll just snuggle into him, taking comfort in his warm, reassuring presence.

But he isn't there.

Is it like the dream? If she pulls back the covers, will she find him—or something, someone else, so hideous that she can't get the image out of her head even now.

The comforter on Trib's side of the bed is still neatly tucked beneath the pillows. It hasn't even been slept in.

He must have fallen asleep on the couch. She left him there with the remote control, and he said he'd be up soon. He just wanted to find something to eat.

She'd considered offering to make him something, but she was just too weary to imagine being on her feet longer than it would take to go upstairs to bed.

Yawning, Annabelle wonders with a twinge of guilt whether she should go down and get him.

No. If she does that, she'll be irrevocably awake, and he might not be able to get back to sleep again, either.

If she stays where she is, she can drift off again for another hour . . .

But not into that same dream, she promises herself as she closes her eyes. She doesn't want to see the dead girl—the one who looks like the stone angel—hiding under the covers in Oliver's bed, in the room where the second Sleeping Beauty was found.

"Indi?"

Awakening to the sound of her name, she's rudely jerked back to reality. Cold, damp, dark.

Juanita's gone now. Dead.

But Kathryn is here, and she's talking again, and her voice is closer than it should be. Kathryn is closer than she should be.

"I did it," she's saying. "I got them off. The cuffs. Come on, wake up. Please—you have to wake up!"

Indi feels her hand, Kathryn's hand, on her shoulder.

No one has touched her in . . .

A long time. Such a long, long time.

It's a simple thing: human touch. So easy to take for granted: that people are there, and they care.

Indi is so overwhelmed by the physical contact that she fails to grasp what Kathryn is actually doing; what she's saying.

She gasps. "You did it? You're free?"

"Yes. It wasn't easy, and it hurts, Indi. My wrists . . ."

"I know. I'm so sorry. Here, put them near my hands, and I'll rub them for you."

"No!" She feels Kathryn recoil in the dark. "No, you can't touch them. They're so sore. Bleeding."

Of course. "I'm sorry. I forgot. But you did it. Oh, Kathryn—we have a chance now. We can save ourselves."

There's a long pause.

Then Kathryn's voice says, in the darkness, "But how?"

"We'll figure it out. I know we will. This is the first step. We're not going to—"

"Indi? Where do you think he took Juanita? Do you think he let her go? Do you think she's already gone for help?"

So Kathryn doesn't know. She didn't hear, or she doesn't remember, or . . .

No. She must know. It's no accident that she finally worked herself free of the shackles now, after he murdered Juanita right above their heads. She may have passed out, but she had to know what was going to happen.

I did. Juanita did, too. She begged. She wanted so badly to live . . .

But she didn't fight hard enough, Indi tells herself. *That's the difference between her and me. I'm going to fight with everything I have.*

Right now, what she has is . . . just Kathryn.

And Kathryn, she realizes, is crying again, softly, in the dark.

It's not right.

Holmes steps back from the bed, aiming the flashlight over her, and then again at the black and white photo print he'd pulled from his pocket.

In the historic photo, the backdrop was simple: a headboard, a curtained window, a fireplace, wallpaper.

The modern room is different. Electronics seem to dominate every surface. The walls are painted a gaudy turquoise color. The bed is made of wood, not iron, and it's in the wrong spot. But he can overlook all of those details.

It's *her*.

She isn't right.

It isn't the hair. The braids might be lopsided, but you can't tell that from the angle of her head on the pillow.

The nightgown is almost exact. Purely by chance, so is the white bedding. And the body's position is identical to the one in the photo. He'd even managed to tug the folded coverlet into the narrow crevice between Juanita's folded arms and chest.

She and the first Sleeping Beauty are identical, with one notable exception: the eyes.

They're still staring at him, bulging, horrified.

"Are you still up? You're supposed to 'Sleep safe till tomorrow,'" he says, quoting the note he tucked beneath her pillow. "You're ruining everything."

She offers him an equally accusing stare.

Not really, of course.

Intellectually, he knows she's not really here. She's long gone, having expelled her last breath on a horrible death rattle.

This is as close as he's going to get to perfection, unless . . .

For a moment, he entertains a spark of an idea.

But no, that would be crazy. He can't find someone else at this late date. As much as he'd like to imagine it—especially with Lindy, the frizzy-haired girl who lit the candle. Or Amanda, or her mother, or . . .

Catherine.

He glances at the window. The sky is still dark, but the sun will be coming up soon. The Akita is still out cold in the hallway, having gobbled down the hunk of steak with a tranquilizer embedded in the bloody flesh. But it won't sleep forever. Nor will the tourists, who will soon be camped out at the curb in front of the house.

Juanita Contreras, with her lopsided braids and ogling eyes, will have to do.

"Unfortunately, it appears I'm stuck with you," he tells the still figure on the bed, and he takes out his phone.

He snaps several photos, using the black and white filter, hoping that will soften the eyes.

Next time, Holmes promises himself as he pockets the phone, gathers the empty tarp, and slips down the back stairs to the French doors.

Next time, at 46 Bridge Street, will be perfect.

From the Sleeping Beauty Killer's Diary
June 21, 1916

The Solstice commenced at 6:24 this evening. That moment found me strolling the midway at Valley Cove Electric Pleasure Park. I visit nightly, occasionally accompanied by a child so as not to arouse suspicion. However, I believe I needn't worry, for I encounter familiar faces each time. Those of us who have the means consider the Pleasure Park a most agreeable spot to while away an overheated June night.

My meandering, however, is purposeful.

There will be three girls altogether. Two would be too few; four would entail additional, and unnecessary, risk. As in science, math, nature, and literature, three establishes a pattern.

Since last week, I have regularly encountered Calliope and many other young women of her ilk. This makes me smile, as the enclosed Tribune *clipping indicates that they are most unwelcome here:*

> While there have been concerns among the upstanding citizenship of our fair village—particularly those of a gentle female persuasion—that the park might draw vagrants and unsavory characters from far afield, management offers utmost assurance that this is a family-friendly endeavor. Undesirables shall be refused admittance.

I engage these ostensible undesirables in conversation—or rather, they engage me. My own intention is no less nefarious than theirs, for time is growing short in my search for the two who will best suit my needs.

I hastily extract myself from those who travel in pairs. Also from any who mention families, friends, or even, in several sad cases, children who await their return with the day's earnings. For my purposes, I seek loners who will not be missed.

When I find them, will I also find the nerve to act?

Yes.

I must do something.

I must.

Soon.

Soon rhymes with June, and tune, and croon, and moon . . .

Senseless poems meander through my brain of late, recited by voices only I can hear, accompanied by music to which I find myself humming along.

I isolate myself wherever possible. I must be careful, lest someone notice that I'm talking to myself and draw the conclusion that I've gone mad.

I have not—of course I have not—and yet the songs and the poems persist:

By the light of the silvery moon . . .

Moon . . . tune . . . croon . . . June . . . soon . . .

Soon.

Moon.

This evening, I attempted to banish imaginary words and music with Amy Lowell's Sword Blade and Poppy Seed *collection. But there was no escape. A sliver of waning silvery moon shone through the pane as I read "The Last Quarter of the Moon." Long after I closed the book and extinguished the lamp, having resigned myself to sweat-dampened sheets in an airless room, these lines buzzed about my head like bloodthirsty mosquitoes, stingers poised to breed endemic disease:*

A desolate wind, through the unpeopled dark,
Shakes the bushes and whistles through empty
    nests,
And the fierce unrests
I keep as guests
Crowd my brain with corpses, pallid and stark.

Hours later, I prowl the house. There is no escaping the smothering heat, or the melody, or the unbearable words, the words . . .

I must do something.

Soon.

June.

Moon.

Chapter 14

Annabelle has given up on sleep. Every time she closes her eyes, she sees that carved granite face resting on Oliver's pillow, and Oliver is missing.

Intellectually, she knows he's safely tucked into his bed on the other side of the wall, yet she can't seem to shake the uneasiness that's crept over her. She'd get up and go check on him if she knew he wouldn't awaken the moment she turned his doorknob.

Even as a baby, he was a light sleeper, rousing at the slightest hint of movement. The hypervigilance made sense later, after he was diagnosed with GAD.

Lying awake, listening to the buzz of insects through the screen, she thinks about the stone angel monument. She'd been disappointed that Ora hadn't been able to shed light on it, and even more disappointed when Lester hadn't e-mailed back. The trip to the mall and the evening with Kim distracted her, as did sleep, but curiosity has taken hold again.

The details flit through her mind.

Z.D.P.

3/31/04.

7/7/16.

Outside, a bird twitters.

Momentarily, others take up the chorus. The long night is coming to an end.

She hears creaking on the stairs: Trib coming up to bed.

Ordinarily, he's lighter on his feet.

Much lighter.

She'd assumed her husband was asleep on the couch, just as she had assumed her son was safely tucked into bed.

What if you were wrong?

She breaks into a cold sweat as the heavy footfalls reach the second floor.

"Trib?" she calls. "Is that you?"

Noxious dread slinks into the silence that follows, and Lieutenant Colonomos's words come back to haunt her: *You haven't had any trouble here, have you?*

The footsteps approach the bedroom door.

Her mouth is too dry to muster a sound, let alone a scream, as the knob turns.

The door opens. A shadowy human form appears.

"Of course it's me. Who else would it be?"

It's just Trib.

Of course. Of course it's Trib.

"It didn't sound like you, coming up the stairs. You usually walk faster."

"It's almost five in the morning, Annabelle. Guess I'm too exhausted for sprints." His weight sinks into the mattress.

She closes her eyes, relieved, hoping she can catch a little more sleep. Instead, the puzzle pieces return to drift through her mind.

Z.D.P.

3/31/04.

7/7/16.

If indeed the second batch of numbers on the statue are a date, and if it refers to July 7, 1916, it makes chilling sense.

Trib cuts into her speculation. "Why are you awake?"

"Bad dream."

She doesn't offer to tell him about it, and he doesn't ask.

She waits for his silence to become deep, even breathing. But after a few minutes, he's still lying awake in the dark beside her. She can feel the tension radiating from his body.

"Trib? What's wrong?"

"Hmm?" he asks, as though she'd disturbed him as he was drifting off. But she knows better.

"You're stressed."

He sighs. "Yeah. Sometimes I feel like it's just too much."

"What is?" As if she doesn't know. It's just like she told Kim. Everything. Everything is too much.

His reply, however, is the opposite: "Nothing. Never mind. Go back to sleep."

So he's not in the mood to talk. That's all right. Neither is she. She rolls over, away from him, staring into the dark.

Z.D.P.

3/31/04.

7/7/16.

Ora Abrams, asking, *Do you think someone is buried beneath the pool?*

No, Annabelle doesn't think that . . . does she? Even if she did, who would it be? The Sleeping Beauty whose corpse was found in this house?

Aunt Etta was at the service when they were buried. They're all there, in the cemetery.

All right. Then the stone angel isn't likely a grave marker. Maybe it has nothing to do with the Sleeping Beauties, and the date isn't connected with the case. It might not even be a date at all. Maybe the numbers signify something else.

Oh, come on, like what?

Ora Abrams, again, echoing in her brain: *I wouldn't mention anything to Lester.*

Well, of course *she* wouldn't. There's no love lost between Ora and Lester. But when and if he gets back to Annabelle, she'll use her own judgment.

Back to the dates.

Why might 1904 have been relevant to the Purcell family?

George and Florence had married in 1899. Augusta wasn't born until 1910—a long stretch of childlessness, in that era. Perhaps they, like Annabelle and Trib, had endured fertility issues. Or maybe they put off parenthood for other reasons.

What else might have transpired under this roof, in that decade? Floyd had died, the servants had disappeared, and . . .

It hits her.

"Trib?" she says softly, pretty certain he's still awake.

He doesn't reply.

Either he doesn't feel like talking, or he's sound asleep, and she shouldn't wake him. Not for this. Not until she knows for sure.

She gets out of bed and hurries out of the room.

Holmes is utterly depleted.

After leaving Juanita Contreras tucked into the empty bed at 65 Prospect Street, he intended to speed straight home to grab a few hours' sleep. But here he sits in his SUV, still parked behind the apartment house on the adjacent block, brooding.

After all that buildup, he'd expected to feel intensely satisfied. Instead, disenchantment has overtaken him.

"What went wrong?" he asks himself aloud, trying to pinpoint the reason his expectations remain unfulfilled.

Is it simply that a letdown is inevitable after a year's worth of painstaking buildup?

Is it that the family is gone and he knows they won't wake up any moment now to discover his handiwork?

Is it because the gaudy turquoise-painted room was wrong, or because the Beauty herself was all wrong, wide-eyed, refusing to sleep?

"All of the above," he concludes, staring moodily at the gambrel roof of 65 Prospect Street, barely visible through wisps of fog and dense growth along the property line.

He drives away, dogged by an intense dissatisfaction and the need to compensate somehow for all that went wrong. But it's too late. The lunar crescent is fading, and the sun will be up soon—at 5:24, he recalls.

We're going to plant flowers next Thursday morning at sunrise . . .

Hence, the Sunrise Project.

Holmes glances at the dashboard clock as a brilliant scheme takes hold. It's already 5:17.

Schaapskill Nature Preserve is five minutes away. He'll have to hurry.

Slipping into the large bedroom at the end of the long, dark hall, Annabelle reminds herself that she doesn't believe in ghosts.

No, but if she did, this is where she'd expect to find Augusta Purcell's.

Stripped of its claw-tattered fabric—draperies, rug, even the window seat cushion—the room is eerily hollow. The air, as in the rest of the house, wafts with old wood, cats, must, and blooming perennials. But here, it's infused with a hint of something else, too. Annabelle recognizes it from the nursing home whenever they visited Trib's father: a blend of pharmaceuticals, toiletries, and food . . . all, like the lives within, past their prime.

Institutions are depressing. But so is the thought of poor Augusta spending all those years isolated in this house, in this very room, surrounded by memories . . . and by family secrets?

Annabelle hurries across the dusty hardwoods.

The tall windows above the built-in seat face the brightening eastern sky. Dim light filters in to throw ominous shadows from a couple of tall moving boxes that sit beside it. In the far corner are the newspapers she stashed here to get them out of the way in a halfhearted effort to make the house seem tidier.

One stack is carefully separated from the other two by a couple of feet of floor space—and a hundred years. It consists of recent papers that need to be tied and recycled. Annabelle was careful not to mix those in with the other two piles, both of which are fragile with age. One consists of 1916 editions Trib borrowed from the *Tribune* archives shortly after the move, because they contain articles pertaining to this house and its role in the Sleeping Beauty murders.

The third pile draws Annabelle now, however. She picks up the yellowed, crumpled paper on top. Squinting, she can't make out the date, even when she tilts it toward the window. The room is still too dark, the type too faded to see.

She hurries over to press the mother-of-pearl button on the wall. An overhead fixture floods the room with light. In the moments it takes for her eyes to adjust, she thinks of the rainy Sunday last month when Trib knocked out the wall in the master bedroom to make it larger.

"Hey, Annabelle," he'd called, "come look at this!"

She'd been painting the trim in Oliver's room. Her son was supposed to be helping her, but was frightened by the resounding thuds of Trib's swinging sledgehammer, so they'd sent him down the street to Connor's.

He'd sealed off the bedroom with plastic sheeting.

Pushing past it, she found a gaping hole in the interior wall. Bits of plaster and lath clung to what was left of the framing around the perimeter. Trib wore a mask over his mouth and nose, protection from the thick dust swirling in the air.

He held out a stack of newspapers.

"What are those?" she asked.

"Copies of the *Tribune* from around the turn of the century. I found them in the wall. It was pretty common back then to use newspaper as insulation."

"The house was built in the 1860s," Annabelle pointed out. "So this was one large bedroom, and the Purcells built the wall to divide it."

"Exactly. I was feeling bad about tearing down walls, but it turns out we're just restoring the house to the way it used to be."

He asked her to save the newspapers until he has a chance to go through them. The *Tribune* archives are missing copies from certain dates, and he's hoping to fill them in with these.

Annabelle's eyes adjust to the bright light. At last, she's able to see the dateline.

November 12, 1903.

The Purcells had built the nursery seven years before their first child was born. Why?

Maybe it hadn't been a nursery after all.

Could it have served as a . . . what? A dressing room? A study?

That doesn't make sense. The house is enormous, and only Florence, George, and his father were living here at that time. Even with live-in staff still occupying the servants' quarters, there would have been several vacant bedrooms on the second floor.

A nursery would be logical, given that there are no windows and it opened only into the master bedroom.

Either Florence and George were being extremely pro-active, or in late 1903, they found themselves expecting a baby.

That's certainly plausible. They'd been married three years by then.

Is it possible that Annabelle overlooked something when she was searching? Yes.

Is it possible that the 1905 census taker failed to in-clude not just a houseful of servants, but a toddler born to George and Florence before Augusta Amalthea came along? Or that whoever answered the door at 46 Bridge Street that day failed to mention the child?

Anything is possible, Annabelle supposes. But plausible?

It's more plausible that if they were indeed expecting a baby, the pregnancy hadn't gone to term—a sad fact of life, then and now. Or that the child hadn't lived very long.

It doesn't solve the mystery of the stone angel, though.

If indeed it's meant to memorialize the Sleeping Beauty who was found in this house in July 1916, then Augusta must have known her identity, and chosen—or promised—not to tell.

Schaapskill Nature Preserve is right next to the Pleasure Park ruins. Holmes doesn't have time to leave the car at the shopping center and hike down the highway. Nor does he park at the fishing pier and paddle over in the rowboat. The river is still shrouded in early morning fog, but it'll burn off quickly once the sun comes up.

It shields him now as he boldly drives between the stone markers leading to the preserve, bumping west along the rutted lane. Amanda had mentioned the bike path the day he bought the chocolate bars. Years ago, it was a railroad track, but it's long since been paved over to create a riverfront trail used by bicyclers and runners.

He turns off the headlights as he draws closer to the spot, and pulls off into a thicket where the vehicle will be well concealed. He'll go the rest of the way on foot, staying away from the road.

He steps out of the car and begins moving toward the water and the faint bleat of a foghorn. The misty woods are alive with the chatter of birds and insects—and, as he slips closer to the bike trail, of women and children. He can hear them talking and laughing, but he can't see them through the trees until he's dangerously close.

There they are, about a dozen of them altogether: mothers and daughters, their faces too shadowy to discern in this light even if he thought he might recognize them.

Only one matters.

He looks for her as the group traipses back and forth to a couple of large SUVs, removing plastic flats containing bright-colored annuals. Then they break up into smaller groups and begin to plant flowers along the edges of the path.

Occasionally, someone jogs past, or a bike whizzes by. Invariably, the approaching runner or cyclist calls out a terse warning—"On your left," or "Coming up behind you!" And invariably, Holmes notices, with growing irritation and restlessness, the mothers and daughters either don't hear, or simply ignore the warning.

"Is it just me?" someone whines, eventually. "Or are these people trying to mow us down?"

He recognizes the voice. It's Amanda's mother, Bari.

What a pleasure it would be to silence her by slicing her throat good and hard. Would it make up for this morning's disappointment?

He feels in his pocket for the razor blade.

It wouldn't even matter if he hacked away through muscle and bone until he cut her head right off. He doesn't need it, or her. She doesn't have to be presentable.

She isn't a Sleeping Beauty. Her eyes can gape, or he can gouge them out. She's utterly dispensable.

His fingers tighten around the handle of the blade that's nearly an exact replica of the one on exhibit in the historical society. S.B.K.'s actual weapon was never found, but it would have been very similar, Miss Ora Abrams once said, to the one on display.

As far as Holmes knows, S.B.K. used that weapon only three times.

Before and after the summer of frightfulness, the killer lived an exemplary life.

And that, Holmes reminds himself, is how one quite literally gets away with murder.

After months of meticulous planning, he's allowed himself to stray into dangerous territory.

This is a public place. There are potential witnesses. Even if he managed to discreetly grab the woman or her daughter and drag her off the path, he'd have to cover a lot of ground to get her back to his car.

And what then?

He can't take her to the icehouse. He has no use for her there.

Nor can he leave her dead in the woods, where someone will come across her in no time. That discovery would, in turn, preempt, or even eclipse, his Sleeping Beauty's debut.

Still, he can't simply go on his way and allow this intense dissatisfaction to fester. That would lead him further into temptation, and next time, he might not have the presence of mind to curtail his urges. He has to figure out what was missing this morning, so that he can get it exactly right next week at 46 Bridge.

Reluctantly, he loosens his grip on the blade.

As he lets go, his fingertips brush something else

tucked into his pocket: the buffalo nickel wrapped in a scrap of muslin.

As he slinks away through the trees, heading back to his SUV, a new idea takes hold—one that may, indeed, allow him to remedy the situation.

If Barnes weren't sleeping on her sofa downstairs, Sully would have gotten up an hour ago. That would have been a full hour after she'd awakened from a nightmare about Manik, for the first time since she arrived in Mundy's Landing.

Barnes will probably assume his presence here brought it all back. Or maybe she'll just let him think that, if he gets on her nerves today.

But the more she's considered the situation, the more she realizes that it was likely triggered by her afternoon at the historical society. Throw an unsolved case at any detective—even one who's determined to get away from it all—and that detective is going to plunge right back into crime-solving mode, with all the accompanying baggage.

The night sounds beyond Sully's window may not consist of sirens and traffic barely muted by twenty stories and a layer of glass, but she might as well be back in the city. Her head is aching, her body is tense, her mind racing over the facts.

No, it isn't her case. And everyone involved is just as dead as the victims themselves. The killer will go unpunished. Unlike in Manik Bhandari's case, justice will never be served.

So what's the point of losing sleep over this?

A fifty-thousand-dollar reward?

Hell, maybe that's all the incentive she needs.

She keeps going back to the three unidentified girls buried right next door in Holy Angels Cemetery.

Yesterday, she'd promised herself she'd take a walk over to the cemetery. Maybe now is a good time. The sun will be up soon, and the tourists probably aren't stirring yet.

She gets out of bed, throws on her clothes, and heads into the bathroom. Splashing cold water onto her face—because it takes too long to wait for hot—she sees that her green eyes are once again underscored by a lovely shade of purple. Her tousled red hair valiantly resists her attempts to wrestle it into a barely presentable drugstore elastic band.

Good thing it's only Barnes, she thinks as she creeps down the stairs carrying sneakers that are still wet—and perhaps a little smelly—from yesterday.

The living room is dark and silent. She tiptoes past the couch, not allowing herself to glance in that direction. She doesn't want to feel guilty about Barnes being unable to stretch out his lanky body. He'll sense her weakness and go for the jugular, and the next thing she knows, he'll be sleeping in her bed and she'll be on the couch tonight.

Crossing the threshold into the kitchen, lit by the bulb beneath the stove hood, she can still smell coffee. Last night before bed, after searching the cupboards hoping to find a stray can of Maxwell House and turning down the tea she offered to brew for him instead, Barnes strolled to the mini mart a few blocks away to buy some.

"Gas station coffee?" she asked when he came back with an extra large cup and a couple of Krispy Kremes.

"It's better than the stuff we make at the precinct."

"That's not saying much," she pointed out.

Now, yawning deeply, she decides that it's not fair the man can drink a vat of undiluted caffeine and sleep like a baby.

She wonders if she dares set the old-fashioned teakettle on the flame before she goes out the door. It would be

nice to have water hot and waiting when she gets back—
but it might whistle and wake up Barnes.

Then again, so what if it does? This is, after all, her
vacation cottage. He's a mere squatter.

She runs water into the kettle, sets it on the stove, and
turns on the burner. After a *click-click-click*, it ignites.
She checks her watch, wondering if she can be back here
in the seven or eight minutes it will take to boil.

Definitely. The cemetery is right next door, and it's
not as though she's going to exhume the bodies. She just
wants to take a look at the graves to see if anything jumps
out at her.

Which isn't exactly a comforting thought when you're
talking about a cemetery, she thinks, starting for the door,
but—

"Going somewhere?"

Sully gasps.

"Dammit, Barnes!"

He's been here all along, fully dressed and sitting quietly at the kitchen table in the shadowy corner.

"Is that localese? Good morning would be nicer, but
I'll go with it. Dammit, Gingersnap!"

"Not funny. What are you doing up?"

"Having coffee." He sips from a paper hot cup. So it
wasn't last night's brew she smelled after all.

"You're becoming a regular down at the gas station,"
she observes.

"Nope, it was closed. But there's a Dunkin' Donuts on
Colonial Highway. Open twenty-four hours."

"So I guess New York isn't the only city that never
sleeps?"

"A Dunkin' Donuts drive-through does not a city
make." He sips again. "But if you're headed in that direction, I'll ride along. I could use a refill."

"It's not where I'm headed."

"No? I'll ride along anyway."

"We're not riding, Barnes. But come on if you're coming."

"Where are we going?"

"You like graveyards?"

"You're kidding, right?"

"Wrong." Sully reaches back to turn off the burner beneath the teakettle before stepping out the door. This might take a while.

Ora Abrams startles from a sound sleep.

What on earth was that?

A muffled thumping noise barged into her slumber . . . unless it was just part of her dream?

No. In the early morning light, she can see Briar Rose perched at the foot of the bed, facing the closed bedroom door, spine straight, tail and ears twitching. Ordinarily, she'd be stretched out across the quilt, eyes closed, paws splayed and belly up.

She, too, was awakened by something.

The cat leaps from the bed and goes to the carpeted platform post beside it, where she stretches her front paws and begins scratching her claws.

Another thump, directly below.

The cat stops scratching. Ora's breath catches in her throat.

That's the special exhibit room. The one she ceremoniously unlocked yesterday for the steady stream of visitors. All day, all night, they paraded slowly past the case that holds the museums prized bloody relics.

Ora's volunteers took turns policing the crowd, making sure no one snuck photos or lingered too long, holding up the line. Many paused to take notes and ask questions, looking for clues.

Maybe one of those would-be detectives resented

being hustled along and came back for a closer look, or to snap forbidden pictures.

Technically, a few photos aren't a problem. Ora established the rule against photography more to preserve the room's air of mystery than the items within, having found little evidence that camera flashes damage artifacts.

That doesn't make it acceptable that an overzealous visitor—harmless or not—is sneaking around after hours—or rather, before hours, Ora amends, now that a new day has dawned. Should she go down and confront whoever it is? By the time she makes her way across the floor, he's sure to flee.

Maybe she should simply call the police. But if she does that, they'll become even more of a nuisance than they were yesterday—poking around, asking questions, acting as if they were expecting to find her violating the maximum occupancy laws.

They're lazy, she thinks. That's their problem. If it weren't for her, they might not even have jobs. They should be grateful for their fat overtime paychecks, but instead, they're resentful for the extra work caused by—

The thought is shattered by the unmistakable sound of glass breaking on the second floor.

Ora's old heart takes off at a gallop, but her legs won't seem to move. She manages to reach for the telephone on her bedside table and hurriedly dials.

"Nine-one-one. What is your emergency?"

"It's Ora Abrams over at the historical society. Someone has broken in. Please hurry!"

Holmes's Case Notes

Visiting the museum this morning was genius—pure genius—and as gratifying as my predawn adventure at 65 Prospect. Perhaps more so.

I went in through the basement window, same as before. This time, I wasn't interested in prowling around or spooking Ora Abrams.

I found the door to the special exhibit room locked, as is always the case at night and even, most of the time, during the day. But of course it was propped wide open to visitors all day yesterday in honor of Mundypalooza, just as it is every year. I've visited many times. I've committed the contents of the room to memory and knew exactly where to find what I needed.

Ora likes to make a big show of ceremoniously unlocking that door every summer as if opening a portal to King Tut's tomb. But the old-fashioned lock is original to the house, and it's laughably easy to pick with a skeleton key. I've been doing it for years.

Miss Abrams uses a brick as a doorstop to prop open the door to the room. She likes to point it out to visitors, mentioning that it once lined the sidewalk in front of the house at 65 Prospect Street.

As expected, the brick lay on the floor just inside the door frame. Upon entering the room, I made sure that the nightgown and ribbons were there, preserved beneath the backlit glass, just as I remembered. Next, I opened the window overlooking the annex roof, ready to make my getaway.

Then it was time. I took great pleasure in heaving that brick through the glass display case. Careful not to cut myself as I reached in, I grabbed the coveted items and fled.

As I escaped into the night, I wondered whether the commotion had awakened Miss Abrams or if she'd slept right through. The answer quickly became evident, much to my delight.

Pity I seem to have cast a pall over tonight's gala.

Chapter 15

Beyond the mist-wisped steeple of Holy Angels Church, a low orange smear tints the opaque heavens, casting first morning light over the little cemetery. Tombstones rise from dewy grass in clusters, their age evident at a glance. Modern markers, with glossy inscriptions and a flecked granite palate, are well-tended by the bereaved, bearing flags, wreaths, and blooming annuals. The oldest graves, weathered rectangles and crosses in monochromatic whites and grays, are unadorned and long-forgotten . . . with three exceptions.

Sully and Barnes stand shoulder-to-shoulder—rather, shoulder to hip—gazing down at the trio of flat concrete slabs etched with crosses and the year 1916. The spot might have been difficult to find if not for countless cellophane-wrapped bouquets heaped there over the past several days.

The same thing happens in the city on sidewalks, subway platforms, and yes, building stoops where people die sudden, violent deaths. Those makeshift memorials spring up amid fresh grief or—for those not personally acquainted with the victims—amid fresh media hype.

Here in Mundy's Landing, hype aside, Sully finds it poignant that a host of strangers have paid their respects to three girls murdered a century ago.

During the short stroll over here from the cottage next door, she'd briefed Barnes about the case, as if they're working it together. To her surprise, he didn't tease her or ask why she cares. He just listened attentively.

"So what's your theory?" he asks now, staring down at the Sleeping Beauties' final resting place.

"If we can figure out who they were, then we might be able to figure out what happened to them and why."

Barnes nods. This is familiar territory for them. "So you're using some modern profiling techniques."

"Exactly. Victimology 101: which three traits do serial killers look for when they're hunting?"

"Availability, desirability, and vulnerability."

"Exactly. Ideally all three, but at least one of those traits has to be present. So think about them." She gestures at their gravestones. "Back then, it was such a big deal that no one ever came forward to identify them. It's almost as if people thought they'd materialized in this town in some enigmatic fashion, like they'd been . . . I don't know—"

"Raised by wolves, dropped from the sky by aliens?"

"Exactly. The truth is that their families may not have known or cared that they were missing."

Again, he nods. They deal with that on the job. Apathy is just as disturbing, in its own way, as dealing with distraught relatives frantic over a missing loved one.

She'd studied the museum's trove of period newspaper articles. Many included not just their physical descriptions but macabre post-mortem photographs published in an effort to identify them.

"Or maybe the three girls' families just never saw the headlines, Barnes. Maybe they lived an ocean away."

"You're right. The girls could very well have been recent immigrants. There were more than nine million here at that time."

She looks at him. "You know that fact off the top of your head because . . ."

"Because I'm a genius and you know it."

"So you made it up."

"Nope, true. I chaperoned my nephew's school trip to Ellis Island last month."

"Okay, so nine million is a lot of immigrants, and I'm guessing they were still fairly concentrated in the Northeast at that point."

"They were."

"How lucky am I to have an immigration expert involved in my case?"

"It's not exactly *your* case, Gingersnap."

He's right. Somehow, she keeps forgetting that. But her mind won't stop working it.

She can think of any number of reasons a missing person's family could have missed the newspaper coverage back then, and she resumes the topic with Barnes, who— for that matter—is playing along.

"If the girls were immigrants, wouldn't someone here have seen and missed them?" he asks.

"You would think. Maybe they were farm girls, and their families lived in a rural area without access to newspapers."

"Could be. Or they were too poor to buy them."

"Or they were illiterate."

"We're most likely talking about three different families," he points out.

"Yes, but it's not really a stretch, when you consider the odds that the girls themselves were probably living a lifestyle that made them vulnerable to predators."

"Just like today."

"Right. So what kind of woman is most available, desirable, and vulnerable?"

He answers without hesitation: "A prostitute."

"Exactly. When I was going through the archives, I noticed that there was no speculation in any of the newspaper coverage that the victims might have been prostitutes."

"Sign of the times?"

"And probably because they were found sedately posed in virginal white nightgowns, looking like innocent young 'schoolgirls'—that's what the press called them, and it stuck, just like 'Sleeping Beauties.'"

Based on statistics in similar cases she and Barnes have worked over the years, Sully is guessing that the victims might not have been schoolgirls, virginal, or particularly young. Nor were they innocent, in terms of chastity, purity, and all the qualities young ladies of a certain era and good breeding were presumed to possess.

"So you're thinking one or all of those 'schoolgirls' might have been working girls?" Barnes asks her.

"It would explain why no one recognized them even if they'd seen them before. The offender was essentially disguising them after he killed them. Prostitutes don't walk the streets in chaste white nightgowns, looking all fresh-faced with braids and ribbons."

He raises an eyebrow.

"Get over your sick self, Barnes. The vast majority of them don't. And I'm sure they didn't back then."

"But would there really have been prostitutes in this small, all-American town back then?"

"Good point. Most small towns have a seamy underbelly. And prostitution was actually legal in some places until the First World War."

"Not in New York State. Not that it matters. But I doubt Mundy's Landing had a red light district—and if it did, it was tiny. Local working girls would have been recognized by someone, if not everyone, even with schoolgirl disguises."

"Okay, so they might have been just promiscuous, reckless young women passing through town, looking for a less than wholesome good time. And once you consider that factor, the case loses some of its inscrutability."

"Not all, though."

"Not by a long shot. It's still pretty freaking bizarre, right?" She turns away from the graves.

The sun is up now, lighting the sky and spilling across the ancient trees and historic rooftops of The Heights. Among them are three houses that may very well have contained evidence overlooked by investigators a hundred years ago.

Barnes yawns loudly. "Ready to head back? I need to go get more coffee."

She nods and they begin walking, weaving in and out among the graves, heading toward the small clapboard church that lies between the cemetery and Church Street.

Sully thinks about the killer, whose anonymity is far more fascinating to her than that of the victims.

Turning her profiling technique on him, aware that that an offender's behavior during a homicide is going to be present somewhere in his lifestyle, she ponders aloud. "Think about it, Barnes. He dressed the girls in nightgowns. He tucked them into bed. Who does that?"

"A parent," he says promptly. "Or a caregiver, anyway."

"And the note beneath the pillows—'Sleep safe till tomorrow.'"

"His version of 'Good night, sleep tight, don't let the bedbugs—'"

"Not exactly. It's a line from a William Carlos Williams poem."

"He wrote 'The Red Wheelbarrow.'"

"Wow, I see someone paid attention in high school lit," she says, impressed. "What about 'Peace on Earth'?"

"It would be great, but don't hold your breath."

"That's the name of the poem, Barnes. It was new at the time, published only three years earlier in *Poetry Magazine*."

"Never heard of it."

"Right, even though you paid attention in lit class and Williams is a Pulitzer Prize–winning poet. Which means that back then, the poem was completely obscure."

"So we can assume that the killer was fairly well-read and had access to *Poetry Magazine* at a time when media was limited. This is a small enough town that you should be able to narrow down the suspects just knowing that."

"If he lived here, why were there only three? Why start suddenly, execute three evenly spaced murders, and then stop cold?"

"Maybe he was transient, and he moved on to a different town," he says.

"But if he had, the bizarre signature would have followed," she points out. "And if it had, someone, somewhere, would have made the connection. Killing young women and staging their bodies is one thing. But transporting the corpses to the bedrooms of private homes while the residents were sleeping isn't just eerie, it's brazen and risky."

"True. Why take that chance?"

"I think he was closer to this community than anyone guessed at the time," Sully theorizes. "And those dead girls might have been props."

"Meaning . . . ?"

"Meaning his underlying motive wasn't just killing for the thrill of it."

"What was it?"

They've reached the edge of the cemetery. The low black iron gate creaks as Barnes opens it for her, and swings shut with a bang.

"It could have been blackmail," Sully speculates. "Or terrorism."

"Interesting concept." He follows her along the cobbled path bordered by the church, with its peeling white clapboards and stained glass windows, and the tall hedgerow separating it from the yard of Sully's rented cottage.

"So you don't think he randomly selected those three houses based on opportunity or access? You think he chose them deliberately, because he wanted to send a message to the people who lived in them?"

"It makes sense, doesn't it?"

"About as much sense as everything else."

By all accounts, the shell-shocked folks who discovered the bodies were truly shaken and mystified by the crimes, as were their families. They had no idea who could have done such a terrible thing, and they had never seen the dead girls before.

Or so they said.

Sully and Barnes have reached the sidewalk. Down the street, a teenage paperboy pedals past, hurtling bagged copies of the *Tribune* onto porch steps. An SUV rounds the corner onto Church Street. It slows and the driver gives a wave as he pulls into the driveway directly across from them.

"Morning, Sully," he calls through the open window.

"How's it going, Ron?"

"You're on a first-name basis with the neighbors?" Barnes asks as they cross the long front lawn toward the cottage. "What's next? Are you joining the block party committee?"

"Shut up, Barnes."

"See that? You're not even on a first-name basis with me."

"That was Ron Calhoun. The police chief. Remember him?"

"Eh . . . I meet a lot of people," he says with a shrug,

but she knows he's only kidding. Then he asks, "How's Lieutenant Colonomos? Been seeing a lot of him since you got here?"

"No. He's busy. They're all busy," she says, and regrets it, knowing Barnes is bound to bring up the meatball bribe again.

Naturally, he does.

"You know," she says as they walk back into the cottage, "there's something to be said for being a cop in a town where that's the worst that can happen."

"If that was true, Gingersnap, then you and I never would have heard of Mundy's Landing."

Only serious swimmers drag themselves out of bed to get to the gym when the pool opens at daybreak.

Some mornings, it's so crowded that Annabelle has to share a lap lane with several other swimmers. She doesn't mind, as long as everyone is up to speed and not there to float or chat, which is usually the case at this hour.

But sharing a lane robs her of the delicious solitude that allows her mind to wander, making the swim as therapeutic for her mind as for her body.

Today, as she anticipated, all six lanes are empty. Many of the regulars have left town, and others have backyard pools of their own. With the entire pool to herself, and the lone teenage lifeguard surreptitiously checking her cell phone, Annabelle ponders the unsolved mystery as she rhythmically pulls herself through the water.

Z.D.P. . . .

She'd been certain until now that the P stands for Purcell, and the Z might be Zelda. But the swim has pried her mind from the path of least resistance, and she considers other options.

Maybe the letters aren't someone's initials after all. Maybe they stand for something else: a personal abbreviation, an acronym, a symbol for . . . what? Where do you find a cluster of three letters?

Had Augusta Purcell gone to college? Could she have belonged to a sorority?

Annabelle had, and is familiar enough with the alphabet to know that Z.D.P. would be Zeta Delta Rho.

But if you were going to the trouble to memorialize a Greek organization on a statue, wouldn't you use the triangular symbol for Delta, instead of a "D"?

Yes, you would.

Think about Augusta, about what her world was like. She lived for over a century, she was reclusive, and independently wealthy . . .

Could Z.D.P. be a stock market abbreviation?

Annabelle is tempted to stop swimming and look it up on her cell phone, tucked into her gym bag in the locker room. She should have thought of it before, but she was stuck on the assumption that the letters are initials. And, for that matter, that the numbers are dates.

A birth date and death date for a twelve-year-old.

Because nothing else makes enough sense. Not in that house, made notorious on 7/7/16 . . .

The body was discovered the next day, though.

If the statue is a reference to the crime, shouldn't the date be 7/8/16?

The girl wasn't killed in the house.

She died somewhere else, likely before midnight—on 7/7/16. She's buried in Holy Angels Cemetery.

Angels . . .

The statue depicts an angel. Is it supposed to be her?

Was she born on March 31, 1904? Were her initials Z.D.P.?

Is the angel supposed to represent all of them? Are Z, D, and P the first or last letters of each of their names?

But how would Augusta know?

And what do the dates mean?

Annabelle pushes through the last few laps, her thoughts dizzying as her kick turns at the end of each length. She hurries to the locker room and quickly towels off, then grabs her phone.

She intends to open a search window to check for sororities and stocks, but a pop-up window alerts her that she has a new e-mail.

She clicks her in-box instead.

Dear Ms. Bingham,

If you'd like to discuss the statue, I have some time this afternoon.

Sincerely,

Lester Purcell

After promising he'll remain on the line with her until the police arrive, the 911 operator instructs Ora to stay in her room and asks whether the door is locked.

She's uncertain. Living alone, she rarely bothers with interior locks—one less thing for her arthritic old hands to fumble around with.

"Can you lock yourself in, ma'am?"

"Yes."

Ora hoists herself out of bed and grabs the walking stick propped against the bedside table. She moves as stealthily as possible—until her bare foot comes down squarely on a squishy pile of fur.

Ora nearly loses her balance. Briar Rose emits an unearthly howl and disappears under the bed skirt.

"Ma'am?" the operator says in her ear. "Ma'am!"

"Yes. I'm okay," she whispers, her heart pounding wildly.

"We have an officer arriving momentarily. Just stay where you are. Did you lock the door?"

"I'm about to." She makes her way over and turns the lock, listening for movement below.

She hears nothing. A chill prickles her skin as she realizes that whoever broke in might be right on the other side of the door, listening for her as well.

Not only that, but he broke something in the room directly beneath. That's where she keeps a couple of china pieces once owned by the Browne family—the Limoges pitcher and chamber pot from the room where the first Sleeping Beauty was found. They're displayed on an antique dry sink. The prowler must have knocked into them.

Unless he broke a window? If someone needed to make a fast getaway from that room, he could jump out onto the low roof of the annex building.

What if he came after the time capsule? Imagine if it's been stolen on the very day it's to be opened. She would never forgive herself. The people of Mundy's Landing would never forgive her.

She endures an agonizing wait, though it's probably just a matter of minutes before she hears footsteps ascending to the third floor.

There's a sharp rap on the door. "Ms. Abrams? Are you there?"

She reaches for the knob to open it, and then hesitates. What if it's the thief himself?

"Who's there?" she calls, moving her walking stick from her left hand to her right, prepared to brandish it in self defense if need be.

"Officer Ryan Greenlea from the MLPD, ma'am."

Ryan Greenlea—yes, he's one of the local boys. She hurriedly unlocks the door with her left hand, then realizes it might be a ploy: the intruder using a name she'd recognize.

"When and where did you and I first meet, Officer Greenlea?"

"Pardon?"

"I'm making sure it's really you. Tell me where we met, and how."

"We met right here a few years back, when I was working on my Eagle Scout project. I built the wheelchair ramp to the side porch."

That's correct, but he was photographed for a community service article in the *Tribune*. A prowler could have seen it . . .

But this is silly, wasting precious time. Tentatively, she opens the door and peeks through a crack. Yes, there he is, looking scarcely old enough to have earned a Boy Scout's pocketknife badge, let alone a police badge that comes with a loaded gun. Yet she's grateful for the weapon holstered at his hip, just in case . . .

"Ms. Abrams—are you all right?" His eyes dart warily around the room behind her. "Are you alone in here?"

"Yes, of course I'm alone. You didn't catch the thief, then?"

"There's no one down there, but—"

"I didn't imagine it, young man, if that's what you're suggesting. I may be getting up there in years, but I'm not senile."

"No, I'm not saying you imagined it. I found a window wide open downstairs, and—"

"In the room right underneath us?" she cuts in anxiously. "The window was open? Not broken?"

"No, it was open, without a screen. Unless you left it that way?"

"I didn't. Did you see the time capsule when you came in, or did they get it?"

"No, it was there."

One concern alleviated, she moves on to the next. "I

heard glass breaking. Was it the pitcher? The chamber pot? Both?"

"Neither. The big display case in that room is shattered."

"Oh no." Her stomach lurches. "Is anything missing?"

"I just glanced at it. I wouldn't be able to tell. You'll have to come look."

A few minutes later, she has her answer.

The museum's most precious items were in that case. They're hardly valuable antiques, but they are priceless.

And now they're gone.

It hasn't been a good morning so far.

Deb Pelham drank one too many margaritas last night at girls' night out, then slept through the alarm this morning. After scrambling to get ready for her nine o'clock shift at the animal hospital up in Hudson, she remembered that she's responsible for feeding the Yamazakis' dog down in Mundy's Landing.

Since the divorce, she hasn't been able to make ends meet on her vet tech salary alone, so she supplements her income as a pet sitter. But as much as she loves Rita the Akita, she could do without the out-of-the-way stop this morning.

In fact, she feels that way most mornings. She tends not to mind the nightly detour on the way home, though, when she has more time. It's relaxing after a long day to enjoy some solitude in a large, empty house than to rush home to the small apartment she shares with a roommate, her roommate's rambunctious puppy, and two dogs of her own.

The Yamazakis are among her favorite clients, not just because she likes them and their dog, but because she loves old houses. Theirs is large, impeccably clean, and comfortable. Unfortunately, she didn't get to hang around there last night, thanks to all those people making note of her every move.

Mrs. Yamazaki had warned her there would be a crowd, and said it was the reason they were leaving at the last minute. As soon as she saw what was going on, Deb didn't blame her. She got in, and she got out, ignoring the crowd.

It would be nice to find that they've magically disappeared overnight, but she has a feeling they haven't. As she follows a string of cars getting off the highway in Mundy's Landing, she realizes she's barely going to have time to hit the drive-through for coffee after she feeds Rita.

Not good.

It gets worse by the moment as she crawls slowly into The Heights. She's going to be late for work even without the coffee stop.

Traffic seems to be snarled on State Street, the block that runs through the heart of The Heights, perpendicular to Prospect. As she inches toward the intersection, Deb sees a police car blocking access to the street. Worried that something has happened to the Yamazaki home—a fire, a break-in, vandalism—she searches in vain for a place to park her car. It will be faster to walk in, as painful as she finds the thought, given her tequila-ravaged physical state.

Spotting a trim woman wearing yoga pants, out for a brisk morning walk, Deb rolls down the window and sticks her head out.

"Excuse me," she calls. "Do you know what's going on down there?"

"There was a break-in."

Uh-oh. "Do you know which house?"

"It wasn't a house, it was the historical society. Do you live on the block?"

"No, I just need to stop by a friend's." She almost said she needs to feed a dog for vacationing owners, but you don't go around telling strangers—even harmless-looking ones—that a house is empty.

Not that Deb's purpose, presence, and lack thereof escaped the crowd gathered outside the house last night. Thank goodness the break-in hadn't occurred there.

"You're probably going to have to wait a while," the woman tells her. "It's an active investigation and they don't want people getting in their way. The street is blocked off on the other end over on Fulton Avenue, too. My sister lives down there, and I was supposed to stop off for coffee, but the cop told me they can't let anyone through right now unless you're carrying ID that shows you live on that block."

"Oh no. Are you serious?"

The woman nods. "I guess you're out of luck. Sorry."

Deb thanks her and rolls up her window, left with no choice but to head to work.

Poor Rita the Akita is the one who's out of luck. At least the poor thing is crate trained. But she's going to be famished by the time Deb gets back there tonight.

I'll stick around for a while, she decides. *I'll take her for a long walk, and I'll play with her.*

In fact, if the police presence keeps the gawkers at bay, she might even spend the night, as she has before, in the Yamazakis' daughter's vacant upstairs bedroom.

From the Sleeping Beauty Killer's Diary
June 22, 1916

*More than two years ago, browsing the shelves in the
public library, I came across a recently published volume
of poetry by William Carlos Williams. I have long since
committed my favorite to memory. The last stanza is
particularly thought-provoking of late, as my brain grows
more addled and my need to act more urgent.*

The Sisters lie
With their arms intertwining;
Gold against blue
Their hair is shining!
The Serpent writhes!
Orion is listening!
Gold against blue
His sword is glistening!
Sleep!
There is hunting in heaven—
Sleep safe till tomorrow.

*The sisters—the trio of stars that glitter in
Orion's Belt—will be united soon in eternal sleep,
and I am Orion himself, the hunter. Fitting that the
constellation is invisible at this time of year—ever
present, yet ever elusive, lurking in broad daylight.*

I must do something.

I shall.

Calliope will become the first of the sisters.

*She was raised in a San Francisco orphanage that
was demolished in the great quake a decade ago, at
which point she fled the West Coast in terror. She got
only as far as a brothel somewhere in the Midwest,
and there she stayed, she informed me, until it was
shut down when prostitution was outlawed over a
year ago. She worked her way east and arrived in*

New York only last month. She lives in a crowded tenement on the Lower East Side where not one of her neighbors, she said, speaks a word of English.

The second sister has assumed the name Liberty. She speaks only broken English and recently emigrated from Sicily. She is a lovely creature with long, wavy tresses she wears flowing down her back. Her features are delicate, although her nose is quite crooked. Broken, she confided, not once but twice. The first time, by the father she gladly left behind in Palermo; the second, by her loutish American husband, a navy sailor. She pointed to a faint bruise on her wrist and told me that he'd bestowed that gift the night before he left to go to sea.

I inquired as to his current whereabouts. She shrugged and indicated that he'll likely be gone for quite some time, as it now seems likely America will enter the war in Europe. Left to her own devices in his absence, she hopes to earn enough money so that when he returns, she will be gone.

I neglected to inform her that will, indeed, be the case regardless of her finances.

Time is growing short. I have arranged to meet Calliope on June 29—the date of the new moon, when the night will be at its darkest, away from the midway's electric glare.

That allows a week for me to finalize my plan. I only hope that I can keep my wits about me in the interim. My head aches constantly, riddled by fatigue. One melody loops like the endless roll on the parlor's player piano:

By the light of the silvery moon . . .

June . . .

Soon . . .

The song is punctuated by voices—of poets, of demons, of people who surround me. The relentless din has transformed my daily life into a living hell, courtesy of the third sister: the monstrous Zelda.

Chapter 16

Annabelle isn't surprised when the doorbell rings at precisely one o'clock. At the house closing back in May, Lester Purcell had been visibly perturbed that she and Trib arrived at the attorney's office five minutes late.

They could have been much later, considering that Annabelle had been called to the middle school that morning. Oliver was in the nurse's office with yet another one of his stomachaches—code for panic attacks. It turned out he was trying to avoid health class, where the teacher was about to show a movie depicting the evils of tobacco. Students who'd already seen it were gleefully talking about its graphic, disturbing images, meant to scare kids so much that they'd never start smoking.

But of course, everything scares Oliver.

Annabelle called Trib from the school nurse's office and told him to go ahead to Ralph Duvane's office without her.

"It's not a party, Annabelle. It's a real estate closing. You have to be there."

"No kidding, Trib," she bit out, conscious of the nurse and Oliver listening. "I'll get there as soon as I can. I'm just trying to handle something here."

"I'll come handle it."

"No, I've got it."

"It doesn't sound like you do."

Just another tension-fraught day in the life of parenting Oliver, topped off by meeting Lester Purcell, forking over more money than they've ever spent—or even have—and taking ownership of a Murder House.

Now Lester is here. Annabelle hurries from the kitchen to answer the door, stepping around boxes, shoes, and baskets of clean laundry she's been trying to find time to fold all morning. What will he think when he sees the house in such a shambles? Maybe he'll regret having sold it to them.

Good thing it's too late for him to change his mind.

Good thing, too, that she made it back from Kim's house in time to answer the door.

After making arrangements for Lester to visit, she'd decided it wasn't a good idea to have Oliver here when he arrived. If her son doesn't like laid-back Steve Reed, imagine how he'd react to the cheerless Lester Purcell. Anyway, she'd rather he didn't overhear her discussing the murders—especially since she hasn't even had a chance to tell Trib the latest.

She was planning to discuss it with him when she returned from the pool, but he was dressed, with his car keys and go-mug of coffee in hand, ready to head out to the office an hour earlier than usual.

"I have a lot to do," he said, kissing her good-bye in passing, "and I have to leave early tonight because of the gala. Oh, and my tuxedo shirt is hanging in the bathroom. I was hoping the shower would steam out some of the creases."

"I'll press it for you if I can figure out which box has the iron," she promised.

She searched fruitlessly for it all morning in between other chores, then made lunch for Oliver and walked him down the street. She'd told Kim she had a couple of errands to run and didn't want to drag him around with her.

"Catherine is here," Kim said. "She can keep him occupied."

"He can just watch TV, or hang around in Connor's room and play video games."

"Let me phrase it differently: he can keep Catherine occupied. She's been horrible all morning. We've been at each other's throats. Having Oliver here will help."

Annabelle left him there second-guessing her own judgment. Which is worse: Oliver meeting Lester? Or being forced on a teenage girl who will only resent her mother, and possibly Oliver as well?

Guess I'm about to find out, she thinks, unlocking the dead bolt.

She opens the door just as Lester is about to press the doorbell again.

"You *are* home."

"I *am* home," she agrees mildly. "How are you, Mr. Purcell? It's good to see you again."

People are still milling around out on the sidewalk in front of the house. She wonders whether anyone recognized him. Probably not. He, like his aunt Augusta, avoided the press.

"I'm well," he says, and they shake hands. His is so cool and dry that hers feels, by contrast, as though it's been pulling taffy.

She'd envisioned that he'd show up in a bow tie and tweed jacket as he had at the closing, but today he's casually, if drably, dressed in brown slacks and a tan dress shirt. His gray hair is neatly combed, and his gaunt face bears a humanizing hint of stubble.

Annabelle leads him toward the back of the house, cautioning him not to trip over a stepstool sitting squarely in their path. She'd climbed up to change a bulb in the overhead fixture earlier, only to realize she couldn't reach anywhere near the towering ceiling. When she stuck her head into the natatorium to borrow Steve's stepladder, he was standing on top of it.

He's not here now, though. He was leaving just as she walked Oliver down the street. "Going to lunch?" she'd asked him, and he'd laughed.

"I did that two hours ago. When you eat breakfast at five, you're hungry for lunch by eleven. I'm on my way to the hardware store. I'll be back soon. Well, I'll try. Damn traffic is a nightmare today."

"No rush," she said, and meant it. She'd been trying to figure out how to show Lester the statue with Steve hanging around. Now they'll have the natatorium to themselves for a little while.

As she leads the way to the back of the house, she thanks Lester for coming.

"Not a problem," he assures her. "It's been quite a while since I've stepped over that threshold."

She glances to see if his face betrays any trace of emotion, or resentment. His utter lack of expression is equally disconcerting.

Ora's words echo back: *I wouldn't mention anything to Lester.*

Yes, well . . . too late to reconsider.

"Ora?"

She looks up to see Rowan Mundy in the doorway of the kitchen, looking concerned.

"I just got here and heard what happened. Are you all right?"

"I wasn't physically harmed," Ora tells her. "But several items were stolen from the special exhibits room."

She nearly admits the truth—that she'd prefer to be

lying in a hospital bed right now to sitting here staring at a long-lukewarm cup of tea and mourning her lost artifacts.

"Thank goodness you weren't hurt, though." As Rowan sits beside her, Ora remembers that she knows a thing or two about grappling with armed and dangerous intruders.

"No. Whoever broke into the museum this morning wasn't a killer. He was a thief. But the way I feel now," she adds darkly, "that's nearly the same thing."

As soon as the words are out of her mouth, she regrets them.

"I'm sorry, dear," she tells Rowan. "That was insensitive of me after all you and your family have been through."

"It's all right."

"I'm just upset."

"Of course you are." Rowan touches her arm. "It's a violation."

Her empathy sounds genuine, but Ora suspects it's gratuitous. Surely she's thinking about the close call she and her loved ones experienced in December—and about the casualties.

Ora considers pointing out that she herself no longer has a family or even a house to call her own. This old building is her home, and its relics—including Rosie, of course—are her nearest and dearest. This is all she has in the world. To her, the loss is fresh and devastating. To think that after she's spent the better part of a lifetime guarding her treasures, someone could boldly walk in here and steal one of them . . .

"What happened is awful," Rowan is saying, shaking her head, "but at least it doesn't seem to have kept people away. Marcia says they're coming in even after they hear that the special exhibit is closed today."

Marcia, a fellow volunteer, is manning the door today. Rowan was supposed to be here this morning, but was delayed taking her daughter to the doctor.

Ora, who's known Katie Mundy all her life, considers asking how she's feeling. Rowan had mentioned yesterday that she'd been sick. But she doesn't have the heart for conversation right now, and she's sure the girl is fine. Otherwise, her mother wouldn't be here.

"Yes," she tells Rowan dully. "People are still coming."

But today, she couldn't bear the sight of them. She didn't want to watch all those strangers traipsing through the house or answer their questions; didn't want to share with them her insight or anecdotes, let alone her prized collection.

He might have been among the hundreds of visitors she met yesterday. He might very well have walked through the special exhibits room and decided to come back later and help himself to its contents. Maybe he came back today to gloat, or to look for something else to steal.

That's not going to happen. Officer Greenlea told her that the police are heavily patrolling The Heights as it is.

"I know the gala is tonight," he said. "You're going, aren't you?"

"I was supposed to, but now . . ."

"Don't worry about the museum, Ms. Abrams. I'll make sure an officer is stationed right here for the duration, and that someone escorts you into the house afterward. You can't be too careful."

Just yesterday, Ora would have argued with that. But he's right. She thanked him and told him it would be much appreciated.

"I'm really sorry about your loss," the young cop said at the door, after concluding his investigation and writing up a lengthy report.

It didn't escape her that he'd uttered the same words people say when someone has died. She appreciated them, along with the irony when it struck her later: she's grieving the stolen muslin nightgown perhaps more than anyone ever grieved the dead girl who wore it one hundred years ago today.

Sully and Barnes spent the better part of the morning preparing for this evening's gala. It took her all of five minutes to pick out a dress from Rowan Mundy's closet, while Barnes spent well over an hour selecting a tux at the nearest formalwear rental place, located in a mall across the river. They wisely opted to grab lunch at the food court, correctly assuming that the restaurants back in town would be swamped.

Upon their return, they find the Village Common alive with activity. The cafés are indeed jammed. Throngs of pedestrians browse merchandise on sidewalk sale tables. A magician performs in one corner of the sun-splashed park and a yoga class stretches on another.

They can't find a parking spot anywhere near their destination, the Elsworth Ransom Library. They leave the car back in the driveway on Church Street and walk back to town.

A group of teenagers loiter against the bike rack out front of the library, which is located on Fulton Avenue in the heart of the hubbub, facing the square. Several women perch on the wide stone steps licking ice cream cones and chatting, watching their toddlers climb up and down, up and down, clinging to the railings with sticky hands.

Beyond the large glass doors lies a hushed sanctuary.

The elderly woman at the desk calls out to Sully and Barnes like long-lost travelers. "Hello, hello, do come in! Have we met?"

"No, I'm Sully, and this is my friend, Barnes."

The woman introduces herself as Miss Agatha Beanblossom—inserting the *Miss* the way Sully would have inserted *Detective*. But of course, she opted not to flash a badge or mention that they're here to investigate a case. Because they're not, according to Barnes, who is along for the ride and refusing to admit that he's just as tantalized by the old mystery as she is.

Everything about Miss Beanblossom is gray, Sully notices. Her hair, her clothing, her eyes—even her pale skin tone, probably tinged with blue as she shivers in a wool sweater beneath the air-conditioning duct fluttering papers on her desk.

"So what brings you and Barney into the library today, Sally?"

Fighting back a smile, Sully doesn't bother to correct the mispronunciation. "We're fascinated by your local history and we came to do some research."

"Oh, this isn't the historical society anymore. It used to be in the basement here years ago, but now it's over on Prospect Street."

"I know, but we were hoping you might have a collection of books on local history," Sully says, as the other half of her *we* rocks back and forth on his heels and inspects a mosquito bite on his forearm, "and we'd love to use a computer to look up some information, since we don't have a connection where we're staying."

Miss Beanblossom is delighted. "It's so nice to see young people making good use of the library. Come right this way."

"*Young* people?" Barnes mutters as she laboriously hoists herself from her chair and reaches for her cane.

"Embrace the compliment," Sully returns, sotto voce.

Miss Beanblossom insists on giving them a tour of the cavernous rooms. She points out the dark woodwork and ornate plaster moldings, original fixtures, marble fireplaces, and tall windows with stained glass panels. They admire it all—loudly, because the old dear is hard of hearing, and dutifully, as Sully is anxious to get down to business with her research. As for Barnes, he's "not a fan of old things," he reminds her when they finally find themselves alone in the research alcove.

"Oh, Barney, you young people have no appreciation for history and culture. Now hush." She indicates the placard on the wall. "Can't you see this is the quiet room?"

"Can't you see we're the only ones here other than Miss Fartblossom?"

"Behave yourself," she says, but she grins as she opens a search engine on the computer, with Barnes settling into a chair beside her to peruse a stack of local history books.

He goes through them, keeping an eye out for anything that might pertain to the Sleeping Beauty murders. Every so often, he looks up to share some historic tidbit with her—none of it relevant in the least.

After an hour of this, Sully cuts him off when he says, again, "Here's something interesting—"

"Is it about the case this time? Because I really don't want to be treated to details about yet another shipwreck."

"It's about one of the houses involved."

Okay—that's better. She looks up expectantly.

"It says here that the house at 46 Bridge Street was rumored to be haunted by the ghost of a young girl. There are eyewitness accounts from people who saw her filmy white figure lurking in a window on the top floor. They said she was the ghost of a teenage girl named Augusta Pauline Purcell who committed suicide in the house on the Fourth of July in 1893."

"Are you sure about the date? Because an Augusta Purcell died in the house before the new owners bought it a few months ago," Sully tells him. "She was over a hundred years old."

"Did your pal Nick tell you that?"

"No, my pal the old lady at the historical society told me that, when I was there yesterday."

"Maybe you got the wrong name."

"I didn't. But maybe she was named after the other Augusta Purcell. What book are you reading?"

Holding his place with his finger, he closes it to show her the cover.

"*Ghostly Tales of the Hudson River Valley*?" she reads the title aloud. "What does that have to do with anything, Barnes?"

"It's interesting, and it's got great illustrations. And it's really old."

"How old?"

He turns to the copyright page. "It was published in 1915. I guess that explains why nobody thought the ghost at 46 Bridge Street was a Sleeping Beauty."

"Right—it hadn't even happened yet. Listen, Barnes, I like ghost stories as much as the next ghoul, but you're supposed to be helping me look for clues."

"Did you find anything yet?"

"Only that I was on target when I guessed that Mundy's Landing was hardly a hotbed of illicit activity back in 1916. There might have been ghosts, but there were no hookers."

"So if the victims were working girls, then the killer must have trolled for them in the cities where they were."

"They'd been dead less than twenty-four hours when they were found, so they were killed nearby. I'm wondering if they were already in the area. Maybe there was some sort of convention nearby, or a carnival, a sports tournament . . ."

"Right. Something that would make prostitutes gravitate to Mundy's Landing."

"Let's go through the local history time line for June 1916," she suggests.

Five minutes later, they have their answer: Valley Cove Electric Pleasure Park.

"Bingo. Hundreds of strangers were descending on Mundy's Landing every day," Sully says.

"Sounds familiar." Barnes shoots a pointed look toward the window overlooking the Village Common.

"I'm going to guess the killer was among them—and so were his victims."

"So there you have it." Barnes pushes back his chair, stretches, and yawns. "I need a nap."

"No, you need coffee. You can get some on the way. Let's go."

"Where are we going?"

"First we're stopping at my favorite bakery. You can get your coffee there. Then we're going to the police station."

"So that you can visit your—"

"No," she cuts in. "So that we can look at the crime scene reports."

"What makes you think they'll let us do that?"

"What makes you think they won't?"

In the kitchen, Annabelle offers Lester a glass of iced tea, and is surprised when he accepts. She finds two clean glasses, makes room for them on the counter, and opens the fridge, conscious that he's taking in the kitchen in all its disheveled glory.

"I'm sorry about the mess," she says. "We're still getting settled, trying to figure out where everything goes."

"Well, there's certainly no shortage of space."

"No," she agrees, deciding now isn't the time to mention that space doesn't necessarily equal storage. "There's just been a shortage of time."

As he runs his fingers over the old Formica countertop, she wonders whether he's testing for dust or feeling nostalgic.

"Did you consider keeping the house after your aunt passed away, Mr. Purcell?"

He doesn't invite her to call him Lester. Nor does he

hesitate to answer the question with a decisive "No. I'm on a fixed income, and I live alone. Even if I wanted this much house, I certainly couldn't afford to heat it or maintain it."

I'm not so sure we can, either, she thinks, and changes the subject, asking where he's spending the summer.

"I rent an apartment just outside of town, over near the college campus. During the year, students live there. When they leave, I arrive."

"That sounds like a good arrangement," she tells him as she pours the iced tea, adding, "I used to coach swimming at Hadley."

"Mmm," he says again, and she realizes he isn't interested in her. He's interested in the house, or maybe just in the statue.

Time to get to it. She asks him what he knows about the stone angel.

"Not a lot. Why are you asking about it, Mrs. Bingham?"

"You can call me Annabelle."

He responds with a noncommittal "Mmm." And then, "Do you think it's . . . notable?"

"Notable?" Frowning, she turns to look at him.

"I went through everything in the house after Aunt Augusta died. The statue looked ordinary and I'd assumed she bought it from a garden statuary shop, but I suppose I could have been wrong."

Annabelle realizes, with a trace of amusement, that he's thinking he may have overlooked a lost masterpiece, like the Michelangelo sculpture in one of her favorite childhood novels, *From the Mixed-Up Files of Mrs. Basil E. Frankweiler.* That possibility hadn't even occurred to her, and she's fairly certain it's not the case.

"Do you remember when the pool was built?"

"Yes. I remember that my father was opposed."

"Why?"

"Because my aunt was eccentric, and Father didn't think an indoor swimming pool was a wise use of . . ."

"Money?" she contributes when he trails off.

"Money, time, space, resources."

"I thought she built the pool because she had arthritis, and the doctor told her that swimming would help."

"That's the case, yes. But my father told her that she could have done that at the local Y."

Annabelle doesn't point out that there is no local Y, and never has been, as far as she knows. Lester's father sounds as judgmental and ornery as she'd assumed Lester himself to be. Now, however, she can't help but feel a bit sorry for him.

"I can imagine that your aunt might not have been comfortable in a public place. She was pretty reclusive."

"Reclusive, and exclusive."

Annabelle raises an eyebrow. "What do you mean?"

"My mother always said Aunt Augusta didn't trust many people, but my father didn't mince words. He said she just didn't like people, and so she excluded them from her world as much as possible."

"Outsiders, you mean?"

"I mean *everyone*." He shakes his head. "She was estranged from family. She never worked. She had no friends."

"So she and your father weren't close?"

"My father wasn't close to anyone. It isn't his way. But he had acquaintances and colleagues."

"Did he ever see your aunt?"

"He'd look in on her, but not very often. They were two of a kind. He didn't want to be here, and she didn't want him here. She liked to be alone."

Alone with her memories, and, perhaps, with her secrets.

"My father passed on when he was in his eighties, and

I took over with my aunt. But again . . ." He shrugs. "She wasn't comfortable having anyone inside the house."

"Some people are like that."

She finds herself wanting to ask him more about his past, and his family life, but senses she'd better tread carefully. He isn't quite the grouch she expected. Perhaps just reserved, and socially awkward. Maybe it runs in the family. Like his aunt, he never married, and keeps to himself.

She hands him the iced tea. "I'd invite you to sit down to drink it, but . . ." She gestures at the table, which, along with the chairs, remains piled with the contents of moving boxes. She's been trying to put things away all morning, but hasn't managed to make a dent.

He shrugs and takes a sip.

"I've been wondering how much you know about your grandparents, Mr. Purcell?"

"Pardon?"

"I can't help but be curious about the nursery."

"Nursery?" He eyes her over the rim of the glass.

"The little room off the master bedroom."

"Oh, that. It wasn't a nursery. It's been empty for as long as I can remember. There was a crib in the house when I was a little boy, and my father said it was his, but it was in a different room, down the hall."

"Maybe that room was used as a nursery for your aunt, then. Or for other babies."

"I can assure you that there weren't very many babies in this house, Mrs. Bingham. Just Aunt Augusta and my father, and their father before them, back in the eighteen hundreds."

"Your great grandmother died giving birth to him, right?"

"I think that's right."

"And your grandfather had an older sister who was

also named Augusta, but she died in her teens, back in the late 1800s."

Lester tilts his head and looks at her. She can't tell whether he doesn't know what she's talking about, or is wondering how she knows all this.

He says nothing.

"There was a lot of sorrow in your family, Mr. Purcell."

"Every family has its share of sorrow. Back then, it was common for people to die young."

"That's true."

He's cagey, but not closed off. Does she dare ask another personal question?

Yes, she dares: "Do you know whether your grandparents lost a child before your father and your aunt Augusta were born?"

"No."

"No, they didn't? Or no, you don't know?"

"I don't know for certain, but I'm almost positive they didn't." He sips from the glass, looking uncomfortable.

"I'm sorry, Mr. Purcell. I don't mean to pry. I'm just . . . I love this house, and I'm fascinated by its past."

"The house's past? Or my family's?"

"They're intertwined, aren't they?"

"Not irrevocably. My father certainly managed to extract himself."

The implication is that Frederick had made an escape—from the house, the family, the past—while his sister had not.

Lester's eyes shift to the left and right as if he's making sure no one is eavesdropping before he sets the glass on the counter and says, "Tell me more about the statue."

"I can show you. It's right in there." She gestures at the door, then adds, feeling a bit foolish, "I guess you know that."

"Like I said, I didn't spend much time here, Mrs. Bingham."

They cross through the mudroom. Lester sniffs the air and informs her that it smells like cat.

"Your aunt fed strays. They keep coming around."

"I thought I got them all. Just don't take the damned things in. They'll destroy the place."

She has to bite her tongue to keep from saying, *Maybe you should have included a clause in the real estate contract about that, too.*

Not feeling quite so sorry for him now, she wonders what he means about getting them all.

She opens the door to the natatorium, explaining, "We're having some work done to restore the pool. Watch your step."

"I'm glad someone will get some use out of it after all these years. You said you coached swimming?"

"Yes." So he was paying attention after all. She can't decide whether she likes him or not.

You don't have to decide, she reminds herself as they pick their way across the cluttered floor along the side of the pool. It shouldn't really matter what kind of person he is.

But she wants to like him. He's the only living link to the Purcell family, and she's become attached to them. To Augusta, anyway, and to Florence.

"Did you ever know your grandmother?" she asks him, knowing she lived into the 1930s, while his grandfather had died well before the Great Depression.

"Not really. She wasn't well. We visited her a few times, but it was a long trip. We didn't make it very often."

"I thought you grew up here in town."

"I did. My grandmother was . . . like I said, she wasn't well. She was hospitalized in a sanatorium down in Rockland for as long as I can remember."

"Tuberculosis?" she asks, thinking of her own grandmother.

"Insane," he says flatly.

Florence? Her Florence?

"You mean it was an asylum?" At his nod, she asks, "What happened? Was it dementia, or . . ."

He shrugs. "I was a little boy. It wasn't something we talked about around the family dinner table. All I know is that my grandmother was mad. Institutionalized all my life, and for what was left of hers."

As she digests that, he covers the last few steps to the pedestal and examines the statue, then looks up at her.

"Why are you so curious about this statue?"

"Because of what's written on it."

He raises a white eyebrow and returns his gaze to the statue, apparently looking for it. He's on the wrong side—which means he didn't know there was an inscription, or he's faking ignorance.

"Here," she says, walking over to show him.

He peers at the letters and numbers etched in the base, and shakes his head. "I'm farsighted. What does it say?"

She reads it for him, though from memory, as the inscription is blurred to her as well.

"What does that mean?" he asks her.

"I was wondering if you knew."

He shakes his head. But she can see the wheels turning in his brain. The significance of the date 7/7/16 hasn't escaped him.

"I thought maybe those were the initials of someone in your family. Z.D.P. I know there were several women named Griselda—Zelda for short. Do you—"

"How," he asks, narrowing his eyes, "do you know that?"

"I looked it up online. It was readily available in public records," she adds hastily.

"But why waste all this time on my family when you have one of your own?"

"I wouldn't call it 'all this time.' It only took a few minutes."

"But there are certainly plenty of other, more productive things you could be doing with those minutes." He flicks a meaningful gaze toward the rest of the house, allowing the words to sink in.

He might be rude, but he's right.

She does have other things to do. The place is a mess, her son is . . . well, he's not a *mess*. Not at this particular moment, anyway. Her marriage isn't a mess, either. Still, she hasn't been particularly attentive to Trib lately.

Maybe it's time to let go of the mystery—at least for now.

Waking to cold, damp darkness, Indi faces the ugly truth again.

She's imprisoned by a maniac, chained to the wall in a dungeon where no one will ever find her. Juanita was murdered, and—

"Kathryn?" Indi calls, remembering the rest of it. "Kathryn!"

No response.

She's out cold again. With her, Indi knows, it's never just falling asleep; it's losing consciousness. Kathryn had precious little physical stamina to begin with.

This brutal incarceration is taking a toll even on Indi.

But there's hope now. After Kathryn freed herself from her shackles, they formulated a plan. When he comes back, Kathryn will pretend she's still cuffed to the wall. If he lowers the ladder to descend, Indi will distract him by feigning an injury. Then Kathryn will grab the ladder and swing it at him with all her might. The element of surprise should work in their favor.

It isn't a perfect plan, but it's all they've got.

"Kathryn?" Indi says again, needing the human contact,

and missing Juanita. "Answer me, please! I need to talk to you."

The darkness is so still.

"Kathryn! Please wake up! Please!"

She can feel the emptiness, almost as if she's all alone here, which . . .

Wait a minute. Am I?

Could Kathryn have managed to escape while Indi was sleeping? Is she going for help right at this moment?

But she'd have woken me up to say she was going to try. There's no way she'd have left without telling me she was going.

"Kathryn? Are you here?"

A terrible thought takes hold.

What if he crept back in and took Kathryn away while Indi was sleeping?

I'd have heard him, though, wouldn't I? I'd have heard a struggle, and she'd have screamed . . .

Maybe not. Maybe Kathryn didn't make a sound— maybe she was already unconscious, or so frightened that she fainted. And Indi has been so weak that maybe she, too, is passing out.

"Kathryn!" she screams hoarsely. "Kathryn!"

No reply. Fresh dread creeps over Indi as she realizes that she's alone in the dark.

Holmes's Case Notes

Six months ago, I used cash to buy three identical nightgowns from Macy's in a busy Albany shopping mall. If the sales clerk thought it was an odd purchase, she didn't let on. She barely acknowledged me, jabbering on the phone with a difficult customer as she rang up the sale.

I assume that my predecessor encountered a similarly distracted salesperson when purchasing the three nightgowns at Waldman Brothers Department Store just a few miles from that very spot. Otherwise, surely a clerk would have come forward when news of the murders hit the newspaper.

Until today, of course, I had no proof that S.B.K. obtained the merchandise in that particular place. But in a vintage issue of the *Tribune* dated just after New Year's, 1916, I spotted an advertisement for Waldman Brothers' January white sale featuring "fine muslin nightgowns daintily trimmed with lace." The ad included a sketch of a woman wearing a garment that was strikingly similar to the ones found on the Sleeping Beauties. Yet another clue, long overlooked by the authorities and masses.

The stolen scrap of fabric I keep wrapped around the buffalo nickel in my pocket wasn't large enough to make a comparison. But now that I can examine the actual nightgown alongside the ad, I see that I was, indeed, correct in my assumption. They are one and the same.

This garment was found on the Beauty at 46 Bridge on July 8, 1916. Originally white, it has since faded to a lovely buttery shade. There are faint splotches of brown just beneath the lace neckline: blood. The satin ribbons, too, are yellowed and lightly stained with her blood.

Those stains hold the key to Beauty's identity. All it would take is modern forensics and a DNA sample from her only living relative, right under their noses all along. But of course they don't know where to look.

And I'm not about to help them.

Chapter 17

It's bad enough that Annabelle has to walk past the strangers milling around in front of her house in order to collect Oliver from the Winstons' house on Thursday afternoon. But as she walks up Bridge Street, she can hear Kim and Catherine screaming at each other from a few houses away, their voices spilling from an open window.

"I keep telling you, Mom, I didn't know she was going!"

"Why would I believe you this time after I keep catching you in lies?"

"Because I'm telling the truth! And I haven't lied about anything big. It's just—"

"A lie is a lie, Catherine."

"I just *can't even*. You have to let me go."

"No. Absolutely not."

Wincing, Annabelle picks up her pace, hoping Oliver is still plugged into a video game in Connor's room. Thank goodness for headphones.

But no more electronics for him today, she reminds herself. *I'll spend the rest of the afternoon with him.*

Lester's visit may not have answered her questions about the statue, but she's resolved something far more important.

As a competitive swimmer, she learned how to tune out the noise and focus on the immediate challenge. That's exactly what she's going to do.

She'd allowed herself to get caught up in the lives of strangers and events that unfolded under her roof a century ago, instead of focusing on her own household and the people she loves.

Probably because it's much easier to deal with long-dead people than with an anxiety-ridden son and an over-worked, preoccupied husband. Yes, and the past, for all its trauma, is much easier to face than the complicated present, let alone an uncertain future.

She remains curious about the history behind the statue, the house, and the unsolved crimes. But she's ready to spend the afternoon with Oliver and the evening with Trib. She's looking forward to date night. It's been much too long.

As she walks up the sidewalk toward the Queen Anne Victorian, she sees that the Winstons' front door is open wide, with only the screen door to keep the world at bay. Such is life when you don't live in a Murder House.

Ah—old habits die hard.

You're not supposed to be dwelling on that anymore. It isn't a Murder House. It's home.

Besides, Annabelle thinks as she knocks on the Winstons' door, it would be easier to forget it's a Murder House without a crowd of bystanders lurking by the fence.

Dreading the prospect of walking past them again, she'd considered driving down the street. But she coached herself through, just as she used to coach her college swimmers. *Come on, don't let them get to you. Hold your head high and do what you have to do.* She felt the strangers' stares as she walked past and was glad she remembered to put on sunglasses to avoid eye contact, but she was determined not to let them intimidate her.

"Kim?" she calls through the screen door, over the sound of arguing. "I'm here."

Her friend breaks off, mid-tirade, to call, "Annabelle? It's open. Come on in."

She steps over the threshold into a house that's as lovely and put together as its mistress. The place is magazine perfection, with vases of fresh-cut flowers, framed family photos, and antique collectibles. Kim painstakingly decorated it herself with period furniture, paint, and fabrics in a warm palette of reds and golds.

Our house could look like this, Annabelle thinks as she makes her way toward the kitchen. Not overnight, but in time, and on budget. She remembers visiting yard sales with Kim when the boys were little. Her friend learned how to strip and refinish furniture she'd bought for a few dollars, but you'd never know it's secondhand, seeing it in these charming rooms.

I can do that, too.

Inspired, Annabelle feels as though she can do anything.

About to walk into the kitchen, she nearly crashes into Catherine, who comes barreling out.

"I'm sorry, Mrs. Bingham," she says, but she doesn't slow down or look back.

"Catherine! Get back here! We aren't finished with this conversation!"

"I am."

"Don't you dare leave this house!"

"I'm not leaving. Not while you're here, anyway. I'm going upstairs." Her footsteps are already bounding up the flight. A moment later, her bedroom door slams above.

Kim sighs heavily. She's standing by the sink, looking pretty in a petal pink T-shirt and white cutoff shorts, but with a haggard expression that catches Annabelle off guard.

"Are you okay?" she asks.

"*I'm* okay. *She's* a beast."

"What happened?" Annabelle doesn't really want to know, but she feels as though she should ask.

"I ran into her friend Jessica's mother when I went to get my nails done this morning. She was getting her nails done, and talking about the gala tonight. She's going, too."

"And . . . ?"

"And Catherine is staying at her house because we're not going to be home and I didn't want her here alone. But now she and Jessica are going to be on their own, and—I don't trust them." She shakes her head. "Lord knows what they'll be up to, unsupervised."

"What about—" Annabelle breaks off as her cell phone rings in her pocket. She takes it out and checks caller ID. "Uh-oh."

"What's wrong?"

"It's Katie Mundy. My sitter for tonight." She answers the phone, hoping Katie is just checking on the time. "Hello? Katie?"

"Hi, Mrs. Bingham."

The moment Annabelle hears the hoarseness in her voice, she knows she's going to cancel—and she's right.

Hanging up a minute later, after telling Katie to feel better, she looks at Kim. "Strep throat."

"Oh no."

"Oh yes. She just came from the doctor. There goes the gala. For me, anyway. Trib is speaking, so he'll have to go."

Kim is shaking her head. "No. Catherine can stay with Oliver."

"You don't let her babysit."

"Not for people I don't know. I'd rather have her being responsible at your house than on her own here, or God forbid at Jessica's, where they'll be having boys over or sneaking out or getting into the mother's liquor stash."

"Why would you think—"

"Every time I see the woman, I smell booze on her breath. Even in the morning. She's bad news, and so is her daughter. I don't want Catherine over there. She'll babysit."

"What if she doesn't want to?"

"I don't care what she wants. Unless—did Oliver say something about last night?" Her eyes narrow. "Was she mean to him?"

"No! Actually, he said she was great."

"Really?"

Not really. What he'd said was that Catherine was great at the video game they were playing.

"She told me not to tell anyone, though," he told Annabelle as she tucked him in.

"Tell anyone what?"

"That she plays games. It's our secret. And I didn't mean to tell you. So please don't tell, Mom. Because when Catherine gets mad at people, she does mean things to them."

"Like what?"

"Like she takes their favorite stuff and hides it until they give her money to get it back."

"Is that what she does to Connor?"

He nodded.

"I don't think she'd do that to you," Annabelle said, "but don't worry. I won't tell."

She, like Oliver, may not have ever experienced sibling conflict firsthand, but she recognized that what Oliver was describing wasn't malicious behavior. Just typical big sister tyranny—extortion and all.

"I'm glad Oliver said she's great," Kim says now. "At least that means she's capable of being a decent human being. I haven't seen that in a long time."

Annabelle considers that. "Maybe you should just let

her stay home on her own for a change, Kim. Maybe she's
feeling smothered."

"I can't do that."

"Why not?"

"Because I'm worried."

"Because of Brianna Armbruster? That wasn't—"

"It's not just that, Annabelle. It's been so hard lately.
Just me and her, day after day, with Connor gone, and
Ross never home—I have to deal with her on my own,
and I swear I just don't know what to do with her."

"She's a good kid, though." Annabelle can't help but
feel as though Kim is overreacting.

Then again, who is she to even consider that?

"She's always texting with kids I don't know and with
boys, and you can't imagine the way she'd dress if I'd let
her, Annabelle . . . and she hates me so much she keeps
threatening to run away. I'm afraid she's going to do it.
That, or get herself into some kind of trouble."

Seeing the vulnerability in her friend's eyes, Annabelle nods. "Okay, I get it. If you think she won't mind,
I'd love to have her babysit for Oliver. Thanks you for
saving our date night."

"Thank you for helping me save my kid," Kim tells her
with a sad smile.

Nick Colonomos isn't available when Sully and Barnes
arrive at the police station, Barnes holding a cup of
coffee, Sully a cup of tea and a box of cookies courtesy of
the Gingersnap Sweet Shop.

According to Wilbur Morton, the lieutenant is over at
the historical society, investigating a theft.

"A theft? In broad daylight, with all those people
around?" she asks incredulously, having seen the line
stretching out to the sidewalk again today.

"No, early this morning. But Miss Abrams has been

beside herself, and Lieutenant Colonomos went over to talk to her. He's going to post an officer there tonight during the gala."

"Is that the gala we're attending?" Barnes asks Sully.

"No, some other random gala here in town."

"Always with the sarcasm. Do you see what I have to put up with?" he asks Wilbur, shaking his head.

"Nobody held a gun to your head to get you here," Sully points out. "But don't you piss me off, because I have one."

"See that, Wilbur? Now she's threatening me."

Wilbur smiles, digging into the box of cookies Sully handed him. "I think she's a breath of fresh air. We could use someone like Detective Sullivan around here."

"Careful what you wish for," Barnes tells him.

Ignoring that, Sully tells Wilbur that they're here to look at some old case files. She doesn't bother to clarify that they're not connected to the one they investigated here in December.

Wilbur leads them to a large storage room filled with file cabinets and rows of shelves lined with cardboard evidence boxes, tells them to holler if they need help, and shuts the door behind him.

Barnes turns to her with an admiring look. "Nice job."

She shrugs. "Don't ask, don't tell. Let's find 1916."

It doesn't take long. One long shelf is devoted to the Sleeping Beauty murders. Each box is carefully labeled. They peruse the contents, looking for victimology clues that might have been overlooked a century ago.

Within the file containing the original autopsy reports and medical examiner's photos, Sully finds a clue at last.

"Barnes. Look at this autopsy report. One of the victims was significantly younger than the others. The other two had recently finished growing and they had one or more wisdom teeth."

"Meaning they were anywhere from seventeen to their early twenties. What about the third?"

Sully taps the report, shaking her head. "Barely in puberty, and her second molars were just erupting. She was a kid, Barnes. Probably about twelve years old."

In the pocket of a room that has—presumably—been unoccupied for over a century, Annabelle expertly wedges her utility blade between the window frame and bottom sash, fused by a dried riverbed of yellowed paint. Oliver stands at her side watching as she attempts to free this final sticky strip of the second-to-last window in the second-to-last room on the third floor. They started in the large ballroom and worked their way to this small warren of bedrooms at the rear of the house.

One by one, they've opened every window, allowing the warm June day, scented by a neighbor's newly mown grass, to spill into the space. Annabelle imagined a simultaneous release of the stagnant air trapped here, steeped in the Purcell family's somber legacy.

"This is a tiny bedroom," Oliver observes as she slices the blade down through the crack to open it. "I can't believe two servants had to sleep in here."

"Two or maybe three," she reminds him.

He's been asking endless questions about the way things used to be in the "olden days"—long before her time, she felt compelled to point out several times, grinning.

This productive mother-and-son afternoon seems to have been a much-needed balm for both of them, even if the conversation made it hard for her to entirely forget about the Purcell family and the Sleeping Beauties. Not that she discussed any of that with Oliver, who seems to be warming up to this old house at last.

"Ready?" he asks as she carefully removes the blade and steps back.

"Go ahead."

He gives the bottom sash an upward tug, then a hard shove, and another, until it slowly groans a few inches past the top panes.

Warm, verdant air flows in through the open space above the sill. Annabelle inhales deeply, envisioning the last of the contaminated indoor air rushing out, diffused in the waning afternoon breeze.

"Good job." Smiling, she holds out her fist to bump his outstretched one.

"Dad's going to be really happy when he finds out you fixed all these windows," he decides as they head down the hall to the final maids' room

"You mean *we* fixed all the windows. We make a good team."

"What are we going to do after this?"

She checks her watch. "In about five minutes, I have to jump into the shower to get ready to go out tonight. You and Catherine are going to have a great time, though, while we're gone."

He looks pensive.

Time to change the subject. She opens the door to the last room. "Wow, this one is the tiniest of all! Look, Oliver!"

He peers over her shoulder. "Are you sure it was a bedroom? There's not even room for a bed or any stuff."

"Beds were smaller back then. People were smaller, too, for that matter. And they certainly didn't have much stuff."

"I feel bad for them, don't you?"

She nods, glad for his empathy and for his interest in history.

He pokes around as she sets to work on the room's lone window, cutting through the dried paint all around the sash.

"I don't think this was a bedroom after all, Mom."

"Why not?"

"Because there's a lock on the outside of the door."

"Really?" she asks absently, scraping away the last bit of old paint.

"I bet they used this room for storage. I bet they did have some stuff. And they put it in here so to keep it safe, like from older sisters and everything."

"Mmm, could be."

"Want to see the lock?"

"Sure." Finished with the window, she turns to see that he's in the hallway, inspecting the door frame. She takes a quick peek at the large, sturdy old-fashioned slide bolt fastened to the outside of the door, and then a quicker peek at her watch.

"Why don't you go ahead and open that window, Oliver? Then we'll be done up here."

He goes over and gives it a tug. Shoves. Strains. "It's stuck."

"Here, let me."

"No, I'll do it."

She lets him try again, to no avail. He finally allows her to help, but she, too, struggles. It won't budge.

Perplexed, she steps back to look at it, and hears Steve, way downstairs, calling her name.

She sticks her head into the hall. "We're up here!"

"I just wanted to tell you I'm heading out. There's wet grout, so be careful if you go in there."

"Wait, Steve, can you come up for a second?"

Her son sighs heavily behind her, still not a fan of the man.

"Shh, I just want him to help us with this," she hisses. "He's stronger than the two of us put together."

Oliver grumbles a denial as Steve's steel-toed boots ascend two flights and cross the hardwood parquet floor of the ballroom.

Annabelle beckons him down the hall through the open doorway.

"This is some place," he says, with a low whistle and shake of his head. "I bet they threw some killer parties up here."

Cringing at his word choice, she explains what they've been doing and asks if he can open the stuck window.

"No problem," Steve says, relishing his he-man status. He asks them to step back and gives the window a little push, as if expecting it to slide effortlessly open. Within moments, he, too, is struggling with it. He asks for the utility blade and works it around the edges just as Annabelle did, but that doesn't help.

"It's okay." She checks her watch again. Trib will be home soon, and she has to get ready. "I'll have my husband take a look."

"But I don't understand why it's—oh!"

"What?"

"There are security pins, see?" Steve points to the spot where the double hung windows meet. Just above the sash of the lower window, inside the jamb where it would slide upward, someone drilled a pair of holes and inserted metal pins. Discolored with age and about the diameter of a thumb, they jut a few inches from the casing on either side, resting flush against the top of the lower sash to keep it in place.

"These are in here good and tight," Steve says, examining them. "If I had a pry tool, I could get them out for you."

"Why are they even there?" Oliver asks, alongside Annabelle, peering over Steve's shoulder on tiptoe.

"Good old-fashioned security measure. The pins keep the windows from being opened. You see them in a lot of old houses. You didn't find them in any of the other windows?"

"No," Annabelle says. "Just here."

"This was a storage room," Oliver adds, forgetting to dislike Steve for a minute. "They used it to protect their stuff, right, Mom?"

"From their older sisters, apparently," she says with a grin.

"Sisters can be a pain," Steve agrees, smiling beneath his backward baseball cap.

"The door's got a cool lock and I think Connor needs to get one for his room when he gets back from camp."

"Where's the lock?" Steve asks, looking at the door.

"Oh the other side. Want to see?"

"Sure."

Annabelle trails the two of them to the hall to re-examine the ornately carved antique hardware affixed to the door. Oliver closes it and demonstrates how the bar slides into the metal groove on the frame. As she stares at it, Annabelle is struck by something she didn't notice before.

"That's not a lock," Steve tells Oliver. "It's a bolt."

"What's the difference?"

"A lock has a key, but anyone can open a bolt. Even a sister. The weird thing is . . . it's on the wrong side of the door."

"That's exactly what I was just thinking." Annabelle frowns.

There's only one reason you'd put a bolt on the outside of a door: to lock someone inside. Between that and the window pegs, she can't help but wonder if the room was used as some sort of . . . cell?

She doesn't voice the thought aloud, but she can tell Steve is thinking the same thing as he looks from the lock to the window, and then at her.

He shrugs. "To each his own, I guess. Listen, I have to go. I'll be back tomorrow. Remind me to see if I can pry those prongs out of the window so you can open it. Bye, guys."

He disappears down the hall, crosses the ballroom, and heads down the steps.

"Can we go down the servants' stairs like you said, Mom?" Oliver asks as she stands staring from the lock to the window pins, lost in thought.

"Sure, come on."

She opens the door across the hall to the shadowy back stairway. It descends to a landing with a door to the second floor and then on down to the kitchen, allowing the servants to come and go without disturbing the family or their guests. She'd told Oliver about it while they were working on the windows,

Now, however, he takes one look at the steep, cob-webby space and pulls back with a shudder. "I don't want to go down there."

Frankly, she doesn't, either. But now that he's seen it, the last thing she wants is for him to envision it as some sort of foreboding dungeon waiting to swallow him. She feels around on the wall for a light switch. There isn't one, just as there are no switches, lights, or even electrical out-lets here in the servants' quarters. Nor are there window screens as there are in the ballroom and throughout the rest of the house.

That confirms what she'd already suspected: that this part of the house was never updated. It's been basically sealed off like Ora Abrams's time capsule, apparently frozen in time ever since the servants left around the turn of the century.

"Mom? Can we go down the regular stairs?" Oliver asks.

"Sure." She firmly closes the door on the back stair, and, once again, on the past.

Sully's shoulders ache from sitting hunched at the metal table in the case files room, and her eyes burn from strain-ing to make out faded, old-fashioned notes. But she and

Barnes have uncovered a second important clue in the Sleeping Beauties murders.

All three victims were killed by a barber's razor slicing straight across beneath the jawbone in a calculated, methodic cut. They'd died quickly.

On two corpses, those slashes were the only wounds.

But on the youngest victim, there were several deep gashes in the torso—classic overkill.

Poor little thing, Sully thinks, staring at her face in the post-mortem photos. She thinks of Manik Bhandari, who died crying for his father, and wonders if this child did the same thing.

Trying to shake the ugly thought, she tells Barnes, "He must have known her. She must have mattered to him."

"Or she was a surrogate for someone who did. I can't believe no one ever caught this."

"It was the dawn of criminology. Profiling wasn't a sophisticated science—if it even existed at that point."

"I mean in recent years."

"These aren't public files. We're lucky we have access."

"You and your smooth talk and your bakery cookies." He shakes his head. "I'm impressed."

"Hold the applause, Barnes. We haven't figured out who she was, or how he knew her, or who *he* was. And I hate to say it, but we should leave soon to get ready for the gala. I just want to double-check one more thing."

"What is it?"

"The date on this report for the order of his victims. Was the youngest one first, second, or third?"

He rubs the stubble on his chin. "I'm guessing the first. He killed her in a rage, then killed two more as surrogates."

She back flips through the report and her eyes widen. "Guess again."

"Third. Practice makes perfect. He realized that the

younger and more vulnerable his victims were, the easier it would be for him."

"Wrong."

"She was the second victim?"

Sully nods. "She was the one found at 46 Bridge Street on July eighth."

Despite having endured a long day on the heels of a sleepless night, Holmes effortlessly covers the last bit of terrain on the way to the little stone icehouse. He isn't dressed for hiking, nor is he carrying a backpack. He wasn't even planning on visiting his Beauties until the weekend, and in fact meant to head home to grab some much-needed sleep.

But his morning adventure at the historical society left him oddly invigorated, and he sailed through his usual obligations fueled by adrenaline and coffee.

He glances over both shoulders as he unlocks the padlocked door to the icehouse.

Inside, he inspects the spot where he killed Juanita Contreras and is pleased to see that not a drop of blood mars the floor.

He tugs open the trapdoor and turns on his flashlight.

Indigo Selena Edmonds stares up at him. Her eyes are large and frightened, her face gaunt.

"Hello there. I brought you a little gift."

He turns to retrieve the ladder. He lowers it into the hole and climbs down. As he moves his foot from the bottom rung to the floor, it encounters . . . something.

A large bundle of rags lie at the base of the ladder.

This makes no sense. Where did it come from?

Turning to question the girls, he sees that Indi is staring down at it, her face frozen in horror. And Kathryn . . .

Kathryn's shackles are empty.

Reality dawns.

Holmes bends over to roll the bundle of rags.

It's Kathryn, stiff and cold.

He can see at a glance that she damaged her wrists so violently in the process of working herself out of the shackles that she severed an artery and bled out through the open wounds.

He opens his mouth, and a guttural cry comes out.

"Noooo!" he howls. "Nooooooo!"

From the Sleeping Beauty Killer's Diary
June 29, 1916

I must do something.
I must.
The refrain marches through my aching head as ominously as German armies through Europe, heedlessly trampling tendrils of reason and fleeting wisps of drowsiness. There is no longer refuge even in sleep because there is no sleep. I reach often for my books, hoping the written word might temporarily quell the ones in my brain.

In the wee hours this morning, as I lay restlessly with a newly published volume by a poet named Robert Frost, I was captured by the opening line of a poem entitled "The Road Not Taken."

Two roads diverged in a yellow wood.

Leafing back twenty-three years to the first entry in this journal, I marvel at my precocious precognition that my own road would diverge not in a yellow wood, but in a gleaming White City.

In Chicago, I was tempted to turn my back upon obligation and bravely charge along a new path: to study astronomy and poetry, to explore the world beyond the confines inflicted upon me.

Instead, I dutifully returned to Father and Mundy's Landing, my astronomical aspirations and poetic fervor relegated to mere hobby.

Having lived with the regret—and the consequences—of that choice, I have reached another fork in the road. This time, I am determined that cowardice will not prevent me from seizing opportunity that may not come again, for as the poet wrote:

And both that morning equally lay
In leaves no step had trodden black.

Oh, I kept the first for another day!
Yet knowing how way leads on to way,
I doubted if I should ever come back.

I must do something.
I must DO SOMETHING.
I MUST DO SOMETHING!

Chapter 18

In the bedroom, Annabelle painstakingly pulls her new black cocktail dress over her head, careful not to muss her hair or makeup. She's kept things simple—lipstick, a bit of mascara, some styling gel in her hair before she blew it dry after her shower. But as Trib swapped places with her in the bathroom, he told her she looks beautiful.

The dress swishes around her bare legs as she crosses to her jewelry box to find her grandmother's pearl earrings and necklace. She's worn them only twice before: on her wedding day, and to her mother's funeral. Both events were fraught with tense emotion. So, as it turns out, is this one.

She can't shake the thought of that third-floor room with the window fastened closed and the door bolted from the outside. Was the bolt added after the servants had vacated the house? Were they sent away because the Purcell family had something to hide? Why did Florence Purcell live out her life in an asylum? What dark secrets did Augusta and her brother Frederick keep over the years?

When Trib got home from work, she and Oliver had escorted him upstairs to show him their handiwork.

"Great job getting all the windows open," he said.

"All but one, Dad." Oliver led the way to the small

room at the end of the hall and shared his storage room theory. Annabelle caught Trib's eye as he noticed that the sliding bolt was on the wrong side of the door. She saw that he, too, was unsettled by it.

Back on the second floor, with Oliver out of earshot, he suggested, "Maybe it was meant to keep children from getting into something dangerous. Guns, or booze— maybe the parents were bootleggers."

"The lock is right above the doorknob," she pointed out. "It would have been placed much higher, out of arm's reach for a child, if that was the case. I think someone was locked in that room."

"Maybe it was an animal."

"Why the bolt? Animal paws can't open closed doors."

"Some can."

She gave him a dubious look.

"Okay, then maybe there was a fire escape leading up to that window years ago, and they didn't want anyone climbing up and getting into the house that way."

"That doesn't make much sense."

"It makes more sense than assuming the room must have been a makeshift prison. Why are you jumping to that conclusion?"

Hurriedly, she told him about the statue with its cryptic inscription. He was intrigued, but again wasn't particularly concerned. He promised to take a look tomorrow.

She slips her feet into a scarcely worn pair of dress pumps and heads downstairs. Halfway down, she takes them off, wondering how—and why—Kim goes around in heels every day of her life.

Speak of the devil: the doorbell rings just as she reaches the first floor. Shoes in hand, Annabelle opens it to see Kim, Ross, and Catherine Winston. Kim is wearing one of the dresses she bought yesterday, Ross a tuxedo, Catherine, cutoff jean shorts and a scowl.

"There are all kinds of people out in front of your house," Kim informs Annabelle. "And there's a police officer hanging around on the corner."

"That's good. I think."

"Looks like this is the safest place to be tonight," Ross assures her. "There are cops all over The Heights. Did you hear about the burglary at the historical society?"

Annabelle nods. She did hear. Trib mentioned it when he got home, saying the tourists have graduated from gawking to grabbing. Whoever broke in stole several artifacts from the special exhibit, and Ora Abrams is reportedly beside herself, poor thing.

"I'm sure it was just kids. By the way, Annabelle, you look beautiful!" Kim turns to her husband and daughter. "Doesn't she? Look how beautiful she is."

"Drop-dead gorgeous," Ross agrees.

Catherine, glaring as though she wishes her mother would drop dead, offers Annabelle a cursory nod of approval.

"I'm so glad you could come stay with Oliver while we're gone," Annabelle tells her with a pasted-on smile, certain this was a huge mistake.

"It was no problem," Kim says for her daughter as they step into the foyer. "She's happy to be here."

The words fall flatter than Catherine's tone as she agrees, under her mother's prodding glare.

Annabelle thanks her. "Oliver is in his room. Do you want to go up and tell him you're here, sweetie?"

Looking quite the opposite of sweet, Catherine heads up the stairs.

Annabelle looks at Catherine's parents. "She doesn't have to do this. I'm really totally fine with staying here with Oliver myself."

"Don't be ridiculous. She's doing it," Kim tells her.

Annabelle looks at Ross.

"She's doing it," he agrees. "Kim grounded her, so believe me, this is the most fun she's going to have for a while."

"Why did you ground her?"

"The usual." Kim begins ticking off reasons on her fingers. "She lied, she was fresh, she was obnoxious, she threatened to run away, and she—"

"Sometimes, I don't know why you won't let her."

Kim looks at Ross in horror. "*What* did you say?"

"Relax. I was kidding."

"It isn't funny."

"Maybe I'm the one who should run away."

His wife narrows her blue, thickly mascaraed eyes at him.

"Kidding again. Let me guess. Not funny?" Ross rocks back on his heels and shifts his attention to Annabelle. "Um, is Trib ready?"

"I'll go move him along. Have a seat." She waves in the general direction of the parlor as she hurries up the stairs, still barefoot and carrying her shoes.

She finds Trib in their bedroom tying his bow tie in front of the mirror. Closing the door behind her, she hurries over to him.

"Are they here? I need two minutes."

"They're here," she says in a low voice, "but I'm not sure I should go."

"What? Why not? Isn't Catherine here to babysit?"

"She is, but . . . I don't think she wants to be. They're forcing her to do it."

"That's what parents do. They force kids to do things. Anyway, we're paying her, right?" Trib fumbles his tie, shakes his head, and starts again.

"Of course we're paying her." Last night, Annabelle had tucked a twenty-dollar bill into Catherine's hand when she left after playing video games with Oliver, and the girl responded with warm gratitude. She even tried to give it back, but Annabelle shushed her, so that Kim wouldn't overhear, and insisted that she keep it.

Tonight, however, is a different story. Catherine clearly resents being here, and Oliver is bound to pick up on that.

"He's already upset that we're going," Annabelle tells Trib. "He's going to be scared. If she's not in the mood to keep him occupied, he could have a panic attack, and she won't know how to handle it."

Trib, shaking his head the whole time she's talking, swiftly reties his tie and picks up his jacket from the bed. "He'll be fine, Annabelle. I'm sure she'll have everything under control. It's only a few hours, and we'll be two miles away."

"But I don't think it's worth—"

"I need you there," he says, standing in front of her and putting his hands on her arms. "I do. I have to stand up there and speak in front of a roomful of people, and I'm nervous. I need you, Annabelle."

She isn't just Oliver's mother. She's Trib's wife.

She nods. "I'll come. I'm sure everything will be fine. Your speech, and . . . everything else."

Throughout The Heights, couples emerge from their homes in formal attire, get into cars, and drive away toward Hudson Chase Country Club off Battlefield Road.

Even old Ora Abrams leaves the historical society, wearing a sequined light blue gown and a tiara atop her snowy Cinderella bun. She leans heavily on the arm of Mayor Cochran himself. Behind them, a pair of uniformed security guards carries the large wooden time capsule chest to the limousine waiting at the curb. A *Tribune* photographer is on hand to capture the moment, as are scads of loitering tourists, and of course, Holmes.

He notes with interest that Ora, who ordinarily courts media attention along with public support, doesn't even glance their way. The robbery has left her rattled, though not enough to keep her home on perhaps the most notable night of her life. She must be reassured by Chief Calhoun's promised police officer, stationed inside the mansion for the duration of the evening.

That's fine with Holmes. There's only one thing he's interested in stealing tonight, and it's not inside the historical society.

He needs to replace the dead Kathryn.

He'd intended to exercise caution, aware that her turn won't come for a couple of weeks, but panic is building.

What if he can't find a candidate before July 13?

What if, as the date grows nearer, he feels compelled to rush?

That would be dangerous.

Do it now.

Find her tonight.

Holmes walks up State Street and rounds the corner onto Bridge, hunting for prospects. People stroll past clutching workshop handouts and Ora Abrams's yellow maps, making the requisite pilgrimage from one Murder House to another. There are no Beauties among them.

As he makes his way toward number 46, he sees people milling about on the sidewalk, snapping photos of the house. The Binghams have visitors, he notes, seeing an unfamiliar car parked in the driveway. He slows his pace, idly watching the house, remembering that Charles Bingham is slated to speak at the gala tonight.

The front door opens, and there he is with his wife, Annabelle, along with another couple, and—

Holmes stops short, stunned.

Catherine.

She, too, is standing on the porch. She has her hand on the shoulder of a young boy. The two of them wave as the four adults cross to the driveway and get into the car. Moments later, they drive away—bound for the gala, judging by their formalwear.

Catherine ushers the kid inside and closes the door.

Holmes can scarcely breathe, unable to grasp his good fortune. There is no mistaking the message: fate delivered a Beauty to the doorstep of the very house where it all began.

Holmes is meant to claim her tonight.

Sully rather enjoys Barnes's startled expression when she makes her grand entrance, descending the steep flight to the cottage living room. As a fellow emerald-eyed red-head, she could have borrowed just about anything in Rowan Mundy's closet, but this pale green chiffon gown immediately caught her eye.

Now, it's caught Barnes's. "Well, look at you, Ginger-snap. My, my, my." He pretends to fan himself.

"You're pretty dapper yourself there, Barnes."

Not that she's the least bit surprised to see that the man is just as handsome, clean-shaven and dressed in black tie, as he is in his uniform, or worn jeans, or the khaki shorts and scruffy stubble he wore all day. But he's looking plenty surprised, having never seen her in any dress, much less a dress like this, with bare shoulders and a plunging neckline.

Compliments out of the way, they head out the door, picking up their conversation where they left off earlier.

Barnes is still trying to wrap his head around Sully's theory that the second victim—the youngest one, who'd been found at 46 Bridge Street, with the overkill wounds—was the killer's ultimate target. The others, she believes, were throwaway victims.

"So you think he was laying the groundwork with the first victim," he muses, as Sully locks the front door after them and puts the key into the little sequined bag she borrowed from Rowan. "And he was wrapping things up neatly with the third."

"Exactly. He wanted the second one to look like a random kill, too, in order to cover his tracks and deflect attention."

"Isn't that a little extreme?"

Sully raises a *Really, Barnes?* eyebrow.

"You're right," he says quickly. In the grand scheme of bizarre cases they've worked, this MO is well within the realm of possibility.

He hurries to the car ahead of her to open the passenger's side door—a first.

"Gee, Barnes. All I have to do is throw on a dress and you're the perfect gentleman. Maybe I should do it more often."

"Maybe you should." He flashes a perfect smile and closes the door, going around to his side.

"We still don't know who she was," Sully reminds him as he gets behind the wheel, back to the gnawing case.

"Regardless of who she was, you said earlier that his true victims might have been the people who found the bodies. So who were they?"

"At 46 Bridge? George and Florence Purcell and their two young children, Augusta and Frederick."

"And they'd never seen the dead girl before?"

"That's what they said."

"Yeah, well, I'm guessing at least one of them might have been lying."

"I'm guessing you might be right."

"I'm also guessing one of them could even have been the killer."

"I'm guessing you may be right again." Equally familiar with homicide statistics, Sully is well aware that most young female victims know, and are likely related to, their killers.

"Does this mean you'll share the reward with me when we solve the case?"

She laughs. "Dream on, Barnes. But I will share a dance with you tonight if you're lucky."

If the flagstone terrace overlooking the river was a magnificent backdrop for the sunset cocktail hour, then the Hudson Chase dining room is a positively sumptuous one for dinner. With gleaming dark woodwork and floors, richly patterned wallpaper, and delicate crystal chandeliers, the vast room is filled with vases of jewel-toned summer flowers and lit by perhaps more white votive candles than there are stars in the clear summer sky.

"OMG. This place is amazing," Kim murmurs to Annabelle as they take their seats at a round table near the speakers' podium. "Have you ever been here before?"

"Once. For my senior prom."

"Who was your date?"

"Steve Reed."

"Oh no, are you talking about the pool *again*?" Trib takes his seat beside her and sets his folded speech alongside the clustered champagne flute and wineglasses.

"Not this time. We're talking about old boyfriends," Kim says tartly. "And I'd tell you about mine, but I'd rather wait until Ross is here. So don't hold your breath, or we'll have to call the paramedics to revive you."

Trib and Annabelle laugh, but she probably isn't exaggerating. Her husband has made himself scarce all evening, contentedly chatting with anyone and everyone who isn't his wife.

The Winstons have always had a healthy marriage, but clearly, their parenting struggles are taking a toll. Annabelle isn't surprised. She just wishes Kim would stop telling her how lucky she is to have an "easy" kid.

Although Oliver did send them off with surprisingly little fanfare this evening.

When she and Trib stuck their heads into his room to say they were leaving, they found him and Catherine sprawled on the floor in front of Battleship.

"Hey, I can't believe you still have that game, Oliver," Trib said. "I haven't seen it in years."

"It was in the cupboard under my bed. Mom put it there."

Annabelle saw that he'd taken out lots of other old games she'd stashed there after the move, and stacks of books, too. Maybe he was finally growing sick of video games.

"It was my idea," Catherine told them. "I wanted to play something other than Xbox. I've been using my brother's a lot lately—but don't tell him."

Annabelle and Trib smiled at her, and then at each other.

"I told her maybe we could play baseball or something outside for a while," Oliver adds, "but she doesn't know how, and she doesn't really want me to teach her."

"Yeah . . ." Catherine grins. "Not really my thing. Sorry."

"She doesn't seem so surly to me," Trib whispered as they headed down the stairs.

"Maybe this is just an act. Or maybe she only resents her parents, and she likes the rest of us. Who knows?"

Who cares? She felt almost lighthearted as they drove over to the country club.

Even now, having listened to Kim's recap of her latest mother-daughter battle, she's finally managed to put her own troubles behind her.

"So who's sharing our table?" Kim asks Trib, gesturing at the four empty chairs alongside Ross's seat. "Are they VIPs like you?"

"I think it's some of the Mundy family."

"Well, don't let anyone steal my seat, okay? I'm going to go hunt down a glass of wine. And maybe my husband, too."

She leaves, and Trib turns around in his chair to talk to an acquaintance. Annabelle checks her cell phone, making sure there are no calls or texts from Oliver or Catherine. So far, so good.

As she waits for Trib to finish his conversation, she spots Rowan Mundy making her way over with her husband, Jake, who is directly descended from the first settlers. Handsome, charismatic, and athletic, he was a few years ahead of Annabelle in school. The Mundys' story is similar to Annabelle and Trib's. They didn't date in high school, both went away to college, and they reconnected while visiting their hometown.

A vaguely familiar couple accompanies them. The good-looking African-American man towers over all of them, and the striking redhead must be related to Rowan.

But when she introduces them as NYPD Detectives Sullivan Leary and Stockton Barnes, Annabelle realizes they're the missing persons team who tracked the serial killer to Mundy's Landing last winter and helped to save the Mundys' lives.

"Are you being honored tonight?" Annabelle asks as Rowan and Jake pause behind their seats, drawn into Trib's conversation.

Detective Leary throws back her head and laughs heartily as she sits down. "God, no. We're just here at the gala because Rowan and Jake had extra tickets. I didn't realize we'd be sitting at a VIP table."

"Don't let Sully kid you," Detective Barnes tells Annabelle. "She always expects VIP treatment."

"Um, who's the one who jets off to five-star resorts in the South Pacific on vacation? Not me."

"Not me, either, unfortunately," he returns. "Not this time."

Detective Leary tells Annabelle she's vacationing in Mundy's Landing, renting a cottage on Church Street for two weeks. "Don't ask me what *he's* doing here," she adds lightly pointing a thumb at her partner. "I can't seem to escape him, no matter where I go."

"You know you can't live without me."

As the affectionate banter continues, Annabelle notices the sparks flying between the two of them and wonders if they're more than just work partners.

"How about you?" Detective Leary asks her. "Are you being honored?"

"No, my husband is one of the speakers. He's the editor of the newspaper."

"So you live here in town?"

"They live in one of the Murder Houses," Rowan pipes up as she takes a seat across the table.

"Oh really? Which one?"

"Forty-six Bridge Street."

At Annabelle's response, the detectives exchange a sharp glance.

"What?" she asks, frowning.

Before they can respond, Stanley Vernon steps up to the podium. Reed-thin, with a bushy gray mustache and a golf course tanned face weathered with wrinkles, the longtime president of the Mundy's Landing Merchants' Association is acting as master of ceremonies this evening. He clicks on a microphone that makes a squeaking noise as he asks everyone to be seated.

Rowan will have to wait to learn why the detectives reacted that way when they learned where she lives.

She isn't so sure she wants to know.

After dark, the Bridge Street bystanders who didn't go to the gala have scattered—out to dinner, listening to the jazz trio performing in the gazebo, or perhaps to bed after a long day.

Sleep is the last thing on Holmes's mind as he creeps through backyards on the next block, following a familiar route to number 46.

From the treeline at the back of the property, he has a clear view of his Beauty in the kitchen. He moves closer, instinctively feeling around in his pocket for his lucky nickel.

The windows are wide open on this warm night, and her voice floats through the screen.

"How about sprinkles?" she asks. "Do you think you guys have any of those?"

Holmes sees that she's leaning against the counter holding a cell phone, rapidly typing on it with her thumbs while talking to a young boy. He's standing on a wobbly-looking chair rummaging through a cupboard.

"Hey, I found sprinkles! What else?"

"Is there any of that marshmallow cream stuff? I love that."

"Nope. There's nuts, if you like nuts. Sometimes my dad puts them on ice cream."

"I hate nuts."

"Me too!" the kid says, as though it's a remarkable co-incidence when, in fact, Holmes also hates nuts, just like Catherine.

Where, he wonders, is his nickel? It isn't in his pocket.

That's a bad sign.

Inside, the boy asks, "What else can we put on our sundaes?"

"Um, what do we have so far?" The girl's gaze doesn't waver from her phone. Holmes will have to rid her of it the moment he gets his hands on her.

Maybe the nickel doesn't matter right now. Things are going so well without it.

"We have ice cream, sprinkles, cereal, and maple syrup," the boy is saying. "I wish it was chocolate syrup."

He's whiny, Holmes decides.

"It's better than nothing, right?"

"I guess. I just hope it doesn't make us sick."

"Why would it make us sick?"

"Because it's kind of weird, and sometimes weird food makes people sick."

"I never get sick."

"That's good, because my real babysitter got strep throat."

"Well now I'm your real babysitter."

"Except I heard you telling your mom that you didn't want to be."

At last, Catherine looks up from her phone. "No," she agrees, "but I'm glad I am. You're a good kid, Oliver. A lot better than my brother."

"I miss him. Don't you?"

"Yeah. But don't tell anyone, okay?" she adds, scooping ice cream into a pair of bowls. "Especially him. And my mom."

For a moment, there's companionable silence.

Then the little instigator asks, "Why do you hate her?"

"My mom?" Holmes can't see Catherine's face, but he admires the way her hair sways on her back as she shakes her head. "She's the one who hates me."

"Are you sure?"

"Positive. Have you heard the way she talks to me? She never says anything nice to me."

"Nope," the kid agrees. "If my mom hated me, I'd probably cry, like, all the time."

"Yeah, that's pretty much what I do."

Holmes sincerely hopes that isn't the case, and he'll bet Indigo Edmonds would agree. Then again, she was pretty shaken up when she realized the other crybaby was dead. Even more upset than Holmes himself.

After his initial shock and dismay, he realized that it was no great loss. Not when there's another, better Catherine waiting to take her place.

She's perfect, he decides, admiring her long blond hair and tiny build. Better, even, than the other Kathryn. She was such a baby, always fussing. It's better this way.

He has no way to dispose of her without taking chances, so he left her to rot. As he ascended the ladder, her cellmate—who has, until now, been a pillar of strength—finally lost her cool. And, perhaps, her mind.

Even now, he can hear Indigo Edmonds's howling shrieks.

"Don't worry," he called down to her before he slammed the trapdoor. "It will only be a couple more days. You're the one who really matters. And you're next."

Driving around the corner onto State Street in her Honda, Deb Pelham is relieved to see that there's no sign of a traffic jam and police blockade at the intersection with Prospect. Even better, the crowd in front of number 65 is considerably smaller than it was last night.

Thank goodness.

Deb uses the remote to release the electronic gate as she drives down the block. The moment it begins to slide open, the onlookers turn and spot her. She ignores their stares and shouted questions as she pulls into the drive-way, just as she did last night.

"Hey, what's your name?"

"Do you live here?"

"Can I come inside?"

Yeah, sure. She'll just turn around and invite the whole gang to join her for a party in the Murder House.

As she reaches to disarm the alarm, she remembers what happened last night. A police officer immediately materialized to question her as she stepped out the front door, asking who she was and what she was doing there.

As soon as she explained and showed her ID, the cop relaxed and smiled at her. "The Yamazakis told us you'd be coming, Ms. Pelham. But we can't be too careful. Burglar alarms have been going off all over The Heights lately."

In light of that news, it's hardly surprising to hear about the break-in across the street.

The alarm, Deb notices, is already disarmed. Did she forget to reset it after she left last night?

Probably. She was thrown off as soon as she saw the cop, and in a hurry to get away from the Mundypalooza crazies and—speaking of crazies—go meet her friends.

Nursing her hangover all day, she's been looking forward to some solitude in a quiet house.

The Akita greets her at the door as she steps into the hall, tail wagging and excited to see her.

"Hey, there, lovely Rita. I'm so sorry, sweet girl," Deb says, kneeling to pet her. "I couldn't come this morning. You must be starved. Come on, let's go feed you."

The dog is happy to chow down, as always, but even more eager to be sprung from her prison after a day in quiet solitude. Leaving half her bowl of food, she waits at the door until Deb gets the leash. She'd been planning to walk the dog through the neighborhood, but revises the plan. She's too tired, and she doesn't feel like parading past the people outside.

Instead, she opens the French doors off the kitchen and takes the dog out into the secluded backyard. She misses having a lawn for her own dogs, as she did back when she was married to Bob. But she sure doesn't miss Bob.

Rita tugs the leash, eagerly sniffing the patio.

"What do you smell, girl? A cat? A squirrel?"

Rita pulls her along onto the grass, then tries to expand the search toward the wooded rear of the lot.

"I hate to break it to you, babe," Deb tells the dog, holding her ground, "but I'm not in the mood to get scraped up and mosquito bitten. How about if you just find a nice spot to do your thing, and then we head back inside?"

The Akita has other ideas, nosing deeper into the pachysandra. Deb steps gingerly, keeping an eye out for poison ivy and sticker vines. Rita is pawing at something on the ground, tail wagging eagerly like a drug-sniffing dog at the airport.

"What do you have, girl? Here, let me see."

Deb spots a small packet lying among the leaves. It appears to be a small wad of light-colored fabric.

At least it's not a dead rodent, she thinks. Her own dogs used to bring her squirrels. Well, the remains of squirrels.

Rita picks up the object in her mouth, willing, at last, to return to the house as long as she can carry her booty.

That's fine with Deb. She's exhausted and ready for bed. There's no way she's driving home tonight.

Back inside the house, she texts her roommate to feed and walk her own dogs. Then, leaving Rita in the kitchen, playing with her filthy little treasure, Deb walks up the back stairs.

She opens the door to Evelyn Yamazaki's bedroom, glimpses her lying in the bed, and cries out, startled.

"I'm so sorry!" Deb presses her hand over her racing heart. "I didn't realize you were here. I was just . . ."

She was just what?

As her mind races for an explanation that doesn't transform her into a guilty Goldilocks, she waits for the girl to sit up and start flinging accusations. Accurate ones, at that.

When it doesn't happen, an icy chill skids into Deb's gut. Her instinct is to flee, but she forces herself to take a closer look at the figure in the bed because she knows. She knows . . .

Hell, everybody knows what happened in this house one hundred years ago today.

And now, Deb realizes, as she backs out of the room, fumbling in her pocket for her phone with a violently trembling hand, it's happening again.

While Catherine was in the kitchen eating ice cream with the kid, Holmes snuck into the house using his key to the back door. He slipped into the natatorium, strewn with construction materials, being careful not to bump into anything.

The statue looms like a sentry in the darkness at the far end of the room. He found the inscription the night he slipped into the house when Augusta was still alive. At that time, he had no idea who Z.D.P. was. It took months to figure it out. Even now, there is no solid proof. Only a series of educated guesses based on evidence he picked up through a meticulous investigation of the events— even the rumored ones—that took place in the spring of 1904.

From the kitchen comes a clattering sound, and water running at the kitchen sink. They must be finished with their ice cream, washing out their bowls.

"It's time for you to go to bed, Oliver," he hears the girl say.

"I'm afraid," is the boy's prompt reply.

"How about if you get to stay up in your room and play video games?"

"I'm not allowed to do that."

"Not when your mom and dad are here."

"You mean I can?"

"I won't tell if you don't. Just turn off the Xbox before you fall asleep so you won't get caught, okay? Because if you do, I'll have to pretend I didn't know you were doing it."

"Okay. Thanks, Catherine." A pause. "You want to come up and play?"

"Not tonight. Go ahead."

"You mean . . . just put myself to bed?"

"Yeah. I mean, my brother does, and . . . you're twelve, right?"

"Right."

"So it's not like you get tucked into bed every night, right?"

The hesitation is a dead giveaway.

After a moment, the kid says, "Right."

To her credit, and Holmes's relief, Catherine doesn't offer to tuck in the big baby. She just wishes him a good night. After a few moments, Holmes hears footsteps padding up the stairs.

In the kitchen, only silence.

Holmes waits five minutes, ten, fifteen.

He replays her question: *So it's not like you get tucked into bed every night . . .*

How about you? he wants to ask Catherine. *Does someone tuck you into bed every night? No? Well I'll be doing that for you very soon.*

Finally, he creeps from the natatorium through the service porch. With painstaking care, he turns the knob on the kitchen door, fraction by fraction, until he feels the latch release and he can edge it open silently enough to peek in.

He thought she must have left the room, but there she is, standing near a table piled high with crap—boxes, folded stacks of clothing, small appliances, books. As oblivious to his presence as she appears to be to the Binghams' household clutter, she is focused, as before, on her phone. Only this time, she's using it to take pictures.

Holmes watches as she snaps a photo or the hallway looking toward the front door, then rotates her back to him to get a shot of the back parlor, visible through the archway. From the corner of his eye, he glimpses a shadow in the hall.

Did the kid sneak down the stairs?

He turns, but sees nothing. He can hear a car passing on the street. The headlights falling through the windows might have cast the shadow. Or perhaps it was an apparition. He's read the ghost stories about the suicidal girl who haunts the third floor.

But I know the truth behind them.

Catherine pauses to type something on her phone, and he hears the electronic swish of a sent text message.

So she is communicating with her friends—sending them pictures, apparently, of the home's interior. He wonders how the Binghams would feel about that—not that it matters. He's about to nip this little photo op in the bud.

Holmes reaches into his pocket and takes out his gun.

Irib isn't exactly "killing it," though Ross Winston just claimed he is, catching Annabelle's eye and mouthing the words across the table between bites of dessert.

Unlike Stanley Vernon, her husband isn't a natural at the podium, striding around with the mike and tossing casual quips like confetti. But he's sweetly earnest and genuine, and his affection for their hometown runs as deep as that of the Mundys and Ransoms, whose roots stretch back over three hundred and fifty years.

A strawberry confection, billowing real cream and dusted with powdered sugar, goes untouched on the china plate before Annabelle as she hangs on her husband's every word. Watching him at the podium, she loves him not in spite of his stage fright but perhaps because of it. All dressed up, his hair neatly combed to one side above wide eyes behind his glasses, he reminds her of Oliver. He's doing his best to put on a brave face and conquer his fear. He's not making it look easy by any stretch— there's no energy to waste on keeping up appearances. She can see the speech shaking in his hands even now, fifteen minutes in, as he welcomes Mayor Cochran and Ora Abrams to the stage.

Ordinarily a commanding presence, the curator is showing her age tonight. She leans heavily on her walking stick as she makes her way to the front of the room, and Dean Cochran's hand at her elbow is more necessary than showy. Which, considering Dean's style, is most unusual.

The mayor gives a short, perfect speech about how lucky he is to be here tonight to witness history and make history anew.

"Are we doing another time capsule?" Kim asks Annabelle under her breath, wearing an evil grin. "Because I can think of a few people—oops, I mean, things—I'd love to bury for a hundred years."

Annabelle wonders if she's talking about the mayor, or her husband. Ross dutifully returned to her side as dinner was served, and all seemed to go well between them until Kim decided to ask the detectives about the Armbruster case.

"My wife worries that it might happen again."

"We have a teenage daughter," Kim said, as if that explained everything. And maybe it does.

Between the salad and main course, Annabelle had wondered aloud to Trib how things were going at home, but let him talk her out of calling to check.

"And now, ladies and gentlemen, the woman who started it all, Miss Ora Abrams."

Taking the stand to resounding applause, Ora reaches up to adjust the microphone like a child straining for the forbidden bookshelf. After making an adjustment, she looks hard at the mayor. "Started it all?" she echoes, deadpan. "Just how old do you think I am, young man?"

The line brings down the house.

Even Trib seems to relax a bit after that.

He informs the crowd that there will be plenty of time later to inspect the historic cache, as the contents will become a permanent exhibit at the museum.

Then he passes a crowbar to the mayor, who passes it to Ora.

"What a moment," she says into the microphone, pronouncing the *h* sound in *what* as many people of her generation tend to do. She struggles a bit as she wedges the tip of the metal tool into the crack beneath the lid of the chest. But of course it's just for show. Annabelle happens to know that the city officials already opened the box this afternoon. The contents, safely tucked beneath a layer of muslin, weren't examined or disturbed. They just wanted to make things easier tonight.

"Welcome back to 1916." Ora's voice, like her hands, quavers with age and excitement as she lifts the lid.

The room is hushed with anticipation.

Stanley leans into the mike, saying, "And now, as Ms. Abrams takes each item from the chest, Mr. Bingham will read the corresponding description."

Ora lifts out a large packet of papers tied together with a ribbon and confers briefly and quietly with Trib. They nod, and he announces, "These are letters to the future, written by Miss Wolken's class at Mundy's Landing Secondary School. They were born in 1904 and many of their names will sound familiar."

He reads off the list of names to murmurs and exclamations of recognition from the audience.

Then it's on to the next item. Ora holds up a newspaper, which Trib announces is the perfectly preserved edition published the morning of July 15, 1916, the day the time capsule was sealed. Even with Annabelle's faulty vision, one bold black word is clearly visible in the front page headline: MURDERS.

Ora puts it aside and removes a glass ball jar filled with

something dark. Trib's chuckle spills into the microphone. "Here's another one that's easy to recognize. It's Mildred Haynes's blueberry preserves. Who wants to try some?"

A ripple of laughter puts him more at ease. He warms to the task, identifying and describing each relic as it emerges from the chest: a pair of women's shoes, a Bible, a dinner menu from the *Titanic* dated a year before it sank, a pouch filled with newly minted 1916 currency, and . . .

Ora holds up a leather-bound book.

"Let's see . . . there should be a couple of books in there that were important in 1916. Is that *Seventeen* by Booth Tarkington? It was a best-selling novel published by Harper that spring. Or is it *Dear Enemy* by Jean Webster? That one was set right here in Dutchess County and it's a sequel to *Daddy Longlegs*."

Shaking her head, Ora turns it to check the spine, then looks at the back, apparently searching for a title. She opens it and shakes her head.

"It looks like a journal. It's filled with handwriting. Let's see . . . the date on the first page is August 1, 1893, and . . . oh my."

Holmes wasn't expecting the girl to believe his whispered ruse. But she takes one look at the gun, another at his face, and she bought everything he just told her. Trusts him. Maybe even recognizes him.

He motions her to be quiet as he escorts her out the back door into the night.

"But what about Oliver? He's upstairs all alone," she hisses as soon as they're away from the house.

"No, he isn't. I already got him out."

"Where is he?"

"Waiting in my car on the next block."

"Do they have guns, too?" she asks, referring to

the mythical band of thieves she believes are prowling through the house.

"Yes. That's why I had to get you out of there right away. Shh, careful not to make any noise. I don't want them to know you got away."

"What were they going to do to me?"

"Don't worry about that, Catherine. You're safe now."

"How do you know my name?" she asks, and even in the shadowy yard, he can see suspicion in her eyes.

A wailing siren erupts in the night and panic sweeps over Holmes.

There's no time to waste. He has to get Catherine into his SUV and away from here.

"Come on," he says. "We have to run."

"But that's the police. They're coming."

"Forget it. I'll carry you."

"What? What are you—"

He slams her in the temple with the butt of his gun, and she crumples to the ground.

Staring down at the old-fashioned script in faded ink, Ora is dumbfounded.

All these years, she could only have dreamed of such a discovery. But how on earth did it get into the time capsule?

Charles Bingham is leafing through his notes, shaking his head. He leans in, away from the microphone he's holding. "I don't see any mention of a journal included in the contents, Miss Abrams."

"I suppose it was a last-minute addition," she says slowly.

Feeling all eyes upon her, she turns the stiff yellow pages with a trembling hand, scanning the dates. A curious rhythm emerges.

The first part of the journal consists of detailed daily entries that span the first two weeks of August in 1893. They become sporadic after that, with many months and often years passing between passages that seem to mark milestone events: a commencement, a wedding . . . the birth of a child.

The final batch of entries span the early summer of 1916, and they are again painstaking, though the penmanship becomes increasingly illegible. From late June into mid-July, a chronicle of the murders, interspersed with fragmented lines scribbled in an increasingly jagged slant as if to mirror the author's descent into madness. Several entries consist only of the foreboding phrase "I must do something," underlined on one page with such a vicious stroke that the pen slashed through the paper.

And then, at the end, a rambling missive—a confession?

If only Ora had thought to preview the capsule's contents before now. She could have grabbed this artifact before it became public knowledge. There's no way to keep it to herself now. The world will know the true identity of the Sleeping Beauty Killer.

"Who wrote it?" Mayor Cochran leans in.

She closes the journal, realizing that she might as well make the most of the moment. *At least*, she thinks, *the news is coming from me.*

After a lifetime of keeping the secret, she lifts the microphone and opens her mouth.

But before she can speak, a uniformed police officer hurries into the room and approaches Stanley Vernon, who is standing off to one side of the podium. The officer whispers something to him, and he in turn motions to the mayor. As the three confer briefly, Ora becomes aware of sirens in the night—and of a cell phone ringing in the audience.

And then another.

Something is happening.

All around the dimly lit ballroom, splotches of electronic glow appear as people take out their phones to look at incoming text messages or answer calls. The crowd stirs, murmurs. Mayor Cochran strides away with the police officer. Stanley Vernon is back at the podium.

"Ladies and gentlemen, the mayor has been called away on . . . an emergency. We're going to take a little intermission and give you an update shortly." He clicks off the mike and looks from Trib to Ora.

"What is it?" she asks, thoughts whirling madly, wondering whether there's any way this sudden commotion can possibly be tied to the journal in her hands. Not likely, considering that it's been locked away for a hundred years.

"I don't know how to say this any other way," Stanley tells them, "so I'll just tell you exactly what I've been told. The body of a young woman just turned up in a bed at 65 Prospect Street."

Holmes's Case Notes

I never knew my father, a predicament shared by
my mother—not in terms of her own father, whose
mental illness was the bane of her troubled childhood, but in terms of the man who impregnated
her. I presume that she knew his name, but as far as
I can tell, I am the product of a one-night stand in
Woodstock, where she was living at the time. We
moved across the river to Mundy's Landing before
I started kindergarten in the mid-nineties, as the
public school district was good, real estate was still
affordable, and Mother had an easy commute across
the river to the boutique where she read tarot cards
and created astrological charts for customers.

As outsiders in a small, insular village, we kept
to ourselves for the most part. I was an excellent
student with a passion for history, as well as an
avid reader. Mysteries were my favorite, not just
modern children's series like Encyclopedia Brown
or the Three Investigators, but classic tales about
Miss Marple, Hercule Poirot, and of course, Sherlock
Holmes.

Captivated by the unsolved local crimes from a
young age, I was determined to unravel the truth as
any of my fictional sleuths would surely have done.

I had long guessed that two of the murders might
have been staged to cover up the third. When I gained
access to records not made public, I found that indeed,
the second Beauty bore telltale signs of a personal
connection to her attacker. That fact, combined with
her young age—another detail I obtained from private
records—led me to believe that the dastardly deed
had been carried out by someone with ties to—or
perhaps, within—the Purcell household.

Upon discovering the inscription on the stone

statue, I knew that Augusta had placed the piece to commemorate the child victim. I formed an interesting theory as to the second Beauty's identity, and visited the Rockland asylum where Florence Purcell was committed when she finally lost her mind. There, I used a creative means to gain access to medical records of her stay. In the written account of Florence's tormented ravings, I learned details that were meant to be disclosed only to medical personnel.

That is how I was able to confirm Z.D.P.'s identity—as well as S.B.K.'s.

Chapter 19

When she saw the police officer scurrying toward the podium, Sully—like everyone else—knew there was trouble. Sure enough, the mayor fled with him, leaving a roomful of people to wonder what in the world is going on.

The speculation doesn't last long.

Annabelle's husband—listed in the program as Charles Bingham, but called Trib by everyone including the master of ceremonies—hurries back to the table, cell phone in hand.

Jake Mundy voices the question on everyone's mind: "What the hell is going on?"

"The pet sitter just found a female corpse at the Yamazaki house, tucked into the bed in Evelyn Yamazaki's bedroom. It isn't Evelyn."

As the others react with horrified gasps, Sully turns immediately to Barnes.

"Isn't that the house—"

"Yes," she confirms, cutting him off, already on her feet. "Let's go."

"But we're not even—"

"I know. But if this is a copycat killer, the locals are going to need all the help they can get."

* * *

Annabelle's heart pounds as she dials their home number.

Beside her, Kim is frantic. "She's not picking up her cell! Where is she?"

"Calm down," Ross tells her. "Maybe she's busy with Oliver."

"She has that phone in her hand every second of her life!"

Trying not to panic as the home phone, too, rings unanswered in her ear, Annabelle looks at Trib and shakes her head.

"Do you want to call Oliver's cell?" he asks, checking his watch.

"He's got to be in bed, and if I wake him up, what would I tell him? I can't say that—"

"Annabelle, you need to call your house!" Kim clutches her arm. "I need to talk to Catherine."

"I just called. She didn't pick up, but I'm sure she just didn't hear it."

"Why wouldn't she hear it? Why wouldn't she hear it?"

"We only have two phones, and it's a giant house. We're always losing track of them."

"Annabelle's right," Trib jumps in. "If we left both phones upstairs and Catherine is downstairs, she wouldn't—"

"They found a girl. What if—"

"No, Kim, that's crazy." Ross puts a firm hand on her arm although he, too, is beginning to look alarmed. "There's no reason to think it's Catherine."

"She's not answering her phone!"

"The two of you are barely speaking to each other right now," her husband reminds her. "She's angry. She's probably ignoring you."

"I texted her that it's a matter of life and death."

"She's probably thinking that everything is a matter of

life and death with you these days, Kim. You're smothering her with all this overprotective—"

"Shut up, Ross! Just shut up!"

Mouth pursed, he shakes his head and looks at Annabelle.

She touches Kim's hand. "I'm sure she's safe and sound at our house with Oliver."

"Your *Murder House*?" Kim flings back at her.

Digesting that, Annabelle grabs her evening bag and looks at Trib. "We need to get home and check on the kids. Please. Right now."

"I guess this means the program is over," Stanley Vernon tells Ora, gesturing at the mass exodus from the ballroom. "I presume your ride has abandoned you?"

She nods, having arrived in Cochran's limo. But as she clutches the precious leather-bound journal and absorbs the news about 65 Prospect Street, getting home the is last thing on her mind.

"I'll drive you. I have to go collect my keys and my wife—and that might take a while," Stanley adds with a fleeting smile that belies the troubled expression in his eyes. "Should I also see about having someone move this chest back to the police station for the time being?"

"Yes, I suppose that's probably for the best, until we figure out what's going to happen with . . . everything."

As he hurries away, Ora sinks into the nearest chair and opens the journal again, flipping to the final entry, dated July 16, 1916.

> *No longer does the phrase* I must do something *screech through my muddled brain.*
> *It is done.*
> *Yet I now find myself wrestling as much with my conscience as with the dilemma of what to do with this damning written chronicle I have created. There were*

times when I questioned my urges to incriminate myself, if only on paper with words meant to be read by no other eyes but my own. However, the writing itself has been cathartic, allowing me to sort my jumbled thoughts, outline my plans, and—perhaps most importantly— safely unburden my soul so that I might avoid the daily temptation to lash out and thus give myself away.

Having unleashed my pent-up rage when I dispatched Zelda from this world, I no longer have use for this journal. I have considered burning it, but the prospect turns my stomach. While I have always believed that I was writing it for my own benefit, much as a budding artist takes brush to canvas, it would be as unconscionable to set flame to these pages as it would be to reduce a vibrant Belle Epoch masterpiece to black cinders.

If I keep it in my possession, however, in the midst of an active police investigation, there is a chance that it might be discovered. I can think of only one safe place to hide it.

Thus, I have reached a decision that is perhaps shocking even to myself.

This afternoon, I am slated to join several fellow dignitaries in placing a large collection of items into a wooden chest that will then be sealed, not to be opened for one hundred years. By that time I will have long gone on to my eternal reward or damnation, having been judged by the almighty power upon which my fate rests and not by those who might read these words and fail to understand why I did what I did.

It is for them that I leave this record. I shall hereby reiterate that my motivation stemmed in love and not in hate. From the moment—

"Ora?"

Stanley Vernon touches her shoulder and she looks up, startled. He's holding his keys, trailed by his wife, Roberta.

"I've arranged for two men who are much stronger than we are to carry this out to the car."

"Thank you." She closes the journal and starts to tuck it under her arm, but Stanley reaches for it.

"Here," he says, "I can put that back inside for safe-keeping. Did you find a signature?"

She did, at the bottom of the last page.

"No," she lies, compelled to guard her secret for a precious while longer.

The drive back to The Heights, which should have encompassed five minutes, takes more than twenty. Everyone fled the gala at the same time, and they're all headed in the same direction. Sitting in the backseat of the Winstons' car in the line of traffic snaking along Battlefield Road, Annabelle holds tightly to Trib's hand. In the front seat, Kim is alternately crying and dialing her phone. She even called the police, begging them to send someone over to 46 Bridge Street.

"They said they would," she frets as Ross steers the car onto State Street at last. "Why aren't they calling me back?"

"Obviously, they have their hands full," he says grimly, gesturing at the scene ahead.

For the second time today, a police barricade has been set up at the intersection of Prospect Street. This time, though, it isn't due to a robbery at the historical society.

Trib has been texting his sources for more information about the incident at the Yamazaki house, which appears to have been staged to mirror what happened there a hundred years ago today. A bit of encouraging news—that the victim is a brunette—is unconfirmed, but it seems to have kept Kim from crossing the brink into hysteria and hurtling herself out of the car.

Now that they're at a standstill, however, she flings open her door.

"What are you doing?" Ross protests before she slams it closed, hikes up her gown, and takes off running toward Bridge Street.

He rolls down his window and calls out to her as she covers only a few steps in her stiletto sandals before twisting her ankle and falling.

"It's okay, I'll go help her," Trib says, already out of the car.

Annabelle takes a few seconds longer, bending to take off her own high heels and grab her keys from her bag. "I'm sure the kids are fine," she tells Ross as she, too, jumps out.

But she isn't really. As much as she's willing to believe that Catherine might ignore her mother's phone calls and texts, would she also neglect to answer the Binghams' landline?

As Trib pointed out, they've occasionally misplaced a handset. But she's almost positive she remembers leaving the downstairs receiver sitting in the charger base this afternoon. Catherine should have heard it ring, and she should have answered it.

But maybe she was wearing headphones. Or maybe she was asleep.

Asleep . . .

Annabelle can't help but think of the girl tucked into the bed at 65 Prospect.

Annabelle's peaceful little neighborhood has been invaded once more. Police radios and sirens drown out the crickets. Whirling red and blue dome lights, spotlights, flashing strobes, and cameras overshadow the porch lamps and fireflies. The media is already on the scene and the gawkers are out in force, clogging the sidewalks and the streets in their frenzy over this incredible development.

"I'm going home," she calls as she passes Trib, trying

to help Kim to her feet. Apparently, she's unable to put any weight on her ankle.

"Annabelle, wait, I'll go!"

She shakes her head, running as fast as she can. If, God forbid, something horrible has happened, Oliver needs her. Nothing is going to keep her away.

Not even the uniformed police officer who steps squarely into her path as she reaches the corner of Bridge Street.

"Wait a minute, where are you going?"

Forced to stop, she pants, "I'm Annabelle Bingham. I live at 46 Bridge. We met at the bus stop the other day, remember? I was going to get my son, and you were directing traffic?"

He nods, still in her way.

"I have to get to him now." She quickly explains the situation, but there's no hint of empathy or urgency in his boyish, freckled face.

He doesn't have kids—he *is* a kid, she thinks.

"I'm sorry," he says, "but I have to keep everyone back right now, because an ambulance is about to come through."

For a dead girl?

She makes a snap decision and pushes past him.

"Hey, wait! Ma'am, this is an active investigation. You can't—"

"My son needs me!" she yells over her shoulder as she runs on.

"Hey, Greenlea, what the hell is going on?" she hears another officer shout behind her.

"She's worried about her kid," the young cop calls back. "She lives in the Murder House around the corner."

"Then go with her!"

Footsteps pound on her trail. He's fast, but Annabelle, still athletic, is faster.

The Murder House around the corner.

The words chase her as she weaves in and out of the crowd. Turning onto Bridge Street, she's reassured to spot her house looking just as it should—not that it means anything. But still.

For once, there's not even a crowd gathered on the sidewalk out front. Drawn to the latest crime scene, they've lost interest, for now, in this one.

The Murder House around the corner.

Sprinting the rest of the way, she prays that she'll find Catherine watching television and Oliver asleep in his bed.

"Ma'am!" The cop's pounding footsteps are still behind her as she throws open the gate and rushes up the walk. "Ma'am, just wait a second! You can go into the house, but I'll go with you. Okay?"

Winded, she nods, stops on the porch, and fumbles with the keys. Her hands are shaking violently.

"Here, let me," Officer Greenlea says, and gently takes them from her. "I'm sure everything is fine."

She nods, allowing him to insert the key into the lock and open the door for her.

"I'm a gentleman," he says, "but I go first this time. What is your babysitter's name?"

"Catherine."

"And your son?"

"Oliver."

He nods, stepping over the threshold, looking around, and beckoning for her to come inside. "Catherine?" he calls. "Catherine?"

Annabelle's heart is racing from the run, and from the fear. "Catherine!"

No reply.

She hurries toward the stairs, telling the officer, "She might be asleep on the couch in the parlor back there. I'm going to check my son's room."

"Catherine?" she hears him calling as she rushes to the

second floor, remembering her strange dream the other night.

But this isn't a nightmare, she reminds herself, reaching for the knob to open his door. This is reality.

Stepping into his room, she sees that there is no stone angel lying on Oliver's pillow.

There is no Oliver, either.

The bed is still neatly made and it's just like the room itself. Empty.

With Barnes at the wheel, Sully had intended to race to police headquarters in Mundy's Landing to see how they could help. But there is no racing along Battlefield Road tonight.

"This has got to be the unluckiest small town in the world," Barnes says, shaking his head as he stares ahead at the unforgiving traffic. "What are the odds?"

"I'd say they're pretty damned high, under the circumstances. This town has gone out of its way to draw attention to the 1916 murders, and that's a double-edged sword. It's not as if they could pick and choose the audience for all that media attention."

"Note to the criminally insane: please disregard this press release."

"Right?" She shakes her head. "Somewhere out there, some lunatic has been waiting to take his turn in the spotlight and prove that he can accomplish what the Sleeping Beauty Killer did. Pure hubris."

"So you think he's going to reenact the crimes at all three Murder Houses on the anniversaries of the crimes?"

"I think he's going to try."

"After this, the cops are going to be staking out the other two locations. How does he think he's going to get past them?"

Sully shrugs, troubled. He must have reason to think it's possible—and he might be one step ahead of them all.

Annabelle was wrong.

This *is* a nightmare.

"Yeah, I need backup at 46 Bridge," she hears Officer Greenlea saying into his phone. "We have two missing kids."

Their quick, frantic search of the house from top to bottom turned up no sign of Catherine or Oliver. Somehow, Annabelle has managed—so far—to keep from dissolving into tears or panic.

"Mrs. Bingham? How old is your son?" the young cop is asking her, blatant shock and concern radiating from his blue eyes. He wasn't expecting to find this. He was expecting to find . . .

Catherine and Oliver, of course. Business as usual.

But then, this *is* business as usual at a Murder House.

"Oliver is twelve."

"*Twelve?*" he echoes. "And your sitter?"

"Thirteen."

He nods, relaying that information to the person on the phone.

She knows how it sounds—a twelve-year-old boy with a babysitter. Especially one as young as Catherine. She should explain, but right now, it's all she can do to remain on her feet and coherent.

"They're on their way," the cop says, hanging up his phone. "Look, I know you're worried about your son. Are you sure he wouldn't have left the house on his own?"

"No. No way. Not at night. Not Oliver."

"And your babysitter . . ."

"She might have. She's been threatening to run away. But Oliver is—"

"Wait a minute—the girl, Catherine, threatened to run away? When? Recently?"

"Yes. Her mother—my friend—said she's been talk-ing about it a lot lately. But that doesn't mean—I mean, I don't think she'd just leave my son."

"No, but she might take him with her."

Annabelle is already shaking her head. "He wouldn't go."

"Forgive me for a second here, ma'am, but if a beautiful thirteen-year-old girl asked me to run away with her when I was twelve, well . . ." He shrugs.

His expression, which had already begun to shift when she mentioned the kids' ages, is now laced with far more objectivity than concern. She supposes she can't blame him, all things considered. But he doesn't know Oliver. Doesn't know that he's the kind of kid who wouldn't—

The front door opens. "Annabelle!"

Trib.

"Kim's ankle might be broken," he calls as she and Of-ficer Greenlea hurry to the foyer. "I had to leave her there. I promised I'd text as soon as—"

He stops short, seeing her with the cop.

"Trib . . ."

"Where's Oliver?" he asks hoarsely, and all she can do is shake her head.

Stepping into the Mundy's Landing Police Department, Sully and Barnes find the anticipated chaos. Called in to aid the tiny local force, a cluster of gray-uniformed state troopers, faces somber beneath their broad-brimmed tan hats, is being briefed in a glass-windowed conference room. Wilbur is so busy on the desk phone that he couldn't bite into a cookie if Sully had brought him one, which of course she has not.

Before she has a chance to ask for Nick, he strides in the door, summoned from a sound sleep between shifts.

"Can we help?" she asks, knowing the answer is going to be no, but feeling compelled to ask.

To her surprise, he says, "Maybe. We've got two missing kids, and they were last seen at 46 Bridge Street. That's the location where—"

"We know," she says quickly, mind racing. "We've been looking into the 1916 case, and we were with the Binghams tonight at the gala. Do the children belong to them?"

"The boy does. He's twelve. The girl is a thirteen-year-old neighbor, and she was babysitting for the kid. Overprotective parents. Don't ask."

She wasn't going to ask. She's seen firsthand the tragic results of underprotective parenting. How can she blame any parent, especially in Mundy's Landing, for taking excessive precautions?

"Does the girl match the description of the one who just turned up on Prospect Street?" Barnes asks.

"No. We've already tentatively ID'd her." He reaches into his pocket, takes out a piece of paper, and unfolds it to show them.

Sully immediately recognizes the missing persons flier she'd seen posted on the bulletin board in the station vestibule.

"It's Juanita Contreras?"

The lieutenant nods. "Looks that way."

Barnes shakes his head. "Tragic."

"It is," Colonomos agreed as he shoves the paper back into his pocket.

Sully and Barnes exchange a knowing glance. Juanita Contreras isn't vulnerably young, she isn't particularly attractive, and her family isn't prominent or local. She barely blipped the missing persons annals leading up to her role in this high-profile case.

"What about the two kids who just went missing? Any leads?"

"My gut tells me that they're runaways. The girl has

been talking about it to anyone who will listen. But I'm on my way over there right now."

"Want us to come along?"

He hesitates, then shakes his head. "I don't think that's a good idea."

"But—"

"I'll call you if I need you," he says tersely as he walks away.

Sully looks at Barnes. The message in his eyes is as loud and clear as the one Colonomos just sent: *You don't belong here.*

"Mrs. Bingham?"

Sitting at the kitchen table as Trib stands in the adjoining parlor talking with Officer Greenlea, who's filling out a report, Annabelle looks up to see Lieutenant Nick Colonomos standing over her.

"I'm sorry about your son."

"Don't say that!" she responds sharply.

"I only meant that I know how hard it is, not knowing where he is right now."

"I know, but it sounded like . . ."

"I'm sorry." He pauses, his dark eyes troubled and lined with dark circles. "I just wondered if you could show me Oliver's room?"

"Sure." She grips the table as she stands.

He puts a firm hand on her elbow to help her—so firm that she's reminded of the presumption by law enforcement that the vast majority of abducted children have been taken by family members, often the parents themselves.

Does he think . . .

Of course he doesn't. And even if he does, hundreds of witnesses will confirm that she was at the gala all evening, along with Trib and Ross and Kim.

The Winstons are, at the moment, being transported to the hospital in an ambulance—perhaps the very ambulance that was so obviously unneeded at the Yamazaki house. They're going not just because Kim injured her ankle, but because she's in the midst of a severe panic attack. Annabelle overheard Trib on the phone with Ross, who said she had to be sedated when she heard that Catherine is missing.

Ross firmly believes she ran away. The police seem to be leaning in that direction as well, despite the fresh homicide.

Trib and Annabelle might be inclined to believe the theory, too—if they didn't know their son so damned well.

"Has Oliver mentioned anything about running away?" Lieutenant Colonomos asks her as they ascend the stairs.

"No. He wouldn't do that. Is that what everyone is thinking?"

"It's one theory."

Reaching the door to Oliver's room, Annabelle turns to face him. Desperate to get through to him, heedless of protocol, she addresses him by his first name. "Nick, you can't make any assumptions based on age or statistics or circumstances. My son is missing. Something is wrong."

He nods and assures her that they're going to do everything they can to find him. But she can tell from his expression that he isn't entirely with her. There's a dead girl around the corner. He has other priorities.

Earlier, she'd left Oliver's bedroom door open in her frantic, futile race to find him. Now, as she steps over the threshold again and looks around, a lump forms in her throat. The room is just as it was when they left for the gala a few hours ago.

Battleship is back on the stack of old games he'd taken out of the cupboard, alongside piles of books.

She remembers thinking he must have grown nostalgic for the childhood possessions she'd stashed away in the cupboard beneath the bed; remembers Catherine saying it was her idea to play Battleship; remembers—

Hide-and-seek.

Nick Colonomos is asking her something—she's hearing words coming from his mouth, but they have no meaning.

An idea has formed in Annabelle's head. An idea so unlikely—and yet not—that she can only grab on to it like a lifeline that may or may not be untethered.

Striding over to the bed, she bends down and opens the cupboard door.

There, stretched on an array of patterned tiles lain across the bottom of the cupboard like a floor, wearing headphones that are plugged into a handheld video game, is Oliver.

From the Sleeping Beauty Killer's Diary
July 16, 1916

. . . I shall hereby reiterate that my motivation stemmed in love and not in hate. From the moment I first glimpsed my wife, I was overcome by emotion the like of which I had never before experienced.

Seventeen years ago, on a warm summer evening, fate propelled me to Springwood, the Hyde Park mansion owned by the family of my old boarding school friend Franklin, a distant cousin of former President Theodore Roosevelt, at that time the newly elected governor of New York.

Teddy was in attendance that night, regaling a rapt crowd with tales of his adventures on San Juan Hill the previous summer.

When I stepped out onto the portico for a breath of fresh air, my eye fell upon a beauty seated with a book on a garden bench. Dressed all in white, with rippling flaxen hair, she looked like an angel. So enchanted was she by the book on her lap that she failed to hear me approach until my shadow fell over the page.

I asked what she was reading before I ever asked her name. The story, she said, was "Sun, Moon, and Talia," a seventeenth-century work by Giambattista Basile. I asked whether she knew the tale was the basis for Charles Perrault's later work "The Sleeping Beauty in the Wood." She did know that, and much more.

Her name was Florence.

Before the night had drawn to a close, I knew that she would provide salvation from the abyss.

We wed the following year. She moved in with Father and me. He, too, was smitten with my bride. Too smitten, though I did not guess that then—or that she would return his affection.

I should have known. Others had always found my father a commanding yet gregarious man, while I considered him overbearing and controlling, as did my poor sister. I fear I turned a blind eye to my sister's plight. At last she escaped his insufferable house—and, I suspect, his nocturnal visits to her chamber—by tying a noose around her neck and hanging herself from the cupola stair rail.

Plagued by guilt after Augusta took her own life, I in turn escaped, embarking alone on the journey the three of us were supposed to make to the World's Fair. It was my first taste of freedom, yet I dutifully returned to Father.

He trampled my youthful rebellion and I submitted to his authority, but always, always, I knew I would flee the moment I had the means. When I met Florence, I fantasized that the two of us would be vagabonds together. She had grown up destitute, a charity case whose benefactors clothed her, educated her, and allowed her to mingle with the right sort of people. She would have me—but only if I continued to live in the world she longed to inhabit. And so I allowed Father to mold me into his own image.

By day, I was a respectable banker, filling his chair at the bank after his retirement, which—aha!— coincided with my marriage. By night, I climbed the stairs to the cupola and trained my telescope upon the moon and stars. I buried myself in the poetry that—much like I myself—had once captivated my wife's attention.

Now she turned away from me in our marriage bed. If we had ever discussed the matter—and we did not—then she might have blamed her distance upon my obsessions, and I, in turn, my obsessions upon her distance.

It matters little now.

Perhaps Florence assumed, when she informed me that she was with child, that I had been too busy or too detached to recall the date of our last physical encounter. But just as her abrupt change of heart beneath a golden harvest moon had not escaped my attention, nor had the affection between my father and my wife.

That, however, appeared to have dissipated due to her delicate condition—small satisfaction for me.

Knowing I could not bear the sight of her until the summer, I gathered cohosh to ensure that she would deliver the child in early spring, just as soon as it had sufficiently developed, not because I wanted it to survive, but because I did not.

It would have to enter the world in order to exit, and I deemed that it would do so according to my command, in the unsettling glare of the rare blue moon.

Watching my wife cradling her swollen womb, I could see that she already dearly loved the life within. I knew, too, that the longer and more deeply you love another being, the more you suffer upon losing it.

I commissioned a builder to construct a small room—a nursery, I called it—adjacent to our bedroom. He wanted to add a window; I told him— and my wife, and my father—that I could not bear to think of the child catching a deadly draft.

In February, Father's favorite cousin, Griselda, passed away. In keeping with family custom, he requested that the child be named after her if it was a girl, and we agreed. Her middle name, my wife said, should be Delphine, after her late mother.

"And what if it's a boy?" my father asked.

"Then perhaps it should be named for its father," I said pointedly, and left the two of them to ponder that.

The child was born according to plan, beneath a full blue moon. I roiled with resentment as I stood at the cradle, much like the neglected antagonist in Perrault's fairy tale who cursed the newborn Beauty.

Intending to erase every bit of evidence that the

child had even existed, I burned the birth document
at the hearth before the ink was dry. Yet I found myself
wrestling with strange bursts of affection for the tiny
creature, even as my father ignored its existence, and
my wife's as well.

Just as he was not man enough to own his
mistakes, I was not man enough to correct them. The
moon waned and still little Zelda, as my wife called
her, was alive.

At Easter, claiming that he pined for warmer
weather, Father abruptly decided to visit an old
acquaintance in the Carolinas, leaving us alone with
the child and the servants. Now man of the house at
last, I finally summoned the mettle to do what had to
be done.

I crept into the nursery one night, unaware that
Florence was in the room, silently watching me
from her rocking chair in the corner. As I pressed
the pillow against the infant's chubby face, my wife
leaped upon me like a snarling lioness.

Time runs short, as do the pages in this journal;
thus, I will not recount the conversation that ensued.
In the end, she begged me to allow the child to live.
I said that I would, under the condition that it never
see the light of day in this small village. Having
endured the shame of my sister's suicide and the
whispers about her motive, I could not endure more
of the same over a bastard daughter.

"If you must send her away, then I shall go, too,"
Florence told me. Yet I knew she lacked the means to
leave, and I shall confess that even then, I could not
bear to let her go.

Desperate, I proposed a solution. We would send
word to Father that Florence and the child would be
joining him in the South for a month, and I would
send the servants away for the duration of her trip.
During that time, I would claim that the child had
died along her journey.

Florence rightfully declared it a preposterous plan. But she was crazed with the need to save her child, and herself. She had nowhere to turn but to me, and she knew she must atone for her dreadful sin. She needed me—and I her.

The plan worked—for a time.

Keeping up appearances, I bid farewell to my wife and daughter on the crowded train platform in Hudson. They disembarked in New York City, where I met them under cover of darkness and transported them back home to the small windowless chamber.

A week later, I announced that the child had died en route to Carolina. A bit later, I reported that my wife had returned alone and bereft. We accepted condolences and went on with our lives, keeping the child hidden away in the nursery where my wife could tend to her, mothering to her heart's content. I provided the servants with a handsome severance, telling them my wife's condition was tenuous and she preferred the quiet, empty house.

I never again saw Father alive. That summer, he suffered a stroke in Georgia, and then another that proved fatal. At last, I was free, yet now encumbered by a dreadful secret. Too late, I came to realize that I might have come to accept the child with Father's pervasive presence gone from my life. But it was too late to undo what I had done. I could hardly produce in public a child who had remarkably come back to life.

Bound by our wretched secret, Florence and I found our way back to each other's arms. In January 1910, not long after the great daytime comet lit the skies as if to herald her arrival, another daughter was born, this time my own. I named her for my lost sister. My affection for Augusta Amalthea eclipsed any glimmer I might once have felt for the illegitimate Zelda, in whose face my father's black eyes glittered, and in whose small body, I knew, his black soul lived on.

I insisted that we move her to the vacant third floor so that my daughter could occupy the nursery. I allowed Florence to fill a small room at the back of the house with toys and every comfort a child could desire. For my own part, I ensured that she would never escape. Some might have considered it a cell and yet, as I reminded my wife every day, I had allowed the child to live. I had allowed the adulteress to stay under my roof despite her betrayal.

Still dependent on my benevolence much as she had been on the benefactors of her youth, she had no choice but to carry on as we had, tending to one child on the second floor and the other on the third.

It was unbearably hot up there with the windows closed in the summer months. In the midst of a terrible heat wave, Florence begged me to remove the locks so that she might let the fresh air into the room. I refused. I didn't trust the girl. Imagine if she escaped to wander the town and share her tale? Florence did not argue. She knew that she, too, would be incriminated if Zelda were discovered.

I did not visit the girl once my own daughter was born, but Florence told me that she shared our love of literature, implying that she, too, escaped her oppressive existence through her books and her imagination.

The years passed, and we conceived a son. Augusta was quite jealous, but I spoiled her by indulging her whims and allowing her to keep a little orange kitten. Every night when I came home, she would tell me of her adventures with Marmalade.

I had forbidden Florence to introduce my precious Augusta to the bastard half sister, and she swore she never would. But one day not long ago, when I asked little Augusta how she had spent the rainy afternoon, she said, "Why, Papa, I played with the angel in the attic."

I knew, when I looked at my wife's face, that she

had betrayed me once again—this time not with her flesh, but with her word.

After our daughter had been soundly tucked in that night, I confronted Florence. She confessed that Augusta had become so frightened hearing thumps from the ceiling above her bed, that she foolishly told her the fanciful tale of a secret guardian angel who lived in the attic. One morning, inevitably, she carelessly neglected to lock the door to the third-floor stairwell, and Augusta snuck up after her.

Blind with rage, I seized the small axe beside the woodstove and brandished it at my wife. She fled in terror, and I chased her to the hall, where I hurtled the axe as she attempted to rush up the stairs. It narrowly missed her, landing with its blade embedded in the wooden newel post.

Had it found its mark, I would have lost everything.

In the sobering light of morning, I realized that Zelda must now meet the fate I had imposed at her cradle. I was no longer too cowardly to carry out my intention, but I knew I must be cautious.

In retrospect, I suppose it would have been simpler to murder the girl and immediately dispose of her body. But my mind has been clouded with fury and, perhaps, delusion. I was compelled to see her lain out like Perrault's Beauty in the Wood, a scene I had envisioned many times over the years.

I remembered Miss Lizzie Borden, and how rumors of a stranger roaming the streets of Fall River at the time of her parents' murder had introduced a shred of reasonable doubt. What if there had been a similar murder in Fall River not long before that of her parents? Then no one would have suspected her of the murders—particularly if a third incident followed. The police would have been caught up in a frenzied search for a madman, and the true culprit would have escaped accusation.

When, in my search for two additional Beauties, I

came across those shameless women at the Pleasure Park, I could not help but think of my wife. I would punish them as I could not punish her when she brazenly embarked on the illicit affair that had nearly destroyed us.

When I had to decide where I would deposit the corpses, I knew that I must choose households similar to our own. Twelve years ago, after Dr. Silas Browne attended Zelda's birth, I detected a glimmer of disapproval in his eyes at my perhaps unenthusiastic response to his hearty congratulations. I bore no vengeance against my neighbors Julius and Sarah Palmer when I chose their household on Schuyler Place. Their children are grown and there are vacant beds throughout their home.

Two weeks ago, when the corpse was discovered at the Browne household, Florence was concerned for our safety. It never dawned on her that I might be behind the dastardly crime.

A week later, I intended to kill Zelda as methodically as I had the whore. But when the time came, it resulted in a considerable mess, and I spent hours scrubbing the room of evidence. For her eternal sleep, it gave me great satisfaction to choose Father's long-vacated bedroom, just steps away from our own at the top of the stairs, and far from my precious Augusta's at the end of the hall.

It was Florence who discovered her, of course.

And Florence who claimed never to have seen her before in her life.

Perhaps she suspects my role.

And yet, perhaps she, too, is relieved that our long nightmare has come to an end.

The guilty have been punished. Justice has been served. I am no coward.

And now, it is time for me to dress for the ceremony on the Village Common, where I shall slip this volume into the chest where it will remain safely hidden.

I close this final entry with my signature and a stanza from Oscar Wilde's "The Ballad of Reading Gaol." He penned the words, quite fittingly, upon his release from a long incarceration.

I shall do the same.

Sincerely,
George H. Purcell

And all men kill the thing they love,
By all let this be heard,
Some do it with a bitter look,
Some with a flattering word,
The coward does it with a kiss,
The brave man with a sword!

Chapter 20

Thursday, July 7

"Mom! Where are you? Mom!"

"I'm right here!" Not taking the time to dry her hands, Annabelle quickly steps out of the first-floor bathroom to find an anxious Oliver standing right outside the door. "I told you where I was going."

"But you said you'd be right back."

She swallows her frustration.

In the week since Oliver turned up safe and Catherine vanished, the path through the daily minefield has been explosive at every turn, and there's no way to shield him from the fallout.

His bewilderment at seeing her in his bedroom that night with a police officer quickly turned to anxiety when the room filled with people, including several police officers.

"Why were you hiding under there?" Nick Colonomos had asked him, once Annabelle and Trib had taken turns hugging their son with relief and managed to calm his nerves. "Did something happen that made you afraid?"

Ah—the mother of all loaded questions.

Oliver hesitated, looking at Annabelle, who nodded and told him to tell the truth.

"I was afraid because my parents were out," he admitted. "I don't like to be alone, and Catherine didn't want to come upstairs with me when I went to bed."

"Why not?"

"She was busy texting her friends."

"So you came up here and hid under the bed?"

Oliver shook his head, explaining that the cubby is his secret hideout. He'd cleared out the stuff Annabelle had stored there and used the old pool tiles to create a floor. He equipped it with a flashlight and a couple of pillows for lounging.

"He likes it there because it makes him feel safe in this big house," Annabelle clarified for Lieutenant Colonomos, who was writing it all down in a notepad, and for the other cops who were there. All those brave, uniformed men, even the clean-cut young Officer Greenlea, were thinking the same thing, she knew: This kid was acting like a big baby.

Greenlea was the one who said to Annabelle, almost accusingly, "So you knew about this hideout? But you didn't look there for him?"

"I didn't know he was spending time in there, no. It didn't occur to me to look there when I first came up."

"And you didn't call out to him when you came into the room?"

"I did, but he was wearing headphones. He didn't hear me. And because Catherine is missing, I guess I jumped to the wrong conclusion."

"Catherine is missing?" Oliver asked in a small voice.

There was no protecting him from the truth, or from his pivotal role in the investigation. He's since been questioned several times, but can shed no light on the disappearance.

Her friends said she'd been texting with them, and that she'd mentioned lately that she hated her mother and wanted to run away from home—most recently, that very morning.

It was a bitter pill for Kim to swallow.

She and Ross have been in seclusion all week at home with Connor, whom they retrieved from camp. They won't let him out of their sight, and Annabelle doesn't dare let Oliver have any contact with him because it will mean subjecting him to Kim's hysteria.

She and Trib have been trying to downplay the fact that Catherine might have been abducted, or that there might be a connection to the copycat crime that occurred the same night at the Yamazaki household.

She's been praying, like everyone else in town, that one has nothing to do with the other. But if the prevailing theory is correct, and Catherine left this house of her own accord, wouldn't she have come home by now? Or at the very least, wouldn't she have contacted her parents to let them know she's all right? Especially since the media has gone into overdrive trumpeting headlines like THE SLEEPING BEAUTY KILLER LIVES and MORE MUNDY MURDER.

Juanita Contreras, the young woman whose body turned up at 65 Prospect Street, had disappeared after leaving work at a White Plains mall about a month ago. No one knows where she's been in the interim, and there are no leads. She'd been dead for well over twenty-four hours when she was found.

The police and the media have been interviewing residents of The Heights all week, trying to find someone who saw something out of the ordinary. But as Trib put it in his editorial, "During these extraordinary times in Mundy's Landing, who among us hasn't encountered a stranger? Now we wonder whether a cold-blooded killer was lurking behind the innocuous mask of a benign face."

There's no doubt in anyone's mind that the person who staged her body at the Yamazaki house might attempt a repeat performance in this house tonight.

Thus, the Binghams have been under police guard all week. Annabelle and Oliver have left only for daily appointments with Dr. Seton, who's helping Oliver process what's happened—to the tune of over two thousand dollars. The rest of the time, they're stuck at home, getting to know various police officers who take turns standing guard over the house—and yes, over the family as well.

It helps somehow that Steve is here, still working on the pool. At least he's someone to talk to. Someone who isn't distraught over a missing child, anyway.

Annabelle has tried to comfort Kim the best she can, speaking to her for hours on the phone. But they both know that if Catherine didn't run away, then something terrible has happened to her. Having experienced a few frantic moments thinking Oliver was missing, Annabelle can't imagine the hell her friend is experiencing.

Trib goes to the office every morning and comes home every night to sleep in Oliver's bed so that Oliver, too frightened to stay alone, can share their bed with Annabelle. Embarrassed, he made her promise never to tell anyone.

"Not Connor," he said, "and not his parents, and not Catherine, if she comes back. Not the policemen, either."

Their incredulous reaction to the fact that he'd had a babysitter had not escaped Oliver.

Annabelle promised.

She wouldn't have been comfortable letting him spend the night alone in his room right now even if he'd been willing. She's been carrying her utility blade around in her pocket, just in case . . .

Just in case a painted window sash needs to be opened?

Just in case a maniac breaks into the house in the dead of night?

But the hypervigilance is wearing thin. She hasn't had a moment to herself in a week, waking or otherwise. Not even in the bathroom, she thinks now as she follows Oliver back to the kitchen, where they were about to sit down to a dinner of canned soup and the last of the crackers.

Trib ran out to the store over the weekend, but they've gone through everything he bought and nearly all the staples. Sooner or later, she's going to have to go to the supermarket.

Later, she thinks.

Everything can wait until later.

Except rest. Seven nights sharing a bed with Oliver have taken a toll. He thrashes in his sleep—when he's sleeping. When he's not, and she is, he wakes her up. And in the rare moments when Oliver is slumbering peacefully, she finds herself lying awake, running over the details in her mind. At this point, she hasn't slept more than an hour or so at a time since last Wednesday night—and even then, she was tormented by nightmares and speculation about the Purcell family mystery . . .

And intruders.

She told Officer Greenlea about the figure she'd seen watching the house a week ago. He was concerned, and took down the information, promising he'd check into it.

But what, she wondered then—and wonders now—does that even mean? You can't hunt down a shadow long after it's faded away.

He's trying to reassure her that the authorities are doing their best to find the culprit and prevent what happened at 65 Prospect from happening at 46 Bridge.

And she's trying to pretend that it isn't inevitable.

"I'm not really hungry," Oliver tells her as she puts two bowls of soup on the table. It's too warm for soup, even with the window fans—unearthed at last—stirring the air.

The silver lining to having been trapped in the house all week: she's managed to unpack and organize the rest of their belongings. She was embarrassed last week, hearing one cop telling another that the kitchen must have been ransacked.

At least now the household is in order, and she's no longer fixated on crimes that took place a hundred years ago. She doesn't dare allow herself to go down that road again. She needs to focus every ounce of energy on getting through today.

And tonight. And tomorrow.

"Would you rather have a sandwich?" Annabelle asks Oliver, opening the fridge to see if there's any cheese, or at least some jelly to spread on the remaining heels of bread.

"No, thanks."

Good. No cheese, no jelly.

"Listen," she says, "I'm not that hungry either, but we have to eat. So let's eat the soup. We'll go to the store tomorrow."

Tomorrow, when the worst is behind them.

Tonight is the night—July 7. After it has passed uneventfully, she can breathe a sigh of relief.

"Are the police still going to be here with us then?" Oliver asks.

"For a little while longer, I think. Okay?"

What is she thinking, asking him if he's okay with that? It's not like they have any choice in the matter.

To her surprise, Oliver says, "I like having them here. I don't want them to go."

She smiles faintly. "Is it because Officer Greenlea played Xbox with you?"

The cop, in his early twenties, is familiar with all the video games Oliver likes to play. He hung around after his shift the other night to beat him soundly at one of them, and Annabelle was grateful for the reprieve.

"It's because I feel safe when they're here," Oliver said. "If they go, I don't want to stay here."

Even a kid without his issues would be skittish in light of what's gone on. Dr. Seton thought it would be a good idea if they could get away from Mundy's Landing for a while. But Trib can't leave the paper, and where would she go alone with Oliver? There are no close out-of-town friends and relatives with whom they would feel comfortable inviting themselves to stay at a moment's notice.

There used to be plenty: cousins, old college roommates, family friends, former colleagues. But Annabelle and Trib have allowed time and distance—and yes, Oliver's anxiety issues—to relegate those relationships to Facebook and annual Christmas cards. Their lives, and their support system, are centered here in Mundy's Landing.

"We could charge a hotel room on a credit card," Trib suggested last week, when they dismissed the idea of reaching out to far-flung acquaintances, with all the accompanying complicated explanations—not to mention the anxiety and perhaps panic Oliver would experience staying under a stranger's roof.

"We're almost maxed out, between the move and all the unexpected doctor bills," Annabelle reminded him.

They decided to scrape together the money anyway, having momentarily forgotten that in addition to Mundy-palooza and the latest media frenzy, it was Fourth of July weekend. There were no vacancies within well over an hour's drive. To find a room, she and Oliver would have had to travel a considerable distance away from Trib, home, and police protection. It might not make sense to stay here, but it didn't make sense to leave, either.

She keeps telling herself that Oliver is better off in familiar surroundings. And she herself is better off if she faces the reality of living here, instead of running scared. This is her home, and she's stuck with it.

No one is going to try anything with an armed cop in the house.

Besides . . .

Her saving grace—the one thought that keeps floating through her mind on a tide of guilt—is that unlike the Sleeping Beauties, past and present, Oliver is a boy.

Does that mean he's safe?

Of course. He's safe, and their family is safe. No one harmed the Yamazakis, and no one harmed those families a hundred years ago.

No one is going to harm us.

Opening the trapdoor for the first time in a week, Holmes doesn't know what to expect.

As tempted as he was to visit Catherine after he'd installed her in the dungeon beside Indigo Edmonds, he forced himself to take an enormous step back.

Grabbing her had been reckless and dangerous. He's gotten away with it, yes. But barely. And only because she'd mentioned that she was considering running away.

That doesn't mean anyone—law enforcement, locals, media, or even her own parents—truly believes that's what happened to her. But at least it's in the realm of possibility.

For now.

He'd snatched her because the opportunity presented itself when he was crazed with frustration over the death of his third Beauty, and delirious with exhaustion. He hadn't been in his right mind.

He is now, and he has been all week.

Well-rested, well-prepared, he's going to move ahead according to plan.

As he opens the trapdoor, a terrible stench hits him.

The dead Beauty.

He left her there to rot, and rot she has.

Holmes smiles. It can't have been a pleasant week in the dungeon. His second Beauty might welcome the alternative.

"Soup's on," Barnes calls to Sully as she sits in the living room reading this morning's *Tribune*, with its bold black headline AREA POLICE ON HIGH ALERT.

"Please tell me it's not soup," Sully says, putting her empty iced tea glass down on top of the newspaper so that the box fan won't blow it around.

In the kitchen, Barnes is setting out the steaks charcoal-grilled on the small Weber he bought for the backyard.

"It's not soup," he tells her. "Everything is cold, except your steak. Because you never listen to me."

"I don't like it rare."

"You made me ruin a great piece of meat."

"Thanks. I think." She sits at the table. He's set it, as every night this week, with a lit votive candle and a couple of yellow wildflowers stuck in what he calls his "Bud vase"—an empty Budweiser bottle.

Barnes opens the fridge and removes a couple of beers, some plastic tubs containing Price Chopper deli potato salad and coleslaw, and a bowl of green pods sprinkled with sea salt.

"Is that edamame?" she asks.

"It is. I miss real food."

"Hey, rigatoni à la Sully is real food," she protested, having cooked her specialty for last night's dinner.

"Okay, A—I wouldn't necessarily say that, and B—I'm talking about Japanese food. And Thai. And Chinese."

"There's Chinese food here."

"I mean good takeout. Tell me you wouldn't kill for some Szechuan Emperor right now."

Yeah, she would.

And when she's in New York, she tells Barnes, she would also kill for the decent night's sleep she's had every night here.

"You can't have everything," he says with a shrug.

"Sure you can. You just can't have it all at once."

Barnes cuts into his steak and proclaims it perfectly done. "Not too red inside, not too charred outside. How about yours? Well done enough for you?"

"We'll see." She stabs it with her fork cuts off a small piece. No blood—always good sign. And a grim reminder. "So what do you think?" she asks Barnes.

"I think that if you're not hungry, you can turn it into a nice pair of shoes."

"What?"

"The steak. It killed me to cook it through, because no one should eat leather, but—"

"I meant what do you think about tonight. And you knew that."

"Yeah. I knew that. But I'm sick of talking about it."

He's also sick of Mundy's Landing. But she refused to accompany him to the Adirondacks, and he refused to leave her alone at the cottage.

So here they are, a week later, settled into this odd semblance of small-town domesticity. They spend their evenings at this table and on the porch swing, recapping days spent searching for leads in Catherine Winston's disappearance and trying to link it to Juanita Contreras's.

Some vacation.

It's not official business, rather an independent investigation of their own volition. But as Ron Calhoun said this afternoon when they saw him getting out of his car, home to catch a few hours' sleep, forget procedure—even with the state troopers on the job, the MLPD needs all the help it can get.

"I'm sick of talking about it, too," she tells Barnes. "But we have to. Time is running out. So what do you think is going to happen tonight?"

Silence.

She watches Barnes cut off another piece of steak, chew thoughtfully, and wash it down with a swig of beer.

Then he sets down his fork and looks at her. "I think your friend Nick Colonomos is going to nab some lunatic trying to move a dead girl into 46 Bridge Street. That's what I think. You?"

"I think you're right. And based on what we know, I'm afraid it's going to be Catherine Winston."

A faraway voice reaches Indi's ears.

"It's time. Come on."

It's Tony, waking her up for school.

She feels him shaking her, and he's hurting her arm. Her entire body hurts. She's sick. She has to stay in bed today.

"Get up. Let's go."

She burrows into the pillow, but there is no pillow. There is no bed. There is no Tony.

Someone is crying.

Not Kathryn. Kathryn died.

Not Juanita. She died, too.

There's someone else, she remembers. Another voice. Here in the dark. Someone new.

The man grunts, close to her ear, and Indi feels herself being lifted.

Her parched lips struggle to form the word. At last, it spills into the dark.

"Why?"

"Because," he says simply, "it's your turn. And because you were born under a blue moon. That's why I chose you."

Blue moon.

Yes.

"Blue moon . . ."

Her mother's voice, singing, drowns out the ugly sound of a blade flipping open in his hand.

"You saw me standing alone . . ."

It's the last sound she'll hear on this earth . . . *Or maybe*, she thinks as she imagines herself swooping into the night sky toward a beautiful full moon, *I'm already gone*.

"Availability, vulnerability, desirability," Sully tells Barnes, the food before her still untouched. "Catherine Winston represented every quality a serial offender would be seeking."

"Exactly. And—carpe diem, right?"

She nods. It stands to reason that he'd have all three Murder Houses under surveillance. It isn't hard to imagine that he spotted her inside 46 Bridge and seized the opportunity.

But there was no sign of forced entry. Had she opened the door to the offender because she recognized and trusted him?

Their profile suggests that he's intelligent and—obviously—obsessed with the original case. That describes just about everyone in Mundy's Landing.

He was carrying a 1916 coin wrapped in vintage cloth, most likely a scrap of fabric from the historical society's stolen nightgown. Forensics has yet to confirm that, according to Nick, who briefed them on various details of the case.

"Are you going to eat?" Barnes asks, gesturing at her plate.

"I'm eating." She picks up an edamame pod. "I'm just trying to get inside his head. What does that nickel tell us, other than that he was obsessed with the original case?"

"That he was ritualistic," Barnes ticks off on his fingers, having been over this countless times before, "and that he probably went through the backyard with the body and dropped the coin there."

"Right. But—"

"Eat, Sully."

"I'm eating." She bites down on the velvety, salt-dappled pod, releasing a couple of tender soybeans onto her tongue before resuming the conversation around a salty mouthful. No need to stand on ceremony with Barnes. "But how can he expect to do the same thing tonight?" she asks. "He has to know the cops will be watching the house."

"He sure as hell does if he reads the *Tribune*."

"He'd have known that all along, though."

"He's blinded by narcissism. He thinks he's going to get away with it."

"Either that, or he's lain the groundwork so that he will. Like the burglar alarms."

Barnes nods. Colonomos told them that Yamazakis' burglar alarm went off incessantly before the break-in. The offender rightly assumed that after so many false alarms, the police response would lose its urgency, or that the alarm would be disarmed.

"The Binghams don't have an alarm system," he points out.

"No, they have something better. Police protection."

"Do you think he'd actually kill a cop? That doesn't fit the MO."

"No, it doesn't." Considering that, Sully raises a bite of meat to her mouth at last, then hesitates. "There must be some other reason he thinks he'll be able to waltz into that house tonight."

"Like what?"

"Like he belongs there."

Barnes shrugs. "Eat, Sully."

"I'm eating."

She bites, chews, swallows.

"How is it? Well done enough for you? No blood, right?"

"No blood," she agrees.

Yet somehow she tastes it anyway.

Watching the sun set over Mundy's Landing from the window of her attic bedroom, Ora wonders where she's going to go from here. When the Sleeping Beauty Killer's identity becomes known to the world, should she act as though it's a surprise to her? Or should she admit that she's known all along?

Great-Aunt Etta pieced together the crime years ago, before Ora was even born. She'd known the players personally and been an eyewitness to the Purcell family drama. She'd heard the rumors of incest involving Augusta Pauline, George's suicidal sister, and of Florence's affair with her father-in-law, and of a little girl living in the attic. People said the house was haunted by Augusta Pauline's spirit, but Aunt Etta was too pragmatic to believe in ghosts.

One night, when bathtub gin got the better of Florence, Etta had snuck a peek at the photo in the locket Florence used to wear around her neck. She believed the guilt-ridden woman wasn't just mourning her lost child, but eventually driven mad over her complicity. In later years, long after George's death, she'd visited her old friend at the Rockland Sanatorium. There, she told Ora, Florence had rambled on, often incoherently, yet in part revealing the tragic truth.

"Why didn't you tell?" Ora asked her aunt.

"Because by then it was much too late, and I didn't see any reason for their surviving children to suffer the consequences. George was dead. Florence had been punished enough. Long after he stopped punishing her, she punished herself."

"But they were fiends, locking a little girl in an attic for all of those years, and then he killed her and two others."

"Yes. He was mentally ill, and a victim of his circumstances, and the era. So was Florence."

"He was a monster, and she was selfish and greedy."

"George was the son of a controlling man who blamed him for his mother's death in childbirth, and who abused his sister until she killed herself. Florence came of age at a time when women were regarded as helpless without a man to take care of them. I understood them. And I watched her transform afterward. She wanted to be independent."

"Instead, she went crazy."

Aunt Etta shrugged. "Dementia runs in some families, my dear," she said pointedly. The conversation took place during a time when Papa was yelling at Rip Van Winkle and the gang to stop making all that noise playing ninepins in the living room.

"Sometimes, it can be a blessing," Aunt Etta added. "It was for Florence. In her lucid moments, she didn't realize she'd unburdened her guilt upon her doctors—and upon me, when I visited her. And upon her daughter."

Yes, Augusta. She had met her sister, Zelda. She knew of her existence. She must have pieced things together, and her mother probably filled in the rest in later years.

The statue, a poignant monument to her lost sister, is proof that she had known. No wonder she isolated herself in that house all those years, guarding her family's secrets, estranged even from her own brother, who presumably didn't know. No wonder she never married, or had children of her own. She had seen those very institutions destroy her parents' lives.

For now, George Purcell's journal still sits, undiscovered, in the chest down at police headquarters. The time capsule has been forgotten in the uproar over the copycat crime that took place last week, and the anticipation of another tonight.

Early last Friday morning, Ora met with Police Chief Calhoun, Lieutenant Colonomos, and Mayor Cochran to discuss what she should do about the remaining Mundy-palooza events. Workshops were scheduled for the remainder of the weekend, and attendees had paid hefty registration fees. There would be an uproar if she canceled.

As it turned out, they encouraged her to go on with the events as planned. Believing the killer might be among the museum's visitors, the police stationed a uniformed officer at the door and a plainclothes cop inside to keep an eye on the crowds.

The remainder of Mundypalooza passed without incident.

Well of course it did.

Because the second crime isn't slated to take place until tonight. Tomorrow morning, rather. Sometime before sunrise.

Staring at the pink-streaked sky, Ora is certain that somewhere out there, a dead girl is being dressed in the bloodstained nightgown stolen from her collection.

lying on the floor in Holmes's upstairs bathroom, the Beauty is almost ready. He took great care to make sure that this one is just right.

He washed the blood from the gash in her throat and the ones he inflicted on her torso, in accordance with the autopsy photographs of S.B.K.'s second victim. He combed her long hair, braided it, and carefully tied the fragile satin ribbons at the tip of each one. Her arms are folded, hands clasped across her breast. Her eyes are closed.

But the nightgown—the one she was supposed to wear, the one Zelda had worn—does not fit.

Fitted in the bust and waist, with a small, constricted neckline, the gown goes over her head, but starts to tear when he attempts to tug it down over her fleshy, wounded torso. Her breasts are in the way.

He could lop them off—but that wouldn't be right. It would ruin his careful replication of the original victim's wounds.

Clutching the garment, he stands over the naked corpse, his thoughts swimming with uncertainty as darkness falls beyond his window and the clock ticks on.

What the hell is he supposed to do now?

"What the hell were you going to do anyway?" he shouts, and clamps his hands over his ears.

"No! Stop it! Shut up for a minute so I can think! I have a plan!"

He'd planned to stash her out behind the detached garage and then sneak her into the house when he was ready. But he'd underestimated the police presence around the house. There are officers everywhere. Even if he gets her to the backyard, how will he ever get her inside?

"You should have known! S.B.K. would have known!"

"You don't know that!"

"Yes, you do! It's proof!"

Is that true? Is this the proof that he wasn't—that he isn't—S.B.K. after all? That his visions of 1916 are mere visions, and not memories?

"No! Be quiet!"

His thoughts spin through the possibilities. He can use one of the nightgowns he bought at Macy's for this purpose. But they feel like cheap imitations now that he's in possession of the real thing.

"So which is more important? Come on, make a decision!"

"Shh! I'm thinking!"

"Is it the Beauty? Or the nightgown?"

He stares at the yellowed, bloody fabric clutched in his

violently trembling hands. This, he could smuggle into the house.

He imagines pulling it over someone else's head. Would it, too, feel wrong? If it feels wrong, will he feel compelled to make a rash, impulsive compensation as he did before?

It has to be right.

"So which is it going to be? The nightgown, or the Beauty? Make up your mind!"

He'd carefully chosen Indigo Selena Edmonds because she shared an important characteristic with Zelda Delphine Purcell: she, too, was born beneath a blue moon. Yes, he'd painstakingly searched birth records for girls born on those rare dates. Of all he tracked down, she was the most readily available.

But what if he can find another child, even more available? What if the child were to share not the blue moon birthday or even the gender, but a body type slender enough for this garment to slip on easily?

"You have the nightgown. All you need is a child."

Holmes paces, twisting the fabric in his hands.

"A child living at 46 Bridge Street."

"I know that."

"A child already inside the house, already tucked into bed in the room at the top of the stairs."

"I know! I know!"

"Then do it."

Holmes nods, turning away from the corpse, forgetting all about Indi.

"Yes," he agrees, "It would be right. It would be exactly right."

Standing sentry in the downstairs hall as it has for over a century, the Purcell family's black walnut clock strikes midnight.

Hearing it, Annabelle wishes she hadn't switched spots with Trib tonight.

He'd offered to share the bed with Oliver so that she could get some sleep for a change, and to her surprise, Oliver agreed—after Trib told him they could watch the Yankees game on the bedroom television.

"Mom never lets me turn on the TV in bed."

"I don't," she agrees. "That's because I'm no fun."

"You're fun," Trib said. "Just not as much fun as I am."

"Have at it, Fun Guy." She handed him the remote and picked up her pillow.

"We will. The little mushroom and I will see you in the morning."

"Mushroom?" Oliver protested as she grinned at Trib's quip, instantly getting the joke. "Why am I a mushroom?"

"Because you're a fun guy, too."

"Huh?"

"Fun guy. Fungi."

Standing there in the master bedroom, joking around with Trib and Oliver, was almost like old times.

Then Annabelle kissed them both good night, and Trib said, in a low voice, "Stay. All three of us can sleep in here."

"No, it's okay. I need to rest. I can't take another day feeling like a zombie." It's hard enough for her to fall asleep in a dark, quiet room. The last thing she needs in her current state of exhaustion is light and noise—and on this hot, sticky night, an extra person in her bed.

As she climbed into Oliver's, she reminded herself that Officer Greenlea—armed and vigilant—is posted right at the foot of the stairs. Two additional officers are outside, one on the front porch and one on the back. Squad cars are parked at either end of the block, and others are patrolling The Heights. Short of a helicopter hovering over the roof and a SWAT team in the shrub border, the Mundy's Landing Police have taken every precaution.

Now, hours later, she can't get her thoughts to settle, can't get past the dread that something is going to happen here tonight.

Downstairs, the clock chimes again: one o'clock.

And then two o'clock.

Three.

Maybe she was wrong. Maybe daylight will come without incident, and she can breathe easily at last.

As the Westminster Quarters chime three-fifteen, Annabelle hears another sound—the faint sound of a voice in the hall. A man's voice, murmuring.

It isn't Trib's.

She turns toward the door just in time to see, in the dim glow of Oliver's nightlight, that the knob is slowly turning.

Sully's insomnia is back, along with the headache.

She may have worked through her sorrow over Manik Bhandari, but she can't stop thinking that another child's life hangs in the balance tonight.

She's certain Catherine didn't run away.

Sully was once a teenage girl herself. At thirteen, she fought incessantly with her mother. She, too, threatened to leave home—yet she never would have followed through.

You don't know Catherine. You shouldn't assume she didn't just take off, like she said.

But if Sully looks at the circumstantial evidence, and assumes that Catherine didn't run away, then she's been abducted.

Who, she's been asking herself, would Catherine have trusted? Who could have come to the door, and the girl would have opened it without question?

Her parents have solid alibis, as do other adults in her life—family, friends, teachers, clergy.

"Don't ever let a stranger into the house," Sully lectures the teenagers who do just that when she and Barnes knock on doors during an investigation.

They flash their badges and ask for the resident adult, but the kids often let them in.

What if someone posing as a cop came to the door at 46 Bridge?

It's a small town, though. Surely Catherine would recognize the local police officers. Even Sully has gotten to know all the faces in her short time here.

All right, then what if . . .

At last, Sully allows in the thought that's been lurking on the periphery like an unwanted intruder:

What if the offender really *is* a cop?

As he crept up the stairs clutching the nightgown, with the antique barber's blade ready in his pocket, S.B.K. knew he'd made the right decision.

"The boy is the one who has to die," he mutters.

A light glows in the second-floor hallway. At the end, his precious Augusta's door is closed. So are the others, including the one at the top of the stairs, across from the master bedroom.

The boy will be asleep inside.

He has to die.

He *deserves* to die, just as Zelda did one hundred years ago. *What do I care? He isn't my son.*

He pushes open the door at the top of the stairs.

And she wasn't my daughter. She belonged to Father, just like this room, and everything else in this house, in my life. Even my wife.

His hand clenching the blade, S.B.K. crosses swiftly toward the figure in the bed.

"What . . . what are you doing?" a frightened voice asks in the dark.

Trembling with anticipation, S.B.K. raises the blade, preparing to strike.

Sully throws on shorts, a T-shirt, and sneakers, and hurries down the stairs. The living room is dark and warm, the box fan whirling in the window.

"Barnes," she calls. "Barnes, wake up!"

She flips the light switch at the foot of the stairs and sees that the couch, made up as always with sheets and a pillow, is empty.

Where the hell, she wonders, did he go?

"What are you doing?" Annabelle repeats in terror, though she knows.

The momentary relief that flooded her veins when she saw who had entered the room is swept away on a tide of sheer terror. Madness torches his eyes, and she can feel the hatred radiating as he stands over her.

"I'm killing you," he says calmly.

She starts to scream, but he shoves something into her open mouth, gagging her with a wad of cloth. His fingers clutch her hair, jerking her head back into the pillow so that her neck arches, exposed.

Annabelle intakes a strangled breath through her nose, her last breath, and she thinks of Trib and Oliver, how much she loves them, how much they need her . . .

Oliver. Oliver needs her. He can't survive without her. He isn't strong enough to endure this.

She has to fight, dammit. She has to fight for her life. She can't let him do this.

Flat on her back, she bends her knees toward her chest, preparing to kick him, hard, with both feet. It isn't much, but it's all she's got left. If she can catch him off guard . . .

But someone else has beaten her to it.

She sees a shadow in the doorway and a flash of movement behind him. Before he can react, she hears the dull thud of something hard hitting his skull from behind in precisely the moment she thrusts her feet into his chest.

The madman is no longer standing over the bed.

Oliver is, holding his baseball bat, panting, wearing a familiar frightened expression as he peers down at her.

"Dad!" he shouts. "Dad! Help!"

Annabelle sits up and fumbles with the gag. Trib bursts down the hall and into the room. He takes in Oliver with the bat, Annabelle in the bed, and the uniformed police officer lying on the floor, unconscious and badly injured from a well-placed blow to the skull. "What happened? Oliver, what did you do?"

"I had a nightmare, so I came to find Mom, and . . . and . . ." He falters.

"You hit a police officer?" Panic edges into Trib's expression. "Oliver, why would you—"

Removing the gag at last, Annabelle finds her voice, trying to explain. "No, Trib, he saved me."

"The officer saved you? And then Oliver—"

"No! Oliver saved me." She gestures at the man on the floor. "He was going to kill me."

"Oliver saved you?"

She nods, folding her son into her arms, her throat choked with emotion. But she manages to say, as she hugs him, hard, "You're the most courageous kid I've ever known, Oliver."

"I'm not. I was scared."

"Everyone was scared. I was terrified. He was going to—" She breaks off, shuddering, unable to fathom how close she'd come to death just moments ago—or that the

child who needs her protection just saved her from the
man who tried to kill her.

I'm out here," Barnes's voice calls through the screen.

Sully finds him on the porch swing wearing only
boxers, his bare feet propped on the railing.

"What are you doing out here?"

"It was too hot to sleep in there. I can't take it anymore,
Gingersnap. I need A.C. I need the city. I need—"

"You need to listen to me for a minute," she cuts in. "I
think I know—"

Her words are curtailed by the sudden wail of sirens
in the night.

"Uh-oh." Barnes swings his feet to the porch floor and
looks at her. "That's not good."

Dread slices her gut. "No. It isn't."

"What were you going to say? What do you think you
know?"

"I think it was an inside job. One of the cops on the force."

"Which one? Colonomos?"

"I don't know. I don't know who. And I'm afraid," she
adds, as the sirens bawl into The Heights, "that it might
be too late to figure it out."

Annabelle has yet to let go of Oliver, who sits beside her
on the couch in the back parlor, bookended by Trib on his
other side. Their trembly hands are clasped across their
son's bony shoulders as they answer questions for a pair
of state troopers, one grandfatherly, the other perhaps
Ryan Greenlea's age.

Ryan Greenlea . . .

Ryan Greenlea?

How can it be?

In the half hour or so that has passed since he attacked

her upstairs, Annabelle still can't fathom that it really happened. Surely any second now, she'll wake up in bed upstairs in the master bedroom—or maybe even back at the cottage off Battlefield Road. Maybe it was just a bad dream, all of it, including the Murder House.

Yet every time she squeezes her eyes closed, she can still hear sirens and troopers' voices and radios squawking and heavy footsteps tromping in the next room, up and down the stairs, overhead. When she opens her eyes, she sees a room bathed in fluid bloodshot light, diluted in its path from the front lawn through unfettered front parlor windows to the back of the house.

A fresh siren wails in the night—an ambulance, she knows. Paramedics stormed into the house on law enforcement's heels. They examined Annabelle and Oliver, proclaimed them shaken but remarkably resilient. She didn't watch them tend to the fallen Officer Greenlea, but she could hear the commotion, and heard them carrying him down on a stretcher just moments ago.

Searching her soul for a scrap of mercy toward the man, she finds none. He may be badly injured, and he's clearly mentally ill, but he violated her home, and he . . .

Catherine.

Catherine is still missing.

The pink light fades away with the siren.

Footsteps descend the stairs, more voices in the hall.

Lieutenant Colonomos appears in the doorway between the parlors. His handsome face has aged a year or two for every day that's passed since she saw him on the street the night Kim was here with her, drinking wine and complaining, as always, about Catherine.

Lieutenant Colonomos beckons the troopers over and speaks to them in a low voice. Annabelle overhears part of it: the troopers are to go help conduct a search of Greenlea's home.

Annabelle is familiar with the small house located off Colonial Highway near the elementary school, where he'd lived with his mother until she died a few years ago. The woman was eccentric—unkempt, outspoken, the kind of person who stands out in a small town. She'd always felt sorry for the boy, but now . . .

He isn't a boy. He's a man.

He attacked her family, and . . .

Catherine is missing. Dear God.

The troopers disappear into the next room.

Crossing over to take one of the vacated chairs, Colonomos asks Oliver how he's feeling.

"I'm okay now. Where's the . . . bad guy?" he asks, after searching briefly for the right phrasing.

"On his way to the hospital. You really clobbered him, kid. The Red Sox could use a swing like that."

"I'm a Yankee fan," Oliver replies, and Colonomos cracks a fleeting, but genuine grin before turning his attention to Annabelle and Trib. He tells them that the investigation is continuing upstairs and it will be a while before they'll have their house to themselves again.

"That's okay," Trib says. "Whatever it takes."

Annabelle wants to ask if there's any news on Catherine. She can't in front of Oliver, though, and there's no way he'd leave their sides right now; no way she'd let him if he would.

If there were news, she reminds herself, he'd tell us right away. Good news, anyway. Bad news . . .

I don't want to know. I'm not ready to hear it.

How would Kim and Ross ever get over something like that? How would Oliver? Or any of them, really?

"So you never had any idea what was going on in Greenlea's head?" she asks Colonomos. A stupid question, she realizes as soon as it escapes her, because of course he didn't. If he had, he'd have put a stop to it. "I'm sorry. I didn't mean—it's just—"

"No, I understand. Believe it or not, he was a good cop. Always said that a detective was the only thing he ever wanted to be, from the time he was a little boy. He lived for the job. I never thought—"

"No one ever would have thought that," Trib says quickly. "I trusted him here with my wife and child."

Annabelle, too, had trusted him. So had Oliver. That's the most frightening realization: that the killer was hiding in plain sight, right under this roof.

Standing on the front lawn at 46 Bridge Street, bathed in the swirling ruddiness of at least half a dozen patrol car dome lights, Sully sees Nick Colonomos step purposefully out onto the porch.

She hurries toward him, leaving Barnes to carry on a somber conversation with a shell-shocked local cop still trying to grasp that a fellow officer was behind all this.

For Sully, who had guessed the truth too late, the shock is laced with guilt and concern for the missing Catherine Winston. The girl's hysterical parents had rushed to the scene just ahead of Sully and Barnes, and were hastily escorted away by a pair of troopers.

"How can we help?" Sully had asked another trooper, stationed along the perimeter of the property as a wave of onlookers and media descended.

"You're NYPD Missing Persons, right? Friends of Lieutenant Colonomos?"

"Yes."

"Well, we've got a missing person, and even if Greenlea was willing to tell us where to find her—which I doubt—he's out cold. Go talk to the lieutenant."

They tried, but Nick was inside the house, and the trooper at the door wouldn't let them in. That's understandable. They're lucky to be on the property, considering they're not technically part of the investigation.

Now Nick Colonomos has stepped outside at last, striding purposefully down the steps toward a cluster of cars.

"Lieutenant!" Sully catches up to him. "I want to help. I know that Catherine Winston is still missing, and—"

"A couple of my guys just found a 419 at Greenlea's apartment. Female."

419—a corpse.

She closes her eyes and curses softly. "Is it . . . ?"

"They don't think so. They turned up some kind of log he'd been keeping. It mentions a location out by the river. I'm meeting them over there now." He throws open the driver's side door of a black police SUV.

"I'm coming with you."

He doesn't argue as she jumps into the passenger's seat. They take off, siren wailing, as officers hold back the throng lining the sidewalk.

Her phone vibrates with a text from Barnes.

Where the hell RU going?

She hurriedly types *To find Catherine.*

A moment later, an answering *Be careful.*

Colonomos speeds west through town. A television news crew is filming on the Common, garish spotlights trained on a reporter standing in front of the historical society. Sully sees them all pivot as the SUV flies past, wondering, undoubtedly, if the unfolding story has taken another turn. It doesn't matter to them whether there's a happy ending, or a tragic one. To them, it isn't personal. To Sully, long immune to media indifference, this case— even though it isn't her own—is personal.

She doesn't know Catherine Winston, and Mundy's Landing isn't home, but . . .

It could be, she realizes as the village proper falls away behind them. *I could stay.*

Barnes wouldn't be happy with her if she did. But Barnes has his life, and she has hers. They're friends, and they're partners, but they aren't anything more than that.

Does she wonder, occasionally, whether something might spark between them if they hadn't mutually sworn off relationships with fellow cops?

Sure. But it won't ever happen, so—

"This is it," Colonomos mutters, turning off the highway onto a dirt access road that runs alongside a large field. "Back there, in the woods."

"What's back there?"

"An old icehouse where he's been keeping them, apparently."

"Them?"

"Juanita Contreras. Catherine Winston. Others."

A sick lump rises in Sully's throat.

Juanita Contreras didn't survive. What are the odds that others did?

Not good.

Colonomos parks at the end of the road and grabs a couple of flashlights. He hands one to her without comment.

She takes it, turns it on, and they head into the dark, foggy woods on foot.

"Do you know this area?" she asks, following him along a tangled, barely discernible path.

"We patrol it. Used to be an old amusement park."

Sully's eyes widen at the eerie coincidence—which isn't a coincidence at all, she reminds herself. "Valley Cove Pleasure Park, right?"

"How do you know about it?"

"I've been doing some research into the Sleeping Beauty case. I thought the killer might have trolled the park for victims."

Perhaps Greenlea guessed the same thing. It's no

accident that the denouement of his copycat crimes has led full circle back to this isolated spot.

She struggles to keep up with Colonomos, hearing an occasional ominous rustling in the undergrowth as they hurriedly make their way toward the icehouse. Harmless woodland critters, she knows, but the woods feel alive with peril.

An owl hoots overhead. A foghorn on some distant harbor sounds a mournful toll. Somewhere behind them, she can hear vehicles, footsteps, the faint voices of other officials rushing to join the rescue mission.

Please, please let it be a rescue, and not a recovery.

Sully's flashlight picks up rubble and ruins: a weedy foundation, a heap of rotting planks, the contorted metal skeleton from some ancient amusement park ride. And then she sees it: a low stone building just ahead.

Colonomos speeds ahead, far more surefooted on the treacherous path, and disappears around the side of the building. When she reaches him, she finds him, panting, inserting a key into a padlocked wooden door.

"Where did you get the key?" she asks.

"Greenlea's pocket," he says grimly.

The lock opens.

He grabs it and hurtles it aside, then pushes the door open.

They train their flashlights on a small, empty room. A ladder and some cleaning supplies are stashed on the far wall.

"Catherine!" Colonomos calls, striding over the threshold. "Catherine, are you here?"

Trailing him into the icehouse, Sully recognizes the sickening smell of decomposing human flesh wafting in the air. Her heart plummets.

Too late.

She thinks of Catherine, of Juanita, of Manik.

Of the dead female in Greenlea's apartment.

Always, always too late.

I can't do this anymore. I'm not strong enough. I'm broken.

Then she hears it: a muffled, barely discernible cry.

It came from beneath their feet. Training their flashlights, they make out a rectangular break in the floorboards.

A trapdoor.

They pounce upon it, prying it open.

The unmistakable stench of a corpse floats up from below, but so does a female voice.

"Help me . . . please . . ."

"We are," Sully calls as Colonomos grabs the ladder. "We're coming."

"Please . . ."

Colonomos lowers the ladder into the hole.

Sully touches his sleeve. "Can I go first? Please?"

He looks at her and nods.

The ladder tilts precariously as she puts her foot on the top rung, despite Colonomos's attempt to hold it steady while aiming a flashlight into the hole.

"I'll go down," he says.

"No, I've got it." She makes her way down the wobbly ladder until at last her foot touches solid ground.

Turning, she sees a child's gaunt, tearstained face blinking at her from the chilly shadows.

"Are you Catherine Winston?"

The reply is nearly inaudible. "Yes."

Sully sidesteps the body on the floor.

Sometimes, it's too late.

But sometimes . . .

Sometimes, it isn't.

And that's what gives you the strength to keep going.

She wraps her arms around the violently trembling girl and hugs her close.

"You're okay," she says. "It's over, sweetie. You're going home."

* * *

Annabelle and Trib sit on their porch steps, Oliver asleep between them with his head in her lap.

The lawn remains lit by whirling red lights, though not nearly as many as before. The crowd on the sidewalk has dispersed.

The first birds are beginning to chirp in the ancient trees high above the mansard roof.

They listen.

And wait.

"What time is it?" she asks Trib.

"Five twenty-seven. The sun will be up in a minute."

"Literally?"

"Literally." He holds up the morning *Tribune*, tossed at their feet a little while ago by their teenage paperboy, who instead of riding by on his bike, was accompanied on foot by his father and a police officer. "The sunrise and sunset times have been printed on the front page for over a hundred years, along with the weather forecast. Today, it will rise at—"

The comment is cut off by his cell phone ringing in his hand.

He looks down at it. "Colonomos."

Please, Annabelle thinks. *Please let her be all right.*

Trib answers the call. "Yes? Did you find her?"

Annabelle closes her eyes and holds her breath.

Please don't let it be bad news. Please.

"That's good." Trib's voice trembles with emotion. "That's really good. Thank you for letting us know."

Annabelle exhales on a sob as he hangs up and looks at her, tears in his eyes. His nod tells her Catherine is safe.

Unable to speak for a moment, they clasp hands across their sleeping son.

Then, around a lump in her throat, Annabelle says, "Five twenty-eight."

"What?"

She gestures at the eastern sky. The rooftops and tree-tops of The Heights glow with rosy golden light.

"When the phone rang, you were about to tell me that the sun comes up at 5:28, and it's going to be a beautiful day. You were probably also going to tell me that you love me," she adds with a smile.

Trib grins. "You took the words right out of my mouth."

Coming soon from
***New York Times* bestselling author**
WENDY CORSI STAUB

BONE WHITE

A Mundy's Landing Novel

Because the past is never really forgotten . . .

Read on for a sneak peek.

Prologue

Hudson Valley
July, 1666

As the crowd begins to jeer, Jeremiah Mundy holds tightly to his younger sisters' hands, steeling himself for the unthinkable tragedy about to unfold.

Thou art a man now, he reminds himself, echoing the last words his father, James, said to him weeks ago, before he and Mother were taken away.

At thirteen, Jeremiah felt in that moment—and feels in this one—like a mere child. Yet of course he promised his parents that he would accept his manly obligation, taking charge of his sisters and the household in their absence. He just never dreamed the absence would endure for weeks, let alone . . . forever.

But forever it shall be.

James and Elizabeth Mundy are sentenced to meet their death today at the hands of the black-clad hangman who, like the others present, only recently arrived in this year-old colony perched on the western bank of the Hudson River. They were originally due last fall, having traveled from England with sorely needed supplies. But a harsh winter set in before the reinforcements could make their way north from the port of Manhattan. Ice rendered the river impassible. The Mundy family and their fellow settlers were left to fend for themselves for nearly five months.

Day in and day out, Jeremiah trudged with his father through a swirling white maelstrom to chop wood and feed a fire that did little to stave the bitter cold. For a long time, there was no way to feed the relentless hunger. The family nearly starved to death.

But they didn't. They were the lucky ones. They found the means to salvation—horrific means, and yet, as Jeremiah overheard his parents saying, what choice did they have?

When at last the supplies and reinforcements arrived in May, only the Mundys remained of the three dozen original English settlers.

"Look there! Satan himself blazes in the Goody Mundy's eyes!" a man proclaims from the crowd behind Jeremiah.

"Ay, and peculiar eyes they be," comes the reply, and he recognizes the rasping voice of the Goodwife Barker, whose bachelor brother was among the first of the winter's casualties.

Peculiar eyes . . .

Jeremiah closes his own eyes: one a piercing shade of blue, the other a chalky gray.

Years ago, back in England, he caught a first glimpse of himself in his grandmother's looking glass and was startled to see that he, like his mother, had one pale iris and one fully pigmented.

"'Tis a rare gift," his beloved grandmother told him, and he believed it . . .

Until now.

Rare, yes. Not a gift, but a curse.

The subject of his mother's "peculiar" eyes came up at the trial—offered as additional evidence of Elizabeth Mundy's guilt, lest there be any claim that her initial confession had been coerced through bodily torture.

Jeremiah had stalwartly witnessed that torture, a public spectacle that unfolded on the riverbank on a gray spring day. The entire colony turned out to watch, bristling with anticipation like an amusement-deprived London audience flocking to the post-Restoration theater.

His father was first to be strapped to the ducking stool as Jeremiah stood helplessly by, apart from the gawkers and gossipers. Their voices and the chirping chatter of woodland creatures were drowned out by violent splashing as James Mundy was repeatedly submerged in the murky current. Each time he sputtered to the surface, he defiantly proclaimed his innocence, determined to let them drown him—until the moment they assured him that his wife would be spared the same punishment if he confessed.

And so he did.

Jeremiah's fists clenched as he listened incredulously to the confession. Yes, he knew it was the noble thing to do and the only option. For either way, his father would die: drowned in the river, or sentenced to death for murder. At least James Mundy had preserved his wife's dignity and her life . . . or so he believed.

They had lied.

Jeremiah's mother had her own turn on the ducking stool. A pair of burly men—the same men who escort her to her doom this morning—held Jeremiah back when he tried to rush to her side. She endured nearly three hours before confessing to the heinous crimes of which she and her husband had been accused.

The trial, now a mere formality, was swift; the verdict unanimous; the sentence so inevitable that the gallows was being built even before the trial had concluded. Again, the crowd has assembled, as eager to know that the devil had been banished from the settlement as they are thirsty for diversion from daily drudgery.

Eyes squeezed shut to block out the horrific sight of the crude wooden structure, Jeremiah desperately searches his memory for the image of his mother's face as it once was—serene, affectionate, exhilarated by the promise of life in this New World. But he can envision it only pale with worry, contorted in pain and terror.

At the telltale pressing of the crowd around him, he opens his eyes to see that it has parted, allowing the procession into the clearing.

Flanked by pairs of the settlement's strongest men, Mother and Father appear even more frail than they were the last time Jeremiah saw them. That was only days ago, when they were sentenced to death after they each confessed to murder—and worse. Far, far worse.

Ten year-old Charity, the elder but smaller of Jeremiah's sisters, begins to whimper. Priscilla, eight, remains as silent and stoic as her brother, grasping his hand firmly.

The magistrate reads the charges in a booming voice and orders that the death sentence be carried out immediately.

Jeremiah shifts his gaze toward the forest on the far end of the clearing. An escape fantasy takes shape: his parents break away and run toward the trees. They disappear into the dense woods and find their way to the water, eluding their captors and the executioner's twin nooses . . .

Suddenly, the throng roars with glee, disrupting the comforting daydream. Elizabeth Mundy has fainted. The brutes at her side pull her roughly upright again and jerk her toward the gallows.

Priscilla remains steadfast at Jeremiah's side, but Charity tugs his hand. "I cannot bear to watch."

Nor can I.

Aloud, he says only, "We must."

With a plaintive wail, his sister wrenches herself from

his grasp and flees, momentarily capturing the crowd's interest.

Torn, Jeremiah knows that he should go after her. But there will be time enough to comfort her when the ordeal is over.

Someone touches his shoulder, and he turns to see Goody Dowling, whose husband and sons are building a home on a plot of land adjacent to the Mundys'.

Her expression is not unkind. "I shall see to the girl."

She hurries away, leaving Jeremiah dumbfounded.

He's scarcely wondered what might become of him and his sisters after today, but when he does allow himself to speculate, he assumes that the other settlers will shun them, forcing them to leave this place.

Where will they even go?

When their family left England a year ago, they were destitute, evicted by their landholder with nowhere to turn in an overpopulated country. Their only hope of salvation lay across the sea. The British had recently wrangled control of the New Netherland colony from the Dutch and renamed it New York, luring settlers like the Mundys with the promise of opportunity, freedom, and abundant land.

Even if Jeremiah and his sisters could afford to pay for passage back to England, they'd be as alone there as they are here. Grandmother is gone and they have no other family to speak of. Certainly no friends.

Here, they may not have family or friends, but they do have a home—if home can be defined simply as land, food and shelter, with livestock in the yard, crops budding in the fields, fish in the river, game in the forests.

What little Jeremiah knows of the world beyond this settlement is formidable and fraught with danger. Mountains and forests teem with feral creatures and un-friendly natives. The neighboring settlements are few and far between, populated by the Dutch, no ally to the English. Having glimpsed the teeming port of Manhattan last year and found it rife with strangers and filth, Jeremiah has no desire to make his way back there accompanied by two vulnerable little girls.

Now, thanks to a stranger's unexpected benevolence toward the imminent orphan and the crowd's murmuring of sympathy as Charity fled, Jeremiah wonders whether he and his sisters may be permitted to stay on in their parents' home after . . .

After today.

It isn't the ideal scenario, yet it's the only one he can possibly fathom. Now, however, isn't the time to plan for the future. Somehow, he must find the strength and courage to focus on the present.

Thou art a man now . . .

His parents stand on the scaffold, side by side, hands bound, facing the crowd.

Father's jaw is set and his gaze is fixed straight ahead, but Mother is searching the crowd as the hangman wraps a length of rope around her skirt, binding her legs firmly.

Her gaze lands on Jeremiah. In that final glimpse of her peculiar eyes, he sees not only the depth of maternal love, but a frantic question.

Before Jeremiah can respond with a nod of reassurance, the hangman blinds his mother with a length of cloth and commands the prisoners to bow their heads for the nooses.

Priscilla's grasp tightens on his hand and he swallows a rush of grief and bile, trying to find his voice.

I must tell her. She cannot die burdened by concern about the fate of her children.

The hangman nods, satisfied that the nooses are fixed. An expectant hush falls over the crowd as he descends a rickety ladder audibly creaking under his weight.

The command is given, and in that moment, Jeremiah finds his voice at last. "Do not worry!" he calls out, and to his own ears, his voice is shockingly strong and sure. "I shall protect my sisters and we shall make you proud and—"

His final message is lost in a roar of approval from the crowd as the platform drops.

Mercifully, the taut rope snaps Elizabeth Mundy's fragile neck, killing her instantly. But James has the brawny build of a man who has spent his thirty-three years enduring long hours of physical labor. His muscular neck sustains the fall and he is left to slowly strangle at the end of the rope, his body contorting with the spasmic efforts to breathe.

His agonizing gasps render the assemblage mute in collective horror. They had turned out to the promise of entertainment, only to bear witness to a grotesque scene that would forever after haunt their nightmares. They scuttle away until only the hangmen and the Mundy siblings remain beside the scaffold.

Her sturdy little body wracked with silent sobs, Priscilla buries her face against Jeremiah's chest, dampening his shirt with her tears. He holds her fast against him, refusing to budge his gaze from their father until at last his struggle has ended.

He watches until his parents' bodies are cut down and hauled away for unceremonious burial.

Only then does he turn away, allowing himself to slump against the broad, sturdy trunk of an ancient tree.

Priscilla looks up at him. "What is going to happen to us now?"

"We shall return to our home and never speak of this again. Not to outsiders, not even to each other, or to Charity. No matter what happens, Priscilla, for the rest of our lives . . ."

He takes a deep breath and looks around. Satisfied no one is in earshot, he repeats for his sister the words he had so foolishly blurted to their mother—the final message she hadn't heard above the roar of the crowd. Nor, God willing, had anyone else.

"We shall never tell."

Chapter 1

July 10, 2016

"**W**e *shall never tell*." Emerson Mundy looks up from the cell phone photo. "That's what it looks like to me, but I'm not sure."

"That's what I thought." Her father nods thoughtfully, removes his reading glasses, and puts them, along with his phone, back into his shirt pocket. "Now what should we have for lunch?"

"Wait a minute, Dad. For one thing, it's nowhere near lunchtime yet, although it is time for you to take your pills, and I'll go get them for you."

"Pills. I'm sick of taking pills."

"You'd be a lot sicker if you didn't take them. And for another thing," she goes on, "you can't just show me this bizarre picture of some old handwriting, ask me what I think it says, and not explain what it is, or what it means."

"I'm not sure what it means, but I can tell you what it is." Jerry Mundy leans back in his worn leather recliner, grunting as he reaches a gnarled hand toward the footrest lever. "It's a page from an old letter I found."

Perched on the arm of his chair, Emerson gives him a chance to fumble for a few seconds before she gets up and stoops to press the lever for him. Up go his feet, swollen from congestive heart failure and clad in the new

Australian sheepskin-lined slippers she'd given him for his eightieth birthday last week.

"Snazzy," he said when he unwrapped them. "I'll be a hit with all the old gals down at the center."

"Well, they're slippers, Dad, so you won't want to wear them out of the house."

"Then I'll just have to have the old gals over to the house to admire them, won't I."

They both laughed, knowing that would never happen. Jerry Mundy might still get out from time to time to play cards at the senior citizen center, but he's never been one to host female visitors—or anyone, really. It's just been the two of them under this craftsman bungalow roof for as long as Emerson can remember, and that covers about three decades, back to a time before her mother left.

"So this old letter, Dad," she says, picking up his empty coffee mug and the newspaper he'd been reading this morning. "Where did you find it?"

"With my parents' things."

"I thought all their stuff was way back in the crawl space."

"It is."

"Please tell me you didn't climb in there today."

"I didn't." He shakes his head. "Not today. I climbed in there last night."

"Oh, Dad." Emerson reaches out and covers his hand—weathered, still tanned from the sunshine of summers past, but not this one—with her own. "The doctor said you need to take it easy."

"I am taking it easy. Sitting around reading old letters, maybe snapping a picture or two so that I can magnify them on my phone . . . that's easy."

She sighs. "Tell me more about the letter."

"It was written over three hundred years ago, which is another reason I took pictures of it instead of carrying it around. It's so fragile that part of it crumbled into dust when I unfolded it."

"Who wrote it?"

"One of our ancestors, apparently. Did you happen to catch the late news on TV last night?"

She shakes her head. She'd been out on a date and hadn't gotten back until the wee hours. Not because they were having a fantastic time, but because the movie was interminable and her date, Tony, had coaxed her into stopping off for an even more interminable nightcap afterward. He'd probably have tried to talk his way into more than a good night kiss at the door, too, if this was her own apartment and not her father's house, with her father conveniently snoring in his chair a few feet from the door.

First dates—ugh. First, and in Tony's case, last.

"One of our ancestors was on the news last night?" she asks her father.

"Not exactly. Remember Mundy's Landing?"

Intrigued, she nods. Located on the opposite end of the country, the village is perched along the eastern bank of the Hudson River about halfway between Albany and New York City.

She'd first heard of it in elementary school, during a lesson on Colonial America. A small group of English men, women and children settled there in 1665. The subsequent winter was so harsh that the river froze, stranding their sorely-needed supply ship in the New York harbor. All but five of them starved to death. When the ship finally arrived after the thaw, the only settlers left alive were a young couple, James and Elizabeth Mundy, and their three children. They had survived by cannibalizing their neighbors' flesh.

The couple swore they only ate those who had already died, but the aghast newcomers—God-fearing, well-fed and unable to fathom such wretched butchery—accused them of murder. They were swiftly convicted and hanged, leaving their children to fend for themselves.

Always a bookworm, Emerson was at that time obsessed with tales about orphans: *Anne of Green Gables, The Secret Garden, The Witch of Blackbird Pond . . .*

The Mundy children seemed, to her, like characters in one of her favorite books. Surrounded by hostile, vengeful strangers, they had not only survived, but thrived. When the village was incorporated nearly a century later, it was named after their illustrious Mundy offspring.

"Do you think we're related to them?" she'd asked her father back then. She knew he didn't like to talk about the past, but there was no one else she could ask. Her paternal grandparents passed away before she was born.

"It's a common last name," he said briefly, "and my father's family came from Ireland, not England."

That was that. She eventually forgot about Mundy's Landing, much as the rest of the world had largely overlooked it for centuries, other than an occasional paragraph in colonial history textbooks.

But something else had happened there. Something Emerson didn't learn about in elementary school.

In the summer of 1916, three horrified local families each awakened to find the bloodied corpse of a young female stranger tucked into an empty bed. The girls were never identified, their murderer never caught. The notorious Sleeping Beauty Murders faded into history until the 1990s, when the local Historical Society invited armchair sleuths to visit and attempt to solve the cold case for a token reward. It's become an annual event, and the still-unclaimed reward has grown substantially. These days, so many people descend on the village for what is now a weeklong affair unofficially dubbed Mundypalooza.

"What about Mundy's Landing?" she asks her father.

"It's been all over the news. You haven't seen?"

"Yes, the Today Show did a segment about it last week. This month is the hundredth anniversary of the murders, so they—"

"No, that's not what I'm talking about." Jerry gestures for the newspaper she's holding.

She hands it over, and he opens it and folds it back to show her a headline. It's not front page news, but close.

COPYCAT KILLER UNMASKED; HISTORIC CRIMES SOLVED

She scans the lead and looks up at her father, wide-eyed. "I didn't know about this, no. What does it have to do with the letter you found?"

"It got me thinking about whether we might have ties to this place after all."

"I asked you about it years ago and you said we didn't, because our ancestors were Irish," she reminds him, knowing his memory isn't as reliable as it used to be.

But his eyes, when they meet hers, are sharp. "Oh, I know what I said."

"You mean it wasn't true?"

"It wasn't a lie, but my father didn't know much about his family at all. He was estranged from his parents and he never wanted to talk about the past."

That trait must run in the family, she thinks, though she didn't inherit it herself. As a history teacher, she loves to talk about the past. A faded, centuries-old letter is right up her alley, and her father knows it.

"My mother's family was Irish," he tells her, "and I think my father just assumed his was, too."

"That doesn't make sense."

"Well, maybe he just wanted to be, and pretended to be, because he had no idea where he came from and he had no way of finding out."

"That's bizarre."

"That he didn't know for sure?"

"That, and the fact that he didn't care to find out. And he did have a way. He could have asked his parents."

"If he was speaking to them. But he wasn't."

"That was his choice. And to never even tell you or your mom why he'd had that falling out with them in the first place . . ."

"He always said some things are better left buried in the past, where they belong. I respected that."

And so should you.

The unspoken message is loud and clear, and she wishes she'd kept her mouth shut. Here he is, finally willing to discuss where they came from and perhaps fill in some of the sketchy family history, and she had to go and critique the dysfunctional relationships. She doesn't expect him to go on with his story, but for some reason, he does.

"Anyway, last night, when I saw Mundy's Landing on the news, it made me wonder about my family. The Mundy side. We never even knew my grandfather had died, but when my grandmother passed away, my father got a letter from a lawyer back east saying he'd inherited their house and everything in it."

"So they never wrote him out of their will?"

"I guess not."

"Did he go back there?" she asks, picturing her grandfather, filled with regret, making the sad journey back to his empty childhood home.

"No, he said he never wanted to set foot in that house again. He just wanted to sell it, so he had the lawyer hire someone to empty it. Everything that had any value was sold at an estate sale, and the rest was sent to my father. I was just a kid at the time, but I remember being struck that an entire lifetime could amount to nothing more than one cardboard box."

"What did your father do with it?"

"Stashed it in the attic. As far as I know, he never even opened it. I found it still sealed with packing tape when he and mom passed away, and I dumped it into our crawl space with everything else from their house."

"Well, *your* parents' lives amounted to a lot more than one cardboard box," Emerson says. The crawl space, tucked beneath the roof upstairs, is crammed with her grandparents' belongings and God knows what else.

"I never did get around to going through any of it."

"Until last night?"

"Yes, but just that one box from my father's childhood home."

"Still sealed. I wonder why he didn't just throw it away."

"I think there was a part of him, deep down, that couldn't let go. I guess that's true of all of us," he adds, and she knows he's thinking of her mother.

Emerson was barely four years old when she left them—just walked out the door one day and never came back. Never looked back. Not a visit, a phone call, a birthday card . . .

Nothing. One day here, the next, gone.

Emerson has no idea what kind of mother she was before she left. Probably a competent one. If she hadn't been, she probably would have left much sooner, or Dad would have kicked her out. Yes, and Emerson would probably have unpleasant memories of her.

Other than fleeting snippets, she has just one solid recollection. She remembers contentedly lying on the floor, chin propped in her hands, watching a beautiful blond woman put on makeup. They were in an alcove off the master bedroom that her mother called her dressing room, and she had a movie star vanity with light bulbs all around the mirror. She was telling Emerson about Hollywood celebrities, talking about them as if they were her friends—especially one guy, John.

Did her mother leave her husband and child to be with him, whoever he was? By the time she grew old enough to speculate about that, she didn't dare ask her father for the whole truth. Not then, and not now. They haven't spoken of her mother in years, and she's pretty certain there are no traces of her left in the house, even in the crawl space.

Years ago, Emerson asked to see a picture of her— preferably one that showed her mother holding her as a baby, or of her parents together.

Maybe she wanted evidence that she and her father had been loved; that the woman had once been *normal*—a proud new mother, a happy bride.

Or was it the opposite? Was she hoping to glimpse a hint that her mother was never normal? Maybe she wanted to confirm that people—normal people—don't just wake up one morning and choose to abandon their loved ones. That there was always something off about her mother: a telltale gleam in the eye, or a faraway expression—some warning sign her father had overlooked. One Emerson herself would be able to recognize, should she ever be tempted to let someone into her own life.

But there were no images of her mother to slip into a frame, or deface with angry black ink, or simply commit to memory. Exhibit A: Untrustworthy.

Sure, there *had* been plenty of photos, her father had admitted unapologetically. He'd gotten rid of everything.

There are plenty of pictures of her and Dad, though. Exhibit B: Trustworthy.

Dad holding her hand on her first day of kindergarten, Dad leading her in an awkward waltz at a father-daughter middle school dance, Dad posing with her at high school graduation.

"Go. You have to go," he said with a tremulous smile on the tear-splashed day she left for college, before he pushed her out the door. "You have a life to live, Emmie. I'll be fine."

He was right. She did have to go, she did have a life to live, and he *was* fine.

For a long time, he was fine.

She left L.A. for Cal State Fullerton, where she quickly bounced back from her homesickness, even spending a semester abroad. She got her Masters at Berkeley and landed a teaching job in the Bay area. She never did come home again, not to live. But every holiday, many weekends, and for two whole months every summer, she makes the six hour drive down to Silver Lake to stay with her father.

It used to be because she needed him, craving that connection to the only family she has in the world. Lately, though, it's increasingly because he needs her.

He pretends that he doesn't. He still wants her to believe that he's just fine without her, able to take care of himself and the house, able to drive and climb stairs and yes, raise the damned footrest on his chair.

The truth is, he's failing fast. But he's too proud to admit it, so she lets him go through the motions. Then, without comment, she does the things he can't do, and he lets her.

"You should have asked me to help you get that box, Dad," she says, shaking her head.

"You're afraid of the crawl space."

"Only because there are spiders in it."

"There was one spider, Emmie. About twenty-five years ago. I'm pretty sure he's gone."

"He was a freakishly huge and hairy mutant monster spider, Dad," she protests with a grin. "Listen, I have to go grab your pills for you."

"Wait a minute. First let me tell you what I found in that box."

"You're stalling."

"You're curious," he returns. "Admit it."

"I'm curious. What did you find?"

"Old pictures, some notebooks, greeting cards and postcards, and papers."

"Letters?"

"Letters, documents, newspaper clippings. It's going to take me months to go through it all and read everything. But that one packet did catch my eye, because I could see at a glance that it was much older than everything else."

"Over three hundred years old, you said?"

"Yes. And as far as I can tell, it seems to have been written by someone who lived in Mundy's Landing."

"One of our ancestors?"

"Could be."

So maybe they're descended from those heroic Mundy orphans after all.

"What does the rest of the letter say?"

"I'll show it to you. It's upstairs. I put it away for safe-keeping." He makes a move as if he's about to stand up.

"I'll get it, Dad. But first, I need to go get your medicine."

This time, he doesn't argue. His breathing seems a little shallow when she returns from the kitchen with a glass of water and medication. When she arrived in June and realized there were too many pills left in the orange prescription bottles in the kitchen, he admitted to occasionally forgetting a dose or two. Alarmed, she bought a plastic compartmentalized box that holds a week's worth of pills doled into day parts. He grudgingly admitted that was a good idea, but drew the line at setting his cell phone timer as she'd suggested. She keeps track of the timing herself, but worries about what will happen when she goes back home at the end of the summer.

Back in the living room, she finds him holding his phone, once again looking at the photo he'd shown her earlier.

"We shall never tell," he muses thoughtfully.

"What do you think it means?"

"It means someone was determined to keep a secret. Now the question is, should we try to find out what it was? Or should we let it stay buried?"

Again, she finds herself thinking of her mother, buried so deeply by her father—and her own memory—that Emerson can't even remember what she looked like.

The mirror yields few clues. She herself is a Mundy through and through, bearing a strong resemblance to her father. They share a long-limbed build, though his hasn't been lean in years, and thick, wavy hair, hers brunette and cascading halfway down her back, his now faded to white. They have the same dimple on their right cheek, the same angular nose, the same bristly slashes of brow. Even their wide set, prominent, upturned eyes are the same, with one notable exception.

Both of Jerry Mundy's eyes are a piercing blue. Only one of Emerson's is that shade; the other, a chalky gray.

"I think," she tells her father, "it's time to do a little digging into the past."